RITTENHOUSE SQUARE

Merla Zellerbach

BALLANTINE BOOKS • NEW YORK

Library of Congress Catalog Card Number: 89-42833

ISBN 0-345-34956-3

This edition published by arrangement with Random House, Inc.

Manufactured in the United States of America

First Ballantine Books Edition: February 1991

To Fred, to Mom,
and to the memory of
my beloved father

In Boston they ask, "How much does he know?" In New York, "How much is he worth?" In Philadelphia, "Who were his parents?"

—Mark Twain

Acknowledgments

THE INSPIRATION FOR the story and characters of *Rittenhouse Square* came from Marcia Nasatir and Ruth Charny.

For technical help and background information, my warmest thanks to many friends and individuals: researcher and travel writer Bernard Friedman; Elizabeth and Frank G. Binswanger, Sr., of Rittenhouse Square; David Marshall of The Rittenhouse; Fred Voigt, director of the Committee of Seventy; author and historian John Francis Marion; David Dutcher, Historian for Independence Hall; Richard Tyler, Historical Preservation Officer of Philadelphia; Nancy Zambelli, Public Relations Director for the Philadelphia Board of Realtors; Rev. John A. Smart of the Church of the Holy Trinity; architect Herbert Beckhard of Beckhard Richlan & Associates; retired *Bulletin* columnist Jim Smart; librarian Ron Taylor of Philadelphia Newspapers Inc.; Jason Cuzzolina of *Philadelphia* magazine; and Lieutenant Jeff Whittock of the Philadelphia Fire Department.

Added thanks to Ralph Merillion and Gary Blos of the San Francisco Fire Department; Officer Don Woolard, Tactical Division, San Francisco Police Department; agent Chuck Latting of the San Francisco FBI office; architect Patrick McGrew; real estate investors Mel Swig, Dan Blatteis, and Dick Blum; the Honorable Dianne Feinstein; Jane and George Sidney of Beverly Hills; Mrs. Jacob Javits of New York; Mrs. Walter Goodwin of San Francisco and Tucson; and Dr. Sherman J. Maisel, professor, economist, author of *Real Estate Finance,* and his wife, Lucy.

A special nod of gratitude to my agent, Fred Hill; and to my wonderful editors, Beth Rashbaum, Robert Wyatt, and (Philadelphia's own) Sam Vaughan.

Prologue

THE YEAR 1987 had just begun, closing off another chapter of world history: the American bombing of Qaddafi's Libyan base; the tragic nuclear accident at Chernobyl and beyond; and, in welcome contrast to the horrors, the dazzling wedding of Britain's handsome Prince Andrew and the vivacious Sarah Ferguson.

Across the Atlantic, in a stylish residential square in the eastern part of the United States, New Year's Day was almost over. At the entrance to a small green park bordered by stone mansions and stately buildings, a young woman stood shivering. Her soft black hair was wrapped in a scarf, her alert, sensitive eyes were hidden behind sunglasses, her striking beauty barely noticeable—had anyone been there to notice.

God, it was cold, she thought, exhaling a stream of white vapor. Why on earth had she come to this place? Yet instinctively she knew why. Every trauma . . . every milestone . . . every love of her life was somehow connected with the Square around her. Faces flashed to mind as if called up on a screen: the well-bred rich girls who taunted her as a child; the highborn mayor who decreed her father's fate; the sensual renegade who helped her bear her grief sixteen years ago, and whom she could not make herself forget; and now the staunch, self-righteous citizens who misunderstood her love, her respect, and her dreams for the spot where she stood.

If only she could *make* them understand. She wasn't taking anything away from them; on the contrary, she only wanted to free them from the past, just as she wanted to free herself. Her greatest desire was to give something back to the city—the city she often hated for its snobbery and conservatism and rigid values but, in a deeper way, revered and cherished. Almost as if it were human, this great metropolis had been her antagonist, holding her hostage to her background, defying her to soar to the top of her profession . . . to erect an empire . . . to amass a fortune.

And despite the awful odds, she was doing just that.

Bundling against the chill, she turned up her fur collar and was starting to head home when a flicker of movement caught her eye. To her surprise, a man in a window across the way stood and beckoned her. She recognized his face, barely changed in their many years apart, waved back, and walked at an angle toward the town house.

PART
I

1
=

THE LAST RAYS of sunlight filtered through the blinds, lingered briefly on the ceramic Jesus over the mantel, then vanished into dusk. Friday, November 8, 1963, would soon fade into nightfall, signaling the welcome start of the weekend. Inside the two-story red-brick row house on South Philadelphia's Snyder Avenue, four figures were sprawled in silence on the living-room rug.

Finally, a voice announced, "Time's up, Frankie."

"Says who?"

"Says me." Vittoria Di Angelo's deep brown eyes were fixed on her brother's concentrating face. He lay on his stomach, propped on his elbows, peering down at the Monopoly board. His twelve-year-old adversary watched closely, patient as a lioness waiting to pounce.

"How do you know his time's up?" Deliberately aloof from the sparring of her younger sister and her older brother, Lisa Di Angelo sat cross-legged, reading the monthly church bulletin as she waited her turn.

Torie frowned. "By the ticking of the clock, dummy. Two ticks make a second, and Frankie's had over two hundred seconds, which is almost half a minute too long. I think he owes a penalty."

"It's *not* life and death, T. D." Peggy Shea, Torie's best friend and schoolmate, had already gone bankrupt. She lay on her back with her knees bent and her hands folded under her head while she tried, as usual, to keep peace between her two favorite people. "It's only a game."

"I know that." Torie's tone was conciliatory. "But what's the use of playing unless you play to win?"

5

"Wanna make a deal?" Frankie tried to inject confidence into his voice but ended up sounding plaintive.

"Sure. Make me an offer."

"I'll trade you Connecticut for Park Place and pay you the difference."

Torie's counteroffer came fast. "I'll give you Park Place for Connecticut and St. James, and I'll pay *you* the difference."

"Double the difference."

"Okay, it's a deal."

Lisa groaned and threw up her hands. "That does it. My assets are going to the bank. You guys can fight it out."

"Stick around, Lis," said Frankie, pronouncing her name "lease." "The game's not over yet."

"Oh, yes, it is, and you know it. One of us always trades with her and she ends up with all the money and all the property. It used to be fun playing with her. None of us gave a hoot who won or lost. But now *she's* gotta win every time. Peggy's right, she plays like her life depends on it. Ever since Mom went to heaven and Torie stopped going to church she's become a real brat."

"I'm *not* a brat." Torie's words caught in her throat. The mere mention of her mother was enough to bring tears. "Please don't stop playing, Lis. I know it's just a game."

"Oh, quit whining. *Someone* has to make dinner. Papa'll be home at six, and the table's not even set. You *are* going to set the table, aren't you?"

"Yeah, as soon as we finish."

"It *better* be soon."

The game lasted another fifteen minutes. Frankie struggled to build hotels on Boardwalk and Park Place, while his sister spread houses along the cheaper property until she was collecting rent on almost every toss of the dice. He soon conceded, threw down his money, and stomped out of the room.

"Hey, Franco-American spaghetti," Torie called after him, "thanks for helping us put the game away."

"Let him go. We can do it ourselves." Peggy began gathering up the bills.

"You don't have to be so protective. Frankie already knows you're in love with him."

"I am *not* in love with him."

"Well, if you marry him, you'll need an awful big house for all his baseball junk and his matchbooks. Whenever people go to a rest'rant or a bar or something, they always bring him matchbooks."

"So what?"

"So there won't be any room for *your* things. He's got so much junk in his room, and so many millions of matchbooks, you practic'ly can't go in there. They're all over the house, too."

"Who cares about—"

"Vit*toria*," came Lisa's irate voice from the kitchen. "I'm waiting!"

"Oh, shush," Torie mumbled.

"I'll help you set the table," said Peggy. "It won't take long if there's two of us."

"We'll do it when Papa gets here."

"But if we—"

"Don't you wanna go up to my room?"

"Of course I do."

"Then c'mon." Torie winked at her companion, her eyes bright and conspiratorial. "I've got a new idea."

"Do you think Frankie might walk in on us?" Peggy closed the door nervously.

"Nah, he never comes in here. He thinks girls just play with dolls and stuff."

"Then tell me quick! What's the new idea?"

Torie opened a drawer, reached under a pile of sweaters, and drew out a cardboard tiara edged in sequins. "Wanna be first lady?"

"No, it's your turn." Round-cheeked and freckled, with eager eyes and metal braces on her teeth, Peggy had an innocent, puppy-dog quality. She adored her pretty friend and wanted to please her any way she could. "Shall I fix my hair?"

"Well, you *don't* look much like a butler."

"Wait a sec." Taking some bobby pins from the pocket of her jeans, Peggy rolled two reddish-orange pigtails into a bun and secured them at the back of her head. Then she tucked in her shirt and bowed from the waist. "At your service, ma'am." Her voice dropped to a whisper. "What's your *idea*?"

Torie stiffened as she assumed a new persona. Her chin tilted upward, an eyebrow rose imperiously, and her tone became sharp and authoritative. "Thanksgiving, Winston. We're going to have a holiday dinner party tonight. The French ambassador and his wife and their two handsome sons will be dining with us. My husband, President Kennedy, my daughter, Caroline, and me, Jackie—let's see, that makes"—she counted on her fingers—"seven for caviar and turkey with all the trimmings. We'll have cocktails in the garden, as usual."

Winston listened attentively, scribbling notes on an imaginary pad as her employer rambled on. She marveled at Torie's ability to create a new scene around the Kennedys every time they started their secret game. In theory, the girls took turns playing the president's wife or daughter and the less-important male roles, but Torie always preferred being female, and Peggy was used to being male, so they rarely bothered to switch.

"Now I'm Caroline, grown into a lovely young woman of nineteen," Torie instructed, straightening her tiara in front of the mirror. "You're the ambassador's son and we're meeting in the garden for the first time." She curtseyed and held out a hand. "How do you do? I'm Caroline Kennedy and I'm going to be a brain surgeon."

The delight on Peggy's face turned to disappointment. Why did Caroline always have to have a profession? Couldn't she just marry some dashing bachelor and live in a mansion on the Main Line? (She was fairly sure the Main Line ran down from the Philly suburbs to Washington.)

With a sigh, Peggy took the outstretched hand and kissed it. "How *do* you do, Caroline. I'm François de la Soufflé. I've heard a lot about you but I never expected you to be so ravishing. And you smell so divine—like a rosebush."

"Yes, it's called My Sin by Levin—a very expensive perfume company."

"And that magnificent dress you're wearing?"

"This old thing?" Torie smiled coquettishly and cooled her neck with an invisible fan. "Just a little ball gown I picked up in Paris. See? It has a wide skirt with layers and layers of handmade lace and a tight-fitting top that displays my small but beautiful boobs. I hope I won't shock the ambassador."

"Oh, no, not at all. Dad will fall head over heels for you, just like all the men do. What do you call that lovely hairdo?"

"An upswing." Torie raised her dark curls off her face and held them in place with both hands. "It shows off my diamond earrings and diamond necklace. Do I really look ravishing, François?"

"Like a princess."

"That's because my father's president of the United States. He makes a million dollars a year."

Peggy's lips pursed in disapproval. "He *knows* your father's president or you wouldn't be living in the White House. My mother says it's not nice to talk about how much money people make."

"What does your mother know about rich people?"

"She grew up in East Falls with the Kellys."

"They're not really rich. They're just Irish—what's that word?—who made a lot of money."

"Immigrants. My great-grandfather was an Irish immigrant. He helped lay the train tracks. My mother says that's a *real* Main Liner."

"Yeah. Well, wait'll you see this!" Rummaging in a drawer, Torie drew out a tattered copy of *Look*. "There's an article in here about the Richardsons, and lots of pictures of their house and all their closets and things."

"Just because you *read* about rich people doesn't mean you know anything. You've never—"

"Tor-*ree*!" Lisa's scream came up the stairs.

Peggy rolled her eyes. "She sounds mad."

"I guess I should go help her. Anyway, you've spoiled the mood. We can't play the game anymore."

"Yes, we can," Peggy pleaded. "You're still Caroline Kennedy. You want to go to Harvard Medical School right after you dance at the Assembly. And I'm François—"

"No, you're not. You're Margaret Millicent Piggytail O'Shea. You've got bands on your teeth and freckles on your nose, and one more year at St. Monica's grammar school. And you're going to be so bee-*yoo*-tiful when your bands come off. All the boys will go crazy for you." Their eyes met and they began to giggle. "Stay for dinner?"

"Can't. I have to get home."

"But it's Friday, and *77 Sunset Strip* is on. Don't you want to see Efrem Zimmerlist?"

"Efrem Zimbalist's father was a famous singer or something. He lived right near Rittenhouse Square."

"Really? I'm going to be a famous actress like Grace Kelly."

"Why do you have to be an actress? Can't you just marry a nice rich guy and have a family?"

"That's all you ever think about—getting married. I can see us in twenty years. You'll be strolling down Passyunk gobbling soft pretzels with your ten children, and this reporter will come up to you and say, 'Is it true, Mrs. Doodlepoop, that you once knew the world-famous Vittoria Di Angelo? What was she like as a young woman?' "

"Oh, criminy." Peggy shook her head. "I'll say, 'She was a pain-in-the-neck know-it-all but she was a lot of fun and she was my best friend.' Anyway, if you ever do become an actress, you'll get married six times and have a terrible life the way all those movie stars do. And if *I* ever get married, at least I'll have a rich millionaire husband."

"Not if you marry Frankie Di Angelo you won't. He'll never be rich."

"How do you know? Whenever—"

"*Tor-ree!* If you're not here in ten seconds, I'm coming up to strangle you . . ."

Saturdays at the Di Angelos' usually followed a pattern. Frankie would sleep or stay in bed till noon, wander down to the kitchen for a Tastykake and a Coke, then stroll over to the schoolyard to shoot baskets all afternoon. He would come back, wash the car, sweep the stoop, and do his other household chores, then disappear with his friends after dinner. Sometimes he stayed out late, but as long as he always came home, his father had no complaints.

Three years younger than Frankie, thirteen-year-old Lisa—Annalisa Marie on her birth certificate—bore him little resemblance, physically or otherwise. Quiet, plump, self-contained, and introspective, she rose early on Saturdays, as she did every day of the week, walked more than a mile to attend early mass at St. Monica's, then returned home and cooked breakfast.

Only thirteen months her junior, twelve-year-old Torie—Vittoria Francesca—spent many of her weekend hours leafing through magazines in the drugstore or haunting the public library. Along with her love of reading, she seemed to combine her sister's penchant for daydreaming with her brother's zest for life. Yet while Lisa would fantasize about visiting their mother in heaven or alleviating the world's suffering, Torie saw herself on the cover of *Life,* delivering her Oscar acceptance speech, or jetting to London to perform for the queen.

Unlike Lisa, Torie was not the least bit religious; after their mother died, in fact, she vowed never to go back to church. Why should she worship a God who had stolen away the person she loved most in the world? Even now, five years later, the pain of the loss was with her almost constantly. Her sister, brother, and father all felt grief, she was sure, but not the way she did. No one missed her mother the way she did. And no one could possibly understand how deserted she felt, how abandoned and alone.

A lingering sense of guilt made the burden even worse. If only she hadn't been listening in the hall that evening back in 1958, hadn't overheard the doctor say that her mother needed a heart operation. Her father's voice had cracked and dropped so low she'd had to put her ear flat against the door to hear his response—slow, choking sobs as he stammered that he didn't have that kind of money.

Well, he had property, didn't he? Why couldn't he sell their house? And the one he owned next door? Yet she remembered hearing him tell someone that he could never part with the homes because of his children. His children! Torie and her sister and brother were the reason their mother was dead. If not for them, Papa could've raised the money to save her.

Or so Torie believed. In truth, however, no amount of money could have saved Rosanna. Even when Frank came up with a partial sum, and her family, the Silvanos, offered to pay the balance, the cardiologist refused to operate. Surgery, he said, would only make the patient's last days worse.

Unfortunately, Torie never learned that fact, for Frank, in his helplessness and despair, could only stammer that God's will was not to be questioned. Torie took the death much harder than her siblings, and although her father tried everything to get her to attend church—threats, punishment, predictions of Hell and damnation, even bribery—his younger daughter was adamant; nothing in the world could budge her.

It wasn't only that she was angry with God. The prayers in Latin and all the rambling rituals and symbolism bored her. It simply made no sense to sit through those long, dull services when she could be reading books and doing so many other things.

"Well, how was Mass?" Frank Di Angelo snuffed out a cigarette and reached for the Saturday *Inquirer.* He was an old-looking forty-eight, streaks of gray rapidly overtaking the black in his hair. Having waited three decades to marry, and having suffered the loss of his beloved Rosanna a mere thirteen years later, he had almost cracked under the strain.

But the blandishments of widows and would-be matchmakers, the flood of attention from friends and relatives, had allowed him no time for mourning . . . and as an unattached man, he had little motivation to resist feminine temptation. Nevertheless, he knew he was in no position to remarry. His first obligations, morally and financially, were to his children—to bring up his girls to be good wives and mothers, and to raise Frankie to take over his small real estate firm. Every chance he got he talked business to his son, explaining financing and negotiating, defining terms and tax laws.

A more tangible goal, one that was rarely out of his mind, was to make the *big* deal—the supertransaction that would enable him to sell the house, buy a better one, and have enough money so that he would never again get caught short, either for the kids or for himself. Sometimes he wondered if he should have been a con man instead of a businessman. Sure, his friends and clients respected him, but respect didn't buy education, or medicine, or pay bills.

Nor did it protect his kids from the world. He often flirted with the idea of moving out of South Philly. Much as he'd miss the colorful street life and his regular beer buddies, the constant reports of crime and drugs made him fearful, and not only for his children. He was, after all, approaching the half-century mark, and the older he got, the more he'd be a target for muggers and youth gangs.

And yet, not everything had changed for the worse. In times past, a Roman Catholic with an Italian surname could go only so far in Philadelphia; that was practically written into the Constitution. But lately, some of the local boys were making it big in music: Mario Lanza, who had died only four years earlier; Frankie Avalon, born Avallone; and Fabiano Forte, better known as Fabian.

The Irish were getting up there, too. Jack Kelly, a *bricklayer* of all things, had made millions in construction, learned to wheel and deal with the Philly Republicans while they were in power, and then later played ball with the Democrats. His daughter Grace had become a movie star and married a prince. And two years ago, an Irish Catholic from Boston had charmed his way right into the White House.

The picture was definitely improving. A man *could* better himself, even an ordinary *paisano* who couldn't sing, box, or play politics and wasn't connected to the mob. If others could do it, by God, so could Frank Di Angelo. That very afternoon, in fact, a deal was brewing . . .

"The service was lovely," said Lisa, cracking an egg into the mixing bowl. "Father James asked if I would help at the cake bake tomorrow. I said I would."

"Why don't you take your sister?"

"Her sister doesn't want to go to a cake bake." Torie pattered into the kitchen, her backless slippers flip-flopping on the lino-leum. "Brrr. Can't someone tell the butler to shovel more coal in the furnace?"

"You and your butlers!" Lisa tossed a contemptuous glance over her shoulder. "Always pretending you're better than you are. Don't you ever think of anything but being rich? You're going straight to H-E-L-L if you don't go back to church and get some divine inspiration."

"Come on, Lis. I think of other things all the time. I just wish we'd had enough money . . ." She paused, feeling herself on the verge of tears again, and not wanting to hurt her father. "Well, to buy nice presents for each other, that's all."

"Your values are shameful."

"They are not. They just happen to be different from yours. I can't see where it does any good to sit around fiddling with beads and praying all day—or baking sponge cakes. It ain't gonna make life easier."

"Don't say 'ain't.' " Frank shook a finger at his younger daughter. He would have liked to be devout and set an example for her, but he secretly shared her views; the services *were* boring. Besides, men were stronger than women. They didn't need crutches like religion. A young girl without a mother was differ-ent.

Lisa stirred the dough. "Have you ever *tried* praying?"

"Of course I've tried. I prayed for Mama to get well and she died. So why should I pray to a God who doesn't listen?"

"He had His reasons for taking Mama. You have no right to question Him."

"Okay, I'll give Him another chance. 'Dear Lord, please bring us a new furnace that really works, and get Papa one of those lean-back chairs like I saw on tel'vision, and bring Frankie a new car, and Lis a new stove, and bring me a new dress all made of silk and lace so I don't have to wear my sister's hand-me-downs.' "

Lisa frowned. "God's not interested in your material needs."

"Then why do *you* pray all the time? Aren't you playing kiss-ass just to get special rewards in heaven?"

"That's enough! I won't have blasphemy in this house!" Frank set down his fork and glared furiously. "You owe Lisa an apology. Right now."

"I 'pol'gize." Torie took a small box of Rice Krispies from the shelf and emptied it into a bowl.

"Since you're too smart to go to church, young lady, what are your plans for the weekend?"

"Homework."

"She never does homework," said Lisa, spooning sugar into a measuring cup. "She reads sexy books and movie magazines."

"I do not."

"Oh, no? I saw that piece of trash with Annette Funicello on the cover. It's right under your pillow where you hid it. Want me to go get it?"

"Tattletale!" Torie grabbed a fork and waved it menacingly. "How'd you like your eyes poked out?"

"Stop that!" Frank slammed down his paper. "Can't we have one meal without you two fighting?"

"I didn't start it," said Torie. "You should see what she's done to our room. She's taken up the whole closet with her religious junk. The top of the dresser's full of rosaries and crosses and statues. And now she's got papers and stuff spread all over the floor."

"I happen to be making a scrapbook. What are *you* going to do all weekend, Miss Vanderbilt? Read those dirty books you're always borrowing from the library?"

"They're *not* dirty. They're novels. My teacher—"

"I *said* that was enough." Frank rose from the table.

"You going somewhere?" asked Torie, watching him walk to the door.

"Yes, I'm going to the mayor's house. I have a meeting at two this afternoon. I should be back by four."

Her fingers tightened around the spoon. "Did you say the mayor's house? On Rittenhouse Square?"

"That's what I said."

"Can I go with you?"

"No, you can't. It's a business meeting."

"Please, Papa, *please*?" She jumped up on tiptoes and clasped her arms around his neck. "Pretty please with honey on it?"

"No," he said, gently disengaging her. "A business meeting is no place for young girls."

"What if I promise to stay in the car and do all my homework? Please? I *promise* I'll behave."

"She never keeps her promises," Lisa muttered.

"I do too! You don't even—"

"Stop that!" Frank's angry voice commanded silence. "All right, Torie," he said resignedly. "Wash your face, put on a dress, and you can wait for me in the car. But not a peep out of you when we get there. I don't want you pestering me to take you inside."

"I promise! I *promise*!" she shrieked, and bounded up the stairs.

"Good riddance," Lisa growled, reaching for a cake pan. "At least she'll be out of my hair for a while."

2

TORIE DI ANGELO shivered with anticipation as their dented Chevy bumped over the old trolley tracks on Seventh and headed north on Broad Street. A few women were still out observing their Saturday-morning ritual, scrubbing away at the short stoops leading up to their front doors. How she used to hate it when her mother performed that dismal chore. The bleach fumes would linger in the air and make her eyes water.

"Why can't the city fill up these . . . God-blessed potholes?" Frank controlled his tongue and jerked the wheel nervously. "What the hell are they waiting for—someone to get killed?"

His passenger didn't answer. She was busy counting all the funeral homes and wondering why so many were concentrated on one street. In only a few minutes they had left behind the crammed-together houses and red-brick drabness of the South

Philly neighborhood where they lived and were entering a brighter, more prosperous district with tall, imposing buildings.

To her surprise, they drove past the turnoff to Rittenhouse Square and continued up Broad toward City Hall. The bustling downtown area known as Center City always fascinated her. She loved the lofty office towers and gray-stone apartments, the dark-suited businessmen hurrying to their destinations, the variety of shops along Chestnut and Market streets. Unlike the South Philly store windows, jammed with hand-lettered signs and over-lapping placards, the Center City windows held neatly arranged displays of stylish clothes, sparkling jewelry, elegant writing papers, leather goods, shiny new toys, delicious-looking candies, cakes, pastries . . .

At the same time, the fine stores reminded her that she was a visitor from another part of town. She didn't really belong here. Her mother, and almost every grown-up she knew, had made very clear to her that wealthy Protestants considered poor Italian Catholics to be inferior. If you weren't born in the right neighborhood, if you didn't pray in the right churches, if you didn't go to the right schools, you would always be an outsider. You would always be looked down on by the people who mattered.

"Where we going, Papa?"

"I thought we'd take a little drive first."

"Oh, goody!" She could never get enough of the sights and feel of Center City.

He slowed the car and peered through the windshield. "You should've seen this neighborhood before they fixed it up. Abandoned houses, decaying buildings—and the river was so full of stinking sewage you had to close your windows when you drove anywhere near it."

"I hate moldy old stuff. 'Member the night I found that big black bug crawling under my pillow? I almost threw up."

"It was just a cockroach."

"Yuck! Someday I'm going to live in a nice new modern house that's all clean and shiny and doesn't have so much dust and clutter that you can't ever find anything. And no spiders or bugs or stinky old mold in the basement."

Or shrines, she thought, with a shudder of disgust as she visualized the altar her father and Lisa had built in his bedroom. The loving memorial, complete with plaster saints, votive candles, and a gilt-framed picture of the Virgin Mary, was grotesque to Torie—a constant reminder of her mother's death.

She looked outside again. "Who fixed this place up?"

"Ever hear of Joe Clark and Dick Dilworth?"

"Sure. They were mayors."

"That came later. Back in the forties, they organized a citizens' group to clean up and save the city."

"Were people glad?"

He chuckled. "You bet they were. I remember going over to Gimbels department store to see the architect's version of the plan. The model was about fourteen feet high, with trees and neat little parks and lots of tall modern towers in place of the Chinese Wall."

"What's the Chinese Wall?"

He glanced at her out of the side of his eye. She seemed so adult at times, he tended to forget she was only twelve. "That was the name they gave to the train tracks that cut the city in half between Market and Arch streets." He tilted his chin toward the windshield. "Right where those buildings are now."

She stared at a cluster of boxy skyscrapers. "Who *put* the tracks there?"

"The Pennsy—Pennsylvania Railroad. It carried trains to the Broad Street Station." He smiled to himself. "Just before they destroyed it in '52, they got the Philadelphia Orchestra to come over and play 'Auld Lang Syne' as the last train pulled away. Thousands of people stood there singing and crying in the rain— I'll never forget it."

He made a U-turn, heading back toward Walnut Street. "When the wall and the station came down, Pennsylvania Boulevard and Penn Center were built in their place. That was the start of the movement that saved the city."

"My teacher said people could buy houses real cheap on Society Hill if they restored them. I still don't understand why they spent all that money fixing up old houses when they could've built new ones." She shrugged. "Anyway, my teacher says it was one of the most successful renabation projects in American history."

"Renovation. She's right." He nodded approval, grateful that his daughter was getting a good education. Not that it mattered, in a way. Pretty girls didn't need to be brainy. They would always have husbands to do their thinking for them.

Torie decided not to pursue the subject. He might launch into a speech that would leave no time for what she really wanted to know. "What's your meeting about?"

Frank swerved into the plaza known as Rittenhouse Square— a green park the size of a city block overlooked by private mansions, apartments, offices, and a venerable hotel. Two smartly dressed women were having an animated conversation as they pushed English prams across the lawn. "It's about business."

"What kind of business?"

He leaned back against the upholstery, knowing she would pester him until she got an answer. "Your cousin Tony got the mayor to consider buying the old Kelsey Building—strictly as a personal investment. I'll be the broker if the deal goes through."

"Why wouldn't it?"

"A lot of reasons. We need approval from the neighborhood association, the planning commission, the fire inspector, and a whole long list of people. Then we have to figure the costs."

"Of what?"

"Of renovating it without changing the way it looks."

"Why don't you just tear it down and put up a new building?"

He debated whether or not to answer, then decided he couldn't blame her for being curious. "People are sentimental about the past, Torie. Like Society Hill you were talking about. You said you couldn't understand fixing up old houses. It's the same principle. Some people would rather *preserve* good things than get rid of them. That's how Mr. Kelsey feels about his building. He wants it saved and restored."

She understood the explanation, but it made little sense. New things were *always* nicer than old things. New dresses were smooth and stylish, not all wrinkled and full of spots. New houses had all sorts of built-in lights, and music that played at the touch of a button, and kitchens with stoves that cleaned themselves, and walls sprayed with chemicals that kept away bugs . . .

She pursed her lips thoughtfully. "Does Mr. Kelsey know that it's the mayor who wants to buy his property? Couldn't that make him raise the price?"

Her query startled him. "Well—it could, ordinarily, but I have an option to buy it for a fixed amount."

"What's an option?"

Frank stopped at the curb and checked his watch; he still had six minutes to use up before he could go in to the meeting. "An option is an agreement between the seller and the buyer. In April, I bought the right to buy the Kelsey Building anytime within the next twelve months for nine hundred and eighty thousand dollars."

"Almost a *million?*"

"That's right. If we restore it for a hundred and twenty thousand, turn around and sell it for a million five, we—the investors—stand to make four hundred thousand dollars."

"Wow!" Torie slapped her cheek, the way she had seen grownups do. "What about the money you already paid Mr. Kelsey? Will that be applied to the purchase price?"

He turned to her in alarm. Where did she pick up terms like "applied" and "purchase price"? Her questions were sharp—too sharp for a twelve-year-old. But then, he and Frankie had always talked business in front of the girls. He had never dreamed that Torie might be listening—much less *interested* in what they were saying.

"Yes, my deposit will go toward the purchase price," he snapped, "and that's enough on that subject. Don't you get any fancy notions about being in real estate."

"I'm going to be an actress." She paused a moment, then turned to him with a pout. "But why *couldn't* I be in real estate, if I wanted?"

"Too many con artists and thieves trying to take advantage of you. No decent man would marry a woman with the qualities it takes to succeed in this business. I've got to go in now."

"Papa?"

"Yes?"

"Will Betsy and Mrs. Richardson be there?"

"How would I know?"

"Papa?"

"What now?"

"If I hide in a corner, quiet as an itty-bitty mouse, could I go with you?"

"No!"

His tone communicated; further pleading would only anger him. At least she had had a ride and his full attention for half an hour. "Will you tell me all about the house when you come out?"

His face softened. "Sure I will, honey."

"Tell me all about the butler and the caviar and the—"

"I will. I've got to go now."

Torie sighed. She pressed her nose flat against the window as she watched her father brush off his lapels and ascend the steps to the town house, one of the dwindling number of private homes on Rittenhouse Square.

To her worshipful eyes the mansion seemed unaffected by time. Its red-brick façade looked bright and fresh, not faded and worn like most of the houses on Snyder Avenue. Below the shingled roof and dormer windows, newly painted shutters added to the well-cared-for look, and a bronze knocker gleamed against a spotless white door.

Unexpectedly, the door opened, and there stood a lady in a print dress, smiling pleasantly. Her eyes lit on the Chevy for a second, and Torie started to wave, but the woman made no response. Perhaps she was embarrassed that she wasn't wearing her maid's uniform.

Still staring, Torie began to make up new scripts for her game. This time, she and Peggy wouldn't be in the White House, they would be in the mayor's house. The Richardsons would be entertaining royalty. Prince Charles would see Torie/Betsy across the room, lose his heart on the spot, and invite her and her family to Buckingham Palace. In a fabulous coronation ceremony, he would crown her his queen. Yes, that would do nicely—to be queen of England. And what a queen she—Vittoria Di Angelo Richardson—would be.

The idea so captured her imagination, she almost didn't notice that the front door had opened again, and the lady in the print dress was walking . . . directly toward the car!

The woman motioned to her to roll down the window. "Hello, dear. I'm Simone Richardson. My daughter's having a birthday party in the garden. Won't you come in with me?"

"But I . . . I wasn't invited."

"I'm inviting you."

Numbly, afraid to believe what was happening, Torie scrambled out of the car and closed the door behind her. Following in a daze, she climbed the stone steps one at a time, her heart beating so fast she thought it would explode. She was sure she would wake up and find she had been dreaming. And yet, her eyes could blink, her ears could hear, her tongue could tickle her teeth. Even in her wildest fantasies, she had never conjured up such a possibility . . .

3
=

A PERSON DIDN'T have to grow up in Pennsylvania to know who the Richardsons were. Along with the Biddles and the Cadwaladers, they had one of the few names outsiders recognized as typically Old Philadelphia. Practically everybody on the East Coast knew that Mayor Matthew Adam Richardson came from one of the oldest Quaker families in Pennsylvania. Somewhat less common was the knowledge that law and finance had been the Richardsons' main occupations until early in the nineteenth century, when Matt's great-great-grandfather Welton, urged by President Monroe to run for the Senate, had achieved that lofty position. Welton's sons and grandsons had continued in political life, their careers marred by occasional scandals but on the whole honorable. The family's long record of public service was so well established in the minds of Philadelphians, in fact, that when a young, idealistic city councilman named Matt Richardson, an honors graduate of Haverford, announced his candidacy for mayor and promised to follow in the reform tradition of Clark and Dilworth, he was swept into office by an easy majority.

Matt Richardson's ancestry, however, was of little concern to Torie that November afternoon as she walked down the hallway of her dream house. Looking everywhere at once, she tried to memorize the wallpaper, the furniture, the paintings on the walls, the carpets, every detail she could capture. Peggy would expect a full recital, and she would get one. Never again could her best friend tease her about not knowing how rich people lived. From now on, she would practically be an expert.

"It's chilly in the garden, dear. If you get cold, I'll bring you one of Betsy's sweaters. What's your first name?"

"Oh, uh, Vittoria." Usually she found it too formal. Today it seemed fitting.

Mrs. Richardson held open a door and Torie passed in front of her, careful to excuse herself. It *was* chilly outdoors, but at that moment she didn't care if she turned into an iceberg. All she could think of was how lucky she was to have put on her best dress, hoping that her father might later take her for a soda.

A dozen boys stood around a glass-topped table on the lawn, balancing plates of cake and ice cream, joking among themselves. The girls stood apart in their own group, chattering quietly.

"Betsy, come here a minute, please."

Torie had already spotted the young hostess. Tall for her age, and slim, she had cocoa-brown hair, her mother's soft skin, and perfect features. She was even more attractive than her photographs.

"Hello," she said, walking over with a smile.

"This is Vittoria Di Angelo, dear. Her father's inside with Daddy and I thought you might want to offer her some cake."

"Glad to meet you, Vittoria. I hope you're not freezing."

"No . . ." She struggled for words—the right words—to show that *she* had manners and upbringing, too. "I'm sorry I didn't bring a present. I didn't know I was coming . . ."

"That's sweet of you, but I've got enough presents as it is."

"Lucky you! I guess it's, uh, the butler's day off, or he'd be serving the cake and ice cream."

"Butler?" Betsy laughed. "We don't have a butler. And if we did, I don't think I'd want him at my birthday party."

Torie felt herself turning crimson. What a stupid remark! What would Betsy think of her? "Well . . . happy birthday, anyway. Are you . . . fourteen?"

"Yes. How old are you?"

"Fourteen."

"Do you live around here?"

"A few blocks away." They could cut off her tongue before she would say "South Philly." "You're prettier than your pictures."

"Oh, thanks. Those photographers get to be a real nuisance. People think it's glamorous to have a well-known father, but you do miss your privacy." She stalled a few seconds, trying to remember her guest's Italian surname. "Is it all right if I just call you Vittoria?"

"That's fine." Betsy introduced the new arrival to her girl-friends, who nodded politely but with an obvious lack of inter-est—in contrast to their gracious hostess. The boys were having their own fun a few yards away, and Betsy was unable to distract them.

"Oh, dear," she murmured to Torie, "I wonder why they formed a circle. I smell trouble."

"What are they doing?" asked a girl in a wine velvet jumper with a lace blouse. Torie tried not to stare, but she couldn't help herself. The jumper had side pockets, a scalloped hem, and tiny pearl buttons. It was the most beautiful dress she had ever seen. By comparison, her wrinkled seersucker, handed down from Lisa, made her want to hide behind a tree.

"I'll bet they're fighting," said another. "Wouldn't you know it'd be Sonny Hopkinson and Nielson Hughes."

"Nielson's cuter than Sonny."

"Yeah, but I wish he'd get a haircut."

Torie listened and watched, understanding little of what was happening except that two boys seemed to be the focus of atten-tion. One had his back to her; the other she could see clearly—a lanky youngster with pale skin and long blond hair spilling over the neck of his shirt. His face was stern and his bright blue eyes seemed to burn like a tiger's.

"Come on, Vittoria," said Betsy, taking her arm. "Let's find out what's going on."

"That's okay. I don't need to meet them."

"They're being rude, and I don't like it one bit." She walked over to the group and put her hands on her hips. "Just what do you boys think you're doing?"

A freckle-faced lad faced her belligerently. "We're playin' hopscotch," he said, winking to his friends as he began to jump around on one foot. "Hippety-hoppity, hippety-hop."

His audience roared with laughter.

"Very funny," said Betsy. "Nielson, will you please tell me what's going on?"

"Tell your girlfriend what's going on, Nielson darling."

The blond boy glowered at the speaker. "Shut that oversized cavern you call a mouth, Hippety-Hopkinson."

"Coax me, baby."

"You're not my type."

"I'll bet you don't say that to Betsy."

"You want a knuckle sandwich?"

"Nielson—Sonny—stop that!" ordered Betsy.

Torie watched in silence, frustrated by her inability to help her new friend. Nielson seemed embarrassed by Sonny's behavior and tried to turn away, but the girls had come over to see what was happening, and Sonny was not about to relinquish the spotlight. "Do you always let your sweetie-pie boss you around, Nielson-Feels'em?"

One of the girls started to giggle, and soon they all joined in—except for Torie, who was waiting to see what Betsy did, and Betsy, who folded her arms angrily.

"Aren't you going to tell her you're sorry?" Sonny persisted. "Kissy-poo and make up?"

Nielson spun around. "Didn't your parents teach you any manners?"

"Ooh, lover-boy's getting mad. My parents did more than that. They got married so I wouldn't be a bastard."

"Sonny Hopkinson, you behave yourself!" Betsy stamped her foot. "And that goes for the rest of you, too! This is my party and my house, and while you're here, you'll act like gentlemen—is that clear?"

Nielson stood rooted to the ground, flushed with anger and confusion. If he answered her, he would lose face with his peers; if he didn't he would be rude.

Betsy apparently sensed his dilemma and spared him the decision. "Sorry I blew up, but I don't happen to like smart alecks." With a firm toss of her head, she returned to the girls, who were quick to rally around her and commend her for her action.

Torie stood apart from the group, alone, embarrassed, aware that she was a newcomer and not a member of their clique. In the excitement, Betsy had unwittingly abandoned her, and although several girls glanced her way, none made any move to invite her over.

Mrs. Richardson appeared briefly, summoned Betsy to take a phone call from her grandmother, and Torie thought about slipping off. But that would be cowardly, she decided, and impolite as well. Better to make the effort. Hesitantly, she approached the girl in the velvet jumper. "Your dress is very pretty," she said, trying to position herself so she wasn't standing outside their circle.

The girl turned to her with a frozen smile. "Yours is pretty too. What's it made of?"

The question came as a surprise. "Well, I don't know. Cotton, I guess."

"It's very chic," said another girl, who could barely contain her giggles. "The latest style. I think I remember seeing it in *House Beautiful.*"

All the girls were snickering now, and Torie knew she was being baited but hadn't the slightest idea what to do about it. If only she could become invisible . . . melt into the ground . . .

"What's your name?" asked a faceless voice.

"Vittoria."

"Victoria what?"

"Di Angelo."

"Sounds like a pizza factory. Do you live downtown? In South Philly?"

"No, I live around here."

"What street?" Questions were coming at her from all directions.

"Walnut," she said, picking the first name that came to mind.

"Wall-NUD?" taunted a new voice, mimicking her accent. "On Suh-sy-a-dee Hill?"

The laughter grew louder, and Torie started to feel sick—sick with shame, sick with embarrassment, sick with anger. Her only thought was to get away before she gave them the satisfaction of seeing her cry.

"You weren't invited to this party, Miss Walnud. What are you doing here?"

"I—Mrs. Richardson invited me—"

"You don't even *know* Betsy."

"Our fathers are friends."

"Is your father his janitor?"

"His pizza maker?"

"I'll bet he's the garbage man."

"He's *not* the garbage man."

"Not the *gaw-bitch* man? Maybe he's teaching the mayor to speak *In-glitch.*" The girls tittered.

"He's—I have to go now."

"To your mansion on *Walnud* Street?"

Tears streamed down Torie's face as she dashed through the hallway of the house and down the front steps to the car. Finding the back door locked, she opened the front and scrambled over the seat. Then she dropped to the floor and buried her face in her hands, letting the mortification and anguish pour out in loud, gasping sobs.

"Hey, *amico*, I can *walk* to the Union League. It's right by City Hall."

"I know where it is, Tony, but why walk when you can ride? And what's a nice dago like you doing in that nest of WASPs, anyway?"

"Gathering honey, I hope. Most of those old geezers don't even see me. If you're not one of them, they look right past you. But I got friends. I got *good* friends." The handsome dark-haired young man in the well-cut suit chuckled and climbed into the front seat of Frank's Chevy. No sooner had he sat down than two small hands reached out and covered his eyes.

"Guess who? No fair peeking."

"Uhh, Sophia Loren?"

"Nope."

"Gina Lollobrigida?"

"Nope."

"Brigitte Bardot."

"You're getting warmer."

"I give up . . . unless . . . unless . . ."

"Yes?"

"Could it be—Vittoria Francesca?"

"You hit the jackpot!" Torie pulled away her hands, leaned forward, and kissed the man on the cheek. She hoped she wasn't overacting, but she had to behave as if nothing had happened. No one must ever find out how cruel those girls had been—especially Tony, the man she loved and was going to marry.

"Sorry we took so long, honey," said Frank. "I hadn't any idea we'd be there two hours."

"That's okay." She had no complaints. The time had given her a chance to collect herself and clean up her face before her father came back. "Got another dime for me, Cousin Tony?"

"A dime?"

"Last time I saw you, you gave me a dime and told me to call you when I was twenty. By the time I'm twenty, phone calls will cost two dimes."

He laughed aloud and reached into his pocket. "I don't know about this kid of yours, Frank. She's getting to be a real capitalist. Here's your dime, Vittoria, and you'd better not spend it all at once. What are you doing there—in the back seat?"

"Papa let me come along for the ride."

"And you ended up at a birthday party. Were you on your best behavior?"

"Oh, yes. Betsy even asked me to call her one day."

"She's quite a little lady," said Tony. "Going to be some catch for a lucky guy."

"Oh? Did you give *her* a dime too?"

"No, she doesn't need my dime. Were the other girls nice to you?"

"Oh, very. We all traded phone numbers." She squirmed uncomfortably, wishing he would stop asking questions.

"What's the name of your friend whose father owns the drugstore?"

"You mean Piggytail? Peggy?"

"I'll bet Peggy doesn't have parties like that."

"No." So many impressions were whirling around Torie's brain, she sat in rapt silence, even forgetting to ask if they could stop at the Melrose Diner for a soda. The experience had been a shattering one, making her feel shabby and worthless and ashamed of being a nobody. She had been ashamed of her father and where they lived, too, and now she was ashamed of being ashamed. If only Betsy hadn't taken that phone call!

Well, someday she would be smarter and richer and more stylish than all those snooty brats put together. Except for Betsy. The mayor's daughter was a princess, and the dumb remark about the butler still made Torie cringe. And yet, the remark wasn't really so dumb. Everyone knew rich people had butlers. Just because the Richardsons were different—maybe they had so many other servants they didn't need a butler. How was she supposed to know about that?

Tony's voice broke into her thoughts. "So Betsy wants to see you again?"

"Why do you keep asking about Betsy? Are you in love with her?"

He shook his head, amused. "No, I'm not in love with her. I'm true to you, Vittoria. But you'd better hurry and grow up. I can't wait forever."

"Don't push, Tony. She's growing up too fast as it is."

Torie leaned forward and rested her chin on the upholstery, anxious to change the subject. "Did you guys make a deal?"

"Not yet. It looks promising but we've a long way to go. What'd you think of the mayor's suggestion, Frank?"

To Torie's relief, the men forgot about her and began to rehash the meeting, talking spiritedly until Frank slowed to a stop before an ornate brick-and-sandstone building with a wide double staircase. Rays of sunlight glinted off the polished brass railings.

Tony got out. "Be a good girl, Vittoria. And thanks for the ride, *amico.* I'll call you in a few days."

"*Ciao,*" said Frank. "I'll be waiting."

Driving home from Center City, Frank was too wrapped in his own reflections to notice his daughter's uncharacteristic quiet. Given the choice, he would never have picked his late wife's thirty-two-year-old cousin as either a friend or a legal adviser. Half of South Philly knew that Rosanna's father, Vito Silvano, had ties to organized crime—and rumors were beginning to circulate that Tony was connected too. Frank would have preferred almost any other lawyer to a member of the Silvano family.

Nevertheless, he had no reason to fault Tony and, on the contrary, still felt vaguely indebted to him. His mind drifted back to his and Rosanna's wedding day. Both sides had strongly opposed the union. The Silvanos thought Rosanna deserved better than a struggling real estate broker, and the Di Angelos thought the Silvanos were mobsters—which most of them were.

After the ceremony, the guests in the Silvanos' living room had divided like the Red Sea. The bride's family ignored the groom's family, the groom's relatives shunned the bride's relatives, and all attempts to bring the parties together failed.

Observing the standoff, fourteen-year-old Tony Silvano had gone into action. Switching on an inexhaustible supply of jokes and small talk, the youngster proceeded to work the wedding crowd as deftly as a politician at a rally. After half an hour or so, the boy's enthusiasm, coupled with the magic of the grape, began to take effect, and the feuding in-laws drifted together.

Then Tony had grabbed the microphone. "Pope Pius couldn't make it today," he teased, "but he wanted me to give the newlyweds his blessings and say that he hopes your life will be like a ship launching. You start out with champagne and proceed on water ever after."

Assorted boos and catcalls had followed Tony's "message," prompting Frank's father to borrow the mike for a retort. As soon as he finished, almost everyone wanted to toast the bride and groom. That evening Frank told Rosanna, "If it hadn't been for Tony, our wedding would have sunk like the *Titanic.*"

The day was amazingly clear in Frank's mind, and the memory made him smile. Tony was no genius, but he *was* persuasive, and he knew how to make people like him. Rosanna had been crazy about her cousin, and when he opened his law practice in 1956, she had prevailed upon Frank to hire him.

Two years later, it was Tony's sad duty to process her will. At the time, he promised Frank a brighter future, boasting that his firm's well-connected friends would soon be "swamping" Di Angelo Realty with business. After seven years, however, Adrian Kelsey was the first client to materialize.

Frank had strong reservations about Tony's ability to make good on his promises and regretted having let himself be talked into investing his total savings of ten thousand dollars to buy the option. But there was no backing out now. Tony still expressed confidence that the building would be sold and had pushed hard to get himself in with the mayor. Frank had to believe it would all work out.

Reaching into his pocket for a plastic container, he popped a Miltown into his mouth. Never before had he needed medicine to calm his nerves, but never before had he risked so much on one man's advice. His fervent hope was that the Kelsey deal would soon be signed and secured—and he could throw the damn pillbox into the garbage.

4
=

PEGGY SHEA PLOPPED down on her bedroom rug, hugged her folded knees, and leaned forward eagerly. "Now tell me again, T. D. Just like you told me on the phone."

Torie sat cross-legged a few feet away, hoping she could remember what she had said. "Tell you *again*?"

"From the beginning."

"Okay. But this is the last time." The recitation began slowly. "I was sitting in the car outside the mayor's house, see, when this butler with a British accent came over, knocked on the window, and told me the Richardsons wanted me to come inside to Betsy's party."

"What was he wearing?"

"A black butler suit. And a diamond pin in his necktie."

"Necktie? You mean ascot?"

"Yeah. Anyway, he opened the door for me and then Simone came over and introduced herself and showed me around. The first thing I noticed was these big, huge chandeliers with thousands of little lights."

Peggy's mouth fell open. "In the living room?"

"All over. But *'specially* in the living room. And the white rugs were so thick, I could hardly see my shoes—"

"I thought you said they had—what's that word?—fancy floors."

"Parquit." She spelled it as she had seen it written: "P-A-R-Q-U-E-T. The parquit's in the hall, not the living room. And then they have this big marble mantel, and chairs trimmed with real gold—"

"What about the birthday cake?"

"That came later. It was chocolate fudge and three feet tall. Two men had to carry it in and set it on the table."

Peggy wrinkled her brow. "I thought you said they wheeled it in."

"I said they wheeled it *out.* After it was cut. They didn't want to get crumbs all over the floor."

"Oh." An apologetic nod. "Then what?"

"Well, then the butler tapped me on the shoulder and said my father was waiting for me, and I had to go."

"Weren't you *furious?*"

"No, not really. The girls have their own group and they all know each other, and I was a stranger. I mean, they were very nice to me. Betsy said we should get together sometime, but I don't think I'll bother."

"Why not?" asked Peggy, a note of fear in her voice.

Torie shrugged, relishing her momentary power. "I wouldn't have much fun with them. I like you better."

"Really?"

"Yeah. You're my best friend."

Her companion blushed with relief. "What else?" she asked. "What about the boys?"

"Dreamy. They all had suits and ties on, and this one blond guy, Nielson, was kind of flirting with me."

"Did you flirt back?"

"I didn't have a chance. Hey, Piggytail, do you realize it's almost seven o'clock?"

"Shoot. I guess you have to go home."

"Not if you don't want me to." Torie attempted a raised eyebrow, a look she had been practicing all week in front of her mirror. "I could call Papa and see if I could sleep over, and then we could play our game. I've got a new idea."

"You do?" Peggy jumped to her feet. "What is it?"

"We could be the Richardsons. One of us would be Betsy—"

"Yes, yes!" Peggy said excitedly. "*You* could be Betsy, and President and Mrs. Kennedy have invited you to the White House to meet Elvis Presley. And I could be . . ."

Less than a week later, on Friday, November 22, 1963, Frank Di Angelo was showing a house to a client when the owner came running into the kitchen. "The president's been shot," she cried. "They've rushed him to a hospital."

"Oh, my God," groaned Frank. "Is he all right?"

"Nobody knows. They've taken him off in an ambulance."

Shaking his head, he took the prospective customer's arm. "Terrible thing, shooting the president. Terrible." He paused a moment, then shook his head again. "But life must go on. As I was telling you, Mrs. Shorenstein, you can't go wrong with this town house. It's a buyer's market right now, and the property values in this neighborhood are going nowhere but up. I can help you find reasonable financing if you're interested."

They walked out to her car, and he opened the door. "No rush, of course. Take your time and think it over. The main thing is for you and your family to be happy. I'll call you in a few days."

His smile faded as the woman drove off. All he could think of at that moment was Torie—her infatuation with the Kennedys, and how she would react to the news. Absurd as it was, the notion that fame and money could protect you from hurt seemed to give his younger daughter comfort. She had somehow convinced herself that the more riches a person had, the more that person would be insulated from the kind of pain she had suffered when her mother died. He had seen no reason to disillusion her. Now he wondered if he should have.

Hurrying to his Chevy, he switched on the radio. ". . . not yet known whether the sniper fired three or four shots. The president has been rushed to Parkland Memorial Hospital, where he is undergoing emergency surgery. We should have word on his condition any minute . . ."

The bulletins continued, each update sounding more and more ominous, until Walter Cronkite's terse report came, thirty minutes after the shooting: "The president of the United States is dead."

Lisa was the first to come home from school that afternoon, shaken, but stoic. "We mustn't question the ways of the Lord," she said, setting down her books. "I'm going to church to say a rosary for the Kennedys."

Minutes later, an unusually subdued Frankie appeared and joined his father in front of the television screen. "What's the latest? Were the Russians involved?"

Frank shrugged. "We don't know yet. Did you cancel your basketball game?"

"Yeah, none of the guys felt like playing. Pretty horrible, huh?"

"Terrible. We're all so vulnerable. Even a president can be dropped by a little piece of steel."

"They got the bastard who did it, though. Some pinko with a cheapie shotgun. I hope they fry his ass."

"That won't bring back—Torie!" called Frank, as a figure slunk past the doorway. "Where've you been?"

"Just walking."

Red, swollen eyes confirmed his fears. His instinct was to reach out and try to comfort her. He sensed she would have liked to curl up and cry in his arms, but she couldn't—not with her big brother watching. "I'm sorry about the president. I know how much you liked him."

"Yeah."

"Want to talk about it?"

"What's there to talk about?"

"Sometimes it helps to get your feelings out in the open." One of his lady friends always used that phrase. He teased her about her social-worker jargon and secretly called it psychoshit, but he wasn't above borrowing a line when he needed it.

Torie bit her lip. "I guess Jackie'll have to move all her clothes and things out of the White House."

"Yes. Lady Bird, Mrs. Johnson, will be moving in."

She looked up, her voice imploring. "Will someone please tell me how they could kill the *president*? Didn't he have bodyguards around him all the time?"

"Yes, but he was a warm, friendly person, and he wanted to ride through the streets and wave to the crowds."

"What if he'd had a bulletproof vest?"

"That wouldn't have helped. The bullets hit his head and neck."

She grimaced as the scene flashed through her mind. "It's not fair. It's just not *fair*."

"Not much in life is fair."

For a quick moment, the injustices of the world seemed almost to overwhelm her. She swallowed hard and tried to speak, but the words locked in her throat and she turned and fled the room.

Father and son exchanged glances. "Want me to try to talk to her, Papa?"

"No, she's a strong little girl." Frank reached for a cigarette. "She'll be all right."

Forty minutes later, Frank climbed the stairs to his daughter's bedroom, rehearsing the dialogue he had carefully prepared. He rapped on her door and entered. "Got a minute?"

Torie shut the book in her hands, shoved it under the pillow, and looked up from her bed. "I'm okay, if you're worried about me."

The sight of her small sad face touched him. Pushing aside a pile of magazines, he sat down on the covers. "I know you're upset, and I'm upset too. Families are supposed to help each other in bad times. I thought if we talked a little, we both might feel better."

"I didn't realize *you* were upset. Would it help you to talk to me?"

"Yes, that's why I'm here. I know how much you admire the Kennedys. I admire them too. Did you know the Bouviers originally came from Philadelphia?"

"Sure, I know everything about Jackie. Her great-great-grandfather came over from France and made all this furniture and stuff. Miss Rashbaum kept talking about it in school today—I don't know why."

"Probably because Philadelphians are proud that one of their own became first lady." He took a long breath, then spoke casually. "If you feel sorry about what happened to Mrs. Kennedy, why don't you write her a letter?"

"A letter?" Her eyebrows shot up. "Why should I do that?"

"Because that's what people do when someone has a tragedy."

"Did people send you letters when Mama died?"

"A few did. Most of them came to see us. I doubt you'd remember. You were only seven."

"I remember." As if she could forget that awful parade of friends and relatives who rang the doorbell every night for a week. And they all brought trays of food: fresh-cooked lasagna, baked hams, macaroni salads, hot garlic bread, pastries, cheeses . . . The rich smells had drifted up to her room and made her want to vomit.

"You can't call on Mrs. Kennedy because she lives too far away," he went on, "but you can write her a condolence note. That means"—how had he worded it in his mind?—"telling her you want to express sympathy."

"She wouldn't read my letter."

"If everyone felt that way, no one would write to her. And that would make her feel no one cared. You wouldn't want that to happen, would you?"

" 'Course not." She nibbled her forefinger. "If I *did* write to her—and I'm not saying I'm going to—what would I say?"

"That the president was a wonderful man. That you're sorry for her loss. That you admired him and you admire her very much. Thoughts like that give people a lot of comfort. I'll help you write it if you like."

"I can write it myself." She sat up suddenly. "Do you have her address?"

"Yes. And if you finish the letter tonight, I'll mail it early tomorrow morning. It could be the first one she gets."

"Do you think she'll answer me?"

"There's a chance."

"Then I guess I'd better get started." Reaching across her bed table, she grabbed a pencil and notepad and began scribbling— too intent on her new project to see her father get up and cross the room.

Bless you for your inspiration, dear Lord, he thought, as he closed the door behind him. I'll never call it psychoshit again.

*   *   *

"Isn't she the most beautiful woman you've ever seen?" Torie stared in awe at the television screen in the Sheas' living room. "She walks with her head in the air like a queen. Do you think she's wearing makeup?"

"Don't be naïve." Peggy's sixteen-year-old sister, Kelly, sat sipping her Metrecal and watching the funeral cortege make its way to Arlington Cemetery. "Wouldn't you wear makeup if the whole world was looking at you?"

"I'd be too sad to think about it," said Peggy.

"I'd wear lipstick," Torie conceded, squinting at the set. "Jackie's is real pale—almost pink. I wonder if she's as sad as she looks."

"Are you kidding?"

"No. Rich people have all these servants around to take care of them and be nice to them and try to please them. I don't think they get sad the way we do."

Kelly shook her head in exasperation. "Money has nothing to do with it when you lose someone you love. Rich people get sick, feel pain, and go to the bathroom just like we do."

"Yeah, but I think T. D.'s right," said Peggy. "If I had a chauffeur and a Rolls-Royce to drive me back to my fabulous mansion after my husband's funeral, and all these famous people making a fuss over me, I'd be lots less sad than if I was sitting in some one-room apartment all alone."

"Oh, brother." Kelly rose and grabbed her glass. "You girls are too young to understand about life. If you'll excuse me, I've got homework to do."

"We'll excuse you." Peggy's face lit up as her sister's footsteps pattered down the hall. "Shall I shut the door?"

"By all means, uh, Winston." Torie flashed a smile. "And tell Claudette to get me out of these *dreadful* black clothes. A person can't sit home mourning all day . . ."

5

=

"CIAO, AMICO." TONY Silvano slapped his cousin on the back and pulled up a chair. "Happy Saint Paddy's Day, eh? Let's have some vino to celebrate. Waitress!"

"None for me."

"A few drops won't kill you, Frank. You worry too much."

"I've got ten thousand reasons to worry." He lit a cigarette and glanced around. At half-past eleven on a Tuesday morning, the neighborhood trattoria was still uncrowded. "Look, Tony. That money I paid for the option on the Kelsey Building . . . you swore to me the investment was as safe as a Treasury note."

"And it is. How many times do I have to tell you?"

"I know what I know. My option's up April 14, 1964—exactly four weeks from today. If we don't sell the building, my money's gone."

"I have a plan." He smiled up at the waitress. "Bring us a small carafe of house red, *bella,* and I'll have the frittata. Frank?"

"Meatball sandwich. What happened with the inspector?"

"I'll get to that. First tell me, how are the kids?"

"They're fine. But I want to hear—"

"Vittoria? Is she doing any better at school?"

"No. She reads library books all the time instead of doing her homework." He exhaled a stream of smoke. "The president's death hit her hard. She wrote a note to Jackie and got a lovely answer—not a form letter. She's been carrying it around like it was a message from God."

"Good for her."

Frank covered his glass as the waitress brought wine. "Give it to me straight, Tony."

"I was about to." The lawyer lowered his voice. "Friday afternoon, Bob Manning, the building inspector; Skip Friend, the contractor; and yours truly went over every inch of that property. I won't go into details, but Manning's a tough old bird, and he insists we can't get rid of the mold and dry rot unless we strip the building to its skeleton."

"Impossible! Adrian would never agree—"

"I told him that. I said Kelsey won't let us touch the outside. Skip swore to him we could clean up the dry rot without gutting the place, but Manning wouldn't listen."

"Oh, my God." Frank wrung his hands.

"Stop worrying, will you? I've played the game a thousand times and I know exactly where we stand. Manning's just waiting for us to make a move."

The older man scowled. "Do you mean what I think you mean?"

"He knows what's going down and he wants his share. It's just human nature."

"It's not my nature. I've been twenty-five years in this business and I've yet to bribe anyone."

"Semantics." Tony made eye contact with a pretty woman across the restaurant. "What you call bribery is nothing more than a small token of gratitude. And there's no law against showing gratitude. Remember, Frank, the sale of this building is going to change your life. Once you've signed the papers, word'll get around that you're a man who handles big properties and who has no time for pissant parking lots and rundown houses anymore. This is the break you've been waiting for—your entrance to the big time."

Frank shuddered. Tony was smooth-talking him again, feeding hopes and spinning dreams, and he could feel himself weakening. Hundreds of real estate transactions had passed through his hands over the years, but they had always been small ones, and with people he knew. He didn't like not being in charge—not knowing exactly what terms and conditions were being discussed, or even what stage the negotiations had reached. And yet, if Tony was right . . .

"What are you suggesting we do?"

"Now that's the Frank Di Angelo I know and love." Tony grinned and filled his wineglass. "Move a little closer, and I'll explain my foolproof plan . . ."

*   *   *

"Are you feeling okay, Papa? You seem under a lot of strain lately."

Frank set down the *Inquirer* and peered over the top of his spectacles. Two days had passed since his brief meeting with Inspector Manning, and he was hoping for good news momentarily. "Things are looking up, Frankie. We should get city approval of the Kelsey Building before too long."

"You think it's going through? You really think we'll be rich?"

"Not rich, exactly. But a lot better off than we are."

"What does Tony think?"

"He's very optimistic."

"He's sure worked hard for us, hasn't he. I mean, there he is, with his fancy Porsche and his custom-made suits, and a new woman every five minutes, and he still thinks about his family. He could've made the deal and socked away the cash for himself, but instead he took you in with him."

Frank held his tongue. Tony was about as altruistic as a cobra. He had come to Frank because he needed ten grand. Period. "Another week should do it. By that time, we—" A ring at the door interrupted him.

"I'll get it. Must be Girl Scouts selling cookies. They're all over the neighborhood." Frankie was back in a moment, looking puzzled. "Some cops to see you."

The paper slid to the floor as Frank stiffened in his chair. He collected himself and hurried to the front stoop. The sight of two uniformed men gave him a cold shiver. Stepping outside, he shut the door behind him. "How can I help you, gentlemen?"

"Frank Di Angelo? I'm Officer Kettner, this is Officer Victor. We have a warrant for your arrest."

"On what charge?"

"Attempted bribery of a public official. We'll have to take you down to the station. Do you want to get your coat?"

"Yes." Calmly and deliberately, Frank walked back inside, took a jacket from the hall closet, and turned to his son. "I have to go with the policemen and I don't know when I'll be home. Where are the girls?"

"In the kitchen."

"Here's some money. Take them over to Pat's for steaks, and don't tell them where I've gone. I don't want them to worry."

"But—shouldn't I call Tony?"

"No, just take care of your sisters."

As they embraced, unexpected tears filled Frankie's eyes, and it took him a second to realize why; he was reacting to his father's behavior. Frank was neither questioning nor protesting. He was responding almost as if he had been expecting the officers' visit. Something was wrong . . . very wrong.

Concern turned to anger as he watched the police escort his father to the car and drive away. Who the hell did those pigs think they were? What right did they have to harass a law-abiding citizen? Swearing under his breath, he slammed the door and strolled into the kitchen, his lips set in a false smile. "Anyone for cheesesteaks?"

Lisa looked up from her casserole. "Are you kidding? I'm fixing macaroni."

"Papa had to leave suddenly." He waved a twenty-dollar bill. "He said I should take us all to Pat's. Special treat."

"Whoopee!" Torie shrieked and threw her arms around his neck. "He sold the Kelsey Building, he sold the Kelsey Building! We're going to be rich, aren't we, Frankie?"

"Uh . . ."

Lisa set down her bowl. "It's something else. I can tell by your face. Something's wrong."

"No, no." He avoided her eyes. "Everything's fine."

Torie drew back. "Something *is* wrong. Better tell us, Frankenstein. Where'd Papa go?"

"Damn you." He knew he was disobeying instructions, but he was too worried to keep his fears to himself. "All right. He went off in a car with the fuzz."

"Jesus preserve us," murmured Lisa. "I hope he won't miss Palm Sunday."

"Was he upset?" Torie asked.

"No. In fact, he acted pretty cool—as if he wasn't even surprised to see them."

"I don't like this one bit." Torie crossed the kitchen, picked up the phone and plunked it on the table. "You better call Tony."

The months that followed dragged by slowly. With an anguished heart, Frank had to tell his eighteen-year-old son that going to college was no longer feasible. If a jury convicted him and sent him to prison, Frankie would have to take full responsibility for the business. Fortunately, Frankie was not disappointed. A high school education was all the schooling he felt he needed, and he was glad to have the opportunity to work with his father, at least until the trial began.

In the spring of 1965, *City and County of Philadelphia* v. *Frank Di Angelo* finally came to trial. Frank knew Tony was defending him the best way he knew how, but his plea of diminished capacity—"Not guilty by reason of mental incompetence"—did not inspire great hopes. Worse yet, the prosecutor's case was solid. Exhibit A, the blank white envelope with the six crisp fifty-dollar bills Frank had handed the inspector inside a magazine, was as incriminating as a smoking gun and a warm corpse.

The morning of the trial, Tony sat with Frank in the bare-walled waiting room. His client's face was drawn and gaunt. "We really got shafted, old friend. That city inspector's office has been a nest of thieves for years. The only reason one of them was clean is because the bastard was a plant. I'd like to shove his goddamn balls down his throat—"

"It wouldn't help."

The lawyer rose to his feet and began to pace. "Why'd it have to be you, of all people? You've never made a dishonest buck in your life. That's how I was able to talk the mayor into using you as our broker. And what does the cretin do? Calls out his task force and tells them to get you."

"No, no, don't blame Richardson. His men set traps, that's all. They didn't know *I'd* walk into one of them."

"Then let 'em slap you with a fine and be done with it." Tony stopped pacing and spun around. "I've made up my mind. I'm telling the court that you were dead set against bribing the inspector. It was my idea and I forced you into it. If they want to send a man to prison, let 'em send the right man—me."

"No, Tony, for God's sake!" Frank's face came alive for the first time. "You mustn't do that. It would only make things worse."

"How can I let you take all the blame? How can I live with myself if you go to prison for a crime I put you up to?"

"Goddamn it, no!" Frank's voice was loud and angry. "No matter what you said, they wouldn't acquit me. But they *would* convict you. The result would be that two of us would go to prison instead of one. And besides, Tony . . ." He tried not to get emotional. "I need you out there. I need you to look in on my kids. They love you."

Relief shone on Tony's face. He owed it to Frank to have made the offer, even if he never intended to sacrifice himself. After all, Frank was right. It wouldn't make the prosecutors any easier on the defendant and would only destroy another life in the process. His life, to be exact.

"I'll do whatever you want—whatever puts your mind at peace." He took Frank's arm as they walked to the door. "We haven't lost yet, *amico*. Not by a long shot."

The small courtroom was jammed with friends, strangers, reporters alerted by the mayor's office that His Honor would be testifying, and a handful of city officials hoping to use the trial to their advantage. Twelve rows behind the defense table, Frankie, Torie, and Lisa, neatly dressed and terrified, sat in grim silence.

After what seemed hours to them, the judge appeared in his black robes, advanced to the bench, and gave instructions to the jury. The room was silent as Tony called up half a dozen character witnesses and, finally, a behavioral psychologist. "Dr. Katherine Feinstein?"

Brisk and energetic in her Harris tweed suit and low-heeled shoes, the woman strode up to the stand and swore to be truthful.

Tony had her recite her credentials; then he approached the witness box. "May I ask if you've had a chance to examine the defendant, Dr. Feinstein?"

"Yes, I have. On four separate occasions."

"And what did you learn from these sessions?"

"I believe that Mr. Di Angelo is suffering from chronic depressive syndrome due to unresolved grief over the death of his wife."

Torie nudged her brother. "Papa's not real depressed anymore. That's a lie!"

"Shhh," he whispered. "Tony knows what he's doing."

"Dr. Feinstein, would you tell the court how this depressive syndrome manifests itself?"

"It affects people in different ways. Mr. Di Angelo suffers insomnia, variations in mood, and recurrent thoughts of death and suicide. He also experiences poor concentration, indecisiveness, social withdrawal, memory loss, and occasional disorientation."

"Would this ailment—this disorientation—be enough to make him act irrationally at times?"

"Obviously."

"Could it impair his judgment to the degree that he might not realize what he's doing?"

"Objection, Your Honor." The prosecutor bounced up. "Defense is leading the witness."

"Sustained."

"I'll rephrase the question." Tony clasped his hands dramatically. "Is it possible that a person suffering from chronic depressive syndrome might make an impulsive gesture . . . grasp at straws, perhaps, without realizing the ramifications of his action?"

"Objection, Your Honor. Counsel is putting words in the witness's mouth."

"Overruled. You may answer, Dr. Feinstein."

"Yes, it's possible."

"Could this person's judgment be further impaired by medication?"

"Yes."

Tony turned to the jury and paused a few seconds, letting the idea register. Then he whirled to face the witness. "At the time of Mr. Di Angelo's meeting with Mr. Manning, was the defendant taking any medication?"

"Yes. His doctor had prescribed a tranquilizer called meprobamate—Miltown. Its main effects are drowsiness, slurred speech, a slowing down of all mental and motor functions. Mr. Di Angelo told me he had taken a pill at lunch that day."

"Thank you, Doctor. No more questions."

The judge's sharp eyes fixed the prosecutor. "Do you wish to cross-examine?"

"Yes, Your Honor." Deputy District Attorney Zeke Raider, a short, stocky man with kinky hair and thick glasses, approached the stand. "Dr. Feinstein," he asked, in a slightly mocking voice, "do you happen to know what dosage of Miltown the defendant was getting?"

"I believe it was twelve hundred milligrams."

"Is that the usual dosage?"

"Yes."

"Could you be more specific?"

"The standard adult dosage is twelve hundred to sixteen hundred milligrams."

"So twelve hundred is the *lowest* adult dosage—the lowest end of the scale. How many times a day does a person take this pill?"

"It varies with the individual."

"As I understand it, the normal dosage is three to four times a day. Are you asking this jury to believe that one single low-dosage tranquilizer was enough to make the defendant behave so 'irrationally' that he sealed six fifty-dollar bills in an envelope, hid them in a magazine, and presented them to the inspector who was holding up the sale of the Kelsey Building?"

Laughter rippled through the room.

"Objection, Your Honor!"

"Sustained."

"Let me ask you this, Dr. Feinstein. You said the cause of the defendant's depression was the death of his wife. When did his wife die?"

"I'm . . . not sure."

"I believe you'll find it was in January of 1958, more than seven years ago. Are you aware that Mr. Di Angelo has had close relationships with a number of attractive women for six and three-quarters of those grief-stricken years?"

"*Objection*, Your Honor!"

"Sustained."

The prosecutor resumed his seat. "No further questions."

On the second day of the trial, Zeke Raider called his final witness. Impeccably garbed in a black suit, vest, and striped tie, Mayor Matt Richardson took the stand. His bearing commanded instant attention.

"Mayor Richardson," the prosecutor began, "would you please tell the court why you agreed to take the time to testify today?"

"I'll be glad to, Mr. Raider." He paused a few seconds, then spoke in his quietly dramatic voice. "As everyone in this courtroom is aware, I am personally committed to rooting out corruption in city government. My task force has researched present-day abuses in the building and construction industry and concluded that crooked housing inspectors and public officials are taking more than eighteen million dollars a year in illegal payoffs from realtors, developers, builders, and contractors."

"Objection, Your Honor. The witness is trying to imply guilt by association."

"Overruled. Continue, Mayor."

"Thank you, Judge Weigel." Richardson rose to his feet and grasped the wooden railing. "As I was telling the court, barely a nail is hammered in this city without someone getting paid under the table for it. The bribe-takers are guilty of succumbing to greed and temptation, but the *real* villains are those who seduce and tempt with their—"

"Objection!" Tony cried.

"Sustained. Strike that last sentence."

"Mayor Richardson," said the prosecutor. "The defendant is charged with attempted bribery of a city official and willful intent to violate building-code regulations with reckless disregard for public safety. Don't we tend to think of these types of offenses as white-collar crime? So-called victimless crimes?"

"They're anything but." The politician swung around to the jury. "You know who pays the price when bribed officials overlook code violations? *You* do, my friends. You and your loved ones are the innocent victims of electrical fires, collapsed arches, rotted support beams. Your children are the ones who get maimed and murdered—"

"Objection!"

"Sustained. Please stick to the facts, Mayor."

Richardson finished his remarks, then made a noisy exit, accompanied by the flashing and clicking of cameras. The attorneys gave their closing arguments, the judge again instructed the jurors, and a short two hours later, they filed back into the courtroom.

"Has the jury reached a verdict?"

"Yes, Your Honor." A well-dressed black man stood and faced the bench. He spoke with no hesitation. "We find the defendant, Frank Di Angelo, guilty on all counts."

There was a flurry of movement as reporters hurried to the exits. The judge rapped his gavel for attention, set a date for sentencing, and adjourned the court.

Torie sat rooted to her seat, pallid and shaken. Having suffered the shattering loss of her mother, she was ill-prepared to face the realization that her beloved father was now being taken away from her too—simply because he had tried to make some money for his family.

Frankie and Lisa, their own grief barely restrained, guided their sister out of the courtroom. "You okay?" asked Frankie, but Torie could scarcely nod her head. All she could think of was that her father had been wronged . . . victimized . . . made a scapegoat. Frank Di Angelo was no criminal. He had been defeated in court because poor people were helpless against rich people—people like Mr. Bigbucks Richardson.

Coping with her collapsed world took all the control she could muster. She knew that for as long as she lived, she would never forget the day her father's freedom was stripped away—stolen from him without charity or mercy by a system that cared more about birth and dollar signs than about justice.

And she made herself a promise: Someday, *she* would be a rich person too. She would be so rich, so famous, so fantastically powerful that nothing in this cruel, unfair world could ever hurt her or her family again.

PART
II

6

=

DESPITE THE IMPASSIONED cries of local politicians and citizens' groups who demanded Frank Di Angelo's blood, a poignant article in the *Evening Bulletin,* under the byline of a reporter named Keith McGarren, proclaimed the ten-year sentence to be unduly harsh punishment. None of Frank's friends or family had any doubt that his own defeatist attitude, his inflexible sense of guilt, and his reluctance to speak out in his own defense had helped solidify the case against him. That knowledge, however, was of little use or consolation.

Once Frank was imprisoned, new scandals erupted, and his case was soon forgotten, leaving his children to try to pick up their lives. Amazingly, Frankie found that Di Angelo Realty survived the uproar, that his father's friends and associates remained loyal to the firm, that the publicity not only generated sympathy for the family but attracted new clients as well.

With life's usual irony, Frankie found himself something of a celebrity in the Italian community. Strangers noticed him, spoke to him, went out of their way to say how sorry they were that a good man had been wronged. Many insisted that a three-hundred-dollar gift could hardly be called a bribe, and ascribed the verdict to anti-Italian prejudice. The surge in business astounded Frankie, for in the year preceding the trial, while he'd been learning the profession from his father, sales had been unusually slow.

Having access to money was a new, intoxicating experience for Frankie, and his first thought was for his sisters. As if trying to blot out their recent unhappiness, he bought them a color television set, a dishwasher, a party dress for Torie, and a gold crucifix charm for Lisa. Then he splurged on a red Ford convertible

49

for himself, rationalizing that the girls could enjoy it too. Shortly after his conspicuous spending spree, Tony Silvano materialized, expressing sudden concern for his "three favorite cousins."

The more Tony tried to tease and joke with Torie, however, the more she felt a growing distrust of the man she had thought she loved—and had fantasized about—for almost half her childhood. His failure to save her father from prison had been a bitter blow; he had not only let her down, he had let down the whole family. Whatever warm feelings she once had for him had cooled and were growing colder.

She was even beginning to suspect that it was Tony who had masterminded the crime—planned it step by step, then conned her reluctant father into taking all the risks. But she kept her suspicions to herself.

Frankie had no such reaction. To his mind, Tony had done his best in court and always had the family's interests at heart. The dapper, smooth-talking lawyer was his hero—charming, smart, successful, and adored by the ladies. Frankie wanted nothing more than to be like him in every way.

Well aware of the younger man's admiration, Tony took Frankie in hand, urging him to order custom-made suits from his tailor, recommending the fashionable London Shop that monogrammed his shirts, sending him to his personal "stylist" for fifteen-dollar haircuts. In return for introducing Frankie to attractive older women known to be generous with their favors, Tony granted his cousin the privilege of picking up all the checks on their double dates.

Lisa and Torie, involved in their own adjustments to a lonely family situation, paid scant attention to Frankie's extravagances. Confused that the wonderful father she loved and respected could also be the sinister man the prosecution had painted so darkly, Lisa took refuge in denial and negation. What happened had been unreal—an illusion. The only reality she could depend on was her religion, and the solace and stability it offered. In the weeks following the trauma, Father James became her confidant, Sister Rhoda her best friend, the church her second home.

Fourteen-year-old Torie had no such haven to flee to. This new tragedy in her life left her even more scarred than the first— and increasingly desperate to protect herself from whatever might assail her in the future. School was a constant torment, for some of her classmates were merciless, hiding ugly notes in her desk, calling her father a killer, threatening bodily harm.

Once, when she left her locker open, she çame back to find her possessions smeared with mustard. Another time, a missing magnifier from the library turned up in her coat pocket—a prank that almost got her expelled.

The harassment continued, and of all her former friends, only Peggy, no less loyal and devoted than before, clung to her—reassuring her that the other girls were jealous because she was pretty, and that the boys only copied what the girls did.

Vowing to tough it out, Torie soon learned to control her emotions, but she would never forget her tormentors. Pain, anger, and resentment welled up inside her, growing and festering and feeding her determination to show her schoolmates, along with the rest of the world, that she was not only as good as they were but a damn sight better.

She would clear her father's name someday, but she wouldn't stop there; her sense of outrage demanded more. She wanted those who had made her suffer to suffer in return. And she wouldn't rest until they did. How she realized her goals didn't matter at the moment, but get to the top she would. Once you were there, once you were covered with fame and riches and power, everyone had to look up to you. More important, no one could ever look down on you—or hurt you—again.

"Aren't they the grooviest?" Peggy Shea leaned her head on her hands and swayed dreamily to the music. "If I was stranded on a desert island, and I could have anyone in the world for a companion, I'd pick Paul McCartney. Or John Lennon."

"Not me." Torie sucked the last drops of Coca-Cola through her straw, set the glass on the table, and looked around apprehensively. The diner was getting crowded, and the waitress would soon be wanting their booth. "I'll take Mick Jagger. The Stones are sexier. Besides, I thought you loved Frankie."

"Sinatra?"

"You don't *know* Sinatra, silly."

"Oh, you mean *our* Frankie. I do love him, but he doesn't even know I'm alive."

"He knows you're alive. It's just that that dumb Tony keeps fixing him up with tramps. I saw a picture they had taken at the Hollywood with their dates. I wish that big jerk would drop dead."

"Don't you even *like* him any more?"

"He's sickening. I don't know what I saw in him for so long. I guess it was a childhood crush."

"He is kinda greasy—like a gangster. He's not a nice person like Frankie."

"Hmm . . . Frankie. There must be *something* I can do." Torie was always looking for ways to repay her friend's loyalty. "Wanna share another Coke?"

"No, we'd better go. I'm broke, anyway."

"This is my last dime. I'll play 'Michelle' for you." Torie slid her coin into the jukebox on the wall.

"Oh, boy, thanks!" Peggy hummed along with the record for several seconds, then frowned. "I've sorta given up on Frankie."

"You can't give up. I know he likes you 'cause he told me so once."

"He did? What'd he say?"

"It was ages ago. I don't remember exactly. We were talking about friends and things, and he said he thought you were cute— or maybe, he thought you *would* be cute when you grew up."

"I suppose he thinks I'm a little girl."

"Well, we'll just have to change his mind. Why don't you get all dressed up with makeup and stuff and come over Sunday? He's always home on Sundays. Steffi's coming over too, and we can watch a movie."

"Ugh. Why do you like her?"

The hurt in Peggy's voice distressed Torie, and she was quick to respond. "She's not a close friend. She's just kind of fun sometimes, and she doesn't have her nose stuck in the air the way those other bitches do. Won't you come over?"

"No, I can't stand her. She's cheap and vulgar. And you'd better watch out. You'll get into trouble running around with that fast crowd. Besides, I'm too young for Frankie right now. I'll probably have to wait three or four years."

"Yeah. But then we'll work on him together—I mean *seriously*." Torie squeezed Peggy's arm as they rose and headed for the exit. "Know what, Piggytail? Someday you're going to be my sister-in-law."

By the spring of 1965, Harvard professor Timothy Leary's nationwide advice to "drop out, turn on, tune in" had its impact on Torie's troubled psyche, and although she remained close to Peggy, she had begun to see more and more of Steffi Adler, a tough, streetwise girl with long legs and frizzy blond hair. Together, Torie and Steffi tried on new personalities, smoked marijuana and hashish, and on three scary occasions, went "tripping" on acid.

At least once a month they would cut school and take the bus to Wanamaker's department store in Center City. Pretending to be shopping for a gift for their mothers, they would spend hours wandering through the aisles, gazing at the counter displays, occasionally watching a smartly dressed woman pay seventy-five dollars for an ounce of perfume or a scarf from Paris with hand-rolled edges.

Steffi taught Torie how easy it was to "accidentally" drop two or three lipsticks on the floor and slip one into her pocket. But when the saleslady began to recognize them and threatened to call security, Torie's brief shoplifting career ended. She had no desire to be involved with the law.

Other days, Torie would ask Steffi to ride with her past Center City, all the way up to Chestnut Hill, where they would hide in a doorway and watch the rich girls in their yellow blouses and blue plaid skirts file out of Springside, the exclusive private school. Several times she caught glimpses of Betsy Richardson walking arm in arm with one of the girls she remembered from the party two years earlier. It seemed like a lifetime ago, and she wondered if Betsy still liked Nielson Hughes—and vice versa.

Particularly vice versa. For reasons she couldn't explain, the proud, intense boy who hadn't the slightest idea of her existence had become more and more of a fixture in her mind. She and Peggy no longer playacted their fantasies (and were embarrassed, in fact, even to discuss their childhood games), but Torie still devised scenarios—schemes that cast her and Nielson in romantic situations where they shared torrid glances, then fell into each other's arms. Kissing and petting were as far as her imagination took her, but marriage and a future were definitely in the script.

One time she even persuaded Steffi to visit the Penn Charter School in Germantown, where they waited more than an hour for a three-second glance of Nielson running for the bus. Bored and unimpressed, Steffi had refused to go there again.

Another time they put on their best clothes and rode up to Rittenhouse Square, where they strolled into the Barclay, pretending to be tourists. A desk clerk gave them each a price list, teasingly suggesting they might like suites. Brochures in hand, they roamed through the *T*-shaped lobby, trying not to stare at the paneled walls with their crystal sconces, the well-worn Persian rugs and high vaulted ceilings, the busboy in his gold-and-green uniform sweeping cigarette butts into a polished pan. An attempt to order martinis in the bar ended their tour abruptly; they left with sharp warnings and a personal escort to the exit.

A veteran of twelve actual sex acts (or so she claimed), Steffi insisted on taking Torie to a Planned Parenthood clinic for birth-control pills. Thus prepared, Torie found herself able, willing, and curious—but reluctant to squander her virginity on one of the faceless jocks from Bishop Neumann High, who wanted little more than to borrow their fathers' cars, drive down to the Lakes, and make out with whatever female happened to be in the front seat. Morality had nothing to do with her decision to wait. She simply wanted to find a boy she liked.

"We got troubles, kids." Frankie chain-locked the front door, dropped a pile of papers on the bench in the hallway, and stepped into the living room. Torie sat cross-legged on the floor, her eyes fixed on the television set.

Lisa came running in from the kitchen. "What is it, Frankie? What's wrong?"

"Take it easy. No big deal." He walked over to his other sister and tapped her shoulder. "Think you could spare five minutes, Your Highness?"

"Huh?" She looked up in surprise. "Oh, hi, Frankenstein. Yeah, I can spare five minutes but I'm going out as soon as this program's over."

"The word is 'yes,' not 'yeah.' What about dinner?"

"I'll get a bite at White Tower."

"The hell you will. You've been going out too damn much lately. And that outfit is disgusting. Your jeans are too tight and you wear enough makeup to paint a circus. Where do you think you're going looking like a whore?"

She glowered at him. "I have a date."

"Jesus H. Christ." He groaned and sank onto the couch. "Papa would break your neck if he knew—and mine, too. You'd better be home by ten."

"Yeah, well, Papa's not here and you're out screwing your head off every night—but don't worry, I'll be home by ten. I always am."

Lisa shifted her weight nervously. Any mention of sex made her uncomfortable. "Will you please tell me what's wrong?"

"All right." Frankie sat up and folded his arms. Acutely aware of his new position as head of the household, he tried to look and sound authoritative, but his tone was heavy with guilt. "I feel really lousy about this. I had to let Delia go today."

"Oh, no!" Torie's face fell. Delia Fleischer had been the office secretary, receptionist, file clerk, and all-around assistant for more than ten years—as far back as she could remember. "How come?"

"Well, I—uh—got a little overextended last month. Too many bills, too many deadbeats at the office. It's only temporary. Nothing to worry about."

"Was she terribly upset?" asked Torie.

"Not really." He smiled to himself at yet another confirmation of his secret observation. Lisa was the great bleeding heart, prattling endlessly about oppressed minorities and starving masses, whereas Torie, who rarely gave such issues a thought, reacted to anyone in trouble with instant generosity. Once, when a beggar had come to the door, Lisa had stood there spouting Christianity while Torie had run to the kitchen and fixed him a sandwich. "Delia already has a job lined up at the bank."

"Then what's the problem?" Lisa rapped her spatula impatiently. "Have you spent all our money on your girlfriends? And that fancy car you bought?"

"That fancy car only costs me sixty bucks a month. Look, I admit I blew it and I'm sorry as hell. I really am, and I'll make it up to you. But right now, I can't afford a secretary and I can't run the office by myself. School gets out Friday and I need both of you to help."

"*Forget* it!" Torie's eyes darted back to the screen. "I'm going to be much too busy with makeup work—unless I drop out of school, which ain't a bad idea. I don't learn anything in that dump anyway."

"Don't say 'ain't.' You *would* learn if you stopped cutting classes." Frankie folded his arms angrily. "And don't give me that crap about makeup work. Teachers don't give homework over summer vacation. Suppose you tell me what you plan to do the next three months that's so important you can't help your family in an emergency?"

"Emergency? I thought we were doing so well—"

"We *were* doing well, and we'll do well again. But at the moment, we're up shit creek." He turned to Lisa. "What about you?"

"It's impossible." Her hands opened in helplessness. "Father James and Sister Rhoda count on me to set out candles and polish the brass and do all sorts of chores around the church. This week they're letting me help Sister Angela pass out books in Bible class. I gave my word I'd be there."

"Saturdays too?"

"That's even busier."

He turned back to Torie. "Looks like you and me, kiddo."

"Okay, okay." She knew she couldn't afford to argue further. If he looked too closely into how she spent her time, she could be in trouble. Besides, he did seem genuinely worried. "I'll help you for a few hours during the day, as long as you don't fuck up my evenings and weekends and give me a lot of shit about what I do."

"I'll give you plenty of shit if you keep talking like that. How many times have I told you nice girls don't use four-letter words? You'll never get a husband with a sewer for a mouth. And I won't butt into your life as long as you're home every night by ten. Can you start work Monday?"

"Yeah, I mean yes—I guess so." A glimmer of a smile crossed her lips. "I wouldn't want you to be up a certain creek by yourself."

"That's my baby sister—all heart." He leaned back on the couch, resisting the urge to hug her and tell her how relieved he was and how much he appreciated her sacrifice.

His head, however, was too filled with self-blame. Papa had left specific orders not to encourage her interest in the family concern, but Papa hadn't foreseen that a number of his cronies would take advantage of his incarceration to delay making payments, that some of the new clients would not be above profiting by a young man's inexperience, or that the young man himself would be so stupid as to blow a small fortune trying to live the way his flashy cousin did. All facts considered, Frankie had no choice. Lisa had commitments to the church. It was either draft Torie or go under.

The first few weeks at the office were slow and tedious, and soon Torie had to work nine to five, or longer, which she hated. Only the realization that the family could lose its livelihood made her show up every day as promised. When school reopened in the fall, she continued to work afternoons, and by June of 1966, after a year of answering the phone, running errands, filing papers, looking over her brother's shoulder, and asking constant questions, she was beginning to get a feel for the business. Real estate was like a true-life Monopoly game; the more property and houses you sold or owned, the more fees and rents you collected.

But it was *ever* so much more complex and in a strange way fascinating. She found herself spending several hours each day reading manuals, trying to understand how inflation, deflation, and swings in interest rates affected costs and rents and mortgages . . . how to structure loans . . . how and where to obtain financing . . .

"Sorry to interrupt your studies, young lady. I'm Jack Slate."

Torie looked up from a desk in the cramped two-room office. A pleasant-faced man was observing her with interest. "Can I help you?"

"I'd like to see Mr. Di Angelo."

"He'll be back in a minute. Want to wait?"

"Thank you." He pulled up a chair and made himself comfortable. "What's your name?"

"Torie Di Angelo. I'm Frankie's sister."

"A very lovely sister, if I may say so. You must get tired of hearing that."

"Umm, not really." The compliment flustered her and so did the stranger. He was too well-dressed and too polite to be from the neighborhood. She wished he would stop staring so hard. "What do you want to see Frankie about?"

"Some property he owns. A small lot in Strawberry Mansion. I represent a firm that might be interested in buying it."

His statement brought a grin. "That's good. I like buyers better than sellers. Are you in real estate?"

"I'm with the Evans Company. We own, develop, and manage real estate in markets throughout the East Coast."

"One of our competitors?"

He smiled tolerantly. "No, we're a fairly large corporation."

Her questions kept the man talking until Frankie returned and led him back to his desk in the other room. She tried in vain to hear what they were saying.

On his way out, Jack Slate stopped by her chair. "Nice to meet you, Torie. I hope I have the pleasure of seeing you again."

"Oh—me too. Did you buy the property?"

"Your brother and I have a verbal agreement. I'll have the

papers ready for him to sign tomorrow." He leaned down and whispered in her ear. "Are you free tonight?"

"Umm—I'll do my best in that matter." Her eyes rolled furtively to the left, indicating that Frankie would not approve. "Did you leave a number where we can reach you?"

"Yes, I did." His manner quickly became impersonal. "Thanks for your courtesy."

"Got any I.D., miss?"

"Yeah, sure." Torie rested her purse on the counter, groped for a wallet, and drew out a card. "Here you are."

The bartender peered down. "Twenty-one's getting younger all the time. What'll you have?"

She perched on the bar stool as if she had perched on a thousand bar stools and announced, "Screwdriver, please."

"Gimme a Schmidt's." Jack Slate waited for the man to move away, then swiveled around. The fancy language and formality were gone. "How old are you, really?"

"Seventeen." It wasn't a big lie. After all, she *had* had her fifteenth birthday in February, and here it was already June. "How old are you?"

"Twenty-eight." He struck a match. "Are your parents very strict with you?"

"They're both dead." At least that was her story. She, Lisa, and Frankie went to visit their father in prison every two weeks, but Torie never spoke of him to others. What was she supposed to say: "My father's locked up"? Then she'd have to explain *why* he was locked up, or they'd think he was a murderer or a rapist. It was far better to bury Papa with Mama, for the moment, and not have to deal with it.

She leaned forward and inhaled her cigarette. "Frankie's sort of my guardian and he's plenty strict. Makes me be home by ten every night. That's why I had to meet you so late."

"Ten o'clock isn't late. How'd you escape?"

She giggled. "I've got a shitproof system. Frankie always goes out about eight-thirty, and Lisa—my sister—goes to bed at nine-thirty so she can get up for early mass. They leave me sitting in front of the TV set, so I just wait about ten minutes and split."

"Doesn't Lisa hear the door?"

"Lisa could snore through a rock concert. Besides, I always leave the set on till I get home."

"What if Frankie comes home first?"

"Frankie almost never sleeps in his own bed. Are you worried he'll get pissed off 'cause you took me out?"

"Big brothers can get very possessive about their little sisters. But you were smart enough to call me, and we're here now, so let's forget about Frankie."

She laughed and blew out a stream of smoke. "Are you scared he might get so pissed off he won't sell you the property?"

"He already said he would."

An impulse seized her. "But after you left, a friend told him the land was worth more than the ten grand you offered. Frankie's going to raise his price."

"He'd better not. Whoever bought that lot twenty years ago didn't pay more than a few thousand for it."

"Why do you want it so badly?"

He squirmed on his stool. "I don't want it *badly*. My firm's thinking about redeveloping the area someday. They told me to pick up a piece of property here and there . . . whatever's available. Frankie'd be an ass not to sell it."

"Are you going to build on it?"

"I thought I just answered that."

"Oh, okay. Fuck business." She smiled at him and lowered her voice. "I've got some good grass in my purse. Wanna get stoned?"

The small room in the Solonex Motel was unlike any room Torie had ever seen. A king-size bed took up most of the space, save for a single stool and dressing table. Above it, in a tarnished frame, a seminude blonde sprawled on a leopard-skin rug.

Torie slipped off her jacket and tried to sound casual. "Nice place. Do you come here often?"

"My first time." He moved toward her and took her chin in his hands. "Are you scared?"

"Of what?"

"Of me?"

"Why should I be?"

"You shouldn't be." His fingers moved down to her breasts. "Let's get rid of these clothes."

"I thought we came here to turn on—"

"We'll turn each other on."

"But . . ." Going to bed with him was definitely in her plans. She liked his looks, she liked his manners, she liked the fact that he was older. She had even sacrificed the last half of *The Red*

Skelton Hour to the challenging task of choosing her prettiest bra and panties. "I need a joint first. I need to relax."

"I'll relax you, baby. Leave it to me." He began to kiss and fondle her, letting his hands roam over her body. Within seconds, he was tugging at her jeans.

"Please, I'm not ready. I need a joint—"

"No, you don't, baby. All you need is some good humping." Before she could argue, she found herself stretched out on the bed, her legs bent and parted. A man she barely knew was lying on top of her, unzipping his pants. "I thought about this the minute I saw you . . ."

She hadn't wanted her first time to be rushed. She had hoped it would be slow and tender and somehow full of good feelings. But it was too late to set up conditions.

A stab of pain made her cry aloud. She felt as if he were tearing her flesh with a knife as he forced himself in, muttered something about how good it felt, then gave a grunt and flopped down on her chest. It was done. Her first sexual experience was over almost before it began.

"You've got a great body, kid," he said, rolling over and closing his pants. "We'd better get you home now."

The moment Torie entered the office the next day she sensed trouble. Pretending not to notice, she murmured, "Hi," hung her jacket on a hook, and dropped into a chair.

Frankie was beside her in an instant, his eyes stern and demanding. "All right, Miss Innocent, cut the crap. Where were you last night?"

"Last night?" A shiver ran up her back. "I was home watching television. Where do you think I was?"

"Why didn't you answer the phone? I called you six times, from ten-ten to ten-thirty."

"I guess the set was on too loud."

"Don't lie to me. You listen for the phone as if your life depended on it."

"Sometimes I get so involved I don't hear too well."

"What were you watching?"

"Uhh, *The Red Skelton Hour.*"

"That's over at nine-thirty." He grabbed her arm and pulled her to her feet. "Suppose you tell the truth for once in your life. What was so fucking important that you had to sneak out last night?"

"Oh, all right." She squirmed out of his grasp. "Some of the seniors had a graduation party and I wanted to go. I knew you wouldn't let me, so I didn't even ask."

"Where was this graduation party?"

"Some girl's house. They picked me up. I don't know the address."

"Torie," he said, his lips trembling with anger, "I'll beat the shit out of you if you don't stop lying to me. For the last time— where *were* you last night?"

Inside his brain, a bomb was about to go off; she could almost hear it ticking. Once before, when she had lied about taking money from his wallet, he had exploded and slapped her around. This time, he looked mad enough to break her bones. "I went out with Jack Slate," she blurted.

"I thought so!" He held his breath. "I looked in and saw him whisper to you before he left. Where'd you go?"

"To a bar. We . . . had two drinks, then he took me home. That's all it was."

"Guys like that don't buy girls drinks without demanding something in return." He drew back from her, afraid of his own temper. The veins in his fists stood out like wires. "Torie," he said, barely able to get the words out, "I know something very bad happened last night. If you tell me it did, I won't lay a hand on you. I swear to God, I won't touch you. I just want the truth so I know what I'm dealing with."

Too frightened to lie further, she lowered her head and nodded. Giant tears slid down her cheeks. "I didn't want to do it, honest I didn't. But he made me. He was very strong and he forced me—"

Without a word, Frankie turned and stormed out the door. Her fingers shook as she grabbed the phone book and found the number of the Evans Company. "Dear God," she groaned, "please let me get to him first."

Torie was nearly frantic when she locked up the office at six that evening. She hadn't heard anything from Frankie since he stomped out with murder in his heart, and none of the messages she had left to warn Jack Slate had been returned. For all she knew, they both lay bleeding to death in an alley.

Half-walking, half-running, she hurried the six blocks to Snyder Avenue, arriving home just as Frankie's convertible pulled up to the curb. "Thank God," she murmured. At least her brother was alive.

Frankie reached over and opened the car door. "Get in."

She obeyed meekly, almost afraid to look at him. When she finally raised her head, she could see that he was exhausted. His shoulders drooped, his hair was disheveled, his face looked white and drained.

"Your boyfriend must be hiding out somewhere," he said in a quiet voice. "I couldn't find the son of a bitch, so you can deliver a message for me. Tell him that lot's not for sale to him or his company and never will be."

"But I already told him you wanted more money for it. I said you wanted a hundred grand."

"A hundred grand?" He snickered. "Sure, I'll sell it for a hundred grand, and the price is not negotiable. If he asks why, tell him I'm just doing to him what he did to my sister."

Her cheeks flushed with embarrassment.

"I've been thinking about you all afternoon," he went on, staring through the windshield, "and I've had to make some decisions—tough ones. It's hard as hell for me to take responsibility for what you did, but I can't lie to myself any longer. I've let *you* down, I've let Papa down, and I've let myself down."

"No, no, it's not your—"

"I've been a selfish, extravagant, irresponsible jerk, I've nearly caused the family to go bankrupt, and I've set the worst possible example for my sisters. I can't blame anyone but myself for what happened last night. If I'd spent more time with you and paid more attention to you, and not let you get so chummy with that hot-pants little groupie—"

"You mean Steffi? She's not my best friend. Peggy is."

"Peggy's a sweetheart. She'd do anything for you—for all of us. I should've encouraged you to see more of her."

"But I *do* see Piggytail."

"Then keep on seeing her and stop seeing Steffi. I'll try to be nicer to Peggy when she comes around—make her feel we love her and that this is her second home. I'll take you three girls to Pat's one night—"

Torie sat up excitedly. "Oh, Frankie, *would* you?"

"Damn right I would." His expression softened as he looked at her. Such a simple offer seemed to give her so much pleasure. The happiness on her face touched him. "Things are going to be very different around here. In the first place, I'll never let you down again. I've got to be Mama, Papa, and big brother all rolled up in one for you, Tor, and by God, that's exactly what I'm going to be—solid as the Rock of Gibraltar."

"I don't want you to change."

"It's too late. I've already changed. I can never undo what happened last night, but I can sure as hell learn from my screw-ups." His voice took on new force. "I made another decision, too. School gets out in a few weeks, and I don't see much reason for you to go back in the fall. You don't go to classes, you're flunking everything, and you're spending too much time with the wrong crowd. I'm going to see the educational authorities and arrange for you to study at home and work with me . . . full time."

She gaped at him. "You mean—no more school?"

"On three conditions. The first is that you come to work every Monday through Friday, and I mean *every* day, from nine to six. If you play hookey even once, I swear on the Bible I'll call the cops and turn you in for smoking grass."

"You wouldn't!" she cried, horrified.

"Try me."

"I'll come to work every day, I promise. You won't have to call the police."

He sighed. "That's up to you. Secondly, no more seeing Steffi and no more dope. If I sniff the least trace of pot on you—"

"No hanging out with Steffi. No turning on. No more drugs."

"And thirdly, last night won't ever happen again. That *was* the first—?"

"Yeah—I mean yes, I swear it!" She looked over fearfully. "Are you going to tell Papa?"

"I'm not telling anyone, and neither are you. As far as the outside world goes, you're a virgin, sweet and pure as the morning dew, and I'll mutilate the first person who says otherwise."

"Oh, thank you, Frankie." She reached for his arm. "I won't sneak out again, I won't use bad language, I won't smoke grass, and I'm going to be a real help to you in the office. I promise I am. You'll see."

The harshness drained from his voice as he turned to face her. "It must be tough for a girl to grow up without a mother. I miss Mama, too, but it's different with guys. It's not as big a deal. Girls, well . . ."

"I love you so much, Frankie."

"I love you too, kiddo." His eyes grew moist as he took her hand and squeezed it. "From now on everything's going to be all right."

7

=

THE RELIEF OF not having to go back to school somewhat compensated Torie for the break-off with Steffi. At the same time, she found herself secretly relieved to be free of her friend's influence. So much of her own behavior, she realized, was no more than an attempt to impress Steffi—to prove that she was equally daring and adventurous, and not the square the other kids thought she was.

Peggy gladly filled the friendship gap. She didn't know why Torie suddenly dropped Steffi, and she didn't care. All that mattered was that Torie had come to her senses. Frankie, too, was pleased that his sister seemed to be on the right track again, and to Peggy's delight, he kept his promise and took the three girls to Pat's cheesesteak heaven the following week.

At first Torie resented having to spend so many hours in the office. Her attitude began to change, however, as Frankie drew her more and more into his work, taking time to explain the various appraisal, financing, and closing processes, making sure she understood the basis of preparing contracts, clarifying some of the complexities of tax laws, and even giving up an afternoon to drive her around and point out all their listings and properties.

Her sharp questions both amazed and concerned him. In his mind, the job was strictly temporary. Her assistance would tide him over a rough period and give her a few years to mature before she married and settled down. He reassured himself that pretty as she was, and growing prettier by the day, some good-looking guy would come along and sweep away whatever thoughts she might have about pursuing a career—an ambition she had never voiced, but one he was beginning to suspect existed.

On a Tuesday morning in late June of 1966, a short, stout man walked up to Torie's desk. "I'm Richard Blum with the Evans Company. Is Mr. Di Angelo in?"

She winced. No one from the Evans Company would be welcome. "Yes, he is, but—"

"Thank you." He breezed past her into the rear office and presented his card. "How do you do, sir. May I sit down?"

Frankie was not uncivil. "Have a chair. What's on your mind?"

"The Strawberry Mansion property. My firm is still interested in buying it."

"And I'm interested in selling. As my sister may or may not have told your representative, the price is one hundred thousand dollars."

"But that's exorbitant!" The man's face reddened. "Jack Slate is no longer with our company. Whatever grievance you had with him . . . there's no reason to penalize our firm."

"I'm not penalizing anybody. That's my price and if you don't like it, I'm quite content to sit with that lot until Hell turns into a skating rink."

"Perhaps you'll reconsider when you see what I've brought." Blum raised his briefcase to the desk and opened it. Inside were ten neatly tied packets of hundred-dollar bills. He looked up smugly. "Mr. Evans has authorized me to pay you fifteen thousand dollars in cash. According to city records, you'll be making a profit of twelve thousand, eight hundred dollars. Your father only paid twenty-two hundred for that lot in '43."

"Sorry, pal, the fish aren't biting." Frankie's voice rose with sudden anger. "Whoever had the bad sense to send Jack Slate to this office is no one I want to negotiate with. Anybody who meets my price can buy that lot. Otherwise, get the hell out of here and don't bother me again."

Torie watched dumbfounded as the shocked visitor wiped his perspiring forehead, packed up his briefcase, and marched out the door. Before she could speak, Frankie glared at her. "And don't you say a word to me," he snapped. "Not a goddamn word!"

*　　*　　*

Less than a week later, Frankie's spirits took a leap. All he would tell Torie was that he had met a beautiful woman in distress, helped her change a tire, and they had quickly become "good friends." Several mornings after that, however, Torie was surprised to find her brother sitting at the breakfast table.

"Are you okay?" she asked, taking a chair opposite him. "Didn't you say you might not be home last night?"

"I just got here. Where's Lisa?"

"Saving her soul, as always. What's wrong?"

"Nothing."

"Come on, Frankie. You're gonna mope around all day if you don't tell me. I'll bet it's something to do with what's-her-face."

"Yeah, Anne. Anne Carter. A real looker, that girl. And sweet . . . charming . . . sexy . . ."

"What happened?"

His chest rose and fell. "Know what a plant is? And I don't mean the growing kind."

"Sure. Inspector Manning was a plant . . . a phony. On television once, the cops wanted to get these bad guys, so they sent in a plant."

"It works the other way, too. When the bad guys want to screw the good guys, they send in a plant. I should've known she was too good to be true."

"How'd you find out?"

"Well, I *did* spend the night with Anne. Woke up early this morning . . . wanted a smoke, so I strolled into her kitchen. I happened to see this list of emergency numbers she'd posted on the wall by the phone. She had the police department, the fire department, and her own office number—which puzzled me because she'd told me she didn't work. Just for fun, I dialed it. I almost swallowed my cigarette when the voice said, 'You have reached the Evans Company.' "

Torie gasped. "Oh, no!"

"Then it all fell into place—how she's been dropping hints about wanting to build a house, wanting a nice lot that wasn't too expensive. And I almost fell for it, too. I would've sold her that Strawberry Mansion property for next to nothing!"

"You didn't—?"

"No." He waved his cigarette. "Thanks to this filthy, dirty habit, your brother is *not* the number-one asshole of the century. Number two, maybe."

"Close call." She bit into a doughnut. "Evans must want that lot awfully bad to go to so much trouble."

"He has as much chance of getting it as I have of growing tits."

"Wait a minute. What if—"

"Forget it. We don't need creeps like that in our lives. We don't need their goddamn money, either."

"The hell we don't! If you don't sell to them, you know what'll happen? You'll sell that lot to someone else. Maybe you'll be lucky and get fifteen grand for it, or maybe you'll be dumb enough to sell it to one of your girlfriends for ten. But whoever buys it is gonna turn right around and sell it to the Evans Company for twenty grand. Or fifty. Or maybe even more. And then you *will* be the asshole of the century. Capeesh?"

"I don't give a shit."

"Well, *I* give a shit, and I'm not letting you throw away a gold mine." She shook her finger at him. "Listen to me, Frankie. You're going to write Evans a letter. Repeat your counteroffer of a hundred grand, tell him it's nonnegotiable, and that if you don't hear from him within a week, the price doubles. Send the letter right away, Special Delivery."

Her vehemence surprised him. All he cared about was salvaging his pride. All she cared about was making money—which wasn't such a bad idea. Maybe they *could* do both—screw the bastard *and* make money. A long shot, but why the hell not? He gave her an amused glance. "A hundred thousand for a lot that cost twenty-two hundred? Don't you think that's a little ridiculous?"

"Of course it is." She tilted her head. "But what have we got to lose?"

The call came two days after the letter went out; Mr. Evans wanted to talk to Mr. Di Angelo as soon as possible. Skeptical and suspicious, Frankie drove to the company's sleek headquarters in Center City. There he met with the chairman, Grant Evans, a vice president, an accountant, and an attorney, all of whom watched their chief executive sign a paper agreeing to buy the Strawberry Mansion property for one hundred thousand dollars. With a copy of the agreement clutched in his hands, Frankie left the building in a daze.

When he returned to his office late that afternoon, Torie took one look at his face and jumped into his arms with a scream.

Too excited to go back to work, they picked up Lisa at St. Monica's and celebrated with steaks at Pat's and blueberry pie at the Melrose Diner.

On Sunday they drove three hours to pay their bimonthly visit to Holmesburg Prison. A minimum security inmate, Frank was allowed to see his children in a small green-walled visiting room. A uniformed guard led the prisoner in and locked the door.

Frankie embraced his father warmly. "You're looking well, Papa." It pained him to see the familiar face so pinched and drawn. Yet the faded denims outlined a trim, solid frame, and the eyes staring back at him were sharp and alert.

"It doesn't matter how I look," said Frank, happily hugging his daughters. "It matters how I feel. And seeing my family makes me feel wonderful. Now sit down. Sit down and tell me how everything's going."

"We're rich!" piped Torie, unable to contain herself. "You know that lot you had in Strawberry Mansion? Frankie sold it for a hundred thousand dollars!"

"That worthless old sandlot? Who bought it?"

"A firm called the Evans Company." Frankie grinned proudly. "They're going to develop that property so they're buying up the block. We asked an outrageous price and told them to take it or shove it. We never dreamed they'd take it."

"We?"

"Uh, your daughter and I discussed it a little."

Frank had no need to ask which daughter. "Such deals come along once in a lifetime—if ever," he said, turning to Torie with a frown. "You can't expect something like this to happen again."

"Oh, no, Papa. It was just a freak accident." The hell it was, she thought. If it happened once, why couldn't it happen again? And again? Yet she understood his concern and played along. "Money doesn't fall into your lap every day."

"It certainly doesn't," he repeated, far from reassured. "Well, maybe God had a reason for sending me to this place. He wanted Frankie to have a chance to run the business and show he's a damn sight smarter than his old man ever was."

Frankie beamed. At that moment, nothing in the world could have convinced him the sale was the result of anything but his own brilliance. "Know what we're going to do with that loot? We're going to hire the best criminal lawyer in the state and get you out of this dump. That's number one."

"No," said Frank, "I won't hear of it. I want you to take that money, buy a new house, and move the family to a good neighborhood, maybe in South Philly, maybe close by—as long as it's near the business and the girls' schools. Don't worry about me. I'm adjusted to being here and I can handle it. That's my decision and there'll be no more discussion." His tone was firm. "Now tell me, Torie, how're you doing with your remedial work?"

"Oh, fine. I'll probably make the honor roll when I go back in the fall." They had agreed not to mention either her plan to quit school or her temporary employment.

"I'll settle for a C average," he said, with a wink to his son. "What about my spiritual daughter? How's the good pastor?"

"Father James sends his blessings, Papa. He said to tell you he prays for you every day."

"That's kind of him. I pray for myself now. There's a little chapel here where I have nice quiet chats with the Lord. It's been a lifesaver for me . . . having a place where I can be alone."

"Why, that's *wonderful.*" Lisa's voice rang with approval. "That's a lot better than getting all that money."

"What's wrong with getting money?" demanded Torie.

"It's what it does to people. Makes them tell lies and pretend to be things they aren't." She scowled at her sister, prim and angelic in a white dress that made her look very much the innocent virgin Lisa strongly suspected she wasn't. "Some people have to play a role all the time. You understand, don't you, Papa?"

"Did you kids come here to see me or to fight?"

"To see you," said Frankie, quickly. "Did I tell you Matt Richardson wants to run for senator? The girls and I are going to make sure he gets his butt kicked in."

"Not this girl." Torie folded her arms defiantly. "Simone and Betsy were very nice to me. I would never do anything to hurt them."

"What about Richardson? Was he nice to you when he took the stand and testified against your father?"

"Papa said we should forgive him, didn't you, Papa? You said he was just doing what he had to do as mayor, and those things he said in court weren't personal against any of us. I hated him at first, but I thought about it a lot and I finally decided you were right. He was just trying to keep his word to clean up the city. In his eyes, he was doing something honorable—trying to save people from *real* criminals. You said so yourself, Papa."

"Yes, yes, I don't want you children to hold hatred—" Frank was stilled by the appearance of the guard.

"Time's up, folks," he said coldly. "You have one minute to say your good-byes."

In February of the following year, 1967, Frankie was able to realize his father's lifelong dream. Leasing the Snyder Avenue house to an elderly couple, he moved his family into a three-story colonial in West Mount Airy, a pleasant wooded district twenty-five minutes north of Center City. His sisters finally had separate bedrooms, and their father would come home from prison to windows that looked out on the lovely trees and hillside of the Wissahickon Creek gorge.

The morning after moving day, Torie sat in her brother's red convertible, peering at the line of cars in front of them. "I wish we could take the bus to South Philly," she growled. "It'd be lots faster."

Frankie shrugged. "Yeah, but I need my car to show properties."

She took out a pad and pencil. "An hour from house to office—two people, two hours, that means four hours commuting back and forth, five days a week. You know, I've been thinking about something. It's crazy for us to be knocking ourselves out selling lots to firms like the Evans Company and letting them develop the property. We could be developing it ourselves."

"We're real estate agents, not developers."

"Any law that says we can't be both? Any law that says we can't have *two* offices—one in South Philly for selling houses and stuff, and a branch in West Mount Airy that *develops* properties?"

"I suppose my sixteen-year-old sister wants to run this new branch by herself?"

"You'll run it, Frankie." She tweaked his ear affectionately. "With your genius mind and supersalesman personality. We'll start out nice and simple with a few small buildings and multi-family units. Then, when we've had a little experience, maybe we'll go on to subdivisions and selling home sites and things."

"And who's going to run South Philly?"

"You'll hire someone, and we won't have to spend four hours a day commuting."

"Ridiculous. Impossible."

"Shit, Frankie, don't you want to be rich? Do you wanna sit

in a crummy office in South Philly for the rest of your life barely making a living?"

"Don't say 'shit.' At least it's a living I'm sure of." He glanced sideways as the traffic came to a stop. "Suppose I did consider your crazy idea. Where would we get the money to open a branch in West Mount Airy?"

"There's enough in the bank now—or almost."

"That account is for investment purposes only."

"Well, isn't a branch office an investment?"

He was silent for several moments. Ever since his traumatic self-confrontation after the Jack Slate incident and his realization that he had driven the family to the brink of bankruptcy, he had gone to the other extreme, becoming almost Spartan in his spending habits. He had sworn to himself never to take chances or to risk their security again—and yet he was enough of a pragmatist to admit that his sister's business intuition had proven remarkably sound. "I don't know. I'll have to give this a lot of thought. Suppose I get drafted and shipped off to Vietnam?"

"They can't draft you. You're needed here to run *one* office, and you'd be even more needed with two. Besides, I don't think the war's gonna last much longer. Did you hear Martin Luther King's speech? And Bobby Kennedy's asking everyone to stop bombing each other so they can talk about withdrawing troops."

"I wouldn't count on it. We're in deep trouble over there, and Johnson keeps making it worse. Before we talk about opening another office, I'll have to consider it very, very carefully."

"I knew you'd say that, Frankie-boy!" She kissed him excitedly. "You're much too smart to get stuck in a silly old rut."

Nineteen sixty-eight was a year of violence. Bobby Kennedy and Martin Luther King fell victim to assassin's bullets; American soldiers massacred men, women, and children in the South Vietnamese village of Mylai; race riots, drug-infested rock concerts, and antiwar demonstrations swept the nation.

By early fall, Frankie had hired Emilio "Jock" Sangiacomo, a free-lance real estate broker, to take over the South Philly quarters. After making sure his new employee could handle the job, Frankie and Torie moved into the larger office he had leased in West Mount Airy, only a twenty-minute walk from their home.

One September evening, Lisa stood frowning as she piled her

brother's plate with pasta. "Do you *have* to bring newspaper articles to the table?"

"We'll be through in a second." He slapped the clipping with the back of his hand. "I still don't get it. After all that hassle, New York City paid this developer four million bucks for twelve and a half acres in Coney Island?"

"Right." Torie set down her fork. "Fred Trump bought the Steeplechase Park site three years ago, in 1965, for two and a half million and wanted to build high-rise apartments, but the parks commissioner said it had to stay zoned for recreational use. Trump argued, made counteroffers, and showed how he could save the taxpayers a bundle by providing housing for the elderly, but the dumb city wouldn't listen. So Trump and his son Donald told 'em to go screw themselves, sold 'em the land, and picked up . . . let's see, one fifty by two point five . . . picked up a sixty percent return on their investment."

"How'd you figure that so fast?"

"Easy. First you subtract . . ."

Lisa listened patiently for ten minutes, not understanding a word of their discussion. Finally she asked, "Will you guys tell me something? If real estate's such a hot deal, how come everyone isn't scrambling to buy property?"

Frankie was astounded. Lisa had never shown the least sign of interest before. "You really want to know?"

"Well . . . yes. Our church just got a nice bequest. Do you think Father Miles should invest in real estate?"

"Damn right I do. But it's risky as hell if you don't know what you're doing. Tell him to call me. That's our business. Will you be sure to tell him?"

"Okay."

"Better warn him that real estate ain't—I mean it's not a liquid investment," Torie added. "If you need to get your money out fast, you could get screwed. And you can't just let a property sit there. You have to know how to manage it and charge rents and stuff."

"What she's saying is that it takes experience. Tell Father Miles—oh, Jesus." Frankie hit his brow with his fist. "We've been so busy jabbering about ourselves, we forgot to ask you: How was your first day of college?"

"Shitty, I'll bet," said Torie. "School's always shitty."

Lisa winced. No matter how often she heard the words, she had difficulty accepting her sister's coarse language. "Not at all.

La Salle is a lovely big campus, and I've signed up for some terrific courses."

Frankie filled his glass with milk. "Like what?"

"Philosophy, Latin, history, and religion—and I'm just about to go upstairs to study. Put the food in the fridge, would you, Tor?"

"Sure. Thanks for the spaghetti. It was good."

"Yeah, it was great." Frankie watched his sister disappear down the hallway. He reached into his pocket for a cigarette and lowered his voice. "Did you talk to her?"

"I tried. Give me a cigarette, please."

"No. I've told you a thousand times, seventeen is too young to be smoking."

"Then I'll do it behind your back."

"Oh, all right—here. What did you say?"

Torie leaned forward for a light. "I tried to do it nicely. I told her you said we could afford to buy some clothes. She wanted to know how that was possible after we just bought a house, opened a new office, and paid her college tuition, so I tried to explain about mortgages. Then I suggested that if she were to slim down a bit, we might trade off and have a double wardrobe."

"What did she say?"

"She laughed. Said she'd have to lose thirty pounds to fit into anything of mine. I told her I'd help her diet, and that she might feel better about herself if she took some interest in her appearance."

"What about . . . you know?"

"Well, I kind of casually brought up the Goretti Gorillas—the schoolgirls everyone makes fun of because they don't shave their legs. Then I mentioned electrolysis, and that she did have a few dark hairs on her lip that could easily be removed—"

"Ohhhh." Frankie groaned nervously. "Think you got through to her?"

"No. She just said, 'I am what I am and you are what you are. I don't try to change you so why do you want to change me?' I couldn't very well answer that, so I didn't."

"Shit." He ground his cigarette into the dish. "What guy in his right mind's gonna look at a fat-ass broad with a mustache? You and I know she's beautiful *inside,* but who the hell's gonna take the trouble to find out?"

"Peggy's mother used to say there was someone for everyone. Speaking of someone, are you going out tonight?"

"Yeah, if I can get a date. Tony gave me two tickets to *2001*. Supposed to be a great film. He's gotta go to some reception with his girlfriend."

"His girlfriend?"

"Sorry, kiddo, Tony ain't sittin' around waitin' for you to grow up anymore. He's got his sights set on a nice rich blue-blooded divorcée from Chestnut Hill. Wait, I take it back. She's not nice, she's a cold-hearted bitch. But loaded."

"You met her?"

"I ran into them in Bookbinder's—long red nails, hair you're afraid to touch, and makeup so thick it looks as if she used a spray can. She ain't no angel, either. Tony told me—before he got serious—if she were a carpet, she'd be labeled 'heavy duty.' But she's got good cheekbones, if you like that kind of sleek plastic look. Personally, I like women with meat on them."

"What makes you think Tony's serious?"

"He called me last week—told me he was hung up on this babe, if she'd get rid of her cat. The damn thing gives him sneezing fits. Today he reported the cat had a new home. So I guess Tony's got a new home too. Sorry to have to break the news."

Torie puffed out her cheeks. "Don't make me gag. How can you still see that schmuck after what he did to us?"

"What'd he do?"

"Are you *kidding*? He was the one who talked Papa into bribing the inspector."

"Don't be ridiculous."

"I'm *not*, Frankie. I was too upset to see it at the trial, but I've thought about it a zillion times since. Papa was such a stickler for honesty. He'd *never* have tried to buy someone off if Tony hadn't put him up to it."

"How do you know? Did you ask Papa?"

"Yes, and he told me to forget it. But he didn't deny it. And you know damn well if it *hadn't* been true, he'd have jumped to Tony's defense. And then Tony did such a shi—, I mean, lousy job at the trial. All of Papa's friends said that *any* decent lawyer could've gotten him off with a lighter sentence."

"Well, I don't see much of him any more. His life-style's too rich for my blood. But if Tony's such a bad lawyer, how come he's rolling in dough?"

"What he's rolling in ain't dough, Frankenstein. Anyway, you'd better get on the phone if you expect to get a date."

"Yeah, I guess . . ." He looked at her with sudden inspiration. "Hey, what about you? Would you like to go with me?"

She started to say she'd adore it, then stopped herself, wondering why the idea hadn't occurred to her sooner. "I'd love to if I wasn't so tired. Peggy wanted to go to the movies tonight, but I had to tell her—wait a minute. Maybe the two of you . . ."

"Peggy?" The idea seemed to startle him. "Me take out Piggytail?"

"She's not Piggytail anymore. She's grown-up now, remember?"

"I keep forgetting. Is she still going to Southern?"

Torie folded her arms in exasperation. "You know very well, Frankie. She's seventeen, just like me. She graduated in June and got a job at Pfitzer's, the big plumbing-supply company. Anyway, I doubt she'd go out with you. She's been seeing a lot of this guy."

"What guy?"

"I don't know. Van something. A football player."

His interest picked up. "They going steady?"

"He keeps trying to give her his fraternity pin but she says she's not ready."

"Then she's fair game. Here, write down her phone number." He watched his sister scribble on the pad, stuck the paper in his folder, and faced the same dilemma he faced at least twice a day. He wanted her opinion on a client, but he didn't want her to know how much he had come to depend on it. Trying to sound offhand, he asked, "Did you happen to see that Valenti file?"

She nodded. "I sure did, and I don't care if he *has* known Papa thirty years. You've carried him way too long. It's time to foreclose and arrange for a property sale. And don't feel guilty. Anyone else would've kicked out that deadbeat months ago."

"Yeah—that's right," he said, getting up from his chair. "Exactly what I was planning to do."

8
=

THE TWO TICKETS stared at Frankie from the table by his bed. He couldn't possibly let them go to waste—not six dollars worth of first-row balcony seats. But he wasn't at all sure he wanted to take Piggytail. On the other hand, two of his regulars had just turned him down; Ruth was washing her hair and Marcia had a date, or maybe she was washing her date. "The hell with 'em," he growled and reached for Peggy's number.

The phone rang twice; Kelly Shea answered and summoned her sister.

"Uh, Peggy? It's me, Frankie. Di Angelo. Hope I'm not disturbing your dinner."

A sudden intake of air and she responded. "No, not at all. Is everyone all right? Anything wrong?"

"Everything's fine. Torie said you two girls were going to a movie tonight but she couldn't make it. I thought if you still wanted to go out, well, I have a couple of seats for *2001*."

"You mean—tonight?"

"Yeah, it starts at eight-thirty. I'd have to pick you up at eight. Can you be ready?"

Peggy swallowed nervously and wondered how many lies Torie had told to get him to call her. Not only had they not had plans for the movies, they hadn't even talked in several days. "Well, sure, Frankie, I mean, yes, I'd love to go. I hear the picture's terrific. I've been dying to see it."

"Great," he said, without enthusiasm. "See you at eight."

Frankie pulled his Ford to the curb outside Peggy's house and switched off the motor. "Wait a minute," he said, reaching for her arm. "It's early yet. Do you have to go right in?"

"I guess we can talk a little." Peggy set her purse on her lap and smiled shyly, wondering if he could hear the thumping of her heart. She still couldn't believe they were actually on a date. "It's been a terrific evening. Thanks for thinking of me."

He gave a self-conscious chuckle. "To be honest, I *didn't* think of you. Torie did. Like that song 'Gigi'—you've grown up before my eyes and I hadn't even noticed. I mean, I've known you so long I hadn't realized you've become a woman. I'm glad she pointed that out to me."

"I'm glad too." Peggy laughed and headed for a safe topic. "Wasn't it great about Arthur Ashe breaking the color barrier?"

"I didn't hear. What happened?"

"He won the U.S. Open today. First black male to win a major tennis tournament."

"That's good news. Maybe they'll let a wop in next."

"Well, I do think the world's improving . . . in some respects."

He snickered. "Tell that to my baby sister."

"She *is* kind of cynical. But in a funny way, she's optimistic too. She once told me that she thinks everyone—even minorities and people who weren't born rich or social—can make a difference in the world if they fight hard enough. She says the problem is that most people just sit back and let the big guys walk all over them."

"What does she want to fight for?"

"Equal justice for all—or something like that." Peggy's tone softened. "You must be very proud of T. D., Frankie. You've been a wonderful brother. She never could've gotten through all the problems without your guidance and stability."

"You really think that? I've sure tried. We've had some rough moments." He thought back two years to Jack Slate. "She was a basket case after Papa left, and that's when she took up with that Steffi character. I used to wonder how you could stay so loyal to her."

"I knew what she was going through. Some of the kids at school were horrible to her—really brutal. At first I was hurt that she spent so much time with Steffi, but then I understood. Steffi was an outsider too. She was wild and cheap and the girls all snubbed her. She and T. D. kind of teamed up against the world. But then when T. D. left school, that was the end of Steffi."

"Thank God."

"I felt that way too." She nodded thoughtfully. "Right after that my dad got sick. T. D. was a lifesaver. She'd come over after working all day and sit and read to him so Mom could get dinner."

"I remember she practically lived at your house for a while. But she didn't mention reading to your dad."

"She does so many nice things for people and she never wants anyone to know about them. She wants everyone to think she's rough and tough, and she isn't."

Frankie shook his head. "It's part of a big shield she puts up so people can't hurt her."

"Don't I know it." Peggy shrugged. "The guys she goes out with all say the same thing. She's warm and friendly, but the minute they try to get close, she snaps shut like a clamshell and won't even see them again."

Her words pleased Frankie, confirming what he already knew. Torie had kept her promise not to repeat the Jack Slate incident. Since that disastrous night she had dated a number of young men, but none had lasted long enough to cause him concern. "Personally, I think she's being smart. She wants to save herself for the right guy."

"Don't we all. I'm just afraid she won't know him when he comes along. She won't let _anyone_ get to first base. I've tried to talk to her about that."

"What does she say?"

"Oh, she laughs and says she'll know when she meets Mr. Wonderful because rockets'll go off and all that jazz. Who knows? Maybe it _will_ happen that way. I hope so—for her sake." She turned to him. "I'd better go in, Frankie. Mom and Dad don't like me staying out late on work nights."

"They're good parents. And they've got a good daughter." He paused, feeling himself at a rare loss for words. Somehow, he couldn't bring himself to feed her his usual line of bullshit.

He walked her to the front door, and felt the strongest urge to kiss her—an impulse that astonished him. "Let's do this again sometime."

"Yes, certainly." She slipped the key in the lock and smiled over her shoulder. "I'd like that very much."

The light was still on in Torie's room when Frankie came home, ran up the stairs, and knocked on her door. "How come you're awake?" he said. "I thought you were so tired."

"I'm reading _Myra Breckenridge._" She set down the book and tried to hide the eagerness in her voice. How could she possibly have gone to sleep without hearing how the date went? "Everything go all right?"

"Swell. She's a nice gal."

"She's a lot more than that. She's a superspecial woman. They don't come any nicer."

Frankie was determined to play it cool. Whatever he said could easily find its way to Peggy's ears. "We got along okay. What about this Van guy she's been seeing?"

"You'll have to ask her about him. Will you see her again?"

"I take it you approve?"

"Damn right I approve. After all those floozies Tony fixed you up with, it's about time you started dating someone worthy of you. But you'd better work fast. Lots of guys are after Peggy."

He didn't doubt it. She had a sweetness . . . a softness . . . an innocence he hadn't seen in a woman in years. "Okay, okay, don't push. I'll give her a call one of these days."

One of these days? His casualness was a pose and she knew it. He was damn interested, or he wouldn't have come knocking on her door at that hour. "I wouldn't think of pushing you. Your love life doesn't concern me in the slightest. By the way, Lisa asked Father Miles about letting us invest their money. He said thanks, but he had other plans . . . whatever that means."

"It means someone else got to him first." He smiled as he crossed the floor. "By the way, the movie was good too."

To Torie's relief and Peggy's delight, Frankie called two days later and invited her for a drive. She was crushed to have to refuse him, but she had a date that evening.

Frankie wasn't sure he believed her. He knew his sister's scheming mind and wondered if the women were in cahoots—playing games and making up stories to get him jealous.

Determined not to be made a fool of, he drove to Peggy's house and parked a block away. After waiting more than an hour, he saw a heavy-set young man pull up in a car and approach the front door. Several minutes later Peggy emerged on the arm of the caller, obviously the football player Torie had mentioned. So there really *was* a Van, and he looked like hefty competition.

Frankie was surprised to find himself disturbed by the discovery, called the next day, and took Peggy out that night. He managed a kiss before bringing her home, liked what he sampled, and made several more dates with her.

Vowing not to interfere in what she hoped would be a long alliance, and fearful that her enthusiasm might deter her brother, Torie told Peggy that she would stay out of their lives completely. She desperately wanted her best friend for a sister-in-law, not only because she loved her, but also because she knew what a stable, supportive wife she would be for Frankie. Setting the stage for a relationship, however, was all she could do. The rest was up to the players.

In a short time, their road to romance became a battlefield. Frankie didn't want Peggy dating others but felt that he, as a man, was above such restrictions. Peggy disagreed vehemently. They broke up and made up half a dozen times before Frankie realized he was on the verge of losing a woman who was becoming very precious to him. A year after their first evening together, they made a pact: Neither would go out with anyone else.

9
=

ON THE NIGHT of July 20, 1969, in the joy and emotionalism of man's first landing on the moon (or so she rationalized), Peggy Shea lost her virginity in the backseat of Frankie's convertible. The happy event was not reported to Torie, who had long ago promised to stay out of their romance, and who was beginning to be too absorbed in her work to notice much else.

By spring of 1970, after serving more than half of his ten-year sentence, Frank Di Angelo was released from prison. His children had seen him regularly yet were saddened by the ways he had changed. Lines of bitterness bracketed lips that rarely smiled, and a mind that had been lively and retentive now seemed scarcely able to concentrate.

Nevertheless, his homecoming was the occasion for a celebration. Lisa prepared his favorite dinner of linguini with clam sauce, veal scallopini, and assorted delicacies from the pastry shop. Torie set the table with candles and flowers, and Frankie said grace, thanking the Lord for bringing their father back to them.

The patriarch's plate of food sat almost untouched, however, as he poked the meat with his fork and tried to acquaint himself with his surroundings. Apart from his time in prison, he had never lived anywhere but South Philly. The adjustment to a new home in a new community would not be easy. Already he missed his friends, his favorite haunts, the familiar streets—even the littered back alleys where he had spent so many youthful hours learning to be a man. "This house is perfect, Frankie," he said, trying to sound enthusiastic. "It's the house I always wanted for you children."

"If you hadn't bought that lot and worked so hard building the business all those years, we'd never have been able to afford it."

"Is the business still going well?"

"You bet. We've, uh, got a few surprises for you."

Frank's eyes narrowed. "I don't like surprises."

"You'll like this—it's a good one. You see, business was doing so well, we opened a branch in West Mount Airy."

"Why?" he asked, startled.

Frankie swore to himself he wouldn't blurt out that Torie had talked him into it. They still had to tell him she worked in the office. Even Lisa had been coerced into silence, unwilling to cause her father further anxiety. "I felt we were ready to grow— to venture into development projects. It's turned out great for us. We're in the black this year."

"We?"

"I mean, the whole firm. Do you remember meeting a real estate agent named Sangiacomo? He's about forty, mustache, wears glasses. Nice guy, and bright. Jock's been managing South Philly for Torie and me—" He stopped suddenly, realizing his mistake.

"Torie?" Frank glanced across the table. He had trouble believing his younger daughter was already nineteen. What a beauty she had become, with creamy olive skin, large brown eyes, and long black hair curling to her shoulders. She reminded him of Rosanna when he first met her. "I thought you were selling hats at Strawbridge & Clothier."

"I was, but I've been working with Frankie since I, uh, finished high school. He's taught me a lot about the business."

His reaction was surprisingly mild. "Why do you have to work? You're pretty enough to get a husband. Don't you want to get married?"

"And turn into a housemaid and a breeding machine? No thanks, Papa." Sensing his disappointment, she softened her tone. "I have nothing against marriage, honestly. But first I want to help Frankie build the company. It's important to me to have a career."

"I don't know why." Frank exhaled and turned to his older daughter; she worried him even more. "What about you? Why didn't you finish college?"

"I thought I explained all that." Lisa tried to keep the annoyance from her voice. His memory was worse than she feared. "Father Miles offered me a job in the church cafeteria. Don't you think feeding the hungry is more important than going to college?"

"I think it's important that you care," he said kindly. Poor Lisa. How hard it must be for her to be so large and unattractive and have such a good-looking sister. "This has been quite a homecoming. Any more surprises for me?"

"We're dying to show you the new office," said Frankie. "Will you go over with me tomorrow?"

"No. I think I'll take a walk around the neighborhood. I see no reason to go back to work. You've been doing so well without me—I'd only be an intruder. Besides, I've become a damn good fixer-upper, and this house needs a lot of carpentry."

Torie caught her brother's eye and shared a wink. What a relief it was to have their father home again and, almost as important, to know that he wouldn't be interfering in the business. "It sure does need work, Papa. One of my windows has been stuck for a month."

He lifted his goblet with a smile. "Thanks for everything, kids. It's great to be home."

The following Monday, Frankie walked into the office and slapped a letter on his sister's desk. "Here's the feasibility study we've been waiting for. Wally thinks we might have troubles with the sewage installation—"

"Who cares what your dumb partner thinks?" Torie tossed the envelope onto a pile and strode over to the coffee machine.

"I'm tired of seeing you working your butt off and letting Wally's company take all the credit. Why do you need a partner on these deals, anyway? We have to get our own name known—make ourselves a reputation."

"We're not ready yet. We make too many mistakes."

"Only when we take other people's advice. It's time for us to make our own mistakes." She handed him a steaming mug, sat down on his desk, and crossed her legs. "And I know just where to start—Snyder Avenue. Has it ever occurred to you that we could tear down those two old houses and put up a multifamily apartment building?"

"Are you nuts? Papa would never touch that house. He and Mama started their life together there. And they saved for years to buy the place next door so they could have some rental income. Where's your sentiment?"

"Sentiment! For those broken-down piles of plaster and bricks? They've got dry rot and cockroaches, the walls are cracked, the paint's peeling, the linoleum's curling . . . I don't know what you're waiting for, Frankie. We're never going to go anywhere unless we start being aggressive and using our equity to make our own deals."

"I've told you twenty times and I'll tell you again: I'm not trying to be Zeckendorf. I'm trying to earn a decent living, stay alive in a cutthroat business, and that's *all.*" He glanced at his wrist. "Oops—gotta run. Tony's meeting me at the draft board to see if he can get my exemption renewed."

"On what grounds?"

"Same as always—sole provider. Hell, he should have plenty of pull now that he's a Democratic ward leader. Shall I give him your love?"

"Yes," she hissed, "and wrap it in a stick of dynamite."

"So, the marvelous Tony Silvano strikes again."

Frankie lit a cigarette and rested his feet on the living-room coffee table. Lisa hadn't come back from church yet, and Frank was upstairs sleeping. "Shit, Tor, you can't pin this one on Tony. He spent half the morning trying his damndest."

"What went wrong?"

"What went wrong is that he's gotten me off before because I was head of the family, supporting my sisters. Now that you're working, I can be spared."

She glared angrily. "You mean it's my fault? Is that what Tony said?"

"Shhh, calm down. No, it's not your fault. Lisa's working, you're working, Papa's back, everything's changed, including the draft laws."

"Have you told Peggy?"

"Yeah. She doesn't want me to go but she understands why I have to. We talked about getting married but her parents think nineteen's too young. And hell, I don't want her sitting around waiting for me. What if I don't come back? She'll have wasted two years of her life."

"Aren't *you* the noble one. You know damn well she loves you and she'll wait. Peggy's not the fickle type. But why put her through all this grief and misery when it's unnecessary? Why put *us* through it?"

"Look, Tor," he said, with a sigh, "if you want to know the truth, I'm scared shitless. I'd sooner dive into a pool of piranhas than go to Vietnam. But all my buddies got drafted five years ago, and it's time I stopped sitting home leading the good life and letting them do the dirty work."

"El crapo, Frankie. You're *needed* at home and any second-rate lawyer who wasn't up to his ass in politics could have made a case for you. Tony's screwed you up just like he did Papa. I'm going to talk to the draft board myself."

"You stay out of this! I've signed the papers, I've agreed to report to camp in eight weeks, and that's final. It's only for two years, and maybe I'll see some parts of the world I'd never see otherwise. Who knows?"

"Like bombed-out villages, and little kids burned by napalm, and jungles full of horrible diseases? You want to get blown to bits in a stupid, stinkin' war?" Torie dropped to the couch and threw her arms around his neck. "Please, Frankie, don't go away and leave us. Talk to another lawyer. We need you here. I love you."

"Hey, kiddo . . ." He took her hands. "I love you too, you know that. If I had any say in the matter, you can bet your ass I wouldn't go. But I haven't any say, so we'll have to make the best of it. I'll be home before you know it—covered with medals."

"I don't want a hero. I want a brother."

"You'll have both. Now go set the table." He turned away quickly, pretending to read, and buried his face in the sports pages. She mustn't see his tears. Real men didn't cry. They did their duty, went off to Vietnam, and if they happened to come home six months later minus their hands or their arms or their legs, they simply shrugged and said, "That's war, baby."

And they were the lucky ones.

The following weeks were tense and chaotic as Frankie struggled to turn the responsibilities over to Torie, bringing her up-to-date on all aspects of running the West Mount Airy branch as well as overseeing the South Philly office. He insisted she hire a man to replace him, and she agreed but pleaded that first she needed to learn more about the business.

Alert and retentive, she absorbed an immense amount of knowledge in a short period—facts and concepts that Frankie explained, despite his conviction that they were too complicated for a woman to understand. To please him, she sometimes pretended *not* to understand, saying, "The new manager can handle that when he takes over." But there wouldn't be a new manager. She would simply stall hiring anyone until Frankie left, and then she would take over herself.

In the meantime, she squeezed as much information out of him as she could, learned to use his reference manuals, to check laws with the state real estate commission, to consult specialists and experts . . . and whenever she was alone in the office, she started putting some of her own plans into motion.

On one such occasion, she rang a number. "May I speak to Miss Peggy Shea, please? Vittoria Di Angelo, president of the Di Angelo Company, calling."

The operator was unimpressed. "Hold on, I'll transfer you."

Seconds later, a new voice came on the line. "Mr. Garner's desk. May I help you?"

"Yes, I'm looking for a Miss Piggytail O'Shea. She's won first prize in our cocker-spaniel-look-alike contest and I have to know where to send the dog biscuits."

"T. D.!" Peggy let out a squeal of delight. "What are you doing calling me at work? You need a new toilet?"

"I need to talk to you. Who's Mr. Garner?"

She chuckled. "Didn't Frankie tell you I got promoted? I'm now secretary to a guy who designs bidets."

"Designs what?"

"It's a kind of basin that the Europeans use to wash their, uh, privates. That's what we sell: bronzed bidets and detachable douche bags. If I work my buns off for the next ten years, I might get another promotion to a guy who makes garbage-disposal units. I should've listened to you back at St. Monica's. It's *not* a woman's world."

"Well, it's going to be. I'll see to that."

Peggy laughed. "God, it's good to talk to you. Between our jobs and our families and the men in our lives, we hardly have time for girl chat any more. As soon as Frankie leaves, let's catch up—"

"That's the reason I'm calling. I've missed seeing you, Piglet, and I need you. I need someone I can trust. I want you to come work for me."

"You *what?*"

"Shhh. I know you can't talk at the office, so shut up and just say yes or no. Do you make more than eight grand a year?"

"Uh, one less."

"Seven plus medical benefits?"

"Right."

"That's not a lot."

"I get by." She lowered her voice. "When I become Mrs. Di Angelo, I'll have to quit working anyway. Did you know your brother wants to raise a baseball team?"

"God forbid. Think of the Christmas presents I'll have to buy." Torie's tone grew serious. "Listen, Peg, I really do need you here. I'll pay you eight thousand starting salary, plus medical benefits, Social Security, and all the stale coffee you can drink."

"But I know zilch about real estate. Frankie never talks to me about business. You expect me to run around selling houses?"

"No, no, in this office, we *develop* properties, we don't just buy and sell them."

"I know it's a dumb question, but what's the difference?"

"Developing is the creative, risky part of real estate. It's also the most profitable. You start with the land—nothing on it but weeds or a rundown old building—and you picture what it could be: an apartment tower . . . a subdivision of homes . . . an industrial park . . . maybe a full-blown shopping center. Then you make it happen. Just like all those pretend games we used to play when we were little, only *this* fantasy comes true."

"How can you afford to build apartments and shopping centers?"

"Leverage. That means you borrow money to make money. And in order to come out ahead, your overall profit has to be greater than the interest you pay on the loan. Capeesh?"

"I'm lousy at math."

"Who cares? You'll be my official secretary, bookkeeper, receptionist, and chief wastebasket-emptier. When can you start?"

"Hey, give me time to think—"

"You don't need to think. There's only one condition to my offer: You mustn't tell Frankie."

"Why not?"

"Because he'd object. Listen, carrothead, you know how square Frankie is about women working. If he had his way you'd be home baking bread and scrubbing floors all day. It's time for you to be realistic. Think of yourself for once in your life. What if Frankie's away *more* than two years? It's a hideous thought, but what if something happens to him? Suppose he gets wounded and you have to support the two of you? Do you want to spend the rest of your life selling toilet equipment? I promise you, the Di Angelo Company is going places . . . and so are you if you come to work for me."

"Well, I'm sure not looking forward to the next two years. If I could at least be with you—"

"That's exactly what I'm saying. Come on, Piglet. You know I can't type, I can't spell, I couldn't write a business letter if my life depended on it. And you're so great at stuff like that. I need you desperately."

"But I can't just quit my job. I'd have to give at least two weeks' notice—"

"Of course you would. Let's see, today's Thursday, June fourth." She flipped the pages of her calendar. "If you speak to your boss this morning, your last day there should be Thursday, June eighteenth, the day Frankie leaves for the army. You'll have Friday and the weekend to lie around on your fanny and eat chocolate bars, and you can start here Monday, June twenty-second. Agreed?"

"What'll I tell my boss?"

"Remember that Mark Twain line your mother always used? 'When in doubt, tell the truth.' What can you lose?"

"Now why couldn't I think of something clever like telling the truth?" The excitement in her voice was mounting. "And I woke up expecting this to be just another day."

"It's a banner day for both of us. Shall we feed our faces at noon and celebrate?"

"Oh, God, I wish I could. But you've got my brain in such a spin . . . How 'bout a raincheck for June twenty-second?"

"You've saved the day, O'Shea." Torie laughed with relief. At least one big problem was solved. "Now go turn in your bidet and your douche bag. I can't wait to start ordering you around."

The morning Frankie left for the army, Torie began poring over all the papers, memos, and lists of instructions he had carefully written out for his successor. The pang of guilt she felt for having lied about her intentions did not lessen her joy at finally having the chance to test her ideas and steer the firm in a far more daring and risky direction.

Her first priority was reorganizing the office, and after three months of familiarizing herself with the files, exploring financing possibilities, researching available properties, and studying every aspect of land planning and subdividing, she started to think about making a move.

"Good God, what are *you* doing here in the middle of the night?"

Torie looked toward the door in surprise. She had been too engrossed to hear Peggy come in. "Seven-fifty A.M. isn't exactly midnight. Hey—great haircut."

"Thanks. Since I now carry the heavyweight title of assistant to the president of the Di Angelo Company, I figure I'd better *look* efficient even if I'm not."

"Quit fishing. You know you're practically running the place. What's Frankie going to think when he comes home?"

"He'll hate it. Men like to say that long hair looks better on a pillow—it's a macho thing. But I wrote him that working women need a hairdo they can wash in the shower, blow dry, and be done with."

"You didn't write him that you changed jobs . . . ?"

"No. Like you said, it would only worry him. He'd be sure the two of us were wrecking the business."

"Good." Torie tried to control her impatience. Small talk at the office wasted precious time, and her dear friend loved to babble. Yet she couldn't hold back a smile. At twenty, Peggy still looked like a teenager. She had the same freckled face, turned-up nose, and, now, short red hair curling at the ears. A beige polyester blouse and brown skirt clung to her frame, accenting a curvy, slightly overweight figure. For a brief second, Torie tried to picture Peggy and Frankie as the passionate lovers she knew them to be. Then, embarrassed by the image, she erased it from her mind. "Aren't *you* in early?"

"I wanted to redo the address file before I got busy. I have a message you're not going to like. Wally Todd phoned right after you left yesterday. He said to tell you the Urbandale School project he and Frankie were working on for so long is finally going through, and that he'll need forty thousand dollars by Friday noon."

"He'll need *what*?"

"He said that you and he have to put the down payment on the land right away or the option will be up and quote, 'We'll be out on our asses.' Unquote."

"Is he crazy? I'm going to give *him* forty thousand dollars? Write him a letter, Pig. Tell him to take his Urbandale School and shove it. Only tell him nicely."

"Don't you think that might be rash? According to the files, Frankie spent almost three years planning that project with Wally. He invested money in feasibility studies, soil reports—"

"Frankie's a softie. He didn't have the heart to break off with that sponger, but I sure as hell do. Tell Wally we want out of this and the other two deals he has going with us, and we expect to be reimbursed for expenses. Now that Frankie's gone, he thinks he can just take over and screw his little sister."

"But shouldn't you write and ask Frankie? Or at least talk to a lawyer?"

"Like who? That great brain Tony Silvano? Send the damn letter and quit arguing!" Torie's lower lip protruded, shooting a stream of air to her forehead. "Sorry, Piglet. These past months have been a bit trying. And now, having that slimy Wally try to sock it to us behind Frankie's back is the last straw."

"I understand. I'll write the letter." Peggy drew a paper from her purse. "On a more pleasant note, I brought you an article from last night's *Bulletin*. I thought you might want to read about Robert Nielson."

"Why would I want to do that?"

"Because you've had the hots for his son ever since you saw him at Betsy Richardson's birthday party. Can you look me in the eyes and deny it?"

"I most certainly can—*not*!" Torie's protest dissolved in a burst of giggles. "How'd you know Nielson Hughes was Robert Nielson's son?"

"I read it somewhere—some gossip column a while back. It stuck in my mind because you were always talking about the guy."

"Guess I wasn't very coy about it. He's still gorgeous—looks like Robert Redford with good skin. I got a two-second glimpse of him about four years ago when I traipsed up to Penn Charter."

"By yourself?"

"No, Steffi was with me." She hadn't wanted to mention her infamous companion.

Peggy smiled weakly. The memory of that relationship still hurt. "What happened? With Nielson, I mean."

"I lost track of him till last year. Then, when Matt Richardson pulled out of the senator race, Connie Morris did a story on the Richardsons for *Celebrity Times*. Maybe that's what you read."

"I doubt it. I can't stand that trashy magazine. And Connie's such a bitch." Peggy leaned in closer. "What'd she say?"

"Oh, that Matt was so upset by all the rumors, he swore he'd never run for office again."

"No one ever proved he had a mistress."

"Right—and lots of people tried, including my beloved brother. I tried to talk him out of it, but he wouldn't listen."

"I know. Frankie could never understand why you forgave Matt."

"I was torn for a long time. I finally forgave Matt because Papa forgave him. Papa said he was a good, decent man just trying to keep his promise to clean up the city. But I'll be damned if I'll forgive the legal system and the society that condemned Papa. They'll be sorry someday. They'll all come crawling to me because *I'll* have the power. All the self-righteous snobs who sat by and pissed in their Pfitzer toilets while their scapegoat went off to prison . . . Hey, how'd I get started on this?"

"I have a feeling it's never very far from your mind."

"You're right." She paused for a sigh. "Anyway, Connie Morris also mentioned Betsy in the story, and that a young man named Nielson Hughes was escorting her to the Assemblies. She couldn't resist adding that Nielson was the son of Janet Hughes and the architect Robert Nielson—who was married to someone else at the time of his son's birth."

"Nielson's illegitimate?"

"Yep. That's why Janet Hughes gave him his father's last name as a first name—and her own last name." Torie's mind raced back to the birthday party, and the scene that was as clear in her memory as the day it happened. She could almost hear Sonny Hopkinson's taunting voice saying, *"My* parents got married so I wouldn't be a bastard . . ."

"That was industrial-strength stupid of his mother." Peggy's brow wrinkled with disapproval. "She didn't have to call him Nielson."

"I think she was right to do it. She had the choice of telling a lie for the sake of appearances, or telling the truth and giving her son his rightful identity. What would you have done?"

"Tried to get Robert Nielson to marry me."

"He *was* married."

"Well, thank God it's not my worry. How old is Nielson?"

"Twenty-one. The article also said he was at Penn studying architecture. I found out he joined a fraternity."

"How'd you find that out?"

Torie felt her cheeks redden. "I called the school. They told me he lived at the Deke house. I phoned there a couple of times and hung up. Once I even heard him say hello—at least, I *think* it was his voice."

"Oh, boy. You've got it bad." Peggy handed her the article. "Well, you might as well get to know your future father-in-law."

"Don't I wish." Torie took the clipping and read aloud, " 'NIELSON IN THE NAVES—By Keith McGarren.' McGarren— why is that name familiar?" She read on:

Robert Nielson, Philadelphia's celebrated master builder and the man mainly responsible for the city's ever-changing skyline, has added another gem to his crown of triumphs: the historic restoration of the Church of The Holy Faith on Locust above 17th.

"I love a challenge," Nielson told reporters at yesterday's press conference to unveil the $1.3 million renovation. "When you build a building, you start with nothing and create your own masterpiece. When you restore, you're taking someone else's masterpiece and trying to bring back its original greatness.

"In the case of this edifice, we had to do a complete history dating back to 1857, when it was built. Our research involved getting sketches and photos of what it looked like, then finding

craftsmen skilled enough to do the frieze work, and to regild
the angels over the altar. In order to uncover the original colors, we had to scrape away seven layers of ceiling paint.'

"Robert Nielson's done a tremendously impressive job,"
said the rector, the Very Reverend Edward V. Johnston. "He's
maintained the integrity of John Notman's Gothic Revival
style, and at the same time, incorporated improvements in
lighting, seating, and acoustics which will allow us to enlarge
our parish activities and better serve the community."

Asked if he felt sad or pleased to have finished the job, the
architect replied, "Nothing I do is ever finished, because I
leave a part of myself in every building I touch. When people
walk through the Church of the Holy Faith, in a sense, they're
walking through me."

The public is invited to celebrate God and Robert Nielson
at a special dedication ceremony on Wednesday, October
14th, at 11 A.M. in the church's English garden.

The final paragraph made Torie chuckle. Reporter McGarren
couldn't resist a jab at the subject's oversized ego—or was it arrogance? She tucked the clipping in her purse and marked the
date on her calendar. There was one way to find out.

10
=

THE STREET OUTSIDE the Church of the Holy Faith was filled
with parked cars. A group of antiwar protesters paraded by on
their way to a rally, their signs and banners held high, their
voices shouting for the United States to get out of Vietnam. Keep
hollering, Torie thought, giving them a thumbs-up. The louder
they screamed, the faster Frankie would come home.

Finding a space for the convertible, she locked the door and
hurried along the pavement, her high heels clicking. The timing

had been painstakingly planned; at half-past eleven the dedication ceremony should be over, and the officials would be milling around greeting friends.

She asked herself what she was doing there, but she could find no logical answer. Despite her absurd fantasy that the famous architect would spot her in the crowd, draw her aside, and whisper, "Whoever you are, you're exciting, beautiful, exactly the kind of woman I've always wanted for my son," she wasn't at all sure what to expect.

A cool breeze stirred her hair. Reaching for a scarf, she wrapped it around her head and tied it under the chin. Usually she was too involved in work to worry about her appearance, but, in the unlikely event that she *did* meet Robert Nielson, she wanted to look smashing—a word she had recently picked up from a society column. The black wool sweater and skirt she wore clung tightly to the generous curves of her five-foot-six-inch figure. A heavy gold-plated necklace with a cross completed her carefully chosen outfit.

As soon as she arrived at the church, she ran a comb through her hair and checked herself in the hand mirror. The image pleased her. Lustrous black swirls fell to her shoulders, framing a delicate oval face. She wore little makeup, only a light tan foundation, cherry lipstick, a whisk of powder blusher, and a thin line of charcoal pencil that made her eyes stand out strikingly, like bright brown marbles. Tony once called her Bianca Neve— Snow White. How she had loved that nickname! And how she had loved Tony—before she found out what a louse he was.

"May I help you?" A woman in a print shirtdress touched her arm.

"Oh, uh, yes." She smiled and slipped the mirror into her purse. "Is it possible to see the restoration?"

"The whole church has been restored. The main chapel is through those doors."

"Thank you." She paused a moment to look about. The complex was divided into three stone structures surrounding a central English-style garden. Sixty or seventy people chatted in small groups on the lawn, sipping punch in plastic glasses. A neatly trimmed hedge and a black wrought-iron fence separated the grounds from the street.

Taking a quick inventory of the faces, and not finding any of particular interest, she headed toward the tower building. Two large red doors opened directly into the chapel, where the unmistakable figure of Robert Nielson stood, with a black-gowned minister, surrounded by admirers.

The honoree was taller than she had expected, crowned by a head of thick white hair and blessed with sharp, regular features. His preening manner left little doubt as to the degree of his self-adoration. She edged toward the circle and watched him as he spoke to the people—smiling, gesturing, pointing out sections of the altar, patiently explaining how he had wrought his miracle.

"How long did the restoration take you?" asked an elderly woman.

"A lifetime," he replied solemnly. "A lifetime devoted to studying, observing, honing my special gifts. No achievement can be judged in terms of days or months. A great master may paint a picture in a matter of hours, but the years he spent developing the skills to do so—ah, those are incalculable."

Torie moved closer, easing her way through the gathering until she was within speaking distance. At the first pause in the conversation, she asked a question designed to get his attention: "Have you ever done anything you're ashamed of, Mr. Nielson?"

"Ashamed?" He peered down at the young lady with curiosity, reassuring himself that she was merely ignorant—or, judging by her jewelry, tasteless. She meant no malice. "I prefer the word 'regret,' " he answered pleasantly. "Yes, I have many regrets. The old cliché about wishing you'd known then what you know now is unfortunately true."

A young man thrust in: "How do you feel about what Le Corbusier did in Pessac?" The architect turned to a trio of students and began what seemed destined to be a long discourse. Not having any idea what they were talking about, Torie slipped through the crowd and glanced around for the exit. Suddenly, she froze.

A few feet away, in the middle of a pew, stood Nielson Hughes, legs apart, arms akimbo. His head was bent so far back it was almost parallel to the floor. The fascination of whatever he was staring at escaped her. All she could see was a wood-beamed ceiling.

Her hands shook as she approached him and noted that his straw-colored hair was still too long, spilling over his shirt collar just as it had at the birthday party. The slouchy schoolboy look of four years ago was gone, however, and he had shot up to well over six feet. A dark gray suit outlined a sturdy athletic frame.

"What do you see up there?" she asked venturing closer. "Bats?"

"It's in the coffers," he murmured, not changing his position. "A slight irregularity. How could he have missed it?"

"I thought a coffer was someone who smokes too much."

He took no note of her presence and continued staring.

His attitude frustrated her. She had drawn on every bit of courage she had to speak to him, and she was not about to leave without his seeing her. An idea flashed through her brain. "Mr. Hughes, may I have a word with you?"

"I'm busy right now."

"It's important."

"Would you mind not disturbing me, please?"

"I'm not budging till I talk to you."

"Oh?" He regarded his challenger for the first time and appraised her with a touch of irritation. "Why didn't you tell me you were beautiful?"

Stay cool, she told herself. One show of nerves and all would be lost. "Does it matter? I want to discuss a business deal." The pale skin she remembered so well was warmed by a golden suntan that highlighted his strong cheekbones and square jaw. Someday he would look very much like his father.

"Yes, it matters. My eyes are trained to appreciate beauty, and human beauty is the highest form because it's the only kind man can't create or duplicate. We'll talk more about it at lunch." He made the statement matter-of-factly, neither waiting for nor expecting an answer. Then he took her arm and guided her to the exit.

The small luncheonette near the University of Pennsylvania was not yet filled with its usual noon crowd. Nielson Hughes helped Torie set down her tray, then glanced about the room. He had been wise, he felt, to avoid the cafeteria on campus. If any of his friends had wandered by, they would have taken one look at that face and incredible body, known exactly what he had in mind, and teased him mercilessly.

"Thank you," she said, as he moved her chair to the table. "I'm glad you have manners. They seem to be in short supply these days."

The girl was uncanny—putting on airs as if she were a duchess. "My mother's a tyrant about details. Tell me, how did you know my name back at the church?"

"Oh, a lady pointed you out. She said you were an architect, and I perked up because I'm looking for one."

"How would she know I'm an architect? I'm still in school."

"She seemed to know a lot about you. Said you were as good as your father."

"That's utter dribble. I'm a damn sight better than my father, and I resent it when people see me as a second-rate carbon copy." He stopped himself. "Sorry, I didn't mean to snap at you. I really don't care to discuss him."

She lowered her head nervously, uncertain how to respond. Then she tried again. "I'm sure it's been difficult for you, growing up in that, er, situation."

Was he hearing correctly? What business was it of hers? It served him right for listening to his groin instead of his brain. Yet with all her cheekiness, the girl had a quality that excited him . . . a sensuality that so stirred his libido he could hardly sit still in his chair.

"I haven't introduced myself. I'm Vittoria Di Angelo."

"Vittoria with two *t*s, no *c*?"

"Yes."

"That's a long name." He chewed his hamburger for several seconds, then asked, "What do people call you?"

"Torie."

"Hmm. Not very original. If my name were Vittoria, I'd want to be called Guinevere or Hepzibah or anything but Torie."

"Don't people call you Niels?"

"They may do it once, never twice. It's like something a drunk would say to a lamppost: 'Niels Hughes—thash my name, fella, and if I may shay sho, you're pretty lit up yourself.' "

She laughed at the unlikely impersonation, relieved to discover a sense of humor—albeit self-serving. "Okay, I know what *not* to call you. What should I call you?"

"Your Excellency isn't bad. Your Highness has a nice ring to it."

"How about plain old Nielson?"

"Superb choice." He smiled with anticipated pleasure, wondering how her lipstick would taste . . . if she reeked of Jungle Musk or Savage Tiger or some other deliciously cheap cologne . . . trying to picture her in a black lace bra and garter belt. "God, you're pretty! You're not married or anything, are you?"

"No, not anything."

"Good. I hate messes." He speared a tomato. "You have the most extraordinary eyes."

"Could we get serious, please?"

"Yes, I have a serious question for you: Where did you grow up?"

"South Philly—until three and a half years ago, when we moved the company to West Mount Airy."

"What company?" The question was a reflex, not curiosity. All he could think of at that moment was how to make her laugh again so he could watch that heavy gold cross jiggle between her breasts.

"Real estate development. We have an office not far from our house. But the project I want to talk about—"

"Do you live with your parents?"

"My mother died when I was seven." Patience, she told herself. He would soon run out of questions, and then she could ask some of her own. The idea she had thought up as an excuse to get his attention was beginning to have real possibilities. "I live with my father, my sister, and my brother, Frankie, who's in the war at the moment. The only good part of his being gone is that I get to drive his car."

"Are you aware that you have translucent skin?"

"Yes—no. Nielson, could we *please* get serious?"

"Certainly." He made a bet with himself; he would have her in the sack within forty-eight hours. "What's on your mind?"

She set down her sandwich and fixed him with steady eyes. "I own two row houses in South Philly. I could earn five times the income by tearing them down and building an apartment. Would you be willing to look at them and give me an estimate?"

He resisted the urge to smile. She was so intense about it all. "Are the houses occupied?"

"Yes."

"Then why tear them down?"

"Because they're old."

"That's hardly a reason. Are they in disrepair?"

"Terrible. Full of dry rot and cockroaches."

"You don't *destroy* structures because they have dry rot and cockroaches."

"Why not, if they're ugly?"

"If we were to tear down every building that someone thought was ugly, we'd have nothing left but streets and sidewalks."

"What if we were to tear down everything that was, say, over two hundred years old, and put up modern buildings in their place?"

She *had* to be joking. "What a clever idea. First we'll bulldoze Elfreth's Alley. Next we'll chop down Old St. Mary's Church where George Washington worshiped, then we'll zip over to Mount Pleasant—"

"I was only teasing. The real problem with Snyder Avenue is that the foundations are shaky, the pipes are rusted, the wiring's frayed, and the tenants aren't safe."

"That's a different matter entirely." He couldn't figure the girl out; she was either very smart or very ignorant, and possibly both. "In that case, I might consider the job. You realize I'm not licensed, don't you?"

She nodded.

"Then let's have a look at your properties, say . . . tomorrow evening? Afterward, we can pop by my place and split a pizza."

"Your place? Don't you live on campus?"

"No, I moved out of the Deke house when I started graduate school. I stay at my mother's. Her main home is in Bryn Mawr, so she rarely uses the town house, and it works out fine for me. It's near the campus and I don't have a car at the moment. Could you pick me up at Meyerson Hall?"

She would pick him up in Siberia if he asked. "What time?"

"I have a seminar from six to seven-thirty, so let's say eight o'clock." He looked down at her plate. "Anything wrong with your sandwich?"

"Umm, no—I wasn't very hungry."

"Care for something else?"

"No, thanks."

"Then let's go. I'll show you where to get me." He rose and took her arm. "Actually . . . I'm not at all hard to get."

11

"YOU DIDN'T TOUCH your dinner. And I 'specially made the stew without mushrooms, the way you like it."

Torie poked a potato with little enthusiasm. She and Lisa were too dissimilar to have a close relationship, but as adults, at least their roles were defined. Hers was to "keep an eye on the business" until Frankie came home; Lisa's was to look after the house. They still disagreed about practically everything but, for the sake of harmony, had learned to keep their thoughts to themselves. "Thanks, Lis, it looks delicious. I'll just have salad, if you don't mind."

"Troubles?" asked Frank. In the six months since his release, his interests had not expanded beyond his family, his carpentry, and the television set. Yet his instincts were sharp, and something in his younger daughter's manner disturbed him.

"There's no fooling you, is there, Papa?" Torie's smile barely masked her anxiety. After leaving Nielson that afternoon, she had spent the rest of the day gathering facts and preparing her dialogue. Maybe this was the opening she had been waiting for. "There is a matter I want to discuss with you. It's . . . about Snyder Avenue."

"What about Snyder Avenue?"

"We've got problems in both houses. The electric wires are so chewed up they could ignite any time, and the foundations are so weak, they wouldn't last five minutes in a fire."

"Can't you put in new wiring?" asked Lisa.

"We have to do something. But rather than waste a lot of money repairing two crumbling old wrecks, we might think about putting out a little more money and building a multifamily

99

apartment. The new unit would bring in five times what we're getting now."

"Did you say a *little* more money?" Like his reformed son, Frank had grown ultraconservative in his spending habits, particularly since his one daring venture had led to such disaster.

"It wouldn't be that much. We can borrow seventy-five percent of the remodeling costs and get a fifteen-year mortgage when the building's finished. It'd be a good investment."

Frank scowled at her. "You're talking about tearing down Snyder Avenue, and that's out of the question. You children were born and raised there."

"I know that, Papa. But it's not a shrine, and we can't afford to be sentimental. If anyone got hurt or killed because of our negligence, they could sue us right into bankruptcy court."

"The answer is no. Absolutely not."

"Out of the question," agreed Lisa. "Our tenants are such nice people. The Stumpos have a little six-month-old baby, and the Quartarolis—well, she's a total invalid."

"All the more reason to worry. If there was a fire, they'd never get out in time." Torie tried to keep her voice calm. She knew her father's stubbornness as well as she knew her own, and she had come prepared. "Personally, I don't care what you do. But if any problems come up, you'll have to deal with the city inspectors yourself."

"City inspectors!" Frank's voice rose in horror. "What are you talking about?"

"Didn't I tell you? That's how this whole thing started. A couple of men were in the neighborhood checking out houses—including ours. There've been a number of electrical fires on the block."

"Oh, my God." Frank rubbed his hands nervously. "Why didn't you say so? We've got to do something right away."

"What about our tenants?" Lisa protested.

"You want me to go back to prison? I can't take chances with the city. If we have to tear everything down and start from scratch, we'll do it. Use your judgment, Torie. Do whatever you have to do and make sure everything's up to code. Lisa and I will go along with you."

Torie exhaled and leaned back in her chair. "Well, okay, Papa, I'll take care of it—if you're sure that's what you want."

*　　*　　*

The predawn hours seemed interminable to Torie as she lay on her pillow, as awake as if it were noon. Thoughts and emotions hammered at her brain, demanding resolution. Family loyalty was not in question; she would give anything she had, including an arm or a leg, for her father or Frankie or Lisa, regardless of their differences. She felt no guilt about that.

Yet she could hardly deny her deceitfulness. Small lies had led to bigger lies until she had wound herself into a thick web. One day her family would appreciate what she had done, but for now, she would have to trust her instincts and live with the falsehoods.

It hurt her deeply that her father, having reembraced Catholicism, seemed to be turning away from her and favoring her sister. He and Lisa had grown so close and so alike in their thinking, they often made Torie feel as if she were an alien— some kind of greedy pagan monster from a different world.

She reassured herself, however, that the rift with her father was temporary, and that the operation that had been churning around in her brain for so many months was well worth a fib or two. The same day Frankie left, in fact, she had notified the Snyder Avenue tenants that when their leases were up on November first they would have to find other housing. Having Nielson work on the project had not occurred to her at the time, but the more she thought about it, the more the idea excited her.

She was positive he could handle the job, even though all she knew about him—aside from his being attractive, almost a prototype of the big, blond, blue-eyed Scandinavian—was that he had gallant manners (when he wanted to), charm that came out in spurts, like water from a temperamental faucet, and total dedication to his profession. No one who spoke to him for five minutes could fail to realize that his world revolved around architecture, almost to the exclusion of everything else. How she fitted into that small circle she wasn't sure, except that he had been struck by her appearance. Perhaps he liked a challenge, and if so, she would be glad to provide one.

Trying to analyze him more profoundly was not in her nature. She could only marvel at how intensely she felt drawn to him, and how certain she was that they had a future. Yet she also knew that any relationship came with built-in barriers. A Main Line architect with a Penn background wasn't likely to waste his credentials on a Catholic Italian girl from South Philly. Never mind that she was bright, ambitious, and determined to be richer than Onassis. The lines separating them were as clear and indelible as the Pennsylvania Railroad tracks.

"Sorry to be late, Torie." Panting and apologetic, Nielson opened the car door and slid onto the seat. "The seminar ran overtime. Been here long?"

"About half an hour. I was just getting ready to leave." A Sherman tank couldn't have moved her.

He took her hand and kissed it. "Forgive me. I've been so looking forward to seeing you."

The gesture left her momentarily speechless.

"I'm a bit wound up," he said, settling back in the seat. "Ever hear of Eric Mendelsohn?"

"The, uh, name's familiar."

"I'm quite taken with his Mossehaus in Berlin. The man had a marvelous way of working vertical elements to emphasize the horizontal. But that's neither here nor there. I only mention him because he always listened to Bach before he began a project. It put him in a special mood. Frank Lloyd Wright was just the opposite. He used to say that as soon as he saw great architecture, an orchestra would start playing in his ear."

"Buildings made him hear music?"

"Not literally, no." Why was he wasting time explaining to her? She wouldn't have the slightest idea what he was talking about. Clearing his throat, he began again. "What I'm saying is that I'd like a few minutes to simmer down and shift gears. How about a drive to Independence Square before we hit Snyder Avenue?"

"Sure. That's easy." She glanced in the mirror, presumably to see if anyone was behind her but mainly to check her makeup. Nothing seemed out of place; her nose didn't shine, her lipstick wasn't smeared, her hair wasn't covering up her earrings. He would never know the pains she had taken to look right for him—spending nearly an hour selecting a beige jersey dress that showed off her figure, then trying on every sweater and coat in her closet until she finally settled on a brown rabbit-fur jacket she had found in the Springside School thrift shop.

Her fingers reached for the ignition. "Have you thought any more about the project we discussed?"

He looked over at her. "Ever read the Bible?"

"Of course I have."

"Then maybe you remember Ecclesiastes—where it says that

there's a time for every purpose under heaven. A time to be born, a time to love, a time to discuss Snyder Avenue, and a time to sit back and enjoy the city."

She laughed. "I think you're trying to tell me something—like shut up and drive."

"I wouldn't put it that way exactly." She was right, though. That's what he meant. The girl was not dumb. She was uneducated and full of pretensions, but she was sharp and caught on quickly. She seemed to understand his need to be quiet and unwind.

"Park here," he said, several minutes later, as they reached the corner of Walnut and Fifth. "Let's get out and breathe some air."

"I'd like that."

He took her arm as they strolled across the flagstone pavement toward Independence Hall. In the shadows of the street lamps, the monuments loomed tall and serene. "The heart of the city looks magical at night. 'Myriad silver-white lines and carved heads and mouldings, with a soft dazzle . . .' Remember Walt Whitman?"

"Yes."

"Extraordinary," he murmured, lost in reflection. "Buildings have a thousand personalities. When the mobs of tourists have all gone home, there's a quiet dignity about these red-brick walls . . . a purity . . . an integrity that blends the past with the present. Did you know that a group of citizens once wanted to tear down these magnificent landmarks? Can you imagine anything more obscene?"

"I—" She started to disagree with him, then caught herself. "Why would anyone want to do that?"

"Back in the 1850s, some morons decided we should have a new city hall. They wanted to surround Independence Hall with a U-shaped mansarded structure. It would have meant destroying old City Hall, our greatest monument in the style of the Second Empire, tearing down Philosophical Hall, and if you can believe it, Congress Hall."

"How did they justify that?"

"They claimed the city was spending more to maintain the monuments than they were bringing in. As if you could put a dollars-and-cents value on these priceless structures. But that's the way the uneducated classes think. They once tried to sell the Liberty Bell for scrap metal. Some of those idiots *still* want to destroy City Hall and replace it with a modern monstrosity. Luckily, its base is rock-solid. Do you know, that's the only thing that's saved a lot of these old buildings?"

"You mean because it would cost so much to tear them down?"

"Yes. I don't understand people who want to destroy beauty and history. They have no soul—no *élan*."

She hadn't the vaguest idea what *élan* was but didn't dare ask, lest he link her with the "uneducated classes" he so scorned. Amazing, she thought, how much self-congratulation went along with revering the past.

One of these days she would answer him, but for now she could only hint at how she felt. In her mind, "historic" and "dilapidated" were practically synonymous. How could those weathered bricks and gray stones with all their fancy scrolls and spires possibly compare with a streamlined modern structure? Their foundations were probably crumbling and rotting just like the houses on Snyder Avenue. Ah . . . but those new high-rise towers were solid and sturdy and almost blinded you with their dazzle—their gleaming steel and glass and granite façades. *That* was power . . . glamor . . . excitement. That was *now*. "I remember a line from Kitty Foyle: 'Philadelphians don't want to feel things until they've had a careful okay from yesterday.' "

The girl was full of surprises. She actually read books. "What does that mean?"

"That Philadelphians distrust anything new or modern. But they don't think *all* old buildings are beautiful."

"Who said *all* old buildings?"

"You did, sort of."

"Playing devil's advocate, are you? All right, forget history for a moment. Forget, if you can, that our nation was born here. Look at Independence Hall with an objective eye. Note the natural balance and symmetry of the tower. And Congress Hall, the jewel in the crown . . . small, self-contained, with its fanlight over the door and iron balcony . . . the distillation of all that was fine and noble in that remarkable period." He stopped himself. "Sorry. I do get carried away."

"Don't be sorry. I know that's your obsession."

"One of my obsessions." His tone suddenly softened. "We're very close to where I live. Are you sure you want to go to South Philly?"

"Could we just drive by quickly?"

"Yes . . . yes, certainly." He guided her toward the car. "You've been kind enough to humor me for the last half hour. By all means, on to Snyder Avenue."

"Don't you want to look around?" Torie tried to hide her disappointment as Nielson rolled up the car window.

"No, thanks. I've seen all I need."

"Does that mean you'll take the job?"

"I don't know yet. I want to think about it." He stayed her hand as she reached for the key. "Before the moment escapes us—I must tell you how glowing . . . how incandescent you look right now. The moonlight coming through the glass gives your skin an astonishing radiance."

His words made her tingle with pleasure. "I guess . . . everything looks better in moonlight."

"Not at all. Quasimodo by moonlight is still Quasimodo."

"True," she murmured, wishing she knew what he meant.

"Those houses out there. You grew up in the one on the left. You and I see it as wood and bricks, but your father and mother made love there. They shared passion in those walls. And passion is the most important, all-encompassing emotion we have. Don't you agree?"

The thought of her mother and father in bed unnerved her; she couldn't deal with the image and didn't want to. "Yes—passion is important. And I feel passionate about this project. When will you give me your answer?"

A hint of annoyance crept into his voice. "Why are you so anxious to hire me? You don't know my work. You haven't seen my designs. You haven't even seen my sketches. The world is full of builders and draftsmen far more experienced than I am."

The question was fair. He had every right to wonder why she would choose a graduate student and total stranger for a project she cared so much about. "I suppose the answer is that I play my hunches. When I saw you in that church, something clicked. Some kind of bell went off in my head and I knew instinctively that you were the man for the job. Don't ask me how. I just knew."

"Well, I applaud your instincts."

"You don't have a passion for crumbling old row houses, do you?"

"I probably should. Row houses are to Philadelphia what apple pie is to America. In early days, they didn't have the materials, the designs, or the technology we have now." He paused to shake his head. "And yet, we're still knocking out the same cookie-cutter houses, only in 1970 we call them model villages or some ridiculous euphemism. Modern developers don't want to beautify or humanize the world. All they care about is profit-and-loss statements."

"Does that mean you'll rebuild Snyder Avenue?"

A glint of amusement came into his eyes. "You never let up, do you?"

"I guess not." She smiled at him. "It's just that I know what a wonderful job you'll do. Besides, you don't have an office and a staff and a lot of overhead, and I can probably afford you."

"You're wrong, there. You can't afford me." The crushed look on her face made him quickly add, "In the sense that my services can't be bought. But I *can* be persuaded . . ."

"How?"

He moved closer and smoothed her hair. It felt as soft and silken as he knew it would. The time was finally coming. "I'm crazy about you, Torie, in case you haven't guessed. I'll be glad to do the job for you, and I won't charge you a cent."

"You won't?" Her voice rose with elation. "You really mean that? You'll do it for nothing?"

"No, not for nothing. For *you.*" Finding her lips, he brushed them lightly. They seemed warm and willing and he lingered there, prolonging the anticipation. Gradually, his control began to slip away and he kissed her hotly. To his delight, her mouth opened to him.

"Vittoria," he whispered into her ear. "My whole being . . . is on fire. I want you very, very much."

Her head was dizzy, her heart was racing. Her body was beginning to pulsate from some strange, secret source. No man had ever stirred or thrilled her that way before. A surge of almost frightening desire made her tremble and go limp. "Hold me tight," she said, half pleading, half commanding.

His tongue thrust hungrily, his hand slipped inside her coat and found her firm, full breast. He kissed her for a long time until he could kiss her no longer. She felt the intensity of her need as his powerful hardness pressed against her—and then he pulled away.

"I'll drive home," he said hoarsely. "It's faster."

12

THE MORNING SKY was gloomy, with bruised overhanging clouds threatening to burst into showers at any minute. Torie barely noticed the impending storm as she tiptoed up the steps to her house.

No sooner had she turned the knob than the front door swung open and Lisa stood glaring at her. "Where've you been? Don't you know it's almost seven?"

"I fell asleep in the car."

"You've been with a man. You've spent the night with a *man*." Lisa's large frame quivered under the shapeless flannel nightgown. "Haven't we been through enough? You want to bring further shame and dishonor on the family?"

"Spare me the guilt trip, Lis. It's none of your—Papa! What are you doing up at this hour?"

"Thank God you're all right!" Frank came rushing toward her. "Lisa woke me. Said you'd gone out last night and hadn't come back. Why didn't you call us?"

"I couldn't. I went to this open house and drank a lot of punch, only I didn't know it was spiked. When I got in the car to drive home, I felt woozy, so I pulled over to the curb. I—I must've passed out."

"You slept in the car all night?"

"Would you rather I'd driven the streets and gotten killed?"

"I'd rather you let us know where you were. I was about to call Tony—"

"What for? To get me out of jail? For God's sake, I'm nineteen years old, I'm perfectly able to take care of myself, and I wish you'd stop treating me like a child."

Frank's eyes blazed at her. "You haven't even the decency to say you're sorry? As long as you're living under my roof, you'll sleep in your own bed every night or you won't sleep in this house at all. Is that clear?"

She started to answer that she would pack her things and be out of his damn house in an hour—but stopped herself. She knew how much such an action would hurt him, and that the break could be permanent. Italian girls, according to custom, left home only in a wedding dress or a casket. Besides, where would she go? What would she tell Nielson? Reason won out over her momentary rush of anger. "I'm sorry, Papa. I would never do anything to upset you. It was just one of those stupid things that happen. Won't you forgive me for causing you pain?"

"I forgive you," growled Frank, tightening his robe and marching toward the kitchen. "But don't do it again."

"I won't. I promise."

Lisa turned to her with a smirk. "You'd better go to church and confess your sins. I'd hate to have to live with your conscience."

"Your concern is touching." Torie's eyes burned into her sister. "And thanks for waking Papa. I'll do you a favor, sometime."

Behind the closed door of her room, Torie tossed her jacket over a chair, slipped off her shoes, and dropped onto her bed. What a night. What a man. Despite all the warnings about how you had to be experienced to enjoy sex, her second encounter had turned out to be the exact opposite of her first. Nielson had been a skilled and patient lover, and she had been so aroused by his caresses that she had no trouble responding.

"You were made for this, Vittoria," he had whispered, as he plunged into her again and again. "I knew the moment I saw you. I knew it would be like this for us."

Three times that night they had made love, and each time her desire had grown stronger. She had longed to cry out her feelings for him; she wanted him inside her, on top of her, all over her, consuming her, so intense was her need for him. And yet, with all his ardor, she had sensed that something was missing. Something personal in this most deeply personal of acts was not there.

Still reflecting as she tucked a blanket around her shoulders, she knew immediately what was missing; he had uttered no words of caring or endearment. Even in their most tender moments, he had praised the softness of her skin, the perfection of her breasts, the proportions of her hips and thighs, yet he had never mentioned how he felt for the woman they belonged to, or that he thought of her as anything more than a well-designed piece of machinery.

That would come, she decided. Their relationship was in its infancy, and now that they had established the physical bond, they could gradually develop the emotional one. Much as she longed to be spontaneous, she knew she had to refrain from telling him she loved him. It was too soon for a blubbering confession, particularly one that might not be returned. Yet love him she did, with all her mind, body, and soul.

The fact that he was cautious only confirmed to her how serious he was. So what if they had different backgrounds? How could anything come between them now? All that mattered was how they felt about each other. They had the rest of their lives to face the obstacles.

"Sorry I'm a little late."

"Here, I'll take that." Peggy shook out the dripping umbrella and set it in the corner of the office to dry. She approached the desk cautiously. "Are you all right?"

"I'm fine." Torie hung her raincoat on the rack and slumped into her swivel chair.

"You don't look fine."

"If I don't, it's your fault. You gave me that clipping."

"Clipping? You went to the church Wednesday?"

"Yes, and Robert Nielson's ego could swallow up the state of Texas. But guess who was there?"

"Oh, no!"

"None other. And we happened to meet accidentally on purpose—and it was just like I knew it would be. We both felt this *tremendous* instant attraction. I didn't tell you yesterday because I knew you'd disapprove. But we saw each other again last night, and, uh . . ."

Peggy scowled. "Does 'and, uh' mean what I think it means?"

"Yes, and I'm not a bit sorry. He'll be calling me any minute now." Her cheeks reddened as she asked, "Do you think people have to know each other a long time to be in love?"

"That's like the beating-your-wife question. If I say no, I'm endorsing instant sex. If I say yes, I'm out of a job."

"Seriously."

"Seriously?" Peggy sat down and scratched her chin. How

could she be honest and not hurtful? If only Torie had had a mother to guide her through her teens, she might not have had so many problems. "I'm sure you're in love with him," she answered hesitantly. "You have been for years. But it's unrealistic to expect him to love you. One day you meet, and the next day you hop in the sack. He doesn't know you don't do that with everyone. Men don't respect women who give themselves freely."

"That's not so," Torie snapped. "He said he was crazy about me. Besides, these are the seventies. Everybody does it."

"You ask for my opinion and then you reject it. The truth is, men like Nielson don't marry women like you and me no matter how long they know us. They marry the Betsy Richardsons and the Frannie Pews and the Dora Biddles of the world. That's just the way it is, so you might as well accept it."

"I'll *never* accept it. That's not the way it is anywhere else. Only here. This city's in love with its own past—like some aging actress who sits home all day getting high on her scrapbooks. People are what they are *now*, not what their ancestors were a hundred years ago. I'll be damned if I'll let this city's screwed-up values ruin my chance for happiness." She exhaled loudly. "Have you checked with Jock about Snyder Avenue?"

"Yes." Her question signaled the end of their discussion. "The Stumpos are moving out October twenty-eighth, and the Quartarolis are giving him ulcers. They don't want this, they can't afford that—"

"Well, tell him to find them something. Nielson's agreed to do the job and he's not even charging me. Oops, I almost forgot. I'm seeing Mervin Lewis at ten. If anyone should call—"

"Don't worry, I'll take a message." Peggy softened her tone. "Look, I didn't mean to make you feel like you're some sort of fallen woman. Nothing's branded across your forehead. Strangers aren't going to point their fingers at you and whisper, 'Guess what *she* did last night!' Although my mother used to say you could tell the good girls from the bad girls by the noise they made when they walked."

"Noise?"

"Yeah, the good girls all went clinkety-clink. They had ice cubes in their pants."

Torie smiled and reached for her raincoat. "Thanks for the explanation. Now I know why the streets are so quiet."

*　　*　　*

A dark-haired man with gray sideburns slid open a glass door. "Won't you come in? I'm Mervin Lewis."

She smiled and shook hands, pleased to find the attorney's appearance as distinguished as his reputation. "What a fabulous office. The lines are so clean and sharp. When I have a big office, it's going to be neat and sparkling just like this. I hate clutter."

"Such strong feelings."

"Hmmm, I guess so. I grew up in a row house where I practically drowned in everyone's junk. My sister and brother were both pack rats. And when my mother died, my father built a big fancy shrine in their bedroom. I still have nightmares about that gorpy altar."

He motioned to a black leather chair. "I know your time is as valuable as mine, Miss Di Angelo. How may I help you?"

She laid a pile of folders on his desk. "I took over our company four months ago when my brother, Frankie, joined the army. I'm here because you're the best real estate lawyer in town and I'd like you to work with me."

"Don't you have a lawyer?"

"My brother used to use my cousin Tony because he was cheap—or said he was—and it always ended up costing us. I've made lots of mistakes since I started working, and I'll make lots more. But I try very hard to profit from them and not repeat them. One thing I've learned is that you don't skimp on legal advice."

"No argument there."

She leaned forward eagerly. "I'd like you to look over these three deals Frankie was working on, especially the Urbandale School project. It's all in the files. I wrote my brother's partner, Wally Todd, that we didn't want to be involved with him any longer."

"Why not?"

"He's been taking advantage of Frankie, and now he's trying to cheat me. I want to make my own deals from now on."

"Isn't that rather ambitious for a lady so . . . forgive me, how old are you?"

"Twenty." Give or take three months. "But I've been in real estate since I was fourteen. Anyway, Wally hasn't answered my letter and I'm not sure how to proceed. If he knows *you're* representing me, I don't think he'll try any funny business."

"I'm flattered by your faith." He set the folders on his blotter. "Is that all?"

"Yes, for now. You won't be sorry if you take me on as a client, Mr. Lewis. I already have a big project in the works, in South Philly. Nielson Hughes is our architect—Robert Nielson's son. He's twice as brilliant as his father, and only half as conceited."

The lawyer laughed and stood up. The girl was amazing; tight-fitting clothes and too much jewelry, but as bright and sharp as she was direct. A certain freshness about her appealed to him. "Very well, I'll look these over. I'm not saying I'll represent you, but I will get back to you."

"Thank you." She smiled and shook his hand. "I'll be waiting."

By late afternoon, Torie could stand it no longer; there had to be some explanation for Nielson's silence. Maybe he had forgotten her last name. Maybe he had lost her card. Maybe he didn't know how to reach her. Finding his mother listed in the directory, she scribbled the number on a pad and called him.

He seemed surprised to hear from her. "Hi, Torie. What can I do for you?"

What could he do for her? After last night? What the hell kind of a question was that? "I thought . . . when you had a minute, we might discuss Snyder Avenue." She couldn't believe the conversation. They were chatting as if they hardly knew each other. "I, uh, have some ideas I'd like to run by you."

"Go ahead."

"On the phone?" Suddenly, she brightened. "Oh, I get it. You're not alone."

"I'm quite alone," he answered. "When can I go out and take a closer look at the houses? Will your tenants let me in?"

"Yes." Still stunned by his attitude, she lapsed into her professional persona. "I'll call them first, and meet you there whenever you say."

"Thanks, but I'd rather poke around by myself. I'm going to try to retain the original foundations and save you some money. Do you have a contractor in mind?"

"No, I was hoping . . ."

"Yes?"

"We *do* have to talk, Nielson. I don't want to retain the foundations if it's going to limit what you can do. With your talent, I'm hoping you'll create something modern and daring and exciting—something people will notice and talk about."

"On Snyder Avenue?"

"Why not?"

His voice was impatient. "For the same reason that you don't build a topless bar next to a church. I have warm feelings for Snyder Avenue. It has flavor and history, and families have seen three and four generations grow up there. I can't turn the neighborhood into a circus. I can't take two old row houses and convert them into a razzle-dazzle apartment complex that'll stand out like earrings on a sow. If that's what you want, you've got the wrong man."

"No, no, I've got the right man. But won't you hear some of my ideas?"

"Such as?"

"Well, I do think that block needs cheering up. I'd like to see you do something eye-catching—maybe black and white and silver, glass-brick walls, if they're not too expensive, oversized windows . . ."

Gads, he thought, all she'd left out was a rocket ship on the roof. Yet he couldn't afford to antagonize her. Not many students got the chance to remodel a real building as a term project. "Can we discuss your ideas later—after I finish the preliminary design?"

She hesitated, wondering if she had made a mistake engaging him. He held the power now. If she didn't like his terms, he could easily bow out and she would be forced to find someone else. Obviously, the choice was either to give Nielson Hughes full command or to hire an established architect who would charge her thousands. "How much later?"

"I don't know. However long it takes."

"All right. I'll stay out of your hair."

"Good." He sounded relieved. "Will you tell your tenants to expect me Sunday afternoon?"

"Yes. I'll tell them." Her voice was almost a monotone. She could hardly believe his attitude; they might as well be two strangers. "Is there . . . anything else we should talk about?"

"Nothing I can think of," he replied. "Thanks for the call."

Peggy sat at her desk, shuffling papers and pretending not to have overheard. Resisting the urge to dash over and offer consolation, she waited till Torie made herself a cup of coffee and returned to her chair.

"Wanna talk?" she asked, crossing the office.

Torie swiveled around. Her face was colorless; her eyes betrayed her confusion. "What's with me, Pig? Am I the biggest fool in the world?"

Peggy offered a cigarette, then lit her own. "No. You're simply in love with a man who's got a thousand other things on his mind. He's got years of work and study ahead of him, and all he wants from a woman right now is to get laid. I have a hunch he'll want to see you again. But any relationship with him has to be on his terms."

"*Everything* has to be on his terms," she said, pounding her fist. "Even the damn project. I'm going to call him back and tell him what he can do—"

"Don't be foolish." Peggy's voice was firm. For the moment, they had switched roles. "This morning, when you said you'd hired a graduate student, I thought you were out of your mind. But the more I think about it, the more I'm convinced it was a stroke of genius."

"You are?"

"Look at it from Nielson's point of view. This is his first commission—probably part of his degree—and he can't afford to blow it. He's going to get the best advice and the best possible help he can get. I'll bet anything you'll have the top brains at Penn working on those plans and it won't cost you a cent."

"Honestly?"

"Isn't it obvious? His name will be attached to this project for the rest of his life. If he screws up, he'll never live it down."

Her anger faded as quickly as it had flared. "I hadn't thought of it that way."

"Well, think of it. I also suspect that Nielson Hughes may one day follow in his father's venerable footsteps and become so famous that his first work, the fabulous Snyder Avenue apartments, will become a national landmark."

Torie was aghast. "You really think that's possible?"

"Anything's possible. At the very least, the curiosity about the building will have PR value. Don't let pride and emotion drown your good sense."

"What should I do?"

"Not a damn thing. If he calls you for a date, fine. If he doesn't, be cool."

"How can I be cool when I'm out of my stupid skull in love with the man?"

"You have no choice. Be cool or lose him. I know what I'm talking about. *Trust* me."

"Trust you," she repeated gloomily. "All right, great wise one, maybe he will build us some sort of national monument—who knows? But I'm still furious. How can you love a man and want to strangle him at the same time?"

"Welcome to the club," said Peggy, chuckling as she walked back to her desk.

Torie felt miserable when she left the office late that afternoon. Part of the problem, she realized, was exhaustion. A few hours of fitful snoozing between frantic bouts of lovemaking did not a night's sleep make. The greater part of her sadness, however, was the realization that she loved a man who had taken her as casually as he would take a slice of pie. She had been his dessert for the night, nothing more.

In such a mood, going home to face her self-righteous sister and a father who disapproved of almost everything she did would only depress her more. The downpour was heavy, the streets were slick and not conducive to pleasure driving. Nevertheless, instead of taking her usual route, she found herself moving along East River Drive toward Center City. More by instinct than design, she turned off at Walnut and headed for Rittenhouse Square.

Several minutes later, she sat watching the rain stream down her favorite town house. The Richardsons still lived on the south side of the Square, in one of the few private homes facing the park. Most of the other houses had been converted into apartments or offices.

She couldn't help wondering about the Richardsons. Betsy would be twenty-one now, the same age as Nielson. Last she heard, Betsy had finished Vassar College and was working in the art museum. She probably hadn't moved away from home yet—and why should she? Where in all of Philadelphia could you find a better address?

Try as she might, Torie couldn't stop thinking about Nielson—wondering if he and Betsy still saw each other, still talked on the phone, still went to parties together. How it hurt her to swallow Peggy's words . . . to accept the fact that she could never compete with anyone rich and wellborn.

But circumstances were changing. Torie, too, would be rich some day . . . richer than the Biddles and the Pews and the Rich-

ardsons all put together. Then Nielson would come to his senses
and realize how much he loved her. She would toy with him at
first and make him pay for his snooty indifference. But after a
short time she would end his suffering and marry him. She would
buy a whole apartment building on Rittenhouse Square and she
would have so much money and so much property that he would
never have to work another day . . .

The deluge lightened, and Torie's gaze widened to take in her
surroundings. William Penn's original plan for Philadelphia, she
remembered from her school days, had called for five open parks,
one at each corner of the rectangular city, and one in the middle.
Center Square had long since been paved over to build City Hall,
but Franklin, Logan, Washington, and Rittenhouse squares remained standing.

She liked the fact that *her* square was named for David Rittenhouse, an eighteenth-century astronomer, inventor, and Renaissance man who had much more going for him than just rich
ancestors. Paul Cret, the French architect who had designed the
park, had done so brilliantly, she thought, dotting the paths with
benches and balustrades, laying out the central flower bed, and
crowning the plaza with a long shallow pool. At one end of it,
a lovely bronze lady rose from a pedestal, her index finger pointing to the sky. What was she trying to say?

Nearby were the stone urns and famous animal sculptures that
children loved to climb on while their nannies stood and gos-
siped. The lion looked mean and ferocious as his powerful claws
grasped the thick hide of a reptile. Maybe that was the lesson
for the kiddies: Do unto others before they do it to you.

On Eighteenth Street, the east side of the park, sat the Barclay
Hotel, where she and Steffi had so unceremoniously been booted
out of the bar. Its twenty-one stories of faded brick and masonry
seemed as dull and uninspiring now as they had then. A doorman in a gold-trimmed uniform stood by the entrance, awaiting
the next taxi or limo, his umbrella poised to protect the well-
coiffed head of any guest who might have to suffer the single step
between car and awning.

Next to the Barclay stood the Rawley Institute of Music, as
sacred to Philadelphians as Vatican City to the Romans. Aca-
demically, she knew, it ranked high, but architecturally, all she
could see was a squat three-story building of sand-colored stone,
with carved friezes and plaster swirls on the roof.

Brrrrrrack! The crunch of the wrecker's ball was so real in her mind she could almost hear it. Was she mad? Had she totally lost her senses to dream of demolishing that hallowed structure? What about replacing it with a gleaming skyscraper of glass and steel and marble? What would those stodgy Main Liners say if they could read her mind? Paranoid old fossils. They would cheerfully strap her to the Pennsylvania Railroad tracks and applaud her decapitation for even *thinking* such thoughts.

Across the park from the Barclay, the Church of the Holy Trinity occupied the north corner of the street known as West Rittenhouse, and adjoining it, on the north side of the Square, Walnut Street hosted five unsightly buildings. What purpose did it serve to retain those mildewed antiquities with their sagging foundations and prehistoric plumbing? Why couldn't other people see what she saw? Why was she so at odds with the rest of the world?

Or was she? Could it be the reverse? Maybe *they* were the misfits—the pigheaded patriarchs who refused to recognize progress and all that modern civilization deemed brilliant and creative. Worshiping the past made no sense anymore, in times when the new was more practical, more functional, and infinitely more beautiful.

But she well knew the futility of her fantasies. When it came to renovating landmarks, particularly on Rittenhouse Square, not even God could sway an Old Philadelphian.

13
==

"WHAT ARE YOU doing tonight?"

Nielson's voice on the phone gave Torie a start. She hadn't heard from him in two months—not since that gloomy October afternoon when she had made the mistake of calling him, thinking they might have something to say to each other.

"Who is this?" she asked coolly. As if she didn't know. At

least twenty times she had picked up the receiver to call and see how he was doing. And twenty times she had set it down again.

"It's Nielson. I have your preliminary design ready. When do you finish work?"

"Around six."

"Meet me in front of Meyerson Hall at seven?"

"Yes—okay." Idiot! she told herself. What happened to all those vows to play hard-to-get?

A click and he was gone. The thought of seeing him that night gave her a tremor of pleasure, and when the phone rang again, she grabbed it eagerly, thinking he might have forgotten something.

"Miss Di Angelo? Mr. Mervin Lewis calling. One minute please."

Another voice came on the line. "Torie? It's Mervin. I have some news for you."

"Good, I hope." His statement brought her back to reality.

"Not so good, I'm sorry to say. I looked into those deals your brother was working on. Two of them appear to be washouts, but the third, the Urbandale School project, is alive and healthy. Your ex-partner bought the land himself. He's about to sign a very profitable contract."

"Oh, no! I thought it was a scam."

"That was a costly thought. Since you opted to drop out of the deal, he's under no obligation to give you a cent." The lawyer's tone was stern as he added, "I'm sending these files back to you, Torie, and I suggest you keep them as reminders. You told me you learn from your mistakes, and these were whoppers."

"What . . . were my mistakes?" she asked, crushed.

"Your first was writing a letter in the heat of emotion. That's a 'never' in any business. Your second was to break off a partnership without getting legal advice. And your third was coming to me. It's absurd for you to be paying my high fees at this stage of your growth. I'd be happy to suggest several attorneys who can take care of you for a fraction of what I charge."

"I . . . guess you're right," she said, still stunned. "Would you send me their names with your bill?"

"I'd be glad to," he replied, "and best wishes for your project."

* * *

Why, Torie wondered, heading down Twenty-third Street toward Center City, did good news always have to be followed by bad? Was there some unwritten law of nature that you had to pay for every happiness with unhappiness? It seemed that way. No sooner had Nielson lifted her spirits than Mervin Lewis had shot them down. His news had been a particular blow because she had felt so strongly about Wally—and she had been wrong. Damn it all. If she couldn't trust her instincts, what *could* she trust?

Still preoccupied, she drove across the rickety Walnut Street bridge and found herself on the grounds of the University of Pennsylvania. Light from tall street lamps reflected off the cluster of Victorian brick buildings that formed the entrance to the campus.

Arriving at Meyerson Hall a minute past the hour, she parked by the curb and fixed her eyes on the door. Seven-fifteen came and went, and when Nielson had not appeared by seven-thirty, she began to wonder if she had misunderstood him. Reviewing their conversation, she clearly recalled his saying that he would meet her at seven. She also remembered that he had kept her waiting for their first date. Perhaps he was habitually late—one of those people too disorganized and too self-involved to consider the value of anyone else's time.

A rap on the window made her sit up. The sight of Nielson in a blue cashmere sweater and gray slacks dissolved whatever annoyance she had felt.

"Sorry to be tardy," he said, smiling and opening the door. "Hop out and I'll take you inside."

"Another seminar?"

"No, I was engrossed in a tape—an interview with Philip Johnson. Ever hear of him?"

"I don't think so." She had decided not to pretend with him anymore. If they were to have a relationship—and she firmly believed they were—she had better start being truthful.

"It doesn't matter." He led her into the building and followed her up the stairs, his eyes suddenly mesmerized by the rhythmic sway of her hips. He hadn't been with her five minutes and she was already starting to get to him—so much so that he wondered if he could wait till they got home. "Turn right at the top landing—yes, go in there. That's my studio."

The section she entered was brightly lit and devoid of furniture, save for a drafting table, a desk with a tape recorder, and a cabinet piled with supplies. He watched her glance around the room, entranced by her silhouette, her delicate profile, the shine of her hair, the sway of her breasts as she bent to examine the blueprint—and abruptly, he switched off the lights. "Those things glare too much."

"But how can I see your designs?"

"My designs," he said, reaching out for her, "should be very apparent. I'd almost forgotten how lovely you are."

"Nielson, you can't—"

"Why can't I? We're alone in here." His lips silenced her as he kissed her easily, then with growing intensity. The force of his desire made her draw away. A student workshop on a college campus was no place for . . .

"You smell like wildflowers," he murmured, pulling her back to him. He found her lips again, ignoring the feeble protest she offered, and parted them with his tongue. His hands slid down to her buttocks and began to stroke.

Her resistance was fading rapidly as she felt herself responding to his movements, pressing up against him and feeling his arousal, then tightening her arms around his neck, surrendering her control until there was none left to surrender.

"That's it," he said, excited, "don't hold back. Show me you want me as much as I want you. Here"—he slipped off his sweater, rolled it up, and placed it on the floor—"put your head on this."

Unthinkingly, she lay down on the makeshift pillow, and he was there beside her, unbuttoning her blouse, dropping her straps off her shoulders, and lifting her breasts from the bra. Her nipples hardened to his tongue, and she felt the joy of his warm, caressing hands.

"It doesn't matter where you are when you feel passion," he whispered. "You have to give in to it or the moment is lost forever."

"Do you feel passion now?"

"Yes. Seeing you—tasting you—touching you arouses me wildly. I have to be inside you . . ." He drew up her skirt, letting his palms slide along her thigh, then back up to her waist; he pushed down her pantyhose and felt her naked belly. "Your skin is pure silk . . . you have a body made for love."

"For your love, Nielson. I don't want anyone else—ever."

His fingers crept inside her panties, and the welcome moistness echoed her words, telling him she was as anxious as he.

Shedding his slacks, he mounted and thrust himself into her, slowing his movements until he could bring her up to his own feverish peak. They rose and fell in quickening rhythms and suddenly she clung to his back and cried out his name. And then they lay breathless, clutched in each other's arms, their bodies locked and spent.

"Turn right next block, at Panama." Nielson opened the window and poked out his head. "Mmm, that wonderful cool night air. Did you know Senator Pepper once lived on Panama? It's the most amazing street. You drive along expecting to find a crumbling old alley, and instead, here's this oasis of charm and history. My mother was incredibly lucky to get this house. Here we are. Park at the curb."

He hurried around and helped her out. "These were all working people's houses in the twenties, except for that one on the corner. See over there?"

"The place with all the gewgaws?"

"Yes. That's one of Frank Furness's finest Victorians. You've heard of the Furness family? Horace Howard edited Shakespeare and his sister married a Wister. Old Philadelphians, the Furnesses, though not quite as old as the Wisters. Everything Frank did was expansive, extravagant—"

"Pretentious?"

"No, not at all. Meticulous attention to detail doesn't make it pretentious. Notice the oval windows, and how gracefully the cherubim and seraphim are worked into the pediments. What a monument to an age when architects weren't afraid to be flowery—when they could express their art by decorating buildings. Contrast this with today's trend to austerity."

"What's wrong with austerity?" she ventured. "I love to see tall sleek skyscrapers with no frills."

"There's a place for those. There's always a place for good architecture of any style." He stopped before a small gray-stone house with ironwork balconies. "Let's go inside."

She followed him up three steps and through the door, feeling instantly uncomfortable, as if she were a trespasser who had no right to be there. A strong sense of *déjà vu* took her back seven years to Betsy's birthday party and a flood of similar sensations. Even the furnishings reminded her of the Richardson house.

The living room looked like a picture in a decorators' manual: overstuffed chairs and couches upholstered in a bright floral print, draperies of matching fabric, spindly-legged tables laden with porcelain figurines. A painting of a handsome, aristocratic lady dominated the mantel. "Is that attractive woman your mother?"

"Yes, but I loathe that portrait. It makes her look hard and stern and she's neither. Would you like something to drink?"

"No, thanks. That sandwich filled me up."

It should have, he thought. Thank God none of his friends had been around to see her spread mayonnaise on a hoagie. She was probably the kind of girl who poured catsup on filet mignon.

"Can I see the design?"

"Of course. I keep forgetting." He started to unwrap a blueprint, then rolled it up and set it back on the floor. Moving toward her, he reached around her waist. "I have a better idea. Take the plans home with you, look them over at your leisure, and when you're ready, give them to your contractor."

"But shouldn't we—"

"Shhh," he said, touching his finger to her lips. "You know what we should be doing and so do I . . ."

Later that night, Torie lay happily nestled in Nielson's arms. The big lace-canopied bed was too sissyish for a man, she thought, and she wondered if his mother ever entertained in it. The rich *did* live better than other people—a good deal better. The sheets were the softest cotton she had ever felt, the pillow cushioned her head as if she were floating, the quilt was light and warm and not the least bit cumbersome. "I wish I didn't have to go," she said, kissing his chest.

He brushed back her hair. "Does your father wait up for you?"

"No. But if I'm not home by two or three A.M., my sister wakes him up and they make a big scene about it."

"How narrow-minded. I'm not your first lover, am I?"

She blushed. "You're my second. The first was years ago and it was awful." Perhaps she could turn Jack Slate into an embellished Tony. "He was kind of a family friend, a lot older than me, and he promised to wait for me to grow up. But then he went off and married some society lady with a ton of money and I hear she nags the pants off him. Serves the"—she almost said "bastard"—"jerk right."

He laughed and smoothed her cheek. "You're a charmer, Torie. I like the way you go after what you want. You don't play games and you don't try to manipulate. Don't ever lose that wonderful directness."

"In that case, tell me about *your* love life."

"It's not too exciting. There's only been one person I ever cared about." And always will, he thought. But Betsy wasn't the kind of girl you took to bed—at least, not until she became your wife. "I haven't seen much of her lately."

"Someone you knew in high school?"

"Even earlier."

"Do you want to marry her?"

"Marry is a very permanent-sounding word. I can't think about that now." Yes, he would marry Betsy. He had never loved anyone else, and neither had she. They had sworn to wait for each other, however long it would take.

"Why don't you see her?"

"I told you, I have to finish school. We both have a lot of growing up to do. Marriage is a long way off."

Torie felt a happy glow. He couldn't possibly still like Betsy or *she* would be the woman lying in his arms. "Nielson, do you ever, umm, turn on?"

"Turn on?" The question brought a terse reply. "I'll take the fifth."

"The fifth," she repeated, puzzled. "You mean you prefer booze?"

Jesus, he thought. "No, I don't prefer booze. When I'm studying and working, I don't choose to muddle my brain with drugs."

"Have you always wanted to be an architect?"

"Yes, ever since I was a boy. My mother used to drive me around the city pointing out all the buildings she loved—not only Independence Square and Elfreth's Alley, but lesser-known places like Grumblethorpe—isn't that a marvelous name?—the old Wister home in Germantown."

"Did your father ever talk to you about architecture?"

"No."

"Does it bother you to talk about him?"

A sharpness edged his voice. "Why should it?"

"I don't know." She knew very well. She also knew enough to change the subject. "My father and I aren't close anymore. He prefers my sister, who cooks for him and takes care of the house. But I had to start working full time"—she hesitated a moment, then decided they shouldn't have secrets from each other—"when Papa went to prison."

"Your father went to prison?"

"On a bribery charge. He was framed. I took over the business after my brother left. I didn't want Frankie to go to Vietnam, but he felt he had to." A worried look crossed her brow. *"You* don't have to go to war, do you?"

"Not unless they put me in chains and drag me there. I've applied for C.O. status—conscientious objector. That war is a bloody outrage."

"It sure is." For a moment, she bristled with resentment. Here was Nielson, safely ensconced in his fancy town house, thanks to the advice, no doubt, of his mother's high-priced lawyers. And there was Frankie, off fighting for his life in a stinking jungle. Yet what else was new? The rich were always sticking it to the poor.

"I'm working on an antiwar rally and demonstration for next month," he announced. "Joan Baez is coming out. We're going to send a strong message to the White House."

Her antagonism suddenly melted. "What a super idea. Maybe we can go together."

"It's *not* a social event." The girl was beginning to rattle him. He extricated himself from her arms and sat up in bed. "Look, Torie, shouldn't you run on home before your father starts getting nervous?"

"Yes, I guess I'd better." Stung by his curtness, she told herself he didn't mean to sound harsh—he often snapped at her without thinking; then a minute later he'd be smiling and talking as if nothing had happened. Dressing quickly, she combed her hair and repaired her makeup in the bathroom. When she came out, she found him sprawled on his stomach, his breathing loud and regular, his head half-buried beneath a pillow.

With a sigh, she reached for her coat and purse. She had found her way to the door after their first night together. No reason she couldn't do it again.

Late the next afternoon, alone in the office, Torie nervously lifted the phone. She had spent most of the day studying Nielson's blueprints and, fully aware of the hours and effort he had put into them, hesitated to offer even the most minor criticism. And yet she had to. The plan was not what she wanted, not even what she liked. It was what she had feared he would do—design a dull, practical building that would blend into its surroundings. Blend, hell, it would practically *disappear*. The result would be about as different from the splashy Torie Di Angelo production she had envisioned as anything could be. "Nielson, it's Torie. Do you have a minute?"

"Yes. How are you?"

He seemed almost friendly after their second night together. Soon he might even recognize her voice. "Fine, thanks. I enjoyed being with you."

If he shared her reaction, he didn't feel the need to mention it. "You didn't call to tell me that. What's on your mind?"

This time she was prepared for his gruffness. "I have a few questions about the design. Would you have half an hour to meet with me?"

"No. What's your question?"

Damn him! It wasn't anything they could discuss on the phone. "I need to show you on the plan, point out to you—"

"Point *what* out to me?"

All right, she would do it his way. "Well, those balconies, for instance. I thought we agreed—"

"We didn't agree on anything."

"But they're so unnecessary. And why red bricks? Everything in this city is red brick. Can't we—"

"Torie, I'm telling you for the last time. 'No house should ever be *on* a hill. It should be *of* the hill, belonging to it, so hill and house can live together in harmony.' Frank Lloyd Wright said that and it applies to Snyder Avenue."

"Well, it so happens I have a quote for *you.*" She reached for her notepad. "Architect Herbert Beckhard said, 'New buildings need not be replicas of those adjoining, or even sentimental exercises in reminiscence. They—' "

"Didn't you promise to stay out of my hair?"

"Yes, but you're being opinionated and stubborn. Why can't you hear me out and then make up your mind?"

"Because," he exploded, "you haven't the vaguest notion what you're talking about! Your idea of beauty is a massive rectal thermometer that incorporates nothing of the past, has no relation to its environment, and gleams like a pile of old auto fenders. You have all the taste and refinement of a warthog."

"Shut up, damn you!" His condescension angered her more than his words. "How the hell would you know what I think? What *anyone* thinks? You're too busy listening to yourself prattle on and on about ancient history and Old Philadelphia and all your sacred Main Line values—"

"Do tell." Suddenly he was calm again. Somehow he had to save face, save the project, and yet keep her from ruining his plans. "In that case, I'll just tear up the blueprints. For five or ten thousand dollars, you can buy another set."

"Wait!" She struggled for control. "Isn't it possible to have a civilized discussion? I have *reasons* for my suggestions."

"I'm sure you do. But tell me this: Do you think da Vinci listened to suggestions when he was painting the *Mona Lisa*? 'Hey, Lennie, open that eye a little wider, put some teeth in that smile, attaboy!' Do you think Michelangelo listened to suggestions while he was carving David out of a chunk of marble? Do you think Baron Haussmann listened to suggestions when he lay out the parks and boulevards of Paris?"

He paused for emphasis. "I've spent two months on these plans. If you were to try to replace them, you'd not only pay a fortune, you'd never be able to duplicate their excellence. Once the building's done, you can paint the inside orange and green polka dots for all I care. But the outside must be mine and mine alone. Does that sound unreasonable?"

"Not unreasonable," she said, "just selfish and stubborn. Very well, Mr. Hughes, we'll do it your way. I bow to your superior wisdom and genius."

"It's time you did," he snapped, and slammed down the phone.

Lisa's piercing shriek shattered the late-afternoon stillness. Torie jumped up in bed, thinking it was morning and time to go to work; then gradually her mind came into focus. Having spent the day interviewing builders and contractors, she had come home from work exhausted, lain down for a few seconds, and fallen into a deep sleep.

Grabbing her robe, she rushed downstairs and found her sister slumped in an armchair, staring at the wall, her eyes glazed with shock. "Lisa!" she cried, shaking her arm. "What is it? What's wrong?"

No answer came forth, only Lisa's voice muttering, "Eternal rest grant unto him, Oh Lord . . . perpetual light . . ." One hand clutched a rosary to her chest and the other grasped a letter.

Torie snatched the paper and saw only the first five words: "We regret to inform you . . ."

"Oh, my God," she gasped, "Frankie! Oh, my God! It's a mistake—" She forced herself to read further: ". . . killed in action . . . upholding the honor of his country . . . remains to be shipped . . ."

"No," she murmured, "no, Frankie, please . . ." As the realization struck, she staggered forward and crumpled to the floor.

PART
III

14

THE OFFICES OF Carpi & Silvano, Attorneys at Law, occupied the third story of a yellow-brick building on Christian Street, a short distance from South Philly's open-air Italian Market.

Dressed in a subdued clergy-gray suit, Torie turned the brass doorknob and entered a well-appointed waiting room. Not bad, she thought, glancing around. Tony could afford wall-to-wall carpets and gold-framed paintings now that he had a rich wife. She hoped the rumors of her bitchiness were not exaggerated.

"Miss Di Angelo?" A receptionist peered over her granny glasses. "Mr. Silvano's expecting you. Go right in."

"Thank you." Tucking her purse under one arm, she started toward the door, when suddenly it opened. "Vittoria!" cried Tony, rushing toward her. "Let me look at you. How long has it been—five years? Six years? You've grown into the glorious woman I knew you would be. How *are* you, *bellissima?*"

"Hello, Tony." Torie let herself be embraced. "I've been better."

He sobered instantly and closed the door behind them. "I can see that. You're pale as a ghost. Sit down and make yourself comfortable. Can I get you anything?"

"No, thanks." She set her purse on her lap and crossed her legs. "I'm sorry—I know you just got back from a long trip. I guess you haven't heard—about Frankie."

"Has he been hurt?"

"He's been killed. We got a letter last month—killed in Vietnam. I knew he'd have to be a goddamn hero and get himself blown up."

"*Dio mio!*" Tony sank into his chair. "My deepest condolences. I—don't know what to say. He was my friend—my little brother—I loved Frankie."

"He loved you, too." Emotion choked her for several seconds; then she sat up stiffly. "But life must go on. There's still Papa to think about."

"You told him?"

"We weren't going to. Lisa and I decided to say Frankie was wounded. But Papa knows us too well. He saw right through us." She stopped to dry her eyes. "He took the news terribly. Said he'd been expecting it every day. Frankie was always the leader of his group, always the first to fight for what he believed in. Papa said it was God's will—and then he had a stroke. We brought him home from the hospital two days ago."

"How is he?"

"Terrible. He cries all the time."

"Poor Frank. And Lisa?"

"Lisa hasn't changed. Once she decided Frankie had gone to heaven to be with God and Mama, she made peace with herself. Now she says God did Frankie a favor by taking him early."

Tony nodded. He was still good-looking, still effusive and charming, but he seemed much older than she remembered. His coal-black sideburns were streaked with silver, his brow furrowed, his deep brown eyes set in beds of wrinkles. The sight of him filled her with bitter memories of the trial. "And you, *cara.* What do you think?"

"What do I think?" His question brought her back with a jolt. "I think this whole goddamn war is fucking madness, and that Frankie gave his life for nothing. That's what I think. And if there *is* a God somewhere in this wretched universe, He's no friend of mine!"

"*Dio mio,* forgive her." Tony's voice rose in shock. "You must have faith in God. Without that, there's nothing. Believe me, I know what you're going through. I've been through hell myself. But I've never questioned the wisdom of the Lord."

"*You've* been through hell?" She looked up in surprise. "I'm sorry, I've been so involved in my own sadness. What is it—business problems?"

"My wife's leaving me," he announced in solemn tones. "Grace and I—we're very different. She'd like to be married to a Republican senator from the Main Line, not a Democratic ward leader from South Philly. I tried my best; I offered to give up politics and move my office to Chestnut Hill, but even then,

I'd never be Anthony Biddle the Third. I'll always be plain old Tony Silvano the First, and that's not good enough for her."

"Is there anything I can do?"

"Thanks, *cara*, no—except be my friend. I'm very lonely. This terrible news about Frankie—maybe we can console each other. One night—we'll have dinner."

Even in her grief, the irony of the situation struck her. Had Tony been more forceful with the draft board, advised Frankie to be a conscientious objector like Nielson, or cared enough to wield his influence, he could easily have gotten him a deferment. And here he was using his *death* as a reason to ask her out. "I can't think about that now. We have legal matters to settle."

"I understand." His voice was once again professional as he rose and walked over to his files. "Frankie wrote a new will before he left. Did you know that?"

"No." The information pained her. "You mean—he thought he might not come back?"

"He knew it was possible." Tony extracted a folder and began to leaf through it. "Frankie wanted you to have his car, Lisa to have his records and stereo equipment, and all his personal assets to go to Peggy. By the way, how's she taking it?"

"She's a wreck. We all are. She showed up at the office the other day—she works for me now—but she couldn't even get through the morning. Every time we looked at each other, we burst into tears."

"I'm so sorry, *piccola*. One last legal matter: Frankie left a codicil in his will. He wanted to be sure his share of the business went to you."

"But Papa owns the business—"

"Yes. Your father's will leaves the Di Angelo Company to Frankie and you, his cash and savings to Lisa, and the house to be divided among the three of you. With your permission, I'll suggest he sign the company over to you now. By paying some minor gift taxes, you'll avoid having it go into probate when he dies. In fairness, perhaps the house should go to Lisa."

"That's fine with me."

"I'll need a few weeks before I call you in again." He came around his desk and kissed her hand. "Give my love to Lisa and Papa. You know how to reach me if you change your mind about dinner. We could both use a little happiness."

"Don't be sad, Tony." She managed a smile. "You won't be lonely for long."

* * *

Four weeks after Torie's meeting with Tony, the Snyder Avenue dwellings had been stripped to bare foundations. The new building was in the first stages of construction when she stopped by the site, as she did every day at noon. She had neither seen nor spoken to Nielson since their angry words two months earlier. This Friday, however, she saw him standing by one of the steel beams. "Hello," she said, walking over.

"Hello," he said absently. "There's no reason in the world they can't make those double-glazed windows open and close to save on air conditioning."

"What windows?"

"The ones that—" He looked up suddenly. "Oh, it's you. Where on earth did you find that jackass of a contractor?"

"The firm comes highly recommended. They've been in business forty years."

"Then they've had forty years of doing shoddy work and screwing their clients. He's trying to—oh, I forgot, you don't care about details. All you want is the finished product and to get those renters in as fast as possible. Can't afford a negative cash flow, can we."

She turned away as her eyes began to cloud. No matter how stoic she tried to be, almost everything—even the words "negative cash flow"—reminded her of Frankie. "I don't care, Nielson. Do whatever you want."

"What did you say?" he asked, staring.

"I said do whatever you want. I have to go. I'll see you later."

"Wait a minute." He grabbed her arm. "Are you feeling all right?"

"I'm fine."

"You're not fine. You've been crying. You look as if the Jolly Green Giant just kicked over your sand castle. What's wrong?"

"I told you it's nothing. I can't talk about—oh, Nielson," she cried, bursting into tears. "My brother, Frankie, was killed in Vietnam."

"Dear God! Come here. Come here." He folded her into his arms. "Why didn't you say so? I'm frightfully sorry. You've been keeping it all inside, haven't you."

She clung to him tightly as her body shook with sobs, and the grief she had tried so hard to repress came flowing out.

"That's good," he soothed, stroking her hair. "It's good for you to cry. I know it hurts, but it hurts more to hold it back.

Think of death as a part of life. Frankie will always be with you, in your heart. We'll make our building a monument to him. Would you like that? Frankie—Franklin—what about Francis? St. Francis Tower. Would he like to be canonized?"

The idea of Frankie as a saint made her smile even as she wept. "Yes—he'd love it. Papa will like it too."

"Then it's settled." He released her and handed her a handkerchief. "Have you had lunch?"

"I'm not hungry."

"You will be. We'll pick up a nice zinfandel, a loaf of French bread, and some Brie, and we'll have ourselves a picnic. Where would you like to go?"

She sniffed, wiped her eyes, and looked up gratefully. "Rittenhouse Square?"

A squirrel scampered across the grass and stopped a few feet from the bench where Torie and Nielson sat in thoughtful silence. Probing a discarded bag, the creature found a half-eaten doughnut, grasped it in its tiny fingers, and began to nibble, its whiskers bobbing and shaking with each bite.

"It must be nice to be a fuzzy little rodent," said Torie, setting a plastic cup on her lap. "No worries except whose garbage you're going to eat next."

"Or who's going to eat *you* next. I wouldn't trade places with him." Nielson's gaze shot past a trio of hippies lazing on the lawn to a pretty nurse strolling arm in arm with an elderly man. Then he looked upward. "Wouldn't you rather be something noble and solid and lasting?"

"You mean—like a building?"

"That thought did occur to me. I know you don't share my passion for historical structures, and yet you wanted to come to Rittenhouse Square. You must have *some* feeling for the beauty of this place."

"I have strong feelings. I think it's one of the loveliest spots in the world."

"Well, for once we agree." The girl puzzled him. Could she possibly have acquired some taste in the few months since he had seen her? "I often come here myself, to sit and daydream. I'd give anything to be able to breathe new life into some of these classic buildings."

"Really?" Could he finally have come to his senses? "What would you do, for instance, to the Barclay?"

"The Barclay. King of hotels. What a challenge to rebuild and restore—to retain the integrity of the old structure and at the same time utilize the best of twentieth-century technology. First, I'd install modern heating—"

"I mean to the outside."

"The façade? I'd clean it up, that's all. Some new paint here and there. If money was no object, I'd reinforce the foundation and add two floors of luxury features: a roof-top restaurant, maybe a health spa—"

"What about the other buildings? Would you tear down the decrepit ones and put up new ones?"

"Tear down! Are you crazy?" So much for his hope she might have changed. "You can build glittery new skyscrapers anywhere. Why destroy something precious that doesn't need to be destroyed? Our survival as a civilization depends upon preserving our links to the past. Give me free rein and twenty million dollars, and I'll give you the Hughes-revitalized Barclay, the most elegant old hotel in the world."

"I believe you." His confidence no longer surprised her. Nor did the fact that he could see Rittenhouse Square only as it was and always had been, instead of how it could be. She wasn't quite sure how *she* would improve it, except that she would streamline and brighten and modernize. The setting was far too lovely to be wasted on a clump of medieval ruins.

"Do you have to go back to work?" The wine had relaxed him and he was starting to feel aroused. Strange, he thought, how two such incompatible minds could have such compatible bodies.

"Yes. I wish I didn't."

"Well, then, come over when you finish. I can't cook dinner, but I'm a black belt at sending out for pizza."

"Double garlic on mine—if you can stand it." She laughed, and he joined her. It was the first time she had laughed since the funeral, and the release was exhilarating. So was the excitement of knowing she would be with him again—in his mind, in his arms, and in his bed, if only for a few hours.

He took her hand as they walked to the car. And she felt like a child again, suddenly lighthearted . . .

The St. Francis Tower was completed four months later, in the summer of 1971. It could have been done in half the time, the contractor told Torie, had Mr. Hughes not been so demanding and disagreeable. Thank God he was, she thought. Nielson had held the man to his word, insisting on the high-quality workmanship and materials he promised. The result was that the property that had cost her $210,000 to build was now appraised at twice the amount.

The brick tower with its tall windows and grillwork balconies was far different from what she had wanted, yet better than what she had expected. Somehow, the classic, dignified structure seemed to uplift the whole neighborhood, and as Nielson had promised, it was *of* the block, not just on it. Two of the ten units had already been leased, and Peggy was busy handling phone inquiries.

On a Friday evening in early August a group of friends, a few politicians, and some reporters gathered in the model apartment to celebrate the opening. Torie had been seeing Nielson regularly for five months. She would "accidentally" bump into him at the site and be sure to praise him and the building's progress; then they would meet later at his house. He was content to be with her whenever the mood suited him; she was happy to be with him whenever he asked.

"Excuse me, please." Torie smiled at the couple she was chatting with and hurried across the room. Nielson had just entered, his face set in a grimace. "Good evening, Mr. Hughes. Couldn't you at least *try* to look happy?"

"Why should I?" His frown deepened as he glanced around him. "What a bloody waste of time. I only came because you were so insistent. I hate these damn parties with everyone sucking up to the press. An apartment in South Philly is hardly front-page news. How'd you get all these people here?"

She shrugged. "I just invited them. You did such a wonderful job. You deserve the recognition."

"Look, if you must grovel to the media, introduce me and get it over with." He checked his watch. "I have to leave in ten minutes."

She knew better than to argue. "Yoo-hoo—hello!" she called out, tapping her glass. "Could I have your attention for a minute? I'd like to introduce the brilliant architect of the St. Francis Tower, Mr. Nielson Hughes. He has another engagement, so if you have anything to ask him, now's the time."

"What's your next project?" queried a reporter.

Nielson stood with his arms folded, the same hard expression on his face. "I don't know. I'm still in school."

"What made you choose South Philly?"

"My client chose me."

A young woman with a notepad smiled coquettishly. "Do you have a favorite architect, Mr. Hughes?"

"No."

"What about your father?"

There it was. The inevitable question, the one he had been dreading. "He has nothing to do with me or the St. Francis Tower. We are separate people with separate careers. My work must be judged on its own merit."

"And yet," the woman pursued, "you were hired because of the similarity of your styles. You can't deny that being who you are gives you an edge in your profession. The first commission of Robert Nielson's son would make news even if it were a chicken coop."

Blood rushed to his head. "I wasn't hired for that reason."

"That's not what it says in the press release. See for yourself."

Glaring angrily, he grabbed the sheet and read: ". . . conserve the warmth and flavor of the historic neighborhood . . . multi-family apartment . . ."

Then he saw it: "Nielson Hughes . . . schooled in the classic tradition of his famous father, Robert Nielson, makes a promising architectural debut with his first commission." Crushing the paper in his fist, he spun around to Torie. "Did you write this excrement?"

"Yes, but I didn't—"

"This is a *Nielson Hughes* building," he cried out, brandishing the release. "It is *not* a building built by Robert Nielson's son. You know how I feel about being compared with my father—riding to glory on his coattails. How could you do this to me?"

The rage in his voice made her tremble. "I didn't mean—I didn't think—but it's true, Nielson. You *are* schooled in his tradition. I didn't mean—"

"You didn't mean what—to exploit me?" He slammed the paper to the floor. "No wonder the press showed up. You'll do anything to get cheap publicity. You don't give a damn about my work. You never did. It was always the name . . . the connection. From now on, I want nothing more to do with you or your building!"

Stunned and speechless, she watched him stride out the door. Her instinct was to dash after him, but too much was at stake. Forcing a smile, she turned to the crowd. "I'm sorry. I . . . I guess I touched a nerve. Nielson Hughes really is a genius in his own right. I hope you'll forget about this incident and enjoy the rest of the party."

A waiter handed her a glass of champagne and the chattering resumed. Seething inside, deeply hurt, angry, and embarrassed, she managed to repress her feelings and play out her role as hostess. When she finally packed Lisa and her father into Peggy's car, reassuring them all that she was not upset, she locked the model apartment and drove straight to Panama Street.

Nielson was home. No question about it. His new MG was parked at the curb and she could see his bedroom light. Standing at the door, she pressed the bell, pounded the knocker, shouted at him to let her in, to no avail.

After ten minutes, pride took over, and she climbed into her car and sped toward the expressway. Death would almost be a relief. It might even make Nielson feel guilty for two or three seconds.

But no, she reflected, slowing down, he wasn't worth dying for. He had behaved unforgivably, publicly humiliating her, creating an ugly, emotional scene with his selfish outburst and almost ruining her party. He was the one in the wrong, and yet she had stood on his doorstep for almost a quarter of an hour, making a fool of herself trying to appease him and offer an explanation.

And for what? He was easily the most infuriating man she had ever known. She would count herself lucky if she never saw or spoke to the bastard again.

15

NIELSON HUGHES'S DRAMATIC outburst at the gathering was, if not good sense, at least good copy. By trying to divert attention from his famous heritage, he had accomplished exactly the opposite. Under the heading ROBERT NIELSON KIN IN PARTY FRACAS, a story on the second page of the Monday *Inquirer* began:

> An informal celebration in a model apartment of the new St. Francis Tower in South Philly ended in drama and conflict Friday night when the building's architect, Nielson Hughes, publicly cursed developer Torie Di Angelo for using his father's name to get publicity.
>
> Inflamed by Di Angelo's press release linking him to master builder Robert Nielson, the 22-year old University of Penn student shouted, "You don't give a damn about my work. It's only who I am. I won't ride to glory on anyone's coattails!" and stalked out in a rage.

Four paragraphs later, the piece concluded:

> Di Angelo appeared shaken by the incident. Hughes was unavailable for comment.

"Yes, I saw the article." Torie set down her briefcase and hung her jacket on the coatrack. "No, I'm not suicidal. Yes, I'm furious at him. Yes, I still love the son of a bitch. Anything else or can we get to work?"

"To work, boss." Peggy grinned in relief and wondered why she had bothered to worry all weekend. Torie was strong, resilient, and well fortified with pride. No matter how sharp the pain, she wouldn't let it show. Even Frankie's death, devastating as it was, had not stopped her for long. Work was her release, her therapy. Work was also her passport to achieving the goal she voiced so often: to be rich, powerful, and, most important, "hurt-proof."

What folly, thought Peggy. Torie would never be hurt-proof no matter how hard she tried. She cared about people too much. She had cared enough to put aside her own despair to give love, patience, and support to her best friend when she needed it. Even now, eight months after the tragedy, Peggy still looked to Torie for the strength to go on. And it was always there for her.

She forced a cheerful tone. "You realize that lover boy's temper tantrum was the best thing that could've happened to us, don't you? You can't *buy* that kind of publicity. I've already had six new inquiries on the Tower."

"Any word from John Loder at the bank?"

"Not yet."

"Call me the second he calls." She sat down at her desk and tried to concentrate on her next project—a land deal involving the building of a small subdivision. During the years her father ran the company, he had always been a cautious investor, never borrowing funds when he had to pay the bank's going rate, but occasionally using low-interest government loans to buy inexpensive parcels, like the Strawberry Mansion lot. Over the decades his few assets had appreciated dramatically, but Frankie had never allowed anyone to touch them. Now Torie was busily refinancing them to free the funds for new developments.

Luckily, she had had the weekend to herself, and time to think about life without Nielson. So much of their recent togetherness had been her doing—planning to be where he would be at specific hours of the day and making herself available. How degrading that role was, in retrospect, and yet she had never minded. Seeing the man she loved was worth whatever it cost her in pride and inconvenience.

She had even been scheming to get him involved in her new project, but working with him now was unthinkable. She would be damned before she would—what was his word?—"grovel" anymore. Her decision was as firm as it was overdue.

" 'Scuse me, T. D., I forgot to ask if you got past page two this morning." Peggy laid down the newspaper, folded to the society section. "It's bargain day. You get two ex-boyfriends for the price of one."

Torie stared at the picture of a handsome couple in formal dress. Their arms were linked and they were laughing happily over a caption reading: "The Anthony Silvanos (Grace Pringle Pennington) at the ballet reception." She handed back the paper. "That jerk hasn't been my boyfriend since I was fourteen and saw what he did to Papa."

"Didn't you say his wife was leaving him?"

"That's what he told me. Poor baby. So sad—so lonely. So anxious to console me about Frankie. So anxious to take me to a quiet, intimate restaurant, and make me conquest number eight hundred and forty-four. What a bullshit artist."

"Maybe he and his wife reconciled—"

"Yeah, and maybe turtles can fly. I'd swear he invented that whole story. By the way, Papa invited him to our party. Did he ever show up?"

"No. His secretary phoned and said he'd be out of town for the weekend. Short weekend, I guess, since he made it back in time for the ballet Saturday night."

"What about Betsy Richardson?"

"She sent a polite refusal. Probably asked Nielson about the party and he told her not to bother."

"Ooh!" Torie exhaled loudly. "What is it with me, Pig? There must be millions of sweet, kind, unneurotic men out there in the big world. Why do I fall for the mentally defective?"

"Why not? Love is the most popular form of insanity . . . Whoops—the phone." She ran to answer. "Di Angelo Company. Yes, she is, Mr. Loder. Please hold."

Torie lifted the receiver eagerly. "Hi, Mr. Loder. I hope you have good news for me."

"I think we can accommodate you," a deep voice replied. "I read the paper this morning about the St. Francis Tower. I didn't realize your architect was Robert Nielson's son. You've got yourself a nice chunk of equity."

"So it seems." She saw no reason to mention that it was heavily mortgaged. "We're filling up so fast it's making me dizzy."

"Good for you. I hope you know what you're getting into, Torie. Borrowed money has made a lot of real estate investors rich, but it's put just as many in the poorhouse. They're the ones you never hear about."

"I know the risks. I understand."

"Well, in that case, you've got yourself a loan. Can you come in this morning at eleven?"

"Yes," she said, barely suppressing her excitement. "I'll be there."

Torie acquired the loan by using a small South Philly property as equity, by presenting a sound marketing plan to develop Melrose Park, a fifty-two-house subdivision in an industrial section of the city, and by convincing John Loder that since her own funds were at risk, she was deeply committed to making her first big development project a success. She knew that once she proved her capabilities and showed the bank concrete examples of profitable deals, she could start to increase her borrowing power.

Melrose Park took almost full-time dedication, and a year later, while the country was still reeling from the Watergate scandal, Torie called on a panel of Navy officials. Pointing to the sale of the Strawberry Mansion lot, the construction of St. Francis Tower, and the successful completion of Melrose Park, she was able to convince them that despite her youth and relative inexperience, she could build their 220-unit housing project with efficiency and economy.

The announcement of a ceasefire in Vietnam in January of 1973 rekindled feelings of rage and resentment at her brother's useless sacrifice. The fact that a well-connected WASP like Nielson, along with so many others in his position, had completely escaped going to war only renewed her determination to make society pay.

An obvious next step in her career was to close the South Philly and West Mount Airy branches and open a single headquarters large enough to combine both offices. That September, under a giant banner proclaiming the firm's new title, DI ANGELO ENTERPRISES, Torie, Peggy, Jock, his secretary, Jane Riley, and two newly hired salesmen took over the main floor of a three-story house in Center City.

Working days, nights, and weekends, she continued to expand the company, her absorption so complete that she had little time for leisure or recreation. Every few months a new man would come into her life, and she would vow to find her own apartment and give the relationship a chance. But her suitors resented taking second place to a career, and the affairs always fizzled before she could move. Then she would take several weeks to try to catch up on her reading, a diversion she missed.

In the meantime, living at home was convenient and rent-free.

Lisa had learned to leave her alone, Papa was happy just to have her under his roof, and so she stayed.

By late 1974 she had successfully completed the Navy housing project and had three other developments under way. Business was growing slowly and steadily, but not fast enough to satisfy her, so she began to think about using the media. After the unexpected write-up in the *Inquirer,* the St. Francis Tower had filled up almost immediately, her credibility had increased, and people had begun to recognize her name. If personal publicity could generate those reactions, she reasoned, it could also attract buyers, sellers, and the main commodity she needed in order to expand—money.

"You read all the gossip columns, Piglet," she said one morning, several weeks before Christmas. "If a person doesn't happen to be Patty Hearst or Fanne Fox, how does a person get her name mentioned?"

"She gets seen with important people at important places—openings, charity affairs, political events. Or else she gives lavish parties and invites the press, which you haven't the time or money to do." Peggy scratched her head. "If she's really serious, she hires a publicist. It's a legitimate business expense."

"Know of anyone?"

"Give me ten minutes to make some calls."

An hour later, Peggy handed Torie a paper. "I've whittled the list down to three," she said. "Harriet Winch is the first name on everyone's lips. She's an old war-horse, used to be a society columnist. Does mostly charities, benefits, social stuff."

"She's the one they call Harried Witch?"

"None other. Choice two is Tom Conroy. He's been around forever—solid, witty, well liked. Specializes in politicians and professionals."

"And three?"

"Three would be my choice: Ellory Davis. He's sharp, aggressive, ambitious, and gets his own name in the news as much as his clients'. The Old Guard apparently adore him because he brings around authors, TV stars, and all sorts of glamorous celebrities to liven their dull parties."

"Why do you like him?"

"He's relatively new at the game. Spent twelve years as drama critic for the *Bulletin,* then quit about five years ago to open his own PR firm. They say he's selective about his clients, but if he takes you on, he pushes hard. I don't think you can go wrong with Davis."

"In that case, get him here on the double."

Ellory Davis was the antithesis of the hotshot publicist Torie expected. About forty years old, balding, round-faced, and paunchy, he wore a polka-dot bow tie and a pin-striped suit designed to extend—or give the illusion of extending—his five-foot-five-inch frame. Shrewd and patronizing, he sat erect in Torie's straight-backed chair, his chin upraised as he peered through his bifocals. His message was clear: She, not he, was the one being looked over.

"Torie—may I call you that? I've decided I *would* like to represent you," he announced fifteen minutes into the interview. "We can sign a three-month contract starting today. After that, if we're still speaking, we can renegotiate."

"You don't think we'll be speaking?"

"Why count on it?"

"Fair enough." She held out a brass box. "Do you smoke?"

"Unfortunately, I do." He took a cigarette, then leaned forward to light hers. "I'll need a complete business résumé as soon as you can get it to me."

"I'll have it for you tomorrow."

"Fine. Right now, I'd like to get a few facts." He drew out a microcassette recorder and set it on the desk. "These questions may strike you as being none of my business, but I assure you they're essential."

She watched with amusement as he rummaged through his briefcase, then pulled out a printed sheet. She was beginning to tune in to his personality. He was not a warm or likable man and almost seemed to be testing her with his gruffness. Yet he gave her the feeling that every word he spoke, every gesture he made, had a purpose.

"Go ahead," she said. "Shoot."

"Date of birth?"

"Febuary 3, 1951. I'll be twenty-four in two months."

"I presume you mean Feb-*roo*-ary. Married?"

"No. And no prospects."

"That's hard to believe. You're a good-looking woman. No time for romance? Carrying a torch? No one turns you on?"

She laughed. "All the above. I *am* too busy and the truth is pretty corny. I still care about a guy I haven't seen in three years.

Most of the men I go out with, well, frankly, I'd rather be at the libary."

"Li-*brar*-y. Your speech is atrocious. Any regular escorts? Men who can take you to parties and openings?"

"No. That social whirl isn't for me. I'd like to be known for my business skills, not for being seen at parties."

"They go together, ducks. And with that face and figure, you'd be insane to keep yourself hidden. Were you planning to attend the Hooker's Ball when you chose your clothes this morning?"

The man *was* infuriating. "What's wrong with my clothes?"

"Everyt'ing's wrong wid your clothes," he said, mimicking her accent. "Tight jerseys went out with hot pants. Donald Trump can get away with wearing maroon suits and matching shoes, but you can't. You're a lady. Or at least, you're going to be. We'll go shopping together tomorrow. Then I'll take you over to Nan Duskin's to see Adolf Biecker."

She closed her datebook irritably. "Now it's my hair? Look, Ellory, I'm hiring you to stir up interest in my company, not to make me over. I don't have time to become a glamor girl."

"But you *are* a glamor girl. How's your bank account?"

"What bank account? I'm in debt up to my eyeballs. In this business, you can't afford not to have all your money working."

"Then we'll charge. I'll pick you up—say, ten o'clock?"

His stern glance elicited a sigh. "Is it absolutely necessary?"

"Absolutely." He lifted his briefcase. "With the help of God, Saint Laurent, and a few other talented friends, I'm going to mold you into the kind of celebrity the media can't resist. Look at Liz Taylor. She could be standing on a street corner spouting the alphabet and she'd be quoted, misquoted, and featured on the cover of *People*."

"I'm not aspiring to be a Liz Taylor."

"Why not? You have the potential. We call it the four *B*s: brains, beauty, bucks, and balls—and I don't mean the bouncing kind. Have there been any tragedies in your life?"

"Are you kidding?"

"Excellent! Save them up for me. The public loves fighters. Comebacks. Cinderella figures. Oh, and I'm bringing you a tape on proper diction. You're to listen to it and practice half an hour *every* day." He stopped at the exit and turned around. "Would you consider changing Torie Di Angelo to Victoria Dalton?"

"No, I would *not*. And you'd better get out of here before I change my mind about tomorrow."

"Ten o'clock," he said, slipping out the door. "Don't forget your Visa card."

"Ellory Davis, you scoundrel! Where've you been hiding that enchanting creature on your arm?" A large man with thick glasses stood by the entrance to the crowded apartment, wiping his brow. "I salute your loveliness, my sweet, if not your taste in escorts. May I fetch you a libation?"

"Negative, Percy." Ellory brushed away the man's arm. "Crawl back under your rock. The lady's not for sale, hire, or rent."

"Why do I feel as if I'm Eliza Doolittle and you're Professor Higgins?" Torie tossed a helpless look over her shoulder as Ellory steered her across the carpet.

A quick glance around the room gave her a strong sense of Old Philadelphia. Scattered Chippendale chairs with needlepoint upholstery had been moved against the walls to make room for the conservatively dressed guests. Rich brocade draperies with an American eagle design framed several pairs of tall French windows, and a faded embroidery of the hostess's family tree hung by the piano.

"Remember what I told you," Ellory coached. "Richardson's reformers are out. Main Line aristocrats are out. Control of City Hall has passed on to the professional and business people who supported Ponti's grass-roots law-and-order campaign. *These* are the new power elite—the people you want to cultivate." Ellory appraised the heads as carefully as a surgeon studying an X ray. "At least this isn't one of those Gay Nineties parties."

"Gay Nineties?"

"Yes, where all the men are gay and all the women ninety. By the way, you look very nice tonight. I must compliment myself on my excellent taste."

"You mean expensive taste." Her good-natured grumbling confirmed what he already knew, that she was pleased with her appearance. Philadelphia's master stylist had swept her long black curls into a smooth, chic roll, fastened back to accentuate the delicate oval of her face and display a pair of sparkling rhinestone earrings.

The clothes Ellory had chosen—especially the black lace sheath she was wearing, with its sedate, high neckline and long sleeves—were clothes she would never have chosen for herself. Yet she felt comfortable in the dress—understated, smart, and elegant. "Is that the mayor's wife by the piano?"

"Yes, that's dear Tina. Scrape away the Revlon and you'll find Estée Lauder. She does look smashing in that Blass I told you to buy. If you'd listened to me, you'd be—"

"Wearing the same outfit to the same party. And she'd be pissed off."

"Watch your language. And she wouldn't be at all. Matter of fact, I'd have posed you together for a picture. The public loves bitchy items like that."

"A lot of good it'd do me in debtors' prison. Could I meet her?"

"It's more important to meet her husband. Let me warn you: Around women he exudes a kind of smoldering sex appeal. Underneath, he's a cold-hearted sexist. But he's got the energy of a charging bull, and he's shrewd as a French general. I want you to charm him with everything you've got."

"I'll do my best. Think he fools around?"

"I'd probably like him better if he did. At least he'd be human. But I'm sure he doesn't. He's much too calculated to let his libido get out of hand—no pun intended."

Torie chuckled. "Do you think he's good at his job?"

"He doesn't have to be. Ever since '51, our city charter's given the mayor of Philadelphia more authority than any other mayor in the country. So he's powerful—and he's personal. If you want something done in City Hall, you don't call his aides. You pick up the phone and call Ponti. That's why you have to meet him."

Ellory led the way through the crowd to a tall peach-skinned redhead, who embraced him and shook her finger at him simultaneously. "Naughty boy! You promised to take me to that Aubusson exhibit at the Design Center."

"We'll go Monday afternoon, love. Ink it in your datebook; it's a for-sure. Athena Trent, meet Vittoria Di Angelo."

Torie extended a hand. "I feel embarrassed coming to your home uninvited. Ellory was so insistent—"

"Any friend of Ellory's is welcome," she said coolly. "He tells me you're quite an opera buff."

"Well, the truth is—"

"The truth is she's busy as hell, Athena, but I'm determined she'll get that beautiful butt out of her office and serve on a board or two. Lord knows we need new blood . . . too many old fogeys sitting around like clumps of dead wood."

"I'm rather partial to dead wood myself."

The hostess turned away and Torie bristled. "Screw *her*," she growled to Ellory. "I'm going home. Who needs this?"

"You do, ducks. Oh, Cal. Could you spare a moment to meet a lovely lady? Vittoria Di Angelo—Mayor Ponti."

"It's an honor, Mayor," she said, quickly recovering. "I'm one of your fans."

The former fish merchant offered a hearty handshake. He was handsome in a thirties-movie-star way; people often compared him with the late Tyrone Power, with his slick dark hair parted in the middle, his heavy black brows, classic nose, and a mouth that tended to curve slightly downward when not set on automatic smile. He looked directly into her eyes. "Maybe we can get a mutual admiration society going."

"Why not?" she said pleasantly.

They appraised each other like birds in a courtship dance— but mating was not their goal. The mayor was far more interested in who she was than in seduction. Yet she *was* a beautiful woman, and beautiful women expected flirtation. "Don't tell me this gorgeous creature is your client, Ellory. I'll buy whatever she's pushing."

"She's not pushing anything, Cal. She does happen to admire you, Lord knows why, and she's anxious to support your reelection campaign."

If the mayor saw his new supporter wince for a fraction of a second, he gave no indication. "That's very generous of you, Miss Di Angelo. What's your first name?"

"Torie."

"How is it we haven't met before, Torie? What do you do?"

"I'm in real estate development, and I'm fascinated by your proposed changes in the Swig-Mailliard law. Any chance you might extend it to earmark low-interest funds with a fifty percent tax abatement for middle-income housing in the Coppertown area? It would please your constituents."

"My constituents who'd live there, or my constituents who want to develop the district?"

"Both. If I could get, say, a hundred acres of landfill for the area right next to the Melrose Park subdivision, I could give you five thousand well-publicized moderately priced living units for the elderly."

"Including people on welfare?"

"Absolutely. Donald Trump stirred up enough problems for our industry by requiring welfare people to meet special conditions. I'm well aware of the 1968 *Jones* v. *Mayer* decision, when the Supreme Court ruled to uphold the Civil Rights Act of 1866 prohibiting discrimination in renting. My only condition would be that government insurance covered us in case of excessive losses. Could I send you some data?"

"Why not? Send it to my office."

"By the way, I know you're getting heat about developers turning all the rental units into co-ops and condominiums. If we guaranteed *not* to convert, that could be a popular selling point."

The woman was impressive. She was too young to have been around a long time, yet she understood his special interests and spoke to them with intelligence. He was grateful, too, that she had made her pitch openly and without feminine wiles. "I'll look forward to hearing from you, Torie. Any chance you'll be bidding on that Washington Theater site?"

"I haven't heard about it."

"Well, it hasn't been publicized yet, and you didn't hear it from me, but there's a nice chunk of city land coming up for auction next summer. Two blocks of factory, and a third block that includes the old theater and a deserted gas station. Some folks want to restore the Washington and build a performing arts center. Others want to tear everything down for a shopping mall. I'd like to be kept informed—"

"I'll see that you are." A small repayment for your tip, Mayor. They understood each other perfectly.

"I'm glad we had a chance to chat." He gave a quick wave and hurried away, followed by his burly bodyguard. Being seen talking too long to an attractive woman was a problem a politician didn't need.

Ellory grabbed her arm. "Well done, my dear. You're as smooth as a greased eel."

"Praise from the master?"

"Don't get swell-headed. You've a long way to go."

"And I won't get there by being snubbed at cocktail parties. What kind of lies did you tell that Trent woman? I wouldn't sit on her damn opera board if she paid me. I hate opera!"

"Lots of people hate opera. That's not the point." He lifted his chin and straightened his bow tie. "It's a place to go and be seen—period. And one way or another, I intend to get you on that board. Now come with me. I want you to meet the society editor of the *Daily News.*"

Torie let herself be led around the room, taking in a blur of faces, her mind focused on a far different subject. She knew the Washington Theater property as well as she knew the three golden rules of real estate: Location. Location. Location. And what a prime location that was!

Converting an old movie house and a factory into a gleaming new shopping center was exactly the kind of challenge she had been waiting for. And the more controversy and publicity, the better. Putting it all together would take time, dedication, planning, and plenty of what Bernard Baruch once called the secret of his success: OPM—Other People's Money. But nothing was going to stop or discourage her. With a smattering of luck and the grace of the Almighty, happiness was only a package deal away.

16
==

BY SPRING OF 1975, Torie had amassed a thick file of data on the Washington Theater property and was moving ahead as fast as she could. She honored her promise to share information with the mayor, hoping he might help her obtain the needed zoning changes and permits. Her immediate challenge was to find a partner to put up cash for the land.

Thanks to Ellory Davis and her own quickly evident flair for making news, her name was beginning to be familiar to readers of both the social and business sections of the dailies. Heeding Tony's advice, her father had begrudgingly deeded the company to her—a step she took as instant liberation, and license to be as daring as she pleased.

The first three months of the year had been hectic and rewarding, with Di Angelo Enterprises growing faster and bigger than anyone could have expected. Her staff—now enlarged to include three brokers, an architect, an accountant, a surveyor, a land-use consultant, and two secretaries under Peggy—took over the second floor of their office building. The third floor would be available in a year, and by then, Torie felt sure, they would be ready to expand into it.

Although she was still heavily in debt, profits from Melrose Park allowed her to send a handsome check to Mayor Ponti's reelection fund. Approval for the hundred acres of landfill she requested came shortly thereafter, along with permission to build on them.

"This is a project near and dear to my heart," Mayor Ponti had told a press conference. "The new apartments will be available to any adult qualifying for subsidized housing, with no restrictions based on race, color, or amount of credit. The developer, Torie Di Angelo, has given me her personal assurance that these buildings will remain rental units and won't be converted to co-ops or condominiums."

"Is it true you bypassed channels to get building permits?" asked a reporter.

"The previous administration dealt with this situation in a piecemeal fashion. I can tell you—"

"Sir, would you answer my question?"

"I don't bypass channels, Miss Steger. On advice of the city solicitor, council unanimously approved this project. If there were any legal way I could speed up the building of shelters for people who need them, I'd sure as hell do so. Fortunately or otherwise, that's not how city government operates. Next question?"

The day after Mayor Ponti's announcement, Torie took a cab to the Rawley Building, a twelve-story landmark facing Independence Square. Peggy had reminded her, in case the subject arose, that the famous brick-and-marble structure dated back to 1916, when Silas Rawley built it as a showplace for his publishing company. Philadelphia's largest contractors, the Goldman brothers, had bought it in 1958 from Rawley's granddaughter, society matriarch Rebecca Rawley French, and now maintained their headquarters on the tenth floor.

An elevator that seemed to take an eternity carried Torie to her destination. After running a comb through her hair and straightening the jacket of the lime-green Chanel suit Ellory had talked her into buying, she entered the well-appointed offices of the Goldman Corporation.

"Have a seat, Miss Di Angelo," said the receptionist. "I'll tell Mr. Goldman you're here."

"Thank you." Torie raised her wrist to check her watch, hoping to communicate that she was on time and did not like to be kept waiting. Resting on the edge of a chair, she set her briefcase on the floor and tried to appear calm. Calling on a total stranger with a request for eight million dollars was a scary challenge, but one that intrigued her. So much depended on this meeting . . . how she presented herself . . . how knowledgeable and capable she appeared . . . whether or not he liked her . . .

Ten minutes later she lit a cigarette and began to drum her fingers. Sitting around offices always reminded her of Nielson and his infuriating failure to realize that keeping people waiting was rude and selfish. No wonder she had become a stickler for promptness.

An ash dropped to her skirt, and she jumped up, brushed it off, and caught the eye of the receptionist. "Will he be much longer?"

"No, he just buzzed. You can go in now, second door down."

Entering the large office, Torie quickly took in the high ceiling, the oak-paneled walls covered with etchings, the stiff-backed velvet chairs . . . and the round-faced man who stepped forward and offered a hand. "Come in, come in. Have a seat. So you're the young lady people are talking about."

Torie smiled. "That depends what they're saying."

"Well, my wife, Sylvia, told me your name was suggested for the opera board." Approving eyes stared through gold-rimmed glasses. "You should be quite an addition."

"Thanks. It's very indefinite." Torie sat down and appraised her host in return. The ultrasuccessful Mort Goldman was impeccably dressed, of average height, and slightly overweight. His charm and affability did not fool her into thinking he would be an easy conquest.

"She also heard that you were pretty, and she was right." His eyes gleamed merrily. "If I were thirty years younger, I'd probably be chasing you around the office—except that thirty years ago I was sharing a six-foot cubicle with my brother. For some reason, I've always been attracted to Italian women. Jews and Italians seem to have a strong bond . . . we're both *haimish* . . . *simpatico* . . ."

"We both like good food."

"Maybe that's it." He gave a polite chuckle. "Now tell me, what can I do for you?"

Her heart was beating fast. The next few minutes were crucial. "My company, Di Angelo Enterprises, would like to build a shopping mall on the Washington Theater property. And I'm hoping the Goldman brothers will consider becoming one of my partners."

He reached for a cigar. "Will this bother you?"

"No. Thanks for asking."

"You don't think the theater should be restored?"

"Absolutely not. In the first place, we can save the murals and give them a better home. In the second place, the building's a poor example of turn-of-the-century architecture, and an eyesore. Perhaps most important, it's unsafe, a serious fire hazard."

She placed a folder on his desk. "When you look over the submission package, you'll see that my track record is sound, my financial statements are in order, and I've already demonstrated my management skills. You'll also realize that the very attractive parklike shopping mall we propose to build will raise property values in the area, bring in tax monies, and upgrade the community in a hundred different ways. Think you might be interested?"

"I don't know. Tell me more."

"At the risk of sounding like the heroine of a B-movie, Mr. Goldman, I want that property so badly I can taste it."

"Mort."

"Okay—Mort. This is the first time in years that a Center City lot that size has been available. As you know, the market's depressed right now, and I'm convinced that property will double in value in a very short time."

"Go on."

She smiled. "If you'll supply the capital to buy the land, I'll give you twenty percent of the total package. In addition, my company will secure financing—"

"Hold on, young lady. Before you get too carried away, what kind of capital are you talking about?"

"The appraiser's judgment for the value of the completed project is seventy-eight million dollars. Experts say the bidding for that parcel won't exceed eight million. The city wants a ten percent cash deposit at the time of the auction, and the balance within twenty-one days."

"And you'd like the Goldman Corporation to underwrite your bid?"

She tried not to wince as a cloud of foul-smelling smoke blew toward her. "That's what I'm hoping."

"What about construction costs?"

"That's my responsibility. If I can get a commitment from you, I'm pretty sure I'll have access to funds from a mortgage investment trust. I'm terribly enthused about the possibilities. I brought along our marketing surveys and the architect's sketches of the finished mall. Would you like to see them?"

"Perhaps later. You know that construction lenders generally require personal liability, don't you?"

"I'm willing to put up surety bonds. I'll also guarantee that all zoning variances and building permits will be in order the day you're ready to start."

"Well, you talk a good line. But do you really understand all the nuances and complexities of financing a shopping center?"

"Yes, I do. And I have very experienced professionals on my staff who are advising me." It was time to play her trump card. "My proposal contains a list of twelve anchor tenants willing to sign long-term leases. One of them is Londoner's Department Store."

"Oh?" His tone was hard and challenging, as if he was taking her seriously for the first time. "I assume your proposal also gives us the power to control expansion and specifies that Goldman will do all present and future construction work. What about some of your other jobs—for instance, the Melrose project?"

The question was not unexpected. He would be a fool not to ask it, and she was prepared with the answer. "The specifications went out this morning. If your bid's anywhere in the ballpark and we have a deal going, you'll get it."

"I'd want that guaranteed." He reached back and opened the window behind his desk. "Better get rid of this stogie before Sid comes in. Nothing worse than a reformed smoker." Sensing her anxiety, he went on, "If I had to give you an answer this minute, Torie, it would have to be no. To be honest, I still think you're too young and too inexperienced for this kind of transaction. But that's my brother's decision, not mine. I'm just the engineer— the guy who goes out to the sites and makes sure they're not hammering square nails into round holes. We'll have to see what Sid thinks."

She knew what he was saying. Mort was the gregarious brother, the PR half of the team. Whenever the corporation needed a spokesman or an image, it was Mort who stepped forward, as accessible to the public and the media as his brother was reclusive. Nevertheless, insiders knew that it was the gruff, unpolished Sid whose brains and shrewdness had rocketed the firm to its success. "Could I talk to him?"

"Sid doesn't generally see people."

"But you've screened me. You know I'm not a nut—at least, not the usual kind. I could tell him everything he needs to know in fifteen minutes."

"When's the auction?"

"Only two months off. I'd swear not to stay one second longer than fifteen minutes, even if he got down on his knees and *begged* me."

He regarded her with amusement. "You're a persistent young lady."

"And you're the best contractors in town. That's why I want you so badly. If it's not to be, it's not to be, and I do have other prospects. But either way, I'd like to know as soon as possible."

"Fair enough. I'll try to talk to him this week." Seeing her disappointment, he added, "Oh, all right. Come by Thursday morning at nine, and I'll sneak you in before he gets busy. But be warned: Compared to Sid, I'm a marshmallow. He won't be easy on you like I was. Prepare to be on the hot seat."

"I like being grilled. It gets my juices going." She leaned forward to admire the photos on his desk. "Is this your handsome family?"

"Yes, that's Sylvia. Poor woman's put up with me for twenty-nine years. That's my baby, Marcia, her husband, Jake, and my grandsons, David and Stevie. My son Lloyd, and Carol—they're getting divorced. No kids, thank God. And that's my oldest son, Jefferson. He's not married."

"What an attractive group. You must be very proud." She offered her hand. "I hope we'll be seeing more of each other—starting Thursday at nine."

"Bring your boxing gloves."

She chuckled. "If David could face Goliath, I can face Sid Goldman. Don't bother walking me to the door. Your light's flashing."

"Oops—thanks." He waved a quick good-bye and grabbed the

phone. "Hello? What? *No*, Sylvia, I haven't called your mother yet . . ."

Adjusting her dark glasses, Simone Richardson breezed out the door of her daughter's newly opened art gallery, leaving behind a strong odor of whiskey. Betsy fanned the air and watched through the window. Four in the afternoon and her mother was bombed.

With a shrug, she walked into the back room. More pressing matters were on her mind, namely the fifty or sixty guests expected that evening to look over the new crop of art works.

"I'm chilling the champagne, but I had to take out the cheese balls to make room."

A young man in spotted overalls folded his arms and leaned against the refrigerator. Peter Fenwick was a nice friend to have, she thought. They both liked art, they liked working in the gallery, and he was true to his male lover, so their relationship was free of sexual complications. "That's fine. Are the pictures hung?"

"All except this one."

"Let's see—oh, that's Jeff Goldman's painting."

"Hmm. It's not bad."

"I rather like it. Besides, he's a good friend and I promised I'd show it. How about in that corner, next to the still life?"

"You're the boss. Want me to answer the phone?"

"No, just hang the landscape." She hurried to her desk. "Co-Op Gallery. Betsy Richardson speaking."

"Juliet? This is Romeo—remember me?"

The voice was unmistakable. "Nielson! How *are* you? I haven't heard from you in ages."

"It's not my fault. If you'll recall, my sweet, *you* were the one who insisted you needed—what was that wretched term?—your own space, I believe."

"So I did," she said, laughing. "That was right after you got your masters—was it two years ago? Where does the time go? What have you been doing?"

"I'm working in an office with six morons who haven't the slightest notion that the man they leave slaving at the drafting board every night while they go out to get drunk and make love to their large-breasted girlfriends happens to be the world's greatest architect. How about you?"

"What would the world's greatest architect like to know?"

"How's the gallery?"

"Ask me tomorrow. Tonight I'm opening a show of local unknowns. Anything can happen."

"Pity—that you're busy, I mean. We're having open house at the office, and I was hoping to impress you with some of my designs. They're quite remarkable, if I say so myself."

"You usually do."

"Another night?"

"No, Nielson." She lowered her voice. "If we started going out, it'd be the same thing all over again. I'm not ready to make a commitment."

"You realize how patient I've been, don't you? I'm good for another ten or twelve years and then that's positively all. Not one decade longer will I wait for you." He paused a few seconds before asking, "You're not planning to run off and get married, are you?"

"No chance of that. Take care of yourself."

"*Au revoir,* Juliet. Whistle if you need me."

Peggy was waiting anxiously Friday morning when Torie walked into the office. "Tell me quick. What happened with Sid?"

Draping her jacket on the chair, Torie dropped down with a groan. "That man's a holy terror, Pig. I can't believe two brothers are so different. Remember I told you how nice Mort Goldman was? Well, Sid's just the opposite—ill-mannered, blunt, only interested in money, money, money. He wouldn't even look at the architect's sketches until I agreed to rewrite the whole proposal."

"Oh, no. How?"

"For starters, he wants a third, not a fifth of the package. The Goldman Corporation wants to be responsible for demolition and land-clearing as well as construction. He wants to use only his own people, he wants to be able to write immediate checks to suppliers, he wants to be free to pay overtime, he wants signed leases from the anchor tenants, and he wants my firstborn on a silver platter. In return, he'll put up eight million for the land."

"Do you have a construction lender?"

"I told him we did. If I can get a commitment from Goldman, I'm pretty sure we can get Jack Block's mortgage investment trust. Naturally, Sid wants a guarantee he'll be paid off in full as soon as the work's done. No wonder he's so successful. You get screwed before you even climb into bed with him."

"But you made an agreement?"

"God, no. Far from it. Our lawyer and accountants have to look over the changes, then his lawyer, his accountants, and then I'll still have to convince Jack Block. Hmmm. . . . I just had a brainstorm. Get John Loder at the bank, please."

A few seconds later, Torie heard a familiar voice. "Loder speaking. How's my favorite developer?"

"Developing ulcers at the moment. Got five minutes?" She quickly outlined Sid Goldman's offer and asked if she could show him some studies and figures.

"No, I don't think so. You'd be wasting both our time."

His answer jolted her. "But why? My credit record's perfect. I build on time and on budget. I've never had a cost overrun—"

"Small subdivisions are one thing. A multimillion-dollar mall in Center City is another. There's a saying in real estate, Torie. Stack your loans as if they're Ming china; one slip could break you."

"I know that. And I don't intend—"

"You're pushing too fast. Remember, leverage is the developer's cocaine. The more you have, the more you want. Frankly, you haven't got the credits for this type of major deal. Take my advice: Don't fight for a seat on the *Titanic*."

"But it *won't* be a disaster, I promise you. If you'll give me ten minutes to explain—"

"Sorry, not interested."

"You won't even discuss it?"

"Nope. My other phone's ringing."

"*Damn* you," she growled, replacing the receiver. "Oh, what the hell. Getting the loan's no big problem; it's just getting the best terms. Does it ever occur to you, Pig, that this business is ninety-eight percent hype?"

Peggy groaned. "We back to Donald Trump again?"

"The man's a showman . . . a hustler . . . a walking ego. But he's so bloody brilliant. Look what he just pulled off. New York real estate's in a funk. Penn Central's broke. Trump goes to see this guy Palmieri, who's selling Penn Central's assets, and tells him how lousy the property is and how hard it's going to be to get zoning changes to develop it. Palmieri bites, and Trump gets options to buy two of Manhattan's biggest Hudson River waterfront sites for sixty-two million. Everyone says what the hell's that crazy twenty-seven-year-old gonna do with 'em?"

"You're about to tell me."

"None of the other biggies would touch that property; Helmsley, the Tishmans, Zeckendorf . . . wouldn't have any part of it. So while they're moaning and bitching about the real estate slump, Trump's helping Abe Beame get elected mayor."

"How thoughtful."

"Exactly. So Donald's got connections. He assumes he can get zoning approval, government financing, whatever. Then he makes his pitch to Penn Central: He'll buy the land for sixty-two million, as agreed, but instead of cash, he'll pay the money out gradually, as the land's being developed."

"Do tell."

"So here's this giant conglomerate practically in bankruptcy, desperate for cash, and this brash genius walks away from the bargaining table with two of their most valuable properties—and he hasn't paid them a cent. Not a penny. Now why can't I make deals like that? Don't answer."

"I wouldn't dream of it." Peggy started back to her desk, then stopped and turned around. "I almost forgot. Ellory called to say he can get you on the opera board with a five-thousand-dollar donation and your promise to buy two season tickets in the orchestra section. He thinks you should go for it."

"Is he kidding? Five thousand bucks to waste my time sitting around meetings and get my name on the goddamn stationery? Tell Ellory what he can do with his opera board."

"That won't stop him. He'll just scream at me."

"Well, scream back," she said, reaching for the phone. "It's good for your lungs."

17

ON THE FIRST Monday in June of 1975, a lively crowd gathered outside Room 296 on the second floor of City Hall. As required by law, the sheriff's monthly sale of properties had been well advertised.

By nine A.M. the group had almost doubled, and security guards were forced to turn away onlookers. Only city employees, accredited reporters, and serious bidders (who could prove their intent with credit documents) were allowed to stay.

Mort Goldman took Torie's arm as she waved a certified check under the guard's eyes, and passed into the auction room. About two hundred people, 99 percent of them males, took seats on wooden chairs.

At two minutes past the hour, a man ascended the podium, introduced himself as Frederick E. Hill, Sheriff of the City and County of Philadelphia, and explained the conditions of sale: Buyers were required to pay 10 percent of their bid in cash or certified check at the time of the auction, and the balance within twenty-one days.

After selling off several small, uninteresting parcels, he came to the Washington Theater property and started the bidding at $4.2 million. Voices were spirited until the offers reached $6 million, considerably lowered at $7 million, and by $7.5 million, the sole remaining bidders were three men and Torie.

One of her competitors she recognized as Frank Binswanger Sr., patriarch of the prominent real estate clan. Another, Mort whispered in her ear, was Al Wilsey, a Delaware contractor and developer, and the third was a Japanese man with an interpreter.

Binswanger and the Asian dropped out at $8 million, and Mort placed a consoling hand on Torie's shoulder. He liked her and had wanted the deal to succeed. But having urged his brother to participate in the somewhat risky venture, he also felt a sense of relief. "Looks like Wilsey's got it."

"Can't we go a little higher?"

"You know our agreement. Eight million was the ceiling. That's already double what the property's worth."

"But it's stupid to lose the sale for the sake of a few dollars."

"Fifty thousand is a lot of money where I come from. Now show your grit and stop acting like a spoiled child. If you want to play the game, you've got to be willing to lose."

He was right; she couldn't expect to win all the time.

But this was not the time to lose—not after she had spent three months putting together the package, another month finding a bank, actually a savings and loan, to act as permanent lender, and still another month revising terms so the Goldmans would accept them.

"The bid is eight million twenty-five thousand dollars," droned the sheriff. "Any advance?"

"Eight fifty," Torie shouted.

Mort glowered at her. Was she crazy? *His* neck was on the line for the cash. Sid would kill him. "I told you—"

"Shhhhh," she said. "Everything over eight million is *my* responsibility."

"The hell it is! You're gambling with—"

"The bid is eight million fifty thousand dollars. It's against you, sir."

"Eight seventy-five," called Wilsey.

Mort glared at Torie. "Don't you dare!"

"Eight one," she cried. Necks stretched and heads craned to peer at the wealthy bidders.

"Eight million one. This choice piece of central city real estate going at eight million one hundred thousand dollars. It's your bid, sir."

All eyes fixed on Wilsey, who sat in tense concentration. Mort gripped Torie's arm threateningly.

"The bid is eight million one hundred thousand dollars. Any advance? . . . Last call . . . *Sold* to the lady!" The gavel banged, the crowd broke into applause, Torie wiped her face with a hankie.

"Sorry, Mort," she said, as they walked toward the rear. "I didn't mean to give you a heart attack, but I know—"

"You don't know a goddamn thing! Who the hell do you think

you are? You've voided our agreement by your actions, and I'm bailing out. The property goes to Wilsey."

"No!" Her voice was panicked. "Please give me a chance to show you I know what I'm doing. I have the collateral for the extra hundred thousand and that's all I have, not a cent more. I couldn't have gone any higher no matter how much I wanted to—I swear it!"

"*You* have the money? Are you sure?"

"I'm positive." A tear rolled down her cheek. "You've *got* to trust me, Mort. I wouldn't lie about something so important."

Exhaling loudly, he shook his head. Emotions were overruling his good sense, and he knew it. But he hated to see a woman cry—particularly a beautiful one. "All right, all right, wipe your eyes. Let's go sign the papers and be done with it."

"You're home early for a change." Lisa greeted her sister's arrival with a quizzical look. "Don't tell me we have the honor of your company at dinner—"

"Yes, I'd like that. How's Papa?"

"The same as he was yesterday and the day before. Dr. Sandor says his heart is beating on borrowed time. It wouldn't kill you to spend a little time with him."

"I'm here, aren't I? When's dinner?"

"The same as it is every night."

"Can I help?"

"Why the sudden politeness?"

"Oh, forget it. I'll be down at six-thirty." Torie started up the stairs, then casually added, "By the way, I had to mortgage the house today. I hope you and Papa don't mind. I'll pay it off as soon as I can."

"You did what!" Lisa's shocked voice rang through the hall. "You mortgaged this house when you specifically promised not to?"

"I'm sorry, Lis. I had no choice. I overbid on some property, and I needed collateral for a loan."

"But you gave us your *word*. When we gave you our powers of attorney, we stated that you weren't ever to touch this house. Did you forget?"

"No, I didn't forget." Torie dropped her briefcase and sat down on the stairs. "Please don't be upset with me. I said I'm sorry and I really am. I wouldn't have done it if I hadn't gotten into a terrible jam. But I'll have the mortgage paid off in only eighteen months, and then the house'll be free and clear again."

"Eighteen months! What if Papa dies and I want to sell it? I was counting on the money to take with me to the convent."

"You're going to be a nun?" Torie asked, startled.

"Does that surprise you?"

"Well . . . yes and no. Not your decision so much as the fact that you never mentioned it."

"You never asked. And you're never here, anyway. The few times when you are here, you're too self-involved to care about anyone but your self. Yes, I'm going to be a nun, and I'm so anxious to start my new life, I can hardly wait. But I *have* to wait because Papa needs me to take care of him."

"There's no reason for you to be a martyr. I've told you a hundred times we can afford a nurse or a housekeeper. Why do you tie yourself down?"

"Because Papa doesn't want some stranger taking care of him. Would you? I'm joining the Carmelite order headed by Sister Margarita. She knows this house is coming to me, and they're counting on the money to put in a new heating system. They say it gets so cold in winter—"

"Lis, I sympathize with Sister Margarita. Honestly. But it's not right to promise your inheritance while Papa's alive. This is still his house—"

"You're telling *me* it's his house? After what you've done? How do you think he's going to feel about that?"

"He doesn't have to know. I promise you if anything happens to him, I'll get you your money right away."

"And I'm supposed to trust you? I'm supposed to believe your worthless promises?" Her finger pointed menacingly. "You'll pay for your greed, Torie. You're a curse on this family. God was merciful to take Mama early, so she couldn't see the monster you've become."

"Oh, go suck an egg. I'm going up to my room. I don't want any dinner."

"What's the matter, no big parties tonight? No place you can go to get your name and your face in the paper? That disgusting man you pay all that money to—isn't he doing his job?"

"On the contrary, he's doing it very well." Torie spun around to meet Lisa's glaring eyes. Her first instinct was to shout an angry retort, but the sight of her sister's sad homely face filled her with compassion, and she opened her hands in a gesture of conciliation. "Please, let's not fight. I didn't mean to hurt you. We're a family. We have to stick together. Let's not cause Papa any more grief. We owe him that much after what he's been through."

Lisa stood unmoved. "You owe him a lot more than that, Torie. You owe him the pleasure of seeing you grow into a mature woman with a husband and some cute little babies to light up his face. Neither Frankie nor I can give him grandchildren. It's up to you."

"I see. I need a husband and a litter of screaming kids before I'm a good daughter. Is that it?" She exhaled loudly and marched up the stairs.

"That's right, shove your head in the sand like you always do. But you won't get away with this. I'm going to tell Papa."

"Don't bother." Torie stopped at the door to her father's bedroom, gave a sharp rap and turned the handle. "I'll tell him myself."

"Come in, come in." Slowly, and with determined effort, Frank wheeled himself toward the entrance. "You're home early. Is anything wrong?"

"Nothing's wrong, Papa." She bent down and kissed him, overcome, as she always was, with the pain of seeing him so frail and helpless. His hair had turned white after Frankie's death, and the stroke had left him barely able to press the control for the television. Fortunately, his thinking and speech were still coherent.

"I want to share some good news with you."

"You met a nice boy?"

She laughed and pulled up a footstool. "Sometimes I think Italian fathers are worse than Jewish mothers. How do you feel?"

"Grateful to God for my blessings." His eyes were questioning as he looked at her. "Did you see Lisa?"

"Yes."

"I worry about her, Torie. This is no life for a girl, sitting home all day taking care of her father. Can't you talk to her? Take her to some parties with you? She'd make the right man a wonderful wife."

So Lisa hadn't mentioned her decision. "I've asked her over and over to hire a housekeeper so she can have some time for herself, but she won't hear of it. Papa—I want to show you the plans for our new mall."

Worry crept into his voice. "Where are you getting the money to do all these things?"

"The Goldman brothers put up most of the cash. Here, look." She unrolled a sheet of designs. "Londoner's Department Store will go where the theater is—"

"*Most* of the cash? Where's the rest coming from?"

She continued pointing and spoke offhandedly. "That's what I wanted to tell you. Sid and Mort Goldman agreed to pay eight million for the land, but it sold for eight million one, so *I* had to put up the extra hundred thousand."

"Where will you get so much money?"

"I was desperate for collateral. I had to take out a loan on the house."

"But *I* own this house. *I'm* responsible for the loan. What did Lisa say?"

"She was annoyed. She doesn't understand that what I'm doing is for the benefit of the family. In a few years, all these investments will start paying off—"

"Lisa and you had a fight?"

"You're not listening to a word I'm saying! All families have their differences. You can't expect—"

"What I expect from you, Torie, is to think of other people beside yourself once in a while." With great effort, he pushed the designs to the floor. "I don't need to be rich. I don't need to worry about owing money to the bank. I want to die with a clean slate. I want my daughters to love each other. Is that too much to ask?"

"We do love each other. There's nothing in this world I wouldn't do for you and Lis. If only—"

"Get out of my room! Get out of my sight!" Wheeling himself around, he moved across the rug and stopped in front of the window, his white head trembling as he strove to master his anger.

Overwhelmed by sadness, Torie walked to the door. She tried to tell herself it was all Lisa's fault. Papa wouldn't have had to know about the mortgage if she hadn't insisted on telling him. Yet Lisa wasn't the one who had broken her promise. It was her own doing—her determination to succeed no matter whose rights she stepped on—that infuriated him.

How ironic, she thought. The wealth and recognition she strove so desperately to achieve would never bring her what she wanted more than anything else: a simple word of approval from her father.

18

CONSTRUCTION OF THE Center City Mall began in September 1975, twelve weeks from the day of the auction. On a cool Monday morning, Torie parked her gray Mazda across the street from the deserted factory and watched as two large trucks rolled up and a gang of workers started unloading equipment.

A foreman in a zippered jumpsuit spotted her leaning against the fender and shouted over a loudspeaker. "Get the hell out of here, lady! Can't you read signs?"

"I'm going," she called, opening the car door.

"They kicking you out already, Torie?"

She turned to see a hard-hatted Mort Goldman come striding toward her, accompanied by a slim sandy-haired young man with a beard.

"You caught me," she said, embarrassed, "but I couldn't resist stopping by on my way to the office."

"I don't blame you. It's a big day. Have you met my son Jefferson?"

She held out a hand. "I'm Torie Di Angelo."

"Hi," he said, "Jeff Goldman."

"Do you work with your father?"

"No, he's too smart for that." Mort smiled. "Jeff's the white sheep of the family. He's an artist."

"That's wonderful. Are you both sticking around awhile?"

"I'll stay long enough to get the project off the ground—so to speak. The demolition crew's planning to drop the factory with explosives."

"What about the noise? The neighbors?"

"I'm sure they'd rather have one loud boom than weeks of drills and wrecking balls. Besides, we have to work fast—before the preservation societies can slap us with an injunction."

Jeff frowned. "I thought you were going to save the murals, Dad."

"We're sending a team into the theater to rescue them today. In the meantime, we're going ahead with the factory. The workmen need about two days to prepare for the blast."

"Why so long?"

"Well, they have to weaken the support beams, secure any materials that might fly out of the building, then map out the best spots to place the explosives so the building collapses inward, not outward."

"What time will they detonate?" asked Torie.

"Mayor Ponti's pushing the button Wednesday at four. Would you say a few words and introduce him?"

"Why don't you do it?"

"Reporters are tired of looking at this old mug. A lovely young face will be much more appealing."

"Anything for the cause," she said, smiling.

"Good. Now if you two will excuse me, I've got to get back." With a quick wave, Mort turned and headed toward the site.

"Damn!" muttered Jeff, eyeing his watch.

Torie slid into her front seat. "Could I give you a lift someplace?"

"I'm going to a gallery at Fifteenth and Walnut."

"It's right on my way. Hop in."

"Really? Thanks."

She drove in silence for several minutes, aware that her passenger was appraising her with unusual interest. "Is anything wrong?"

"You mean why am I staring at you?"

"Well . . . yes."

"Your profile is terrific. I'd want to paint you if I still painted portraits. Unfortunately, my Roy Lichtenstein period ended six years ago. I wasn't bad as a pop artist, but I was an imitator. I had to find my own style."

"And have you?"

"Not completely. I'm still experimenting. When I came back from Florence I was full of the Old Masters. That's what I went there for, to study craftsmanship and be inspired. Now I'm getting away from that and more into—hey, why am I telling you all this?"

"Because I asked." She stole a sidelong glance. What a refreshing, open expression he had, so unlike the sly leers of the men at the parties Ellory dragged her to. A shower of freckles highlighted the upper part of his face; his smile was earnest and guileless.

He chuckled. "I guess that's the cue for me to say, 'Let's talk about you.' But I'd rather finish what I was telling you about me. What *was* I telling you?"

"About becoming a painter." Except for the beard, he didn't look much like a painter, she thought, with his hair combed neatly off his forehead and his clean white shirt and khaki pants. So many artists felt they had to parade around in exploding hairdos and slummy overalls or no one would believe they were artists. "What style are you into now?"

"I'm kind of groping. But that's okay. I'm still in my twenties."

"Where in your twenties?"

"I'm twenty-eight. And you?"

"I'll be twenty-five soon."

"How soon?"

"February third," she said, careful to pronounce the *r*.

"That's five months away. I don't call that soon. What's wrong with being twenty-four?"

"Nothing." She shrugged. "It's just that people think I'm too young to know what I'm doing. They don't realize I've been learning my profession for ten years. You're lucky to have a father who encourages you. Mine never did. He thinks females were put on earth to make lasagna and babies."

"That'd be a shame."

"What would?"

"To hide you behind a stack of diapers. You must know that you're incredibly beautiful. You could be a model . . . an actress . . . almost anything you wanted to be with your looks."

"Thanks, but I don't think life works that way. Lots of beautiful women sell cosmetics and scrub floors. I wouldn't dream of depending on my face to get what I wanted."

"What do you want?"

"Nothing much. Just all there is."

"I think you mean that."

"In a way. It's strange. I can mastermind a megabucks deal

and convince powerful men like the Goldman brothers to be my partners, yet I can't seem to achieve the one goal that would mean more than anything—I can't please my father."

"Isn't he proud of you?"

"No, but that's a long story." She turned up Chestnut Street and stopped at a traffic light. "Are you going to a gallery where they're showing your paintings?"

"I wish I were. I'm going to help a friend. She just started managing this place, and she wants me to look over some art she's selected before the owner gets there. I sure appreciate your delivering me on time. My car's tied up in the shop all morning."

"I'm glad it is. If you hadn't needed a ride, I wouldn't have met you."

"Do you mean that?"

"Of course I mean it."

"Could I see you again sometime?"

She pulled over to the curb. "I'd like that. You did say Fifteenth and Walnut?"

"Yes. Thanks for the lift." He climbed out, shut the door, then opened it impulsively and poked in his head. "You wouldn't want to go to a concert tonight, would you?"

"Umm, tonight?" Ellory was supposed to be taking her to a restaurant opening.

"Eight o'clock at Patterson Hall. I could pick you up about seven-thirty. Do you live nearby?"

"West Mount Airy."

"That's not far. Ever heard Ravi Shankar?"

"No, but I think I'd like to."

"Hey, that's cool!"

She scribbled her address on a card and handed it to him. "Seven-thirty?"

"Make it seven-fifteen so we can get good seats." He slipped the card into his breast pocket and grinned at her. "It's going to be a long day."

Frank Di Angelo wheeled himself to the front door, then back again to the living room. He knew he mustn't appear eager, but how could he not be? Torie hadn't had a date pick her up at the house in over a year. Working as late as she did, she usually preferred to meet her young men at the office and go from there. Tonight *had* to be a special occasion; why else would she have come home early to bathe and change her clothes?

Despite Lisa's warnings not to "make a big deal" out of a first date, Frank felt his excitement growing. Jeff Goldman sounded like exactly the kind of husband he had always wanted for his girls—a nice boy from a good family who could supply the financial stability and social prestige he had never been able to give them. True, the Goldmans weren't Catholic—far from it—but Jewish people were devout in their own way, and just possibly, living in a religious atmosphere might inspire Torie to return to God.

The doorbell rang and he hurried to answer it.

"Mr. Di Angelo?" The young man on the front stoop smiled warmly and shook his hand. "I'm Jeff Goldman. Very happy to meet you, sir."

Frank returned the smile. He hadn't expected to see a beard, but so what? Abe Lincoln had a beard. Silas Rawley had a beard. "Come in, come in, please. Torie will be right down. Would you like a drink?"

"No, thank you, sir. I'm hoping we'll get to the concert in time to grab ourselves some good seats. It makes all the difference in the world—where you sit, I mean."

"Yes, I'm sure it does. I had this stroke a few years ago and haven't been able to go out much. But I remember when my Rosanna . . ." The sound of footsteps made him stop and look around. He was disappointed to see Torie wearing a simple navy wool dress and carrying a matching coat over her arm. He had expected a vision in red silk or satin. But he had to admit she looked nice.

"Hi, Jeff. We ready?"

"I think so. Hey, you're even prettier dressed up. Great to meet you, Mr. Di Angelo."

She leaned down to kiss her father, pleased to note his beaming expression. He obviously approved of her date—and so, for that matter, did she. Something about Jeff Goldman made her feel like a teenager. "You behave yourself, Papa. I'll see you at breakfast."

"Have a good time, kids." A grin spread across Frank's face as he watched Jeff drape her coat over her shoulders and open the door for her. The boy had manners, good looks, charm—everything. With a deep sigh, he crossed his fingers and rolled himself to the stairlift.

*   *   *

The famous Rawley Institute of Music occupied the corner of Eighteenth and Locust Streets on Rittenhouse Square. As almost every Philadelphian knew, the school had been founded in 1924 by Helen Rawley Patterson, a pianist and music lover who named it for her father, Silas Rawley, chairman of the monumentally successful Rawley Publishing Company.

Funny, Torie had thought earlier, here she was going to a concert at the institute built by the Rawleys with a man whose family owned another Rawley building. Not that it surprised her. Philadelphia's ingrown society was always crisscrossing itself in strange ways. What puzzled her was her own longtime ambivalence toward the rich. On the one hand, she yearned to share their privileges, their financial security, their insulation. On the other, she detested their snobbism and elitism, the kind that had so poisoned her childhood. Could you hate something and desperately want to have it at the same time? Yes, she decided, you probably could.

"I've always liked this Italian palazzo," said Jeff, ushering her through the door. "It was originally a private mansion. There's a great feeling of stability that you don't find in modern structures."

Torie had studied the building well, as she had studied all the buildings on Rittenhouse Square. The stone façade with its inset windows and decorative friezes looked no better now than it had ten years ago. "But it's such a hodgepodge of styles. I'd love to hire an architect to redesign it."

Jeff blinked in surprise as they crossed the lobby. "Are you serious?"

"Certainly. Do you think a structure's sacred just because it's old? We don't revere old stoves or shoes or clothes, unless they're museum pieces. We don't even revere old people. Why should we revere old buildings?"

"Because it's a form of art, and all art has value."

"Even bad art?" He was beginning to sound like Nielson.

"Who's to know what's bad or good? Hey," he said, "why are we getting serious? I don't want to strain my brain, I want to have a good time. Come on." He took her hand and led her up to the balcony. "I've finally figured out where the best acoustics are."

"Right here, I assume," she said, taking a seat beside him.

"Two rows down would be better, but they're filled. Look above you."

Torie glanced up at the ceiling. Round-cheeked cherubs and pink-skinned nudes frolicked across a sky of clouds, flowers, and seashells. To her eyes the mural looked trite and saccharine, like a cheap greeting card. "That's . . . quite a scene. Who painted it?"

"Jean-Claude Massaine was the artist. He worked standing on a scaffold twenty-four feet in the air with his neck crooked. He was quoted as saying his biggest problem wasn't sore muscles, it was perspective. He couldn't quite center the center."

"Only an artist would notice that."

"It's very obvious to me. I could fix it with some trompe l'oeil work, and I've offered my services. All it would cost the institute would be a few hundred bucks for materials and a scaffold."

"That was nice of you. Were they pleased?"

"Yeah, very," he said, snickering. "So pleased they can't get their board to approve it. They're afraid I might screw it up and make it look worse."

It couldn't look worse, she thought, wondering if she should speak up or be silent. Perhaps she could be tactful. "I know you'll disagree, but this auditorium seems a bit bland to me. If it were mine, I'd reupholster the chairs in a pretty bright-colored fabric, replace those projectors with high-tech equipment—"

"High tech? In here?"

"Hidden behind the wall panels. Then I'd build a sound-shell at the rear of the stage, and bring the acoustics almost up to recording-studio quality."

"Is that possible?"

"Sure. I just read about a place that did it. And I'd put in soft, flickering lights—"

"Now you're talking. It's beginning to sound like a disco."

"I don't mean flashy, I mean tasteful and harmonious. The hall should be a backdrop for the music."

He grinned. "Well, we don't exactly agree on what we'd do with this room, but what's fascinating is that we both want to redo it."

"There's either change or there's stagnation."

"Yes, but you have to know when to leave things alone, too. I wouldn't try to improve a Rubens painting or a Beatles song." He handed her a program. "I was thinking this afternoon—I forgot to ask if you liked music. Do you?"

"I love it, except for long-winded operas and loud rock and roll. Say, is that woman waving at you?"

Several people, in fact, were waving at him, and she was amazed to see how many faces he recognized in the small auditorium. During intermission he introduced her to a crowd of his friends, and as she talked and laughed and enjoyed flattering glances, she felt relaxed and happier than she had in months.

The pleasure of being with people of her own generation was a revelation. Ellory's forced forays into the upper strata of society had made her forget that going out could be fun—that you could chatter and giggle and flirt harmlessly, and not give a damn who somebody was or who their ancestors were or how much money they had. Even the girls were refreshing—determined to be "sisterly" now that they had embraced feminism, and bursting with plans for their pro-abortion rally.

After the concert Jeff suggested a stroll through the park. "I've always liked Rittenhouse Square," he said, slipping his arm around her. "It has a special, romantic glow at night—or maybe it's because this is a special night."

She smiled and huddled closer. "It's been a wonderful evening, Jeff. And this is the perfect way to end it. I've loved this spot ever since I was a little girl and got to peek inside the Richardson house."

"A political function?"

"Umm, no." She didn't want to bring up unhappy memories. "Betsy Richardson had a birthday party."

"Hey, I know Betsy. She's a good friend."

"I didn't really know her. It's a long story. But ever since then, I've always felt possessive about the Square . . . as if I'm destined to have some important connection to it. I mean me, personally. Isn't that ridiculous?"

"Maybe not. Maybe you'll buy a condo and live here. Then you'll own part of it."

"It's not . . . a physical ownership exactly. I've thought so much about the music institute and some of these other old buildings. Sometimes I dare to think the unthinkable—that they should be torn down and replaced."

He chuckled. "You want to tear down Rittenhouse Square?"

"Not the *whole* Square," she said, instantly defensive. "But every time I come here I get stronger and stronger feelings that I have to do *something*. And razing homes isn't all that shocking. People have been razing homes to build high rises for ages. Five years ago, Jack Wolgin tore down the Episcopal diocese headquarters for the same reason. In a way, I almost feel the Square's *waiting* for me to give it a face-lift. Is that so terrible?"

"Well, *I* don't mind, but you might get a little static from the natives—something on the order of World War Three." He laughed and stopped under a tree. "What a bundle of contradictions you are, Torie. To look at you, one could easily think you were nothing but an empty-headed society girl who spent all her days buying clothes and all her nights taking them off. Come to think of it, that's not such a bad idea . . ."

"You mean buying clothes or taking them off?"

"Guess." He drew her to him and kissed the tip of her nose. "I'm mighty attracted to you, in case you haven't noticed. I can't remember ever feeling so . . . desirous of anyone. But I don't want to rush things. I'm scared to death I'll come on too strong and spoil it for us. Does that make any sense to you?"

"It makes good sense, Jeff. Let's take our time and get to know each other. Right now, I ought to be getting home."

"What? And leave the scene of your future triumphs?"

She smiled. "Tease me all you want, Mr. Goldman, but one of these years, when you look over at where the old Rawley Institute used to be and you see a spectacular new skyscraper, guess who'll have the last laugh."

"I'm not laughing." He grinned and took her hand. "Need a good art director?"

The Center City Mall launching ceremony was livened by the appearance of Mayor Ponti, the Franklin High School marching band, two string bands, and reporters and camera crews from local television stations. After Torie's brief introduction, the mayor praised her and the Goldman brothers for their "public-spirited dedication to improving the quality of life in our great city," added a dozen more clichés, then began the countdown.

Among the spectators, only Jeff Goldman, watching from behind the podium, realized that the wire from the mayor's beribboned red box ended in a clump of bushes. The operative switch, less photogenic but far more efficient, was pushed at the proper moment by the project superintendent standing in the parking lot.

A series of tommy-gun booms split the expectant stillness, and seconds later the factory began to crumble—first at the sides, then in the middle, releasing an avalanche of concrete and dust. A group of protesters watched from their post beneath the

Washington marquee, while several students waving SAVE OUR HERITAGE signs paraded by, shouting, "Barbarians! Neanderthals!"—even though no one had ever objected to razing the factory. The dissenters' main concern was the theater.

"Hello, Jeff," said Torie, stepping off the podium. "I didn't know you were here."

"Do you have your car?"

"No, I didn't want to have to park so I took a cab."

"Then let's go." He hurried her into his well-dented Ford and drove off, bypassing the crowd.

"You're a lifesaver," she said, once they were on the expressway. "The last thing I wanted was to tangle with the preservationists. Your dad was right; they did get an injunction against tearing down the Washington, and the delay could cost us a fortune."

"Even though you agreed to save the murals?"

"They've changed their tune. Now they want us to spend a million bucks renovating the theater."

He shook his head. "I hate to see the old place go, but as you said the other night, some things have to be sacrificed for progress."

"Did you hear my introduction?"

"You were terrific! Poised, witty, charming. What will I do when you run for mayor?"

"It's president or nothing." She chuckled and rolled down the window. "No fear. I'm much too outspoken to be a politician. Where are you taking me?"

"Home, if you can stand my humble digs. I want to show you some of my work."

"Come up and see your paintings? At five in the afternoon? I don't even leave my office till six."

"Then consider yourself kidnapped. You have two alternatives. You can put up a fight and cause a horrible accident in which we'll both be killed or maimed for life, or you can do as you're told and stay healthy. I think I got that right. Did I forget anything?"

"Sounds pretty threatening to me." She laughed and leaned back against the seat. "In the hands of such a ruthless criminal, I have no choice . . ."

"Did you really fix that soufflé yourself?"

Jeff pushed away the card table and joined Torie on the tattered sofa. "It's easy when you're a vegetarian. The selection's pretty limited."

"I can't even boil an egg. My father says I'll never get a husband unless I know how to cook."

"What do you say?"

"I say I'm going to be rich enough to hire a cook."

"You sure think a lot about money."

"Doesn't everyone?"

"I don't. Greed and materialism are what's wrong with the world. I'd be a communist if it wasn't so much trouble. Money doesn't bring happiness."

"Maybe not—but what's that old saying? 'It's better to cry in a Rolls-Royce than to smile on a bicycle.' I like that."

Jeff's arm crept around her and she moved in closer. "We had a cook when I was growing up. Her name was Denise. The trouble was, Mom and Dad were always dieting, so they had her leave out the butter and cream and all the good things. But then she'd whip up these rich, gooey dishes just for me. And she'd teach me how to make them."

"You see? If your parents hadn't had the money to pay Denise, you wouldn't know how to cook those gooey dishes. You wouldn't be able to afford them, either." She snuggled closer. "I really like your paintings. You have a nice sense of nature."

"That's what I do best—at least right now—only there's not much nature around a two-room attic in Center City. The folks have a house in Unionville they never use, so I go there almost every weekend. It has a lovely little creek, and a lake, and woods . . . I'd like to show it to you someday."

She resisted mentioning that not many communists had second homes. "I'd like to see it."

His arm tightened as he pulled her closer. "Do you mean that? Or are you just a girl who can't say no?"

"Hmmm. I can say no when I want to."

He kissed her neck and her chin, and eased up to her lips. "Now's not the time to prove it."

His touch was so sweet and gentle, he surprised her by reaching under her blouse and unhooking her bra before she had a chance to protest. Her sexual feelings had been dormant so long, she had trouble responding at first . . . but soon she began to relax, and when she did, she came alive and kissed him back.

"Torie," he murmured, his hands gliding down to her hips,

"you're warm—you're beautiful—I care so much about you. I don't want to—"

"But I want you to," she said, whispering the words once whispered to her. "Passion is rare and wonderful . . . we mustn't let it get away . . ."

19

HAVING A MAN wildly in love with her was a happy experience for Torie. She liked being in control, and she liked not being so consumed with desire that she lost all sense of pride. Whoever loved less in a relationship held the power; she had learned that from her one-sided affair with Nielson. In this instance, however, reason ruled her heart—and she found herself making decisions coolly and logically.

At the same time she was growing increasingly fond of Jeff. They spent many nights together after that first evening in his loft, and once Torie explained to her father that Jeff had a "guest room," he made no objections. In some ways, she found Jeff to be the opposite of Nielson—antiwealth, antisociety, unrealistic, and not overly ambitious. But he was kind, even-tempered, and accepting of their differences. As a lover he was tender and sensitive and always made her feel he was making love to *her*, not just enjoying the sex act.

In late December he invited her to his parents' house for a Chanukah supper. Mort was his usual charming self, and Sylvia was pleasant, though far from effusive. Torie came away with the impression that no woman would be good enough for her precious Jeff. He was the dreamer, the idealist, the creative soul—the only one of his generation of Goldmans who cared little for money or possessions.

In her turn, Torie astounded her father and sister by bringing Jeff home for Christmas dinner. Frank and Lisa were overjoyed;

they wanted nothing more than to see her give up the business, settle down, and marry this nice young man—even if he did worship at the wrong shrine.

On New Year's Eve, Ellory Davis insisted on taking the couple to a benefit for the Shubert Theater. After having been seen, introduced to various celebrities, and photographed by three newspapers, they left early and went back to his apartment.

Shortly before midnight, Torie lay naked in his arms. "You were sweet to come with me, Jeff," she said, stroking his cheek. "I'm sure you were bored to death."

"I was more upset than bored. The money those people lavish on themselves is sickening. That necklace on the woman sitting next to us could feed a starving African village for a year."

"You're probably right."

"I am right. The only good thing about the evening—besides being with you—is that I had to wear a suit and tie. I'd forgotten how uncomfortable the damn things are. With your permission, I'm putting them back in storage."

"Go right ahead. You shouldn't have to be uncomfortable. It's about time I stopped letting Ellory drag me to all these affairs, anyway. I think I'll let him go."

"Don't you want to be famous?"

"Sure, but not for going to parties. Ellory's given me a start. Now I'll have to get there on my own."

"Don't fire him on my account, sweetheart." He smoothed back her long silky hair. "He does keep you in the news, and you said it helps business. Why stop something that's working for you?"

"I thought it might please you."

"You please me," he said, gazing down at her. Moonlight drifting through the window cast shadows across her face. He outlined them as if he were making a drawing. "I don't ever want to interfere with your dreams. I know how much they mean to you. I wish I were half Shakespeare and half Elizabeth Browning, so I could speak what's in my heart."

"You don't need them. You express yourself beautifully."

"Not the way you deserve. And I meant what I said. I'm vastly jealous of anything that demands so much of your time and your energies, and yet I know I can't be—anymore than you can be jealous of the hours I spend painting."

"You're wonderfully understanding." Her arms closed around his neck. "I do love you, Jeff. You've brought warmth and fulfillment and a gentleness to my life that I never knew existed."

"In that case, why are we living apart?"

"You know why. It would kill Papa if I moved in with you. He's still back in his own generation."

"Do we have to wait for him to die before we can live together?"

"I don't know." She pursed her lips. "It's not that he doesn't like you. He raves about you—"

"Even though I'm not Catholic?"

"Yes." She laughed softly. "A lot more than your parents accept me for being—what's that funny word?"

"A *shiksa*. Dad talked to me about you the other day."

"I'm sure he doesn't approve."

"Why do you say that?"

"He probably wants for you the same thing Papa wants for me—a nice home, dinner on the table every night, lots of babies. He knows I can't give you those things."

"That's pretty much what he warned me about—your ambition. He said I would always come second. He also said that intermarriages cause a lot of problems. I told him we hadn't discussed marriage, and it seemed to quiet him."

"That's good."

"But it didn't quiet me." He took her face in his hands. "If we can't live in sin, I'll have to make you an honest woman. I love you, Vittoria Francesca. I love you so much I'm willing to take second place to your business, I'm willing to let you schlep me to deadly parties, I'm willing to take on all domestic chores and do everything in my power to make you happy for the rest of our lives. Will you marry me?"

"I—I'm so touched, Jeff. I—"

"Do you have anything against marriage?"

"Oh, no, my parents adored each other. They were the best possible example. I just don't know if I'm ready to get married. I've got so many responsibilities. I have no money—I'm way in debt—"

"I don't care about your money or lack of it. The income from my trust will support us until my paintings start to sell—and even if they don't."

"Oh, Jeff," she whispered, "I do need you. I need your love, and I need to love you. If you really understand this strange force that drives me . . . that I'm in too deeply to let marriage slow me down . . ."

"How many times do I have to tell you I understand?" He bent to meet her lips as a burst of shouts and noisemakers announced the arrival of 1976. "You see? Even the neighbors are celebrating. You won't be sorry, sweetheart. I'll love you just as much on our golden wedding anniversary as I do now—with all my heart and my soul."

The moment Jeff revealed his intentions, the Goldmans welcomed Torie into the family. Once they realized their son was serious, they were wise enough to keep their reservations to themselves. Meanwhile, Torie had her own reservations and spent many nights wondering if she was making a mistake. Rich and prestigious as the Goldmans were, Jeff had no job, no desire to get one, and barely enough income to rent them a small, cramped apartment.

Yet she loved Jeff, she loved the possibility of finally pleasing her father, she loved the idea of marrying into a powerful family, and she could put up with a few inconveniences, knowing that Jeff would eventually come into a large inheritance. Her confidence was bolstered when his parents not only insisted on hosting the wedding but made them a gift of a spacious condominium in one of their Center City apartment towers.

The nuptials took place at two in the afternoon on the second Sunday in March, in the glittering Mirage Room of the Barclay Hotel on Rittenhouse Square. Frank Di Angelo, his wheelchair folded beside him, sat in the first row, sobbing with happiness. Beside him, Lisa nervously clutched her rosary. Self-conscious about her weight and appearance, she had declined to be in the wedding party, leaving Peggy to replace her as maid of honor. Jeff's sister, Marcia, was the sole bridesmaid, followed by her two small sons as ring-bearers.

A crowd of several hundred rose in expectant silence as the piped-in organ began the Wedding March. The bride, exquisite in the Saint Laurent seed-pearl gown Ellory had helped her choose, swept down the aisle on the arm of her future father-in-law. Jeff stood proud and beaming and took her hand as she arrived at the altar.

Judge Julius Goldman, oldest of the three Goldman brothers, performed the ceremony; Father Miles and Rabbi Greenfield looked on and offered brief blessings. After Jeff and Torie were pronounced man and wife, the groom kissed the bride so intensely that the room broke into applause. Lloyd Goldman, his brother and best man, pretended to wrench them apart with great effort. Then, laughing and holding hands, the couple moved into the adjoining Baroque Room for the reception.

Torie stood patiently through the long ordeal, charming the guests with her poise, her naturalness, and her remarkable memory for names—another skill she owed to Ellory's tutelage.

"How about a shot of the four of you?"

"Why not?" Jeff smiled at the *Daily News* photographer and touched his wife's shoulder. "Honey, do you know Simone and Matt Richardson?"

Torie felt a surge of excitement as she stared at the famous pair. Matt looked the same as he had at the trial, only grayer, and she had to remind herself that she had long ago forgiven him, that her father had forgiven him, and that Tony was the real culprit of that disaster. Unfortunately, the slim, pretty woman who had so graciously taken her into Betsy's party was now bloated and clearly inebriated. "I met you a long time ago, Mrs. Richardson. You were very kind to me."

"Bully for me." Her voice was husky, her eyes too glazed to focus. Matt clutched her forearm.

"Felicitations, my dear," he said with no sign of embarrassment. Long years as a politician had taught him to finesse such situations. "You're a lucky man, Jeff. We'll take a raincheck on that picture. Simone sometimes forgets that champagne isn't ginger ale."

"That's easy to do. We appreciate your coming."

"Wouldn't have missed it. Betsy was so sorry she couldn't be here. As you know, she's in a bridal party herself."

"Yes. A lot of people are going on to the Hopkinson wedding this evening. Tell her we missed her."

Torie turned to Frank, sitting beside her in his wheelchair, his eyes glowing with excitement. She had dreaded this moment as much as he had been anticipating it. "This is my father, Frank Di Angelo. Papa, the Richardsons."

"How do you do," said Matt, perfunctorily. If he recognized the man he helped send to prison, he made no sign. "My felicitations, sir. You have a charming daughter."

"Don't you remember me, Mayor? I was in your house once—in your living room. We had a nice talk. Don't you remember me? I'm Frank Di Angelo."

"It's been a few years since I've been called Mayor. Good luck to you, my friend."

Frank tugged at his coattail. "Wait! You testified at my trial but I never held it against you. I've been waiting a long time to tell you that. I didn't want it on your conscience. I understood what you did and why you did it. I forgave you a long time ago. My daughter forgave you too."

Torie blanched and wished she were invisible. Matt seemed unfazed. "Congratulations again," he said with a smile. "Good day to you, sir."

"Good day?" Stung by the abrupt dismissal, Frank watched in shocked silence as the couple disappeared into the crowd.

Torie leaned down. "Forget it, Papa. It's nothing personal. His wife's staggering drunk and he wants to get her out of here before she falls on her face."

"Did you see that?" he gasped. "Did you see the way he treated me? Like I was some babbling idiot. I only wanted to clear him of a burden—to let him know—"

"I'm sure he appreciated it, but he has his own problems. Would you like some wine?"

"Frankie . . ." he murmured, his head shaking, "Frankie knew all along what Mayor Richardson was like, and we wouldn't believe him. Frankie, Lisa—they were both right. I saw the man's eyes today. They looked right through me as if I wasn't there—wasn't even worthy of two minutes of his time. He was ashamed to be seen talking to me . . ."

"That's not so. I told you why he wanted to get away. Papa, this is my *wedding*. Some people are coming. Now will you stop—"

"A curse on that scum! *Maledetto!*" Trembling with anger, Frank wheeled himself over to where Lisa was sitting, talking to Father Miles.

Torie started to go after him, when Jeff's arm reached out. "C'mere, honey. I want you to meet Frannie Pew. She was my biology partner in high school. We dissected our first frog together."

"How romantic." Taking her place by her husband, Torie turned her attention back to the guests. She could see Lisa's worried face as she got up and steered Frank toward the exit. Her expression communicated that Papa wanted to go home, and that was that. Torie would have to invent some reason for their departure.

The last stragglers passed through the receiving line, and an exhausted Sylvia Goldman gave the signal to break up. A nine-piece band and nonstop hors d'oeuvres kept the mood lively for another hour, and by four o'clock, only the wedding party remained. The maid of honor was about to kiss the bride good-bye when the catering manager poked his head in the doorway. "There's a call for Mort Goldman."

"He's dancing with his daughter," said Torie. "I'll take it."

Several minutes later, she returned to the reception. Jeff saw her and hurried over. "What's wrong? You're as white as a sheet."

"Hal, the foreman at the theater site, phoned to say they're ready to detonate but they can't. The protesters have formed a human fence."

"Better let Dad handle that."

"I don't want to spoil the day for your parents. They've both been so sweet and they look ready to drop. Couldn't we go over there? I'm so worried . . ."

"Go there *now*? On our wedding day? Why are they working on Sunday?"

"Because the judge overruled the injunction on Friday. We figured the protesters wouldn't expect us to start the job till Monday, so we'd fool them. I guess our strategy didn't work."

"But, honey, by the time we go home and change our clothes—"

"We'll go just as we are. It'll only take a few minutes, and *then* we can go home and forget all about it. Otherwise—"

"Yeah, I know the otherwise." He sighed good-naturedly. "I can't say you didn't warn me. Okay, let's say good-bye to the folks. Are you sure you don't want to tell Dad?"

"Positive. But let's hurry . . ."

The limousine waiting to whisk the newlyweds to their condominium took them to the Washington Theater, instead. A group of nineteen men and women, their arms tightly locked, formed a line across the entrance.

Torie laid her veil on the seat, gathered up her skirts, and hurried over to where Hal was standing with four policemen.

"Ye gods!" he exclaimed. "You didn't have to leave your *wedding.*"

"It's all over. We're married." Ignoring the stares of the workmen, Torie turned to one of the officers. "Is there some quiet, peaceful way you can remove those demonstrators?"

The policeman took off his cap and scratched his head. "I don't know about quiet and peaceful, Miss, er, Mrs. . . . What the hell, did you two just get hitched?"

Jeff's eyes opened innocently. "What gave you that idea?"

"I asked you a question, Officer."

"You wanna know about the birds and the bees?"

The round of snickers annoyed Torie, and she stamped her foot on the cement, inadvertently breaking off the heel of her right sandal. "Oh, shit!"

The sight of his lopsided bride swearing on the demolition site in her delicate lace gown was too much for Jeff; he covered his mouth and scurried away.

Torie was getting angrier by the moment. "I'll ask you a last time, Officer. Have you talked to the demonstrators?"

"Yes, ma'am," he said, seeing the fire in her eyes. "We've talked to 'em and reasoned with 'em and treated 'em like the fine, upstanding citizens they are. You can see where that got us."

"What are you going to do about it?"

"Well, ma'am, if you have any suggestions—"

"You'll have to force them to leave."

"The tac squad's on their way, but frankly, if I were you, I'd send everyone home and sit down with these people in the morning. Maybe you can get together at the bargaining table."

"We're *not* going home. The law is on our side and it's up to you to see that it's carried out. We're going to settle this right now."

Jeff came running back breathlessly. "Hey, guess who I found over there? Phil Stevenson, my old history teacher. He says they're blocking the demolition because you didn't save the murals as you'd promised. Is that true?"

"Yes, it's true, and for a very good reason. Turned out they're not murals, they're frescoes—pigment mixed with plaster. The paintings are the actual walls."

"I know what frescoes are, honey. Did—"

"We tried everything to save them but we couldn't. The minute we touched that old gypsum, it crumbled to dust. I was just as upset as you are."

"Are the frescoes still intact?"

"For the moment."

"Then you have to be fair. You made those people a promise. You owe them the courtesy of a compromise."

"How can we compromise?" Her voice rose. "Either we spend a million dollars nobody's got to renovate the theater, or we tear it down and put up a handsome new park and shopping center that thousands of people will enjoy."

"There must be some middle ground."

"There isn't! Those damn preservationists with their petitions and their legal maneuvers have tied up this project for months and cost us a fortune. Do you have any idea of my carrying charges on the construction loan? Thank God the judge finally ruled in our favor, and now they want to say the hell with the judge, who cares about the law, we'll do what we want. Over my dead body!"

Two police cars and a paddy wagon pulled up, and a dozen men in jumpsuits, boots, and helmets leaped out. "Sergeant Gill, tac squad," announced a strapping man with a bullhorn. His eyes fastened on the woman in lace. "What the hell's going on around here?"

"Show him the court order, Hal," said Torie, limping toward him with her heel in her hand. "Sergeant, those people have been blocking this detonation since last September, and we're not going to fuss with them one second longer. The theater's wired to blow up, and their lives are in danger unless they move away right now."

The sergeant scanned the paper, then turned to the patrolmen. "You tried talking to them?"

"Yeah, we tried."

"Okay. I'll give the dispersal order." Raising his bullhorn, he shouted, "This is an unlawful assembly. You have five minutes to disperse. If you do not disperse in five minutes, you will be subject to arrest."

"Good God, Torie," said Jeff, "you've got some heavyweight names in that group. You can't have them arrested."

"They're breaking the law."

"Then it's a dumb law. You can't blithely destroy priceless art works. You haven't the right—"

"I have *every* right." She folded her arms defiantly. "The Landmark Committee, the City Planning Commission, and Mayor Ponti himself approved the demolition. The judge gave us a court order. And the longer we stand here arguing, the more those people are costing us. Our blasting crew is already on over-time."

"Screw the overtime!" Realizing what a sight they must be, squabbling in their wedding outfits, Jeff lowered his voice. "Be *reasonable*, honey. One more day won't matter. I'll bet those peo-ple could raise a million bucks in no time if they set their minds to it."

"But I don't *want* them to. Can't you understand? We've been reasonable for six months. Now we need the space."

"So that's why you didn't want Dad to come. You were afraid he might compromise."

"One minute to go," hollered Sergeant Gill. "This is an unlaw-ful assembly. If you do not disperse in one minute, you will be subject to arrest." He watched the group for several seconds, then turned to his men. "They're not moving. Keep it orderly and don't draw your batons. Thirty seconds . . . twenty-five . . . twenty . . . all right, walk slowly and proceed according to rules."

One by one, the policemen went down the line, asking each protester, "Do you wish to leave now?" The answers were all negative, and the officers quietly marched them into the paddy wagon.

As soon as they drove off, Torie slipped off her other shoe and picked up her skirts. "Okay now, Hal?"

"Nothing's stopping us but you two. By the way—congratula-tions."

"Thanks," growled Jeff. "I married this woman for better or for worse, but I didn't expect to cover the whole range so soon." He shrugged and took her arm. "Come on, Mrs. Goldman. We have better ways to spend our wedding night."

20

THE CHURCH OF the Holy Faith was filling up fast. From his seat to the right of the center aisle, Nielson waited impatiently for the ceremony to start. He had never cared for Sonny Hopkinson and wouldn't have made the effort to attend his wedding if he hadn't read that Betsy was to be one of the bridesmaids. The dim hope that she might relent and join him for dinner after the reception was enough to tear him away from his drafting table for a night off.

A flurry of movement caught his attention. Heads stared as an usher led a striking couple to the front pew. The white-haired man settled in his seat, smiled, shook hands around him like a politician, then helped his young wife out of her mink.

"That's Robert Nielson," a lady whispered to her husband. "Wife number five looks like a chorus girl."

Nielson had met his new stepmother once, at a reception honoring her husband's latest skyscraper, and she had greeted him as if he were the Boston Strangler. Not that he cared about her, or any of his father's previous wives for that matter, but she could at least have acknowledged the relationship—that is, if she knew about it.

Craning his neck, Robert Nielson glanced about the church, meeting the eyes of his son, saluting him with a nod, then quickly passing on. You goddamn prick, thought Nielson. He was used to being snubbed by his father—and yet he wasn't. Having lived with the hurt of being ignored by him all through his childhood, he now had to deal with a new set of feelings: the frustration of working in the same profession, living in the same city, and yet having no communication other than a brief hello when they met publicly.

The room quieted as the minister entered the chancel, followed by the groom and best man. Three ushers led the procession down the aisle; then came the attendants—one, two, and sweet Betsy, radiant and lovely in a pink satin gown. Her long brown braids were laced with rosebuds, her eyes were smiling, her figure slim and willowy. For a moment, he felt half-intoxicated. Her beauty had never been more breathtaking.

The bride appeared next—good name, good family, and a face like a bulldog. Sonny Hopkinson deserved her. The ceremony seemed interminable, but finally Nielson took his place in the line of guests waiting to greet the wedding party, and fell into conversation with a balding gentleman next to him.

"I suppose we should introduce ourselves," said the man, offering his card and accepting one in return. "I'm Jim Harris, Bickman Oil."

"Nielson Hughes. Delighted to meet you."

"I see you're an architect. Your first name—any relation?"

"He's my father."

"Hmm. Interesting. His name was bandied about quite a bit at our board meeting. We're building new headquarters downtown. Some say he's the only architect for the job; others think he's overpriced and overrated. What do you think?"

"I think he's excellent. Superb, in fact." Nielson smiled charmingly. "But I'm better, Mr. Harris."

"The name's Jim." Sudden interest lit up his eyes. "What kind of things have you done?"

"Suppose I send you my portfolio. If you approve of my work, I'd like the chance to submit some designs to your board. My services aren't cheap, but my fees are light-years away from my father's."

"In that case, we'd be glad to take a look."

By the time Nielson reached the bridal party, he was feeling a stir of excitement. Bickman Oil was a major corporation, their lot was on some of the most valuable property in the city, and the commission could be in the millions.

"Nielson!" Betsy leaned forward and kissed his cheek. "I didn't expect to see you here. I'd almost forgotten how handsome you are."

"I came to remind you. How long do you have to perpetuate this barbaric ritual?"

"You mean stand in line? I'm stuck till we've greeted everyone."

"Have dinner with me?"

"I'd love to, but I can't. It's Mother's birthday and Daddy has a meeting, so I promised I'd take her to Mirabelle. It's been ages since I spent any time with her."

"Or with me, for that matter. If I call you, will I get the usual answer?"

"No . . . no, you won't." She looked at him as if she were seeing him for the first time. "I'd like very much to have dinner with you."

He felt his pulse quicken. "Tomorrow night?"

"That'd be neat. I'd love to show you my gallery. Is six o'clock too early to meet me there?"

"Not after waiting nine years for a date." He bent to kiss her hand. "*À bientôt*, Juliet. I count the hours."

"I tell you I'm perfectly sober. I had two cups of black coffee and a big, rich dessert."

"I don't care. I won't let you drive to Rehoboth alone." Betsy took her mother's arm. "Why can't you go home and wait for Daddy?"

"Because I want to go now."

"But that's stupid. You had champagne at both weddings, a bottle of wine with dinner, and you can barely walk. I'm driving us back to the Square."

"The hell you are!" Simone grabbed the keys from the parking attendant and slid into the front seat. "I told you, I'm going to the beach house."

"Then I'm going with you." Betsy walked to the other side of the Mercedes, got in, and slammed the door. The three-hour drive to the Delaware coast was bad enough in bright daylight when her mother was sober. At least, Betsy thought, she could try to keep her from speeding, or take over if she started to feel drowsy.

The adrenaline of anger seemed to sharpen Simone's senses, and after many uneventful miles, Betsy found herself beginning to relax. Gradually, however, as they neared their destination, Simone's foot grew heavy on the pedal.

"Slow down, Mom. You're over the line."

"I've been coming here for sixteen years. I could drive it blindfolded."

"We're not in any hurry. Can't you take it easy?"

"You still think I'm drunk?"

"I think you're being reckless. Mom, get over in your lane!"
No sooner had she spoken than a mobile home rounded the
bend; the driver veered to avoid them, and Simone tried to
swerve, but the steering wheel slipped from her grasp. Betsy
lurched for the wheel as their car spun out of control, crashed
through a fence, and somersaulted into a pole. There was a thun-
derous crunch—a hail of metal and debris—and then . . . deathly
stillness.

The phone rang at six o'clock Monday morning. Torie fumbled with the receiver. "H'lo?"

"It's me, Lisa. Sorry to wake you."

She sat up instantly. "What's wrong? Is it Papa?"

"No, Papa's okay. But remember yesterday when we left the
wedding early?"

"How could I forget? I had to lie and say he got sick."

"He was very hurt at the way Mayor Richardson treated him.
He thought you were making that story up about his wife being
drunk, but now he knows you weren't. Torie, it's horrible—"

"*What* is?"

"The Richardsons left the Hopkinson wedding separately,
and when Matt returned home around midnight, the police were
waiting. They told him Simone and Betsy had an accident on
the road to Rehoboth. Simone was killed and Betsy's spine was
crushed. The doctors say she may never walk again."

"Oh, my God . . ."

Jeff awoke to the sound of his wife's groan. He took the phone.
"Who is this?"

"It's Lisa, Jeff. Simone Richardson was killed last night. Betsy
was badly hurt."

"What? How?"

Lisa explained, then added, "I didn't want you to read it in
the papers."

"That's thoughtful of you. What a ghastly shock—after we
just saw them yesterday. How's your father?"

"Better, thanks. Could I talk to my sister for a second?"

"Hold on."

Torie took the receiver numbly. "Y-yes?"

"Don't worry about Papa. He's convinced his curse was re-
sponsible for the accident. He feels terrible about Simone and
Betsy, but he also feels that he's finally evened the score with
Matt Richardson."

"Evened the score? No, no, he *couldn't* have said that!" She slammed down the phone, her brain alive with memories, her mind unable to erase the vision of the lovely young girl whose sweetness and gentleness had once meant so much to her. "Oh, Jeff," she whispered, curling up to him, "hold me tight . . ."

Whistling a chorus of "I'm Getting Married in the Morning," Nielson warned himself not to be overly optimistic, parked his BMW in front of Betsy's Co-Op Gallery, then strolled up to the entrance—punctual, he guessed, for the first time in his life.

To his surprise, a CLOSED sign hung in the window and several rolled-up newspapers lay by the door. He rapped on the glass and called Betsy's name but got no response, so he knocked again, glancing about to see if she might have left a note for him. Her absence concerned him. Even if she had forgotten their date or changed her mind, she still would have opened the gallery.

He hurried to a nearby phone, tried her apartment first, and then her parents' house. "Is Mr. or Mrs. Richardson there?"

"Who is this?" asked the maid.

"Nielson Hughes. I'm a friend of Betsy's. I was supposed to meet her at the gallery tonight, but she hasn't shown up and I'm rather worried."

"Don't you read the papers?"

"The—?" His voice rose in alarm. "I didn't have time. I was on a building site all day. What is it? What's happened?"

"Read the front page," she snapped, and hung up.

Moments later, cold and trembling, a crumpled newspaper clutched in his fist, Nielson burst into Pennsylvania Hospital and raced up five flights of stairs to the intensive care unit. "How is she? I want to see her!"

"No one goes in there," said a security guard. "If you mean Miss Richardson, her condition's stable. Are you a reporter?"

"I'm a friend. Is she conscious? Is she in pain?"

"Last I heard she was sleeping. You can check at the desk."

The head nurse had nothing to add and suggested he go home and listen to his radio. Knowing that he was helpless—that he couldn't even see the woman he loved, the woman he had always loved, and who finally seemed ready to love him in return—he staggered toward the stairway, grasped for the railing, and felt himself go limp.

"My poor, poor darling," he whispered. He took a few steps

and glanced back at the guard. Then he sat down on the stairs, buried his face in his hands, and wept.

Simone Richardson's funeral the next morning was a massive city affair, overshadowed by the still greater tragedy of Betsy Richardson's dark future. Reports from the hospital were grim: The twenty-seven-year-old woman was completely paralyzed from the waist down. Her upper torso was relatively intact, however, and with intensive therapy and a bit of luck, she would probably be able to move about in a wheelchair.

Matt Richardson made a brief appearance, supported by two friends. He held back his tears through most of the service, then wept openly at the final eulogy. Torie, standing in the rear of the hall, signaled to Jeff that she wanted to leave. Why torture themselves watching the poor man's agony . . .

Minutes later Jeff pulled up to their apartment. "Aren't you coming in?"

"I can't, honey. I've got to get to work."

"In that black suit? You look like a grieving widow. People will think you did me in on our wedding night."

"I tried to." She kissed his lips. "You'd better start cooking my dinner. What'd I marry you for?"

"You've got a point. When will you be home?"

"I thought we discussed all that."

"We did. My efficient wife has got our marriage clocked like a bus schedule. Leave at seven-thirty, return at six-thirty. We dine at seven, and if I'm lucky, I get the pleasure of your company for half an hour before you hit the blueprints. Shall we synchronize our watches?"

"Don't hassle me, Jeff. I won't always have to work this hard. But right now—"

"I know, sweetheart. I knew what I was getting into—forgive the phrase. Do you like *latkes*?"

"What are *latkes*?"

"Simply the best potato pancakes you've ever tasted." He climbed out of the car and watched her slide across the seat. "I love you. Drive carefully."

By June of 1976, three months after the tragedy, Nielson still hadn't been able to get through to Betsy. Her father guarded the town house like a fortress—or maybe he was carrying out her wishes. A mutual acquaintance told Nielson she wasn't in a

wheelchair yet but was getting therapy and doing better, even
though she continued to refuse to talk to anyone.

"Your extension's ringing, Nielson."

"Righto." He snapped out of his reflection and reached for
the phone. "Hughes speaking."

"Jim Harris from Bickman Oil. Got a minute?"

"All the time you want." Finally, the call he had been waiting
for.

"Our board met again yesterday and with certain reservations,
approved your preliminary design."

"That's great news—isn't it?"

"Damn right. The only problem is that some of the board
don't feel you've had quite enough experience to tackle a job of
this magnitude, and they've come up with a small proviso. You'll
be our prime architect, but we want your father to come in as
consultant."

Nielson's hand tightened on the receiver. "Why do you need
him? We don't work together."

"I told them that. But they were insistent. They'll only hire
you on that condition."

"Could I talk to your board? Could I explain to them why
that would be an utterly impossible situation?"

"Sorry, old boy, they're adamant. We meet again in ten days,
and I promised I'd have your answer. Think it over. Talk to
Poppa. And get back to me as soon as you can. We're anxious
to fly with this."

Three days later, as Nielson entered the offices of Robert Nielson & Associates for the first time in his life, he felt like a walking
time bomb. The decision to approach his father had been the
hardest he had ever made. What finally convinced him was not
only the fear of losing a major commission but the realization
that the problem was likely to crop up repeatedly. One way or
the other, he would have to deal with it.

"This way, please." A leggy brunette led him past a series of
open chambers where draftsmen and lesser architects labored
over easels and blueprints. At the end of a long hallway, massive
bronze doors opened into a suite filled with modern sculpture,
oversized chairs and sofas, and a circular conference table.
Floor-to-ceiling windows split by marble pilasters overlooked
the heart of downtown and a view that would inspire any architect: a skyline of his own creations.

Near the doorway, a trio of built-in spots highlighted a model of an extravagant beach house, complete with guest cottages, pool and cabana, tennis courts, and landscaped gardens—a retreat the great man was no doubt building for himself and wives to follow. Gold-framed awards and diplomas made a mosaic of the wall behind a round raised platform. On it, the recipient of the honors sat at his desk, unsmiling.

"Hello," said Nielson. He wondered if he should offer his hand, then decided not to. "Good of you to see me."

"I'm very busy. What do you want?"

In the absence of an invitation to sit, he remained standing. "Bickman Oil wants me to design their new headquarters. And they want you to serve as consultant."

"I don't consult."

"I assure you, it wasn't my idea to involve you. But it is an incredible opportunity and could be rather a plum for me. It wouldn't take long for you to approve my designs."

Robert Nielson's expression was impassive as he asked, "Why should I? You're a competitor."

"I'd like to think so, but I'd be deceiving myself. Someday, perhaps. At the moment—hardly."

"The point is: What made you become an architect in the first place? You only did it to capitalize on my name. And now you want my seal of approval?"

"My decision to be an architect had nothing to do with you—except, possibly, that you supplied the genes to propel me in this direction. I've done everything I could to dissociate myself and to make it on my own. I told you, this wasn't my idea. I don't need anyone double-checking my work. But I felt the situation might come up again and we should settle it now."

The older man squinted through his spectacles. "Get it through your head, Hughes, I'm not running a charity for opportunists. There's only room in this city for one architect named Nielson, and that's me. I don't know where you got the idea you could run around getting commissions on the basis of your bastardy, but if you ever try to exploit my name again, I'll ruin your reputation so fast they won't even hire you to build a doghouse. Now get the hell out of here and stay out!"

Cold rage gripped Nielson. A sea of retorts flooded his brain, but he knew the futility of lashing back. Every muscle in his body was taut with hatred for the man who had sired him, the man whose genius he so admired, the man whose character he now despised.

Clenching his fists, he turned and walked out of the office. Robert Nielson was right. Philadelphia *wasn't* big enough for the two of them. He knew what he had to do. In the back of his mind, he had known it for a long, long time.

PART
IV

21

MARCH OF 1977 came quickly for Torie and Jeff, ending their first year of marriage, a year filled with happy moments and major adjustments. His greatest complaint was that her frantic pace left few evenings free for the easy, informal get-togethers and grass-smoking sessions he loved, yet she could always find time for the opening nights and glitzy charity events Ellory dragged them to. If Jeff wanted to see his friends, he soon learned, he saw them in the daytime.

The Center City Mall had proved a far greater challenge than Torie expected. Water easement disputes, union hassles, building delays, and a critical press, along with continued harassment from environmentalists and neighborhood groups, had added months to the completion date. Nevertheless, she finally managed to achieve her goal: the transformation of a shabby stretch of land into a bustling shopping district, and the masterminding of a difficult project which, despite unexpected legal, construction, and other costs, proved profitable to her and her partners.

Even more important was the fact that a large volume of work now came her way via the Goldman brothers. Her company doubled its worth in a short time, and then doubled it again. By the fall of 1977, Di Angelo Enterprises had enlarged its staff to forty-four employees, including first-rate financial, legal, engineering, and architectural consultants, who occupied all three floors of the building. As a growing force in the city of Philadelphia, the company was drawing more and more notice.

"I need to talk to you, Pig." Torie clicked off the intercom, swiveled around, and reached into a cabinet.

Peggy was there within seconds. The trauma of Frankie's death still haunted her reflective moments and always would.

After the initial shock, however, she had thrown herself into her work so completely that she had had little time for musing on what might have been. Torie had purposely tried to fill Peggy's free hours, if not with office work, with errands, chores, and whatever would prevent too much introspection. Peggy knew it and was grateful; thanks to Torie, she was emerging from the tragedy with added strength and maturity.

As Torie promised, too, Peggy had grown with the company and now enjoyed the title of executive vice president. She had her own office and was required to present a smart appearance, with posture and demeanor to match her position. Because of Torie's increasing unavailability and frequent absence on business, Peggy often found herself running the company. "You rang, master?"

Her personality still delighted Torie, particularly now that she could take pride in her friend's professionalism. "Better sit down for this one."

"Oh?" Peggy nodded readiness for whatever. Her loyalty had not diminished since they were childhood soulmates playing fantasy games; if possible, it was even stronger now. Whatever Torie wanted she was ready to give. "You know you're seeing the mayor at ten."

"I know. I've got half an hour. Listen, I had a thought for the Gibraltar Insurance complex."

"I forget which—"

"It's a leasehold deal. We own the land, Gibraltar's leasing it from us, and Goldman's building the buildings. The great thing about leaseholds is that you reap in the dough without getting involved in construction and operation. But Mort wanted our opinion on some of the sketches they're considering. See if this one reminds you of anything."

Peggy glanced at the design, raised an eyebrow, and handed it back. "St. Francis Tower."

"Exactly. Only the architect happens to be *Robert* Nielson and he wants a bloody fortune. Mort told me the man's gone crazy. His fees are astronomical. So I thought . . . possibly—"

"You thought why not see if his son's available. Nielson gets the commission, Gibraltar saves zillions, the Goldmans become heroes, and they're all indebted to little Miss Wonderful. Have I missed anything?"

"Only the question you're dying to ask."

Peggy's gaze was unflinching. "What's the answer?"

"I don't know," she said, suddenly thoughtful. "I won't deny I'd like to see Nielson again. I'm sure we've both changed a lot in six years. But I wouldn't be involved on this project, unless—"

"Unless he asked you to be. And you want *me* to make contact so you don't stick your neck out and get your head bitten off. Right?"

"Damn you! Why are you always three steps ahead of me?"

"Because you're so obvious. Does Jeff know about Nielson?"

"No. His name's never come up."

"Is Nielson in the phone book?"

"His number's disconnected. You'll have to play detective."

"All right, Watson. Give me four or five seconds."

"The mayor will see you now, Miss Di Angelo." A sharp-voiced secretary with turquoise contacts ushered Torie into the second-floor chambers. The decor was oppressive: thick tapestry draperies, stained-wood walls with elaborate moldings, gilt-framed paintings, ornately carved furniture. Definitely not her taste, but then, very little in Center City was.

Cal Ponti stood to greet her. "You're looking lovely as always, Torie. What about those 76ers? Think Wilt the Stilt'll win us the title?"

"Let's hope so." She liked sports but had no time to follow them. "I must've passed twenty-five prisoners standing out in the hall. Don't you ever worry about security?"

"No, our deputy sheriffs keep a close watch. Remember, City Hall isn't only the seat of government. It's also one of the largest courthouses in the country. We've got fifty-eight criminal court-rooms operating almost daily."

"It still seems odd that people who make laws share quarters with people who break them. Ever thought of building a separate criminal justice complex to hold the jail, detention center, and courthouse? Then you and the council, the assessor, the city attorneys, and so forth, could have City Hall all to yourself."

"I'm willing if you'll raise the money." He buzzed the intercom. "Bring my coffee, Lois. Join me, Torie?"

"No, thanks." His relaxed manner did nothing to put her at ease. She had been nervous about seeing him and now she knew why; the aura of power he exuded in his own setting was formidable. "I don't know how you manage to stay so calm under pressure. Don't you sometimes wish you were back in the fish business?"

He smiled. "Some say I never left it. Seriously, my father was smart enough to realize that I handled people better than I cleaned fish guts, and he always sent me out to call on customers. I made a lot of good friends that way—restaurateurs, caterers, retailers—and it paid off. Last election, they supported me ninety-nine point two percent."

She wondered where he got that unlikely statistic, then realized it didn't matter. He believed it, and somehow he had a way of making others believe it too. "I came to discuss an idea that could make you a hero—even a bigger one than you are. It could swell the city tax base and rejuvenate the whole downtown area."

"I'm all ears."

"Good. I'd like to remodel the Bellevue Hotel into a very exciting multipurpose building."

"The old Bellevue-Stratford? That's not a hotel, it's an institution. Every president since Teddy Roosevelt has stayed there."

"All the more reason to fix it up."

"They used to hold those fancy dances there. Remember the story about the Clothier kid wanting to take Grace Kelly to the Assembly? Those biddies on the committee told him, 'No way, José. Not unless you marry the girl.' So little Grace married a prince instead and laughed all the way to the throne. Hell, the old Bellevue's practically a shrine to the Main Liners. Did you know Tom Edison did the original electric work?"

Before she could answer, he went on, "Closed down in '76, over a year ago. Bunch of people died there."

"Twenty-nine, to be exact. But the health department says Legionnaires' disease isn't a threat anymore. Listen to me, Cal. The property's available for eight million, and I'd be willing to pump in another fifty million to give the city a stunning multiuse tower with thirty-five floors of luxury hotel space at the top, ten floors of offices, and two floors at the bottom for restaurants, shops, and ballrooms."

"One of us must be crazy. My figures add up to forty-seven stories."

She leaned forward eagerly. "Yes, I *know* there's a gentleman's agreement that no building can rise higher than Billy Penn's statue on your roof. It's custom and it's tradition, but it's *not* the law. There's absolutely no legal mandate or ordinance that can keep me, or anyone, for that matter, from building a structure taller than forty stories. What's to stop me?"

"Well, the City Council, the zoning board, the art commission, public opinion—you want more?"

"That's why I need your help. I need *you* to speak to these groups. Use your wonderful persuasive powers to convince them that the Center City skyline's about to explode. *Someone's* going to break that 548-foot height limit and it might as well be me."

"You've got the chutzpah for it, I'll say that. But you're not being realistic. That's been the highest peak on our skyline for almost a century. Everywhere in the city, from any location, you can look up and see Billy Penn's statue on top of City Hall. Once you lift that ban, the sky's the limit. Every developer in town'll want to build the city's tallest structure, and next thing you know, poor old Billy'll be drowning in a sea of skyscrapers. Forget the forty-seven floors, Torie. Lop off seven, and I'll do what I can to speed approval."

"But that's not the point. I wouldn't be wasting your time if it were just a renovation. You're the only person who has the power and charisma to convince the citizens that downtown needs a shot of adrenaline. It's practically *pleading* for revitalization. That damn height limit is the one thing that's keeping us from attracting the kinds of major investors and corporations we desperately need if we're to stay competitive with other cities. Right now, you know what we are?"

"Tell me."

"We're a sleepy town somewhere on the map between New York and Washington. Cities are exploding all around us, yet this stupid, archaic tradition condemns us to a skyline of flat-roofed overgrown stumps that the architects literally had to *squash* to build. Our retail climate is pitiful. Can't you see what a dynamic skyline would do for downtown? For the whole *city*?"

"Probably turn us into a Houston or an Atlanta—all glass, brass, and glitter."

"But that's what we *need.*" Easy, she told herself. Don't sound hysterical. "I've worked months on this project, Cal. I've got potential backers, I can guarantee ninety-five percent preleasing for 280,000 square feet of prime office space, and I've got commitments for a first-class restaurant and a designer clothing store. I'd be willing to do whatever it takes—public meetings, discussions, testifying before the council and the zoning board, *anything.* Think what a building boom could do for the local economy. Think of the thousands of new jobs, the increased office and retail space, the tax revenues, the influx of tourists and executives to shopping districts . . ."

"Would you change the façade?"

"I wish I could. I'd like nothing better than to strip it bare and face it in granite. But it's a landmark and I can't, so I'll just build upwards in the same style. The new roof will be an exact replica of the old, turrets and all, only higher. In other words—"

"In other words, you'd expect a tax incentive for improving a historical building?"

"Why not? It's part of my proposal." She placed a folder on his blotter, then added, as if it were an afterthought, "You know, I have a decorator friend who got stuck with a roomful of very elegant office furniture he ordered before a client changed his mind. I was thinking . . . I could probably do him a big favor by taking it off his hands. You might even be able to use it here. As a gift to the city, of course."

"That's very generous," he said, noncommittally. "I'll talk to my aides about the hotel and get back to you. Frankly, though, I think you're crazy."

"Maybe." She flashed her most persuasive smile. "But isn't that how all great ideas start?"

Late that afternoon, Peggy rapped three times and entered. "Well . . . there's good news and there's bad."

Torie looked up from her desk. "What's the good?"

"The good news is that Nielson Hughes is not available, and you're not about to get involved with him and muck up your marriage."

"Don't be silly, I . . . What's the bad news?"

"Bad for him, not for you. Apparently, he was offered the job of designing the new Bickman Oil building some time ago, on condition that Daddy serve as consultant."

"*Oi vay.*"

"Precisely. So he bit the bullet and approached his old man, who promptly became apoplectic, told him to stop trying to cash in on his name, and threw him out of the office. That's the story making the rounds, anyway."

"Oh, God."

"Poor baby was so upset, he packed up and moved to Arizona, where Daddy isn't quite so well known. One of the guys at his old firm says he swore he'd never live in Philadelphia again."

"It's just as well." Torie shrugged. "He really is talented. And at least whatever he does in Arizona will be judged on its own merits."

Peggy stopped in the doorway. "You still haven't gotten that Swedish stud out of your system, have you."

"No comment."

"No comment needed. I read you like a neon sign."

The decision to move to Scottsdale, a luxury resort community on the eastern border of Phoenix, had come hard to Nielson. Much as he liked the idea of living twenty-three hundred miles from his father, he would miss seeing his mother and his friends, and he hated being so far from Betsy and a familiar civilization. Yet the location was ideal. The town, already third largest in the state, was burgeoning like a flowering cactus. Frank Lloyd Wright's Taliesin West campus, along with Paolo Soleri's famous gallery-workshop, gave the community a heightened architectural consciousness. Even more attractive, the city's most prestigious developers had offered him an immediate partnership.

Before leaving Philadelphia he had continued to send flowers, letters, and gifts to the Richardson house. Every attempt to reach the occupants had failed, however, until the morning of his departure, when Matt Richardson called.

"You've known Betts a long time, Nielson. You've been a loyal friend to her. But you'll have to understand what she's going through. She's deeply depressed and won't see anyone."

"I quite understand," he had answered. "It's only that . . . I'm positive I could help her if she'd let me. My feelings go far deeper than whether she can walk or sits in a wheelchair. If you could talk to her and perhaps convince her that—"

"I can't rush her. She's not only dealing with her own affliction, she's carrying the burden of her mother's death. She feels none of this would have happened if she'd been more forceful and insisted Simone not drive—which is absurd, because Simone did what she wanted no matter what any of us said."

"You have my deepest sympathies."

"Thank you. Don't give up on Betts, Nielson. She may come out of this one of these days, and when she does, she'll need her old friends."

"I wouldn't dream of giving up. I've left a standing order with the florist, and I intend to keep phoning until she talks to me."

"That's the spirit; I hope she catches it. And good luck to you out West."

Six months later, Nielson flew home for his mother's birthday. After the party and five straight hours of margaritas, he took a mariachis band to Rittenhouse Square. They gathered outside the town house and serenaded at full volume until the police came and hauled them down to the station for disturbing the peace. Despite the indignities of being arrested, Nielson had no regrets. The next morning Betsy took his call.

Cal Ponti waited eight weeks before getting back to Torie about the Bellevue; his answer was an unqualified no. Her proposal to change the beloved society bastion to a mixed-use building, and to jazz up Broad and Walnut streets by overshooting the traditional height limit, was about as popular as syphilis. In Philadelphia, he reminded her, an unwritten law was just as binding as a written one.

After strong pleas and repeated offers of concessions, Torie was forced to accept his decision. Knowing the mayor was limited to two terms by city charter and would be out of office in a few years, she was tempted to buy the hotel and try again with the next administration. Intuition, however, told her she could better invest her money.

She relinquished her option to the Bellevue (which another developer promptly bought) but maintained her link to City Hall. Interior designers on her staff, in fact, were already drawing up plans to beautify the mayoral office at no cost to him or the taxpayers.

Ponti was pleased by the handsome new furnishings, and to show his gratitude, he passed along a tip that a valuable residential building was in deep debt. Torie investigated, and after a series of complicated negotiations that guaranteed the tenants financial inducements and relocating assistance, she bought her first property on the north side—the Walnut Street block—of Rittenhouse Square.

The realization of her childhood dream thrilled her tremendously, but the euphoria merely honed her appetite for more of that precious location. She phoned several key persons to make her desires known, and the calls paid off. Eight months later, when a second parcel on the block became available, she was alerted early, and was able to buy it before anyone else knew it was for sale. Somewhere in her mind, a vision was starting to take shape . . .

That same year, 1978, saw Di Angelo Enterprises scoop up four Society Hill apartments at a distress sale, acquire a stretch of undeveloped waterfront in South Philly, and win a contract to build a massive housing complex in the heart of North Philadelphia's black community—transactions that kept Torie busy setting up six new corporations in partnership with Gibraltar Insurance.

Her satisfaction at engineering these coups was exceeded only by her determination to keep expanding and to take on new challenges as fast as they came along. As Peggy said, she was on a roll . . . and spinning like a whirlpool.

One night in December, Torie came home to find Jeff reading in bed. "Hi, honey," she said, dropping her briefcase on a chair. "The party lasted later than I thought it would."

He looked up with mild interest. "How'd it go?"

"Well, Jim Wygant got swacked and made a pass at Jan Coleman, who was trying to make time with Ronn Eason, who told his secretary, Zelda, that her breath smelled like ten-day-old Limburger. I don't know about Christmas parties—they seem to bring out the worst in people."

"Maybe they're a catharsis. We all need to get things off our chest."

She stopped undressing and walked over to him. "Is something on your chest?"

He patted the bed. "Sit down a minute."

She perched on the quilt. "Something about us? Something making you unhappy?"

"It's not a big unhappiness. What I'm trying to say in my halting way is that I miss you. I miss taking walks in the park. I miss going out for cheesesteaks and a movie. I miss the ordinary, simple pleasures of life. Sometimes I don't even feel as if we're married. It seems we don't do anything together any more."

"But we—"

"I know. We go to society affairs and public functions and family dinners. By the way, Lisa called and they're expecting us Sunday night."

"What's Sunday night?"

"That's my point. You're so damn involved, you don't even know. It's a tiny little holiday called Christmas. Look, honey, I'm not trying to make problems. But I see that company of yours growing bigger and bigger and sprouting branches and tentacles like some monster plant in a sci-fi movie. I see you getting pulled in deeper and deeper and it worries me."

"It won't always be like this. Once I get where I want to get—"

"Where *do* you want to get? My Zen master had a saying: 'The higher the monkey climbs, the more you can see his butt.' I love your butt, but not from a distance. I don't want us to be one of those 'modern' couples who go their own ways and lead separate lives."

"I don't either." She wrapped her arms around him. "I love you. I don't ever want to do anything that hurts you."

"I'm not hurt," he said, stroking her hair. "Just try to fit your husband into that crowded datebook once in a while. What about this weekend? No one's using the house in Unionville. We could leave Friday night and be back for Sunday dinner."

"I'd love to get away, Jeff, honestly. But I promised Mervin Lewis I'd stop by his open house on Christmas Eve, and I can't antagonize him now that I'm finally able to afford him. And Ellory's got me lighting candles at Christ Church that afternoon."

"Couldn't you cancel?"

"That's only Saturday. I've got a big meeting Sunday."

"On *Christmas*?"

She nodded. "The property owner's coming to be with his mother, and he's only here for the day. It's not *my* idea of how to spend Christmas, but he owns sixty-four thousand square feet in Bala Cynwyd, and unless I can firm up the deal and apply for a zoning change—"

"What about next weekend? Can't we get out of that New Year's Eve party?" Her face gave him the answer, and he shrugged. "Well, I tried."

"I'm glad you did. I *have* been neglecting you, and neglecting myself, too. I'll make a New Year's resolution to do better for both of us. I promise."

"That's all I wanted to hear." He drew her to him and found her ear. "You know, lovebug, I wouldn't mind becoming a father someday. Is motherhood anywhere in your master plan?"

"Of course it is."

"Would you care to project a date?"

She looked to see if he were serious. "You mean the exact day I'll give birth?"

"No, I mean the day you'll stop taking the damn pill."

"That's easy. Give me, say, a year—one year from now. By January first, 1980, I should have the business where I want it, and enough of a staff to leave me free to become a mother. On that day, I'll discard all pills, jellies, jams, and whatever, and devote concentrated effort—if that's the word—to the making of baby Goldman."

"I second the motion."

"It'll be good for the baby, too. I'll be almost twenty-nine, you'll be thirty-three, and all the studies say that mature couples make better parents."

"Just so we don't get *too* mature." He reached under her sweater. "Has anyone ever told you you have great jugs?"

"The florist said I had nice marigolds."

"That doesn't count." He slipped a hand into her bra and found her smooth, full breast. "I'm beginning to feel inspired."

"Me too." She lay back on the pillow. "Do you really think we can make a baby?"

"Maybe not the first time." He kissed the side of her neck, and slid his leg up over her thigh. "But we'll practice till we get it right."

Once committed to the idea of having a baby, Torie felt less obligated to heed Jeff's pleas for immediate togetherness. She knew that as soon as she started "breeding" she would have to relegate her business to second place. Without making a conscious decision to do so, she felt justified in devoting the next twelve months almost exclusively to work.

Because she hadn't discussed her reasoning with Jeff, the stepped-up pace mystified, hurt, and disappointed him. Often tempted to remind her of her New Year's resolution, he forced himself to be patient. The flurry would only be temporary, and she would *have* to slow down when she got pregnant.

Sensing their son's unhappiness, Sylvia and Mort Goldman offered to send Jeff and Torie to a marriage counselor. He declined the suggestion and made them promise not to interfere. As soon as he got back from Washington—he was off to protest nuclear power after the Three Mile Island accident—he and Torie would have a long talk.

And they did, but little changed. One of the few happy moments they shared that year came on December 31, when, with great ceremony, they flushed Torie's pills down the toilet, toasted each other with champagne, and went to bed to create a baby.

To their surprise, Torie did not conceive right away. Not until mid-October of 1980, in fact, did Jeff take a call from the gynecologist. He gave a shriek that echoed through the apartment, then phoned Torie's office, learned where she was, and decided he was too excited to wait till she came home.

Grabbing a jacket, he drove twenty minutes to the North Philadelphia apartment project. A large sign greeted his eyes: DI ANGELO PLAZA. DEVELOPER: DI ANGELO ENTERPRISES. CONSTRUCTION: THE GOLDMAN CORPORATION. She hadn't told him what she had named the development, but he had read it in the business pages some time back and had asked about it. Her reply had been quick: "I named it for Papa. I thought it would please him."

"Bullshit!" he had retorted. "You named it for yourself and you know it. I seem to recall that you're my wife. Why don't you ever think about pleasing me?"

"I do."

"Then stop promoting Torie Di Angelo all over the place. Everywhere I go, I see that goddamn name, and we've been married four years. Are you ashamed of being Torie Goldman? Is it too Jewish for you?"

Their argument had grown bitter, and neither had won points. Jeff rarely lost his temper, but this last insult had been too much. Yet now, getting out of the car and seeing his slim, beautiful wife standing by the skeleton of the building, he felt a swell of pride. How thrilled he would be to have a daughter with her mother's exquisite face and figure—or a son he could take on camping trips and teach how to throw a baseball.

He hurried over to where she was talking with three hard-hatted men. "Jeff!" she exclaimed in alarm. "What's wrong?"

"Nothing." He smiled reassuringly, tempted to blurt out the news but afraid he might embarrass her. "Could we talk for a minute?"

"Yes, of course. You know Al Hart, our architect, and this is Andy and Ray who work for your dad. My husband, Jeff Goldman. See what you can do about the problem, gentlemen. Those sprinklers sound like an awful lot of money if they're not mandatory." She linked her arm in Jeff's. "What is it, honey?"

"Didn't you get a message from Dr. Kerner? Their office has been trying to reach you for days."

"I haven't paid much attention. They just want to tell me the test was negative again." She stopped suddenly. "Oh, my God! You don't mean—"

"Yes, I do," he singsonged. "Congratulations, little mother. You're eight weeks along."

"I am? Is he sure?"

"I didn't ask if he checked with a higher authority."

"What fantastic news!" She grinned and hugged him. "When am I due?"

"Around May eighteenth. Think you can fit it into your schedule?"

"I don't know." She tapped her lip. "That's an awfully busy week. If I can't, will you do it for me?"

"I'll sure as hell help. I'm getting a book on Lamaze. Uh, I guess I'd better let you go back. Your boyfriends are giving me dirty looks."

"They're not paying the slightest attention to us. And they're *not* my boyfriends."

"They don't know that. I know how guys think."

"Oh, come on, honey, that's nonsense."

"Is it? How would you like it if I spent twelve hours a day surrounded by women?"

"That's *ridiculous.* I'm not going to dignify your remarks by arguing." With a firm nod, she hurried back to the building site. One of the men took her arm as she stepped over a pile of lumber.

Jeff stood watching for several seconds, hoping she might turn and give him a wave, but she was immediately immersed in blueprints—too involved to remember he had been there or even why he had come.

Frustrated and angry, he climbed into his car and sped off.

22

"CONGRATULATIONS, MR. HUGHES. Welcome back to sunny Arizona." The freckle-faced young man stood grinning by the Buick. "Got any luggage?"

"My bride's bringing most of it next week. Her father insisted on chartering a plane."

"From what I hear, her old man can afford it."

Nielson climbed into the front seat. "Am I to assume my recent nuptials caused a bit of talk around the office?"

"A *lot* of talk." Jack Winslow slipped behind the wheel and started to drive. "They say your new father-in-law owns half of Philly. Wasn't he mayor or something?"

"Yes, he was mayor." And he did own impressive properties, but that had little relevance. Much as Nielson loved money, the Richardson fortune had never influenced his feelings for Betsy.

"How was the wedding?"

"Quite beautiful. My wife looked every bit the princess she is." His wife. After all these years, it hardly seemed possible. Convincing Betsy to marry him had been the hardest selling job he had ever done.

"Was it a big wedding?"

"Big enough. Twelve people. Betsy wanted it very hush-hush—at least in Philadelphia."

"Why?"

"My wife is partially paralyzed. She gets around quite well in her carriage—I loathe the word 'wheelchair'—but she hates people to fuss over her. She was afraid if the press learned of our marriage, they'd make too much of it."

"Is that why you didn't come back together?"

Be patient, Nielson, he told himself. He disliked answering

such questions, yet he knew he was well regarded by his employees, and naturally they were curious about him. "Yes, that's the reason."

That wasn't the reason at all. Betsy was simply bringing so much therapy equipment, he needed time to convert the extra bedroom into a partial gym. Fortunately, their cramped quarters were only temporary. The new house, the one he had been designing in his mind for months, would soon be on his drafting board.

"Could I ask something personal, Mr. Hughes?"

Nielson glanced sideways. "Haven't you been?"

"I mean about your work."

"What is it?"

"What happened with the Bates Corporation?"

"That's no secret. When I came here five years ago, they offered me a partnership. I was quite proud of myself until I found out they had an entire organization of 'partners' and the title was meaningless. They wanted to add me to their production line of mindless, faceless drones churning out subdivision houses."

"What did you do?"

"Borrowed money, opened my own office, and spent most of that first year drunk or stoned because my genius went unappreciated. Then I heard about the new Native American Museum in the works and offered my services. At first they thought my design was too radical, but I convinced them—"

"You were right. The Sun Pyramid's the biggest tourist attraction here, isn't it?"

"I don't care about tourists. Some love it, some despise it, but everyone goes to see it, and I'm proud of it. Besides being a work of art, it houses a marvelous collection of paintings, sculptures, and artifacts dating back to the fifteenth century. Visitors not only get some idea of the contributions Indians have made to our culture, they also learn about their current plight."

Jack pulled up to a two-story house on a quiet, tree-lined street. "It's sure an honor being able to serve my apprenticeship with you. Everyone says you're going to be famous, Mr. Hughes."

"They're right, I suppose. I need to be in order to work on my own terms. Thanks for the lift." Nielson climbed out of the car and walked off without looking back.

*   *   *

Pregnancy, much to Jeff Goldman's disappointment, had little effect on his wife's work habits. Except for taking a week at Christmas to fly with him to Bermuda, Torie hadn't missed a day in the office since that memorable October afternoon when, in a strange reversal of roles, he had informed her of her condition.

On the morning of May 20, 1981, Torie's pains struck suddenly, and Peggy sped her to the hospital. By the time Jeff arrived, she was in heavy labor.

He stayed more than four hours by her bedside, calming her, reassuring her, regretting he had never been able to get her to take the time to learn Lamaze. At the crucial moment he donned a gown, accompanied her to surgery, and watched the wonder of birth—an experience that touched him profoundly. When the nurse handed him six pounds and nine ounces of healthy, squalling, black-haired son, he wept with joy.

Torie, too, was awed by the miracle of creating life and felt a new surge of love for Jeff and for the tiny being their love had produced. She vowed she would be a good mother and a better wife, and she still found the idea of going to a marriage counselor, as her in-laws kept suggesting, absurd. The solution to their problem was obvious: She had to spend more time at home, and he had to stop nagging and being jealous. What could be simpler?

And yet, she reflected, even as Jeff kissed her and ran off to call the families, she had spent all her life with a single goal. After working harder than she ever thought possible, she was finally on the verge of achieving it. If Di Angelo Enterprises continued to snowball, she would soon—perhaps in as few as five years—be the biggest developer in Philadelphia. How could she give that up? And why should she? Jeff had promised he understood her ambitions; she never would have married him otherwise. What had made him change?

The answer seemed clear to her. Vows uttered in the heat of infatuation were easier said than kept. In his eagerness and innocence, he simply hadn't realized the extent of her commitment, the constant crises, the demands on her time and energy.

Yet there was reason for optimism. The baby would bring them closer and make them realize how lucky they were to have a healthy, precious son to love. Every marriage had its headaches; the difference was that they had agreed a long time ago never to settle their troubles by divorce. Whatever the problems, they would find solutions—and find them together.

"I'd recognize that baby anywhere. He's got the face of an *angelino*, like his mother. He's going to be a killer, Vittoria. Killer Goldman. He's going to be fighting off the ladies from the day he takes his first step. Mark my words."

"I hope not." Torie grinned down at the cherubic infant in her arms. "They're not going to call you Killer, are they, Michael Francis? I hope the girls will at least stay away until you're housebroken."

Tony Silvano threw back his head and laughed. "You're going to be some mother! You don't housebreak kids, *piccolina*. You toilet-train them."

"Well, whatever. Papa looks amazingly well, don't you think?"

Tony followed her eyes across the chapel in the Church of the Holy Trinity. "*Splendido!* Becoming a grandpapa has done what no medicines, no operations, not even prayers, could do for him. All of a sudden, he looks ten years younger. By the way, Grace said to tell you she was sorry she couldn't be here."

Torie held her reply. This was not a day for bitterness.

"So *that's* where you're hiding the future president. Is he behaving himself?" Jeff put his arm around his wife and beamed at his son.

"He is so far. Dry as the desert. You remember Tony, honey—whoops, I should say Councilman Silvano."

"Please, to my friends I'm still Tony. We met at your wedding. My congratulations on the christening. You have a splendid boy. You must be proud."

"Damn right I am. I thought the service went fine, Tor. It was about as nonsectarian as you can get from an Episcopal minister."

She turned to Tony. "We didn't know whether to have a bris or a baptism. The Episcopal church seemed a good compromise, at least to us, if not to our parents. And it's on Rittenhouse Square, where we first fell in love." Shifting the baby to her shoulder, she patted him softly.

"Will you raise him in the church?"

"No. When he's old enough, he can choose his religion for himself."

Jeff reached toward her. "I'll take his majesty for a while. I want to show him off before he starts hollering again."

"Michael doesn't holler, do you, darling." She released him reluctantly, tucking the white satin blanket around his neck. "He exercises his lungs. There's a difference."

"Tell that to my ears. See you later, Councilman."

"By all means. Let's have dinner some night."

"Sure. Maybe Sara Lee Birds Eye will whip up one of her gourmet meals."

Tony watched Jeff cross the room, then lowered his voice. "You look marvelous, *carina.* You'll always have a special place in my heart. And I hear wonderful things about you. Soon you'll own the whole city."

"Not soon. It might take a week or two."

"I may be able to help you there. I owe a debt to your father. I've always felt guilty that I couldn't keep him out of prison in— when was it?"

"Sixty-four."

"Nineteen sixty-four—so long ago. Perhaps I can ease my conscience by doing something for his daughter."

Instinct warned her about Tony Silvano. He *had* no conscience. Every word he spoke, every blink of his eyelids was solely for the aggrandizement of Tony. And yet she was curious. "What do you mean?"

"I might be able to deliver the contract for the new city library building." He paused to savor her reaction. "You interested?"

"You know I am. I've studied the specifications all week. We're coming in with a fair price and the highest standards of workmanship."

"But it'd help to know what the other bids are."

His smugness irritated her. "What are you getting at?"

"Before you do anything, *piccione,* wait to hear from me." His voice dropped to a whisper. "I'll call you tomorrow, as soon as I get the information."

"What information? Don't involve me in anything shady or illegal. I want no part of it."

"*Dio mio!* Would I do anything illegal? *Ciao, bellezza.*" He blew a kiss. "I'll say good-bye to Frank and Lisa."

Torie had not planned to return to work so soon. Michael was barely two weeks old, and she had expected to stay out three weeks. But she felt eager and full of vitality, and credited her fast comeback in part to her decision not to nurse the baby. Despite Jeff's urging, she saw little reason to be tied down to two- and three-hour feedings around the clock—a chore she willingly entrusted to Mrs. Rennie, their capable Irish nanny. As it turned out, Michael took the bottle happily, his parents were able to close their door and sleep through the night, and everyone was reasonably content.

A ceiling full of blue balloons greeted Torie's arrival at work the day following the christening. Her second surprise was a gift from the staff—a handsome English stroller that Peggy had loaded with toys and parked by the window. After hugging everyone within reach, Torie sank into her chair, delighted to be able to move close to her desk again. The long ordeal was over and she was back doing what she loved most.

An accumulation of work kept the phones busy, the intercom flashing, people bustling in and out of her office all morning. Ellory insisted she start an art collection and talked her into buying a Degas painting for her living room—"an absolute *steal* at the price." Lisa phoned to ask if they could take Michael on the nurse's day off, and Torie consented, delighted that her son had brought her back into her father's good graces. One of these days he might even say something nice to her.

The pace slowed at noon, and Peggy buzzed to announce a call from Councilman Silvano.

"Hello, Tony."

His voice was so low she could hardly hear him. "Bid high."

"What? Can you speak a little louder?"

"No. Whatever you were thinking of bidding, bid higher."

"Are you crazy?"

"Trust me, *bella*. The estimates are too low, and the committee fears they won't get a quality job. Whoever comes in with a higher bid right now walks off with it."

"But that's insane!"

"I can't say any more."

She replaced the receiver numbly, staring at the sealed envelope with the bid for the library building. An immediate decision had to be made. Either she ignored Tony's call and sent the proposal as planned, or she hit a few keys on the computer, raised the figure a digit or two, and got a new printout.

Her first reaction was to trust Councilman Silvano as far as she could toss his bulky body. What he had just done was sneaky and dishonest, and having been burned by her father's and brother's mistakes, not to mention her cousin's long history of lies and deceit, she was sensitive to any hint of wrongdoing.

And yet . . . he had seemed so sincere about wanting to make amends. Besides, if anything went wrong, she wasn't the one to blame; he was. He had supplied illegal data she hadn't asked for, and nobody could prove she had acted on it. A few seconds of her time to revise the numbers might mean the difference between a nineteen-million-dollar contract and no contract. And who'd ever know?

Impulsively, she called up the copy on her screen, tapped the keyboard, and printed a new letter. The increase wasn't large enough to make the estimate seem out of line, yet it *could* be enough to do the job. After licking and sealing the envelope, she dropped it in the Out box. Within an hour the bid, now inflated by a quarter of a million dollars, would be on its way.

23

THE WHITE LINCOLN sedan slowed to a stop where the street ended at the waterfront. A husky black man in a chauffeur's cap turned his head. "We're at Penn's Landing, Miz Torie."

Ellory Davis fumbled for his glasses. "Is that the *Moshulu*?"

"Yessir."

"Then that must be the *Welch Princess* right next to it. Oh, dear—a gangplank. What about my acrophobia?"

"Hush, Ellory. Pretend there's a flock of reporters at the top." Torie leaned forward. "Thanks, Moose. We won't be more than an hour."

"Yes, ma'am." He was at her door in an instant, helping her out.

"It's about time you got a car and driver," said Ellory, combing his hair as they walked toward the boat. "But *Moose,* for God's sake?"

"Benjamin Franklin Moose. That's his name. Think antlers."

"Couldn't you use Ben? Or Franklin?"

"He doesn't like them." She chuckled and took his arm. "When I asked him what people called him, he stood up very tall and said, 'Jes' like the old joke, ma'am. Anything I want 'em to.'"

"A real comedian."

"Don't be such a snob, Ellory. Moose came with the highest references. He worked for a very nice couple before they moved to New York."

"Noo Yawk? Watch your diction."

"New Yorrrrk. Anyway, I feel very safe with Moose. It's like having a bodyguard."

"Is that why you hired him?"

"Umm, not exactly. When I asked Jeff to take Michael to the pediatrician last week, he got mad and started yakking about a mother's duty and all that jazz. I told him it wouldn't hurt him to get off *his* ass once in a while, and . . . oh, what am I getting so upset about?"

"Possibly the fact that your husband hasn't done an honest day's work since you've been married. Does he ever sell any of those wonderful paintings?"

"Yes. His sister bought one. And some friends of hers, I think."

"How charitable. Doesn't it occur to your dear husband that you're supporting him?"

She shrugged. "He never thinks about money. He got along fine on the interest from his trust fund when he was sleeping in a loft and eating brown rice. If I weren't working, he'd expect us to live on twelve hundred a month—with a baby."

Ellory stopped at the foot of the gangplank. "That doesn't bode well."

"It's my fault too. I promised to slow down when the baby came, but so many exciting things are happening. The business is exploding all around me, and Jeff can't understand why I wouldn't rather be home changing diapers. Right now, Michael's very happy as long as he's fed, bathed, and cuddled. When he's old enough to need a mother instead of a nursemaid, I'll be there."

"I'm not sure I will. I may not last the night." Ellory groaned and leaned on the gate. "Officer, is there any other way to board this vessel?"

The guard's face was impassive. "Not unless you want to swim around to the other side. Your name?"

"Davis. And this is Miss Di Angelo. Or Mrs. Goldman—for the moment."

"Go right on up, folks."

"That's easy for you to say."

"Be brave, Ellory." Torie took his hand and pulled him gently. "Close your eyes and pretend I'm leading you up the side of a magic mountain. At the top there's a crystal decanter that never empties. What's your favorite wine?"

"That depends." He swallowed nervously and started climbing. "If we're talking white, the Bernkasteler Doktor has it all over the Gewürztraminer, although one is fruity and one is spicy, so it's not fair to compare them. I suppose if someone held a gun to my head, I'd have to say Bollinger Vielles Vines champagne, made entirely from Pinot Noir grapes grown on a single acre of vineyards—"

"You can stop raving and open your eyes. We're here."

"Allah be praised." Ellory blinked, dabbed his forehead with a handkerchief, and surveyed the scene. They were standing on the deck of a yacht, amidst a crowd of chattering guests. The air was balmy, and the noise level high, abetted by a five-piece dance band.

"I see our hostess. Grab on to me and don't let go." Elbowing through the mob, he maneuvered over to where three women stood by the port railing. Two were typically Old Philadelphia. Their short gray hair fell in sculpted beauty-shop waves, their pearls were large and well-matched, their demeanor guarded and unapproachable. Expensively cut dresses framed their slightly overweight figures.

The third woman peered out from under a three-cornered hat. She wore a ruffled blouse and white silk pants tucked into boots. "Ellory, love," she cooed, spinning around. "How sweet of you to come!"

"Felicitations, Tina." He kissed both her cheeks. "Forty years you've been wed to Cal Ponti? *Mon dieu,* this *is* an occasion! Many more happies, my dear. You know Torie—"

"Yes, indeed." The women shook hands. "I'm sorry your husband couldn't make it. I've known Jeff since he was a baby. Don't tell anyone, but he was always my favorite of the Goldman children."

"He's everyone's favorite," said Torie. "He sends you his love and regrets. He's . . . busy with his painting."

"I understand the creative mind. Tell him we're looking forward to his first showing."

Ellory stepped in quickly. "All right, Tina, I give up. Why the outfit?"

She giggled coquettishly. "It was the children's idea. They said we all had to wear colonial naval uniforms. At least you can't miss our family. We stand out like zebras in a herd of mules."

"I see Cal over there . . ."

Ellory followed Torie's eyes, then turned to take leave of their hostess, but she was already busy with new arrivals.

"Let's pay our respects and blow," Torie whispered. "I don't want the press starting in again about my fixing up the ex-mayor's office."

"Don't call him ex. Call him mayor or he'll bite off your head. If you had let *me* handle that situation instead of barging ahead like a rutting rhino—"

"It worked, didn't it? Cal was there when I needed him. Too bad he couldn't get the charter changed so he could rack up a third term. But I think I've got Borland pretty well sewed up."

"*Pretty* well! I could buy a Rolls-Royce or three for what you gave his campaign. Oh, oh, there's Brayton McGarren. I'd kill to get his magazine to do a piece on you."

"I'm not rich or famous enough for *McGarren's*. And anyway, here comes our host." She smiled warmly. "What a handsome admiral! Now I know why we won the war."

Cal Ponti, decked out in a black navy uniform with gold braid, shook Ellory's hand and kissed Torie's cheek. "Beautiful ladies gave us something to fight for, ma'am."

"If I can interrupt this touching dialogue, we both want to wish you happy anniversary, Cal. I don't know how Tina's put up with you for forty years."

"I think he'd be an exciting husband," said Torie. "Not many men have the brains and guts to work their way up to being the most powerful man in town."

"You haven't done too badly yourself. But I was sorry to hear you lost the city library contract. It wouldn't have happened if I was still in office."

"Lost it?" Her throat tightened. "I haven't heard a word."

"One of my aides told me the committee was all set to give

it to you, but your bid was too high—not much, I understand, just enough to swing it to Pennington."

"Who?"

"A small firm in Chestnut Hill: Pennington Contractors."

Her face paled as the realization struck. "Any relation to Grace Pennington Silvano?"

The ex-mayor nodded. "Her son. Tony's stepson. But from what I hear, Tony had nothing to do with the choice. They went strictly by the figures."

"I see," she managed to blurt. So Tony had done it to her again, and done it in such a way that she couldn't possibly tell anyone how stupid—how utterly gullible—she had been.

A new voice broke into her thoughts. "My compliments, Cal. I hope I'll be around for the fiftieth."

"I hope we'll both be around. Torie Di Angelo, Ellory Davis—you know Matt Richardson, don't you?"

"Yes, we met . . ." She stopped self-consciously.

"It's all right, Torie." Matt smiled and patted her hand. "I can't very well forget you. My life fell apart the day of your wedding."

"I'm so very sorry."

"You wrote a beautiful note. I showed it to Betts. It meant a lot to us."

"How is Betsy?" asked Ellory.

"Doing fine. Matter of fact, she got married in April."

"She did?" The host looked puzzled. "Why didn't we hear about it?"

"The kids wanted to keep it quiet. She married her old childhood sweetheart, Nielson Hughes—Robert Nielson's son. They're living in Arizona and he's absolutely devoted to her. Building her a big house completely on the level so she'll be able to get around in her wheelchair."

"Nielson Hughes . . ." Ellory repeated. "Didn't he do something for you, Torie?"

"Er, yes, ten years ago. He designed the St. Francis Tower." Her head was spinning—first, the shock of Tony's betrayal, and now this revelation. She forced a smile. "I'm so happy for Betsy, Mr. Richardson. If I write her a note, would you forward it?"

"I'll do better than that." He scribbled on a card. "Here's her address. She'd love to hear from you—so would Nielson. He started courting Betts, you know, right after the accident. She was at her lowest then, trying to face up to life as a paraplegic.

I was a wreck, myself. The last thing either of us needed was a lovestruck suitor."

The adjective hurt, yet Torie knew it was true. Nielson had always adored Betsy, even when he was making the most ardent love to her. She had suspected it at the time, though she had never wanted to admit it. "I can understand how you felt."

"Betts refused to talk to him, or to anyone, for about ten months. One night he had a few too many tequilas and came trooping over to the house with a mariachi band. They were so loud and disorderly I called the police. It was the best thing I could've done as far as Betts was concerned. She felt I'd harassed a helpless minority. The next day she took her first phone call from one of the poor victims—Nielson Hughes."

"How delicious! This is better than a soap opera." Ellory lit a cigarette and leaned against the railing. "Do go on."

"Well, Nielson had already moved to Arizona. He began calling her every night, and then morning and night, and soon about the only thing she really looked forward to was his calls."

He paused to check the faces of his audience, and reassured of their interest, continued: "I don't know when he first proposed. But Betts said no, she didn't want to saddle him with her handicap. It took more than four years before she broke down and said yes—and frankly, I don't know if she'd have come through all this without Nielson. Even in the beginning, when she refused to see him, it was important to her to know that a man—a very attractive man—still wanted her."

"If I were a movie director, I'd snap up that plot in a minute," said Ellory. "It has everything. Even a happy ending."

"No, a happy ending would be for Betts to walk again." Matt's frown faded quickly. "But you're welcome to try to peddle it, Ellory, as long as I get fifty percent of the gross."

"Forty or nothing. That's my last offer."

"Come on, bigshot." Torie took Ellory's arm and kissed both of the former mayors. "I'll write Betsy tomorrow. And Admiral Ponti—don't *ever* take off that uniform."

Sleep eluded Torie that night. The news about Nielson had startled her at first, but the more she thought about it, the less surprising it became. Nielson had always fancied himself a hero. She remembered very clearly his telling her how he had played the role of Sir Walter Raleigh in a high school skit, only in his version, spreading a coat wasn't good enough; he had to *carry* the queen over the puddle. Being Betsy's knight in armor and rescuing her from the bleak life of an invalid would fit perfectly with his chivalrous self-image.

Still, Matt's disclosure had been a blow. As far as Torie was concerned, no conclusion had ever been written to the chapter in her past titled "Nielson Hughes." The hope that he would somehow, someday, come back into her life now had to be buried and forgotten. The chapter finally had an ending, and personal feelings aside, it was a good one. Nielson married the woman he had always wanted, and Betsy had an adoring husband who loved her enough to take on her tragic affliction.

Torie climbed out of bed quietly, so as not to awaken Jeff, then sat down at her desk and wrote:

Dear Betsy,

I saw your dad at a party tonight, and he told me your wonderful news. Congratulations and I hope you'll be very happy.

I worked with your husband many years ago, and have great respect for his talents. Your father is very excited about the house Nielson's designing for you.

She started to mention Michael, then stopped. No need to remind her of joys she would never know. Instead, she continued:

My work and family keep me running, but I hope our paths will cross before too long. If you ever come home (to your old home, that is) for a visit, Jeff and I would be thrilled to see you. We both send love . . .

Despite all her rationalizing, addressing the envelope to Mrs. Nielson Hughes gave her a pang. Refusing to think any more about it, she tucked the letter into her briefcase, switched off the table lamp, and crawled under the covers.

Now that she had dealt with the second shock of the evening, she was free to go back to the first—Tony's duplicity. Her feelings for him were a mixture of fury and loathing, tinged with self-hatred for her own gullibility. But such emotions were unproductive. The mistake was irreversible, and she had better move to more constructive thoughts.

Try as she would, however, she couldn't switch off her anger. Even as she attempted to force him from her mind, a part of her brain was already framing plans. Tony Silvano had walked over the Di Angelo family once too often. This time she had an obligation to pay him back.

Peggy paced the floor of the office, her hands gesturing rapidly as she moved. "I can't *believe* you could be so dumb. And Tony, of all people! If it had been anyone else—"

"Okay, okay." Torie slammed down a pen. "I was greedy, I was dishonest, I made a colossal goof. I already know what an ass I am. I don't need you to confirm it."

"Then why'd you tell me?"

"Because you're the only person in this bleeping world I trust. I've learned my lesson. I'd have my tits tattooed before I'd do anything like that again. But I *have* to get even with that son of a bitch. Think of something."

Peggy plopped into a chair. "I haven't time to think of something and neither do you. Do you realize what's on your calendar?"

Torie wasn't listening. "How does this sound? We set up a steamy seduction scene. Tony's convinced I'm going to hop in the sack with him, so we meet at the Barclay, where I've misled him into thinking we keep a permanent suite for visitors. But then—what do I do next? How can I cause a scandal without getting myself involved?"

"When you find the answer, let me know."

"Don't desert me, Piglet. Brainstorm for a minute?"

"One minute." Peggy bowed her head and concentrated for several seconds. Then she looked up. "Okay, you've got the schmuck in the sack. Does he have any physical disabilities you can play on? Could you hide his glasses? Does he wear contacts? I read once where a guy put his contacts in a glass of water by the bed, and his girlfriend woke up in the middle of the night and drank them."

"Don't tell me how she got them back."

"What about allergies? We could fill the room with roses—"

"As a matter of fact, Tony *is* allergic. I remember Frankie saying that he couldn't marry his wife unless she got rid of her cat."

"Hold it. A light just flashed. My sister can't go near cats either. Her allergist gives her cat serum. She takes a few drops under her tongue each week to build up her immunity." Peggy leaned on the desk excitedly. "What if you were to sneak some of Kelly's cat drops into his drink?"

"How would I do that?"

"Bring along some booze with the drops already in it. You're not allergic, so they wouldn't bother you."

Torie grinned. "By George, I think you've got it! The perfect crime. No weapons, no witnesses. I'll do it! Piglet, old girl, how can I show my gratitude for that fiendish mind of yours? What if I got you those pretty pearl earrings you saw at Nan Duskin?"

"I wouldn't accept them."

"What would you say if I got them, anyway?"

Peggy's eyes filled with mischief as she walked to the door and glanced back over her shoulder. "Meow?"

24

==

TWO WEEKS PASSED before Torie learned that Councilman Silvano would be representing his district at a meeting in City Hall on July 22, 1981, to discuss the Penn's Landing waterfront project. Dressed in a white Adolfo suit with red trim, she entered the assembly room and spotted Tony chatting at the conference table with his aide, Max Lemo—known to be a member of an organized-crime family.

Seeing her, Tony jumped to his feet. "What a surprise! I never thought such an important lady would attend such a small meeting."

She smiled warmly. "This could be a major redevelopment. I want to be in on the ground floor."

"You will be, *bella*, I give you my personal guarantee." He slapped his cheek with sudden recall. "*Mama mia*, I owe you an apology. I should've let you know about the library building. You got the letter?"

"Yes."

"You were a naughty girl." His voice dropped to a whisper. "If you'd added a few dollars to your secret bid, you'd have walked away with it."

The man was incredible.

"It's my fault, Tony. I should've listened to you."

"Luciano! *Paisano!* District Council Forty-seven's heating up. Lunch next week? I'll call you."

She watched him slap backs for several minutes, then turned to find a chair.

"Sit by me, Vittoria."

"I don't want to get in your way."

"How could you get in my way?" He looked at her intently. "How could you *ever* get in my way?"

She averted his gaze demurely, as if embarrassed by its message.

"You smell like musk," he said, lowering his voice again. "You bring out the animal in me." His face was a mask of innocence as he pushed her chair to the table. To an onlooker, he might have been saying, "I hear we're due for rain."

The meeting had barely started when she felt a foot touch her shoe, then press against her ankle. Struggling not to show amusement, she pressed back. Soon the foot was roaming up and down her calf, and by the time the meeting was over she feared for her pantyhose.

"Shall we continue the redevelopment discussion over coffee?" he asked aloud.

"Thanks, but I have to get back to my office."

"I'll walk you to your car."

The minute they were outside, he asked, "When can I see you? When can we be alone?"

"Oh, no, Tony," she said nervously. "We mustn't even think about something like that."

"What is 'mustn't'? That word's not in my vocabulary. My blood boils for you and you feel the same for me. It's God's will, *carina*. The Lord gave us these feelings."

"But there's nothing we can do about them. We're too well known. We shouldn't even be walking down the street together."

"I'll find a place for us to meet. You're right. It's important that no one see us. Good things become bad things when someone gets hurt."

He sounded like a robot set on Automatic Seduce. She stopped at her car. "We'd better say good-bye, Tony."

"We can't say good-bye. You know as well as I do that we're destined to be together. If we were alone, without these other people on the street, I'd take your hand and show you what you do to me—even now, here, standing on the sidewalk."

The vision seemed to inspire her. "Hmm . . . well . . . I *might* have an idea—"

"Tell me."

"My company keeps a suite at the Barclay for traveling VIPs and small gatherings. If you could take the elevator . . . no, no, forget it, it's too risky."

"What's risky? Tell me and I'll decide."

"I suppose you *could* get off at the fifteenth floor and walk down two flights—"

"When?"

"Well, the lunch meeting should be finished by three. We'd better say four to be safe. Four o'clock—Friday?"

He consulted a black book. "Review board . . . finance committee . . . make it four-fifteen. What's the suite number?"

"Thirteen twenty-one." She looked up guiltily. "Tell me it *is* God's will, Tony. What we're doing isn't wrong, is it?"

"I swear to you, you'll go home Friday a better wife and mother for our having been together. Marriages can grow stale—people tend to take their close ones for granted. When you're full of love for one, you pass it along to everyone."

"I can't deny that."

"*Dopo domani,*" he said, with a wave. "Take care of yourself, *bella.*"

Friday afternoon, Torie strode down the corridor to thirteen twenty-one, turned the key in the lock, and entered the two-room suite. A busy young man at the front desk had confirmed the reservation and paid little attention as she signed the register for Councilman Silvano. In her mousey brown wig, horn-rimmed glasses, and plastic rain slicker, she looked like a typical harried secretary.

Locking the door, she slipped off the coat, spectacles, and hairpiece, rolled them into a bundle, and tucked them into her tote bag. A glance at her watch told her it was exactly four P.M.—fifteen minutes to prepare the scene.

She hurried into the bedroom and set the bottle of serum-spiked champagne and two glasses on a table. Nervously checking her wrist every few minutes, she rolled down the spread and fluffed up the pillows on the double bed. Next, she filled her arms with bath towels and stuffed them in the closet.

Those chores accomplished, she found some romantic music on the stereo, examined her hair and makeup in the mirror, tucked her pink cashmere into her skirt, and sprayed herself with Shalimar. If only she could sneak a cigarette . . . but no, leaving telltale remains in the ashtray would be foolish. The moment she sat down to collect herself, a knock sounded. "Who is it?"

"Let me in, *cara.*"

"Just a second." Her hand was shaking as she opened the door and watched Tony close and lock it behind him.

"Come to me," he said, taking her hands. "This charming child I knew so many years ago has blossomed into a hot-blooded woman. Tell me, dear heart, are you frightened?"

"Yes. A little." Her eyes widened as she looked up at him. "I . . . hope you'll be patient with me. I've never done anything like this before."

"You won't be sorry." He led her toward the bedroom. "Ah, *che bellezza*! I see you were expecting me."

For a moment, she was tempted to plead nervousness, grab her tote bag, and run out. So much could go wrong with her plan. What if he didn't want champagne? What if the cat serum didn't work? What if his wife was having him followed? What if . . .

"Don't be afraid, *bambina.* Tony's here. Nothing bad will happen to you." Mistaking the cause of her fears, he drew her to him and kissed her. She made no protest, having already decided that a few preliminaries were inevitable if she was to be convincing.

"Your lips are sweet," he murmured, "as soft and sweet as I always knew they would be."

The kiss seemed endless. Much as she tried to relax and fantasize that he was Nielson, the thought of Frankie, Papa's imprisonment, and the lost nineteen-million-dollar contract made pretense impossible. "C'mon, Tony, let's get under the covers and have some champagne."

"We'll do whatever you like." He reached for the zipper of her sweater.

"No, no—you get undressed in here, crawl in bed, and wait for me. I'll get undressed in the bathroom."

"You're modest?" he asked with amusement.

"I know it's silly, but I can't help it."

"It's a virtue to be modest. I find it refreshing . . . desirable . . ."

She let herself be kissed again, then pulled away and disap-

peared into the bathroom. Several minutes later, she emerged
still clothed. "I—I need you to undress me. I need a drink. I
guess I'm not as cool as I thought I was."

"It's all right, *bella*." He reached for the bottle and filled both
glasses. "There's no hurry, is there?"

"Well, I just learned this morning that a developer from Texas
is arriving at six." She perched on the bed, took the glass, and
whispered, "Let's drink the whole thing down. I don't want to
waste another second."

"No, no, you're right. We can't afford to. *Salute.*" He finished
the champagne in six gulps and watched her take several minutes
to consume hers. The instant she set down her glass, his hands
were on her, loosening her skirt and pushing it down over her
hips. "We must hurry now so we can take our time when it matters."

"Here, let me." She jumped off the bed and struggled out of
her skirt, prolonging every movement. What had gone wrong?
Why wasn't he reacting? Reaching for the bottle, she refilled
their glasses.

"No more champagne," he said firmly. "Come to me." His
voice was impatient, and she sensed she could delay no longer.
Panic was setting in. What could she do? An attack of guilt? A
sudden case of herpes? A tearful confession that she was too
scared to go through with it?

Kicking off the covers, he reached out and pulled her to his
naked body, his hands tugging at her pantyhose.

"Tony, please—wait!"

"I've waited too long and so have you. I can't wait any
longer." Before she knew what was happening, he had rolled her
on her back and was lying on top of her.

"M-my sweater! I have to—"

"Your clothes *excite* me, *bellezza.* Sometimes being half-
dressed is more sensual—" He stopped in the middle of his sentence and wrinkled his nose, as if smelling a strange odor.
"Damn!"

"Is something wrong?"

"No, just a—a tickle—"

Torie closed her eyes and prayed.

"I don't know what's—ah—ah—ACHOO!" His whole body
shook with the force of the exhalation. A series of convulsive
sneezes followed rapidly.

"You poor dear!" she exclaimed. "Here, drink this. It'll help you."

He wiped his eyes with the sheet and gulped down a second glass of champagne. "*Madre d-dio,* w-what is ha-ha-CHOO!"

Both hands shot up to his dripping nose as he jumped out of bed, ran into the bathroom, and slammed the door. The moment he did so, Torie scrambled to her feet, put on her skirt, corked the bottle, and grabbed the glasses and his clothes. She stuffed everything into her carryall, leaving only his watch and wallet. Then she ripped the sheets and blankets off the bed and threw them into the hall.

Loud foghorn blasts were coming from the bathroom as she dashed to the stairway and ran down thirteen flights to the main floor. After taking a second to straighten her wig, she crossed the lobby slowly and hailed a cab outside, on Rittenhouse Square. Several blocks from her own building she got out, entered through the basement, and stopped long enough to empty her bag into a storage cabinet.

A few minutes later, coatless and purseless, she marched into her office, sat down at her desk as if she had never left the premises, and buzzed the intercom.

"Achoo?" came Peggy's anxious voice.

Torie exploded into giggles. "Gesundheit!"

Late the next afternoon Torie sat at her bedroom writing table, while Jeff, cuddling Michael in front of the TV, watched the fastidious preparations for the wedding of Lady Diana Spencer to Prince Charles. Peggy had just called to report that the contents of the storage locker had been incinerated and to recommend a story of special interest on page two of the *Evening Bulletin.*

Opening the paper eagerly, Torie spotted the headline COUNCILMAN CLAIMS FRAME and read:

In a bizarre incident that has authorities puzzled, City Councilman Anthony J. Silvano, a lawyer and congressional aspirant, told police he was invited to a Barclay Hotel suite at 4:15 P.M. Friday to meet a prospective client, who allegedly drugged and stripped him and stole his clothes.

Silvano, 49, insists that a man calling himself John Pella was part of a plot by political rivals to smear him with scandal. According to the councilman, Pella slipped knockout drops into a glass of champagne. An hour later, Silvano awoke to find himself naked in bed, his watch and wallet intact, but his clothes gone.

Claiming he was under the influence of the drug, Silvano admits he hid behind the door, rang for the maid and gave her a phoney story. "He told me he was from out of town," said Bonnie Predd, 41, a twelve-year Barclay employee. "He said his wife had gotten mad at him and run off with his clothes. He offered me a hundred dollars if I would find him something to wear and not tell anyone. I called security right away."

Silvano's story appears to have discrepancies. Mark Burstein, the reception clerk, told police that a woman with brown hair and glasses, not a man, registered for the suite in Silvano's name. Room service shows no record of having delivered champagne, and police have been unable to locate anyone who fits the description of Pella.

The investigation will continue.

"What are you grinning at?" asked Jeff, switching off the set.

"A funny write-up about Tony Silvano." Torie handed him the newspaper. "Someone stole his clothes and left him bare-assed in a suite at the Barclay."

"Sounds like a jilted mistress, or one of his bimbos. What is it they say? 'When a Republican gets in trouble, it's money. When a Democrat goofs, *cherchez la femme.*' "

"It's obvious *someone* doesn't care for Tony."

"Can't blame them. He's always struck me as being the slippery type. I can't imagine why your father would have him for a lawyer."

"Family loyalty." She took Michael from his father's arms. "Come to Mommy, sweetheart. Why are you such a fussy boy? How're your diapers? Where's Mrs. Rennie?"

"She's gone. Tomorrow is Sunday, her day off, remember?"

"Oh, dear. I think he needs a change."

"I'll do it." He took Michael back again. "You don't know where anything is."

"What kind of a remark is that? I know where his diapers are."

"Forget it." He smiled at his son and set him on his blanket. "I don't want him to hear us argue. Infants are very smart. They sense everything."

"Were we arguing?"

"I wouldn't exactly call it happy talk."

"We *can* be happy, honey, if you'll stop expecting me to be something I'm not."

"I know. It's all my fault." He fastened the baby's diaper and tickled his tummy. "There you are, young man. Ready to go out and bat some balls around? By the way, I'm taking him over to Marcia's tomorrow. His cousins have been asking to see him. I assume you'll be going to the office."

If only she could tell him he assumed wrong, but she couldn't. She desperately needed ten or twelve hours to catch up on paperwork and to think through the Penn's Landing proposal. Within the last five years, suggestions for developing the waterfront had called for a cultural complex, a festival marketplace, a recreation center with an ice rink, even a mini-Disneyland. But since all plans for the city-owned property had fallen through, the area had become a monument to political ploys and procrastination. This time, she hoped, things would be different. "Could I at least spend the morning with my son?"

"Sure—why not?" He hoisted Michael to his shoulder and walked out of the bedroom. "We'll be here till eleven."

25

THE PHILADELPHIA DAILY NEWS was merciless. Monday's front page featured a three-column picture of an angry-looking Silvano shaking his fist in the air. The caption read: "I was framed!"

Under the heading COUNCILMAN CAUGHT WITH PANTS DOWN, the tongue-in-cheek article repeated the attorney's tale of foul play by a "political assassin" who disguised himself as a woman when registering for the suite, then vanished mysteriously, taking a bottle of drugged champagne and Silvano's clothes.

According to police, the councilman could give only a sketchy description of the mysterious "John Pella" and said he had no time to press charges.

Torie read the piece with satisfaction—and then concern. If Tony ever got angry enough to blurt out the truth, the situation could prove embarrassing. And yet, he couldn't change his story now . . . any more than he could admit to being in a hotel room with a married woman.

Halfway into the morning, Jane Riley, her executive secretary, announced a call from Mayor Bill Borland. He was anxious to have her master plan for Penn's Landing so he could set the machinery in motion to designate her as the official developer. After thanking him and reassuring him he would have the proposal by the end of the week, Torie was startled to get another call—from Councilman Silvano. Wary but curious, she picked up the receiver. "Hello, Tony. How've you been?"

"Why did you do it?"

"Do what?"

"Don't play games! How did you slip the poison in my glass? What kind of drug did you give me?"

She wondered if he was taping the call. "I haven't the vaguest idea what you're talking about. If this is a joke—"

"How could you hurt your own cousin—a man who has never had anything but love in his heart for you and your family?"

"Your family loyalty couldn't be more obvious. We were talking just the other day about how cleverly you maneuvered that city library contract for your stepson."

"*Dio mio*, what are you saying? We went by the figures on those estimates. You know what happened. Your bid was too low."

"My bid was too high."

"Too high? Who told you that? Are you going to listen to some gossiping imbecile who got his facts from the janitor? Or are you going to listen to a city councilman who sat on the decision committee?"

"The gossiping imbecile happens to be the former mayor of Philadelphia. And he's not going to care much for your description of him. Bye-bye, Tony." She hung up quickly, delighted to have made her point. If he hadn't realized the reason for her behavior *before* the call, he'd have no doubt about it now.

*   *   *

The week was hectic, and Friday night, after a late meeting at the office, Torie fell asleep in the Lincoln on the way home. Her short rest was shattered by a report on the car phone that fire had broken out at her North Philadelphia property, the newly completed Di Angelo Plaza. "Swing around, Moose. Make a U-turn," she said urgently.

By the time they arrived, police had cordoned off the whole complex. Torie jumped out of the car and gasped. One of the four apartment towers was a bright, blazing torch. Flames leaped from upper-story windows, panicked voices screamed to be rescued, firemen scrambled to set up ladders and hoses.

After identifying herself to the police, she rushed over to where Mort Goldman was standing, next to a red car with a revolving spot. "Mort, I can't believe this—"

He patted her shoulder. "Take it easy. They're doing everything they can. We may be lucky tonight—there's not much wind."

"How'd it start?"

"They think it was a kid smoking in bed." He pointed to a man in a helmet and raincoat. "The chief just sent up a team to chop holes in the roof and let out the fumes so they can go in with their hoses."

"But why? Shouldn't they try to contain the blaze?"

"No. The first thing they do is open up the building as much as possible. Heat rises, and when the smoke lifts, the temperature drops a few degrees. Then the firemen can get in there, see what they're doing, and start knocking the hell out of the blaze."

Torie squinted, her eyes beginning to sting from the thick, black clouds that swirled into the sky. Frightened yet fascinated, she watched the lead man swing a nozzle over his shoulder and start up the ladder, with the hose running between his legs. At the top, he twisted the spout, and a powerful stream of water gushed forth.

"Do you think it'll spread?"

"Not unless the fire gets out of control, and it won't. That steel-and-concrete construction's got too much integrity. The steel's been sprayed with fireproofing, so the building can't fall. But the bricks are a veneer. If it gets hot enough—"

The sound of footsteps made her glance over her shoulder. A familiar figure came striding toward her, his face flushed and anxious. "Jeff! What on earth—?"

"Are you okay?" He stopped to catch his breath. "I've been worried to death about you. You said you'd be home over an hour ago. I thought you'd had an accident."

"Sorry, honey. I got so upset when I heard about this, I made Moose drive right over. How'd you find me?"

"They announced the fire on the news, and I hoped you'd be here. Don't ever do that to me again."

"I'm really sorry."

"Forget it." This was not the time to launch into one of his tirades about her lack of consideration. Under the circumstances, he could hardly blame her for being concerned. "That damn fire's so hot it's drying the sweat on my forehead. What's happening, Dad?"

"They've cleared out all the residents—at least, they hope they have. The chief ordered a safety net in case anyone's still in the building."

Sounds of a scuffle turned their attention to a crowd of evacuated tenants; one man in overalls was shouting and waving his arms. Jeff hurried over to investigate and found himself in the role of mediator. After several tense moments, he was able to resolve the dispute, quieting and consoling the distraught parties.

His face was ashen as he walked back toward his wife and father. All around him, men of every age, mothers cradling babies, children in their nightgowns and pajamas, stood weeping as they watched their homes and possessions fall prey to the flames. Jeff's voice was incredulous. "How could something like this happen, Dad? Aren't there fire codes and strict preventive measures you take when you build a high rise?"

Mort shrugged; his skin was an eerie orange in the light of the blaze. "We distinctly specified a first-rate automatic sprinkler system. The best they make. I can't understand—"

"The . . . sprinkler system wasn't installed." Torie had no choice but to blurt out the truth. Someone would tell him soon enough. "Sprinklers weren't mandatory, except in the basement, and the extra pipes were so costly we'd have been forced to raise rents. Rather than deprive the tenants of the low-cost housing we'd promised them, we put in smoke detectors."

"But automatic sprinklers were in the plans. I specified them myself."

"I know they were. My architect and I studied the design very carefully. We felt that as long as the code required a sensitive detection system, fire escapes, pull-station alarms, and two separate exits on every floor, the tenants would be well protected. We even put hand extinguishers by the exits."

Mort stared at her, rage beginning to narrow his eyes. "You *canceled* the sprinkler systems without consulting me?"

"There was no *need* to, Mort." Torie's voice was high-pitched and strained. "Al was very careful to check with the Fire Prevention Inspections Unit. They wouldn't have given us the permit if they'd had the slightest doubt."

"So you took it upon yourself to tell *my* builders to shortcut the fire-safety specs in order to skim a few bucks off the costs?"

"You can't blame me for this! I followed every law. I did nothing illegal. And I can't understand why the detectors didn't warn the people in time."

"I'll tell you why." Jeff's tone sliced into her. "Most of those people are dirt poor. That man in the overalls told me he needed money to buy shoes for his kid, so he unscrewed the smoke alarms and sold them for five bucks!"

As if to underscore his anger, a sudden gust of wind brought the stench of rotten eggs. "Oh, Christ—gas," groaned Mort, pulling Torie back. "They make it stink so you can tell when it leaks." The chief grabbed his bullhorn. "Clear the building! Get out of the way!" Three firemen hurled themselves onto the safety net; others jumped from windows, leaped off ladders, and came rushing out the entrance. Five seconds of ominous silence . . . and then . . . a shattering boom as fragments of concrete, glass, and brick rocketed into the air. Sparks lit up the sky, spreading and falling like Fourth of July fireworks and finally settling into a heap of steaming rubble.

Pandemonium followed. The crew from ladder one turned their hoses on the pile, while firemen dashed back into what was left of the building, searching for signs of life. The police worked frantically to restrain the crowd, Red Cross disaster crews passed out blankets and first aid supplies, rescue squads labored to revive half-asphyxiated firemen. A TV reporter, determined to capture the faces of shock and horror for the late-night news, slipped past the fire lines and turned his camera on the hapless victims.

Mort Goldman sighed and wiped the soot from his brow. His voice was weary as he turned to his daughter-in-law. "One gas concussion, one apartment tower gutted, God knows how many injuries, and more than a hundred families who've lost everything they had in the world. Add to that the blow to our professional reputation, and enough lawsuits to keep us all in court till the day we die. I hope you're satisfied with the bucks you saved, Torie."

Too shaken to reply, she stood shivering in the night air, clutching Jeff's arm until Mort was out of sight. "Why does your father blame me? The fire wasn't my fault—"

"Wasn't it?" He pulled away from her. "Maybe if you'd put in the sprinkler systems he specified, those people wouldn't be freezing in their nightclothes with no place to go."

"So it *is* my fault. Is that how you feel?"

Jeff's shoulders slumped. "I'm not sure how I feel anymore. I just know I've had it with your drive and your greed . . . your self-centeredness . . . your broken promises. I can't take it any longer."

"What does that mean?"

"It means that we made a mistake. It means that our life is miserable, and our marriage is in the same shape as that high rise you built. I don't know you anymore. The woman sharing my bed is a stranger. I only know you'll never give our relationship the time and nurturing it needs. I'll find a place to stay tonight and pick up my things tomorrow."

"Jeff, I—please! You and Michael are my life—you're the *reason* I work so hard. Don't you remember we agreed we would always talk things out? That we would never get a divorce?"

"That was a long time ago. We were different people then— at least I was. I believed in you. I was sure you loved me enough to make our marriage the most important thing in your life."

"But it *is* the most important thing. I'll do anything to keep you," she pleaded, her voice cracking. "I'll change. This time I mean it—I can do anything I want to do. You have to believe me!"

"I've been believing you, Torie, for over five years." The night air, now that the fire was under control, had grown cold. "I'm tired," he said. "Tired of being walked on and shoved into a corner, tired of living my life only to serve your needs. I have needs too, but you haven't the slightest idea what they are."

"Don't do this to me," she whispered, tears wetting her cheeks. "Come home. We'll talk it over."

"There's nothing to talk over except Michael, and we can do that tomorrow. I have no hatred for you, no anger, no bitterness—only a raw, gaping wound that's going to take a long time to heal."

"Honey, wait! We'll go away together! We'll take that trip to Florence to meet those friends you're always talking about—"

"No. Maybe we can be friends someday, when the hurt dies down. I wish you well, Torie. I wish you only the best." He slung his jacket over his shoulder and walked toward the wooden barricade. "Here comes Moose. He'll see you home."

26

DIVORCE HIT TORIE harder than any of her earlier traumas. Her mother's illness, her father's disgrace, Frankie's death in Vietnam—all these had been situations over which she had no control. But the breakup of her marriage was different. This relationship had been her personal responsibility, and her husband had given ample warning of his frustrations. What a fool she had been not to heed them.

After Jeff walked out, she tried every possible way to mend the breach, even setting aside her pride to plead with him, to offer compromises and concessions—to make deals. His lack of interest eventually convinced her he was determined to end his so-called martyrdom and regain his self-respect. She would gladly take the major part of the blame for their problems, but not all. Much as he had protested living mainly on her income, he had made no attempt to improve that situation by getting a job, or doing anything other than peddle a few paintings to his relatives.

Mervin Lewis urged Torie to seek alimony, assuring her that the senior Goldmans could easily handle it, but she declined, not wanting to force her husband into another situation of dependency. Her decision in late 1982 to settle for minimum child support and joint custody greatly relieved the Goldman clan—all except for Jeff, who hadn't worried. He knew Torie was generous in her personal life, and that she loved Michael enough not to cause a rupture that would hurt him.

The following year, 1983, was a period of great change and adjustment. For the first time in her adult life, Torie blocked off one day a week for herself and her family. Every Sunday she took Michael to see his aunt Lisa and his grandfather, who doted on the boy. Frank had been so shattered by the divorce, however, that he could hardly bring himself to be civil to his daughter. And some days he didn't even try.

On a Sunday in late January, Torie found her sister studying a recipe book in the kitchen. "Sorry to bother you, Lis, but I've got to collect Michael and go home. Papa's not talking to me today. Is he okay?"

Lisa raised her head. "He's okay."

"Does he ever mention me? What does he say?"

"Oh, the usual. That you're ruining your life. That you're chasing fame and money and all the wrong values. That you think you're too good for us now that you run around with society."

"Society! Oh, brother." Torie dropped into a chair. "He should only know. Sometimes I feel like a Ping-Pong ball. Ellory bats me in, and the bluebloods bat me out. I gave a party last week, and you know who came? The politicians I give money to, the lawyers, bankers, and businessmen I deal with, my office staff, and one 'consciousness-raised' young couple from Chestnut Hill. Rittenhouse Square and the Main Liners all sent regrets."

Lisa frowned. "They're not your friends. Why do you even invite them?"

"Because they *are* my friends, in a sense. I know them all; I've been in their homes at board meetings and benefits. Who the hell do they think they are to snub me? Sometimes I get so pissed off, I feel like buying up all their fancy property and renting only to minorities. I can just hear them screaming: 'What? You want wops and spicks and niggers and kikes to walk the same hallowed ground as our sacred WASP feet? You want *their* little bastards to go to school with *our* darling children? Over our dead *bodies*!'"

"Italians wouldn't *want* to live in their snooty neighborhood."

"Then maybe I should rent to rapists, murderers, and junkies. Yes—why not? 'Developer Torie Di Angelo is erecting a dazzling new skyscraper on Philadelphia's most exclusive property.

What will it be—a fancy hotel? Luxury apartments? Office towers?' No, you turkeys. It's going to be a halfway house for drug addicts and ex-cons. Right smack on Rittenhouse Square. I'd laugh till my guts spilled out."

Lisa shook her head. "You're full of hatred and bitterness, Torie. You need prayer. Confession. Time to sit down and search your soul."

"I don't need to search my soul. I know exactly what's in there, and you're right. I do hate and I do resent and I'm going to get even with those snot-nosed sons of bitches if it's the last thing I do. And you can bet your butt it won't be!"

After the visit, Torie calmed down enough to meet Peggy for a walk around Rittenhouse Square.

"It's a year and a half today," Torie murmured, as she pushed Michael in his stroller. "Since the fire, I mean."

"I wish you'd forget the damn fire. Let the attorneys worry about the lawsuits. God knows you pay them enough." Peggy took a wool scarf from her purse and tucked it around her neck. In the thirteen years since she had joined the business, the giggly chatterbox had matured into a quiet, serious-minded woman with a wry sense of humor. "I hate lawyers and all their ruses and injunctions. Pimples on the ass of progress—that's what they are. Likewise those idiot insurance investigators. I can't believe how many times they've gone over the blueprints, the fire inspector's permits, the invoices for the smoke alarms . . ."

"I'll never forget watching my building go up in flames. It made me realize how self-centered and ambitious I'd been. Still am, I suppose. But at least I know it now."

"Self-centered, ambitious people are the ones who get ahead."

Torie laughed. "Whatever happened to idealistic little Miss Piggytail?"

"She grew up. For God's sake, T. D., let go of the damn guilt trip and get on with your life. Your personal life, I mean. All those good-looking guys you meet in your work. Isn't there anyone out there who stirs your blood?"

"Not even a ripple. What about you?"

"I'm too busy to think about men. My boss works me too hard." Peggy grinned. "She works herself too hard, too. Do you realize what you've got scheduled this week? First thing Monday, you've got what'shisname—chairman of the Gersten Park City Authority."

"Bill Hall."

"Right. He told me their competition for the trade center attracted fourteen proposals. How'd you get the nod?"

Torie shrugged. "I figured the other developers would all come in with elaborate blueprints. I just handed him a copy of the authority's bond-repayment schedule marked, 'I can guarantee these payments.' What he cared about, mainly, was keeping those bonds afloat—and I knew it."

Peggy shook her head. "You've got the most incredible instincts . . . like a pig sniffing out truffles. One of these days, you're going to out-trump Trump."

"Nothing wrong with *his* instincts. Look what he did in Atlantic City. Sent a whole team of agents to buy up land for him—quietly, before the boom."

"You saw it coming too. How come you didn't jump in?"

"Because the last thing I need, with my name, is to be associated with gambling. Everyone knows the mob controls most of the action. And *paisanos* control the mob."

"What about Meyer Lansky? Bugsy Siegel?"

"That's my point. The exceptions stand out. I learned a good lesson from my dear cousin Tony. Those boys play dirty and there's not a damn thing you can do about it. I never want *anything* to do with them again."

"You think Trump's connected?"

"Politically, yes, but not to the mob. He's too big. He doesn't have to be." Torie stooped to pick up a rattle and poked her head around the stroller. "I'm warning you, Michael. Toss that out once more, and I'm taking it away from you for *good.*" She turned back to Peggy. "I admire Trump."

"The man's a wizard, all right. But he's got nothing on you, T. D.—except filthy lucre." They walked in silence a few minutes before Peggy pointed across the Square with her chin. "What's the latest on those buildings you've been trying to buy?"

The question snapped Torie out of her reverie. "Didn't I tell you? We finally came to terms on building number three. We're closing the sale Tuesday. The owners of number four are holding out, but I'll get it—it's just a matter of price. And if I can ever convince those old fogies to sell me the Historical Society Library, then I'll own all five buildings—that whole block of Walnut street. Imagine, Pig—*one fourth* of Rittenhouse Square, not counting the park. I can't believe my fantasy's finally coming true. I suppose it all goes back to Betsy's party . . . wanting to belong, to be a part of all this . . ."

"What'll you do with that block if you get it?"

"Improve it—develop it. I've got a million ideas churning around, and the residents won't like any of them. But that's enough business talk. Tell me about your life. Did Kelly's boyfriend ever—" She stopped suddenly, bent down, and picked up the rattle. "All right, Michael Goldman, that's *it*. No more toys in your stroller. This goes right in my pocket. See?" She straightened up quickly. "What were we saying, Piglet?"

"You asked about my sister and the answer is yes." Peggy's mouth curled into a smile. "Kelly's boyfriend *did* get rid of his cat."

Jeff's remarriage in 1984, three years after the divorce, came as a fresh shock to Torie—especially since his second wife had all the qualities his first wife lacked. Seemingly devoid of vanity, talent, and ambition, Fran Saperstein Goldman wanted nothing more than to cook, clean, stay home, and produce babies, one of which almost immediately popped out of her willing womb. Another child came soon after, prompting Jeff to tell a friend: "Most guys marry spoiled Jewish princesses or sweet Italian mamas. I married a spoiled *Italian* princess and a sweet *Jewish* mama," a remark that found its way back to Torie.

What hurt even more was the fact that his Jewish mama made him supremely happy. Despite Jeff's good-natured teasing, Torie knew that he had always resented her lack of culinary talents—a lack she never tried to remedy. She would continue to be "Sara Lee Birds Eye" until she died; swapping recipes was not her idea of creative bargaining.

The custody arrangement made it inevitable that she would see her successor fairly often in the months to follow, and to her surprise, Fran Goldman proved to be a genuinely warm, likable person. Even Michael was crazy about his stepmother and his two new half-brothers, and hard as that had been to accept at first, Torie soon realized it was a blessing. The Goldman clan could give Michael what she could never provide: parents and grandparents who loved each other, cousins close to his own age, and the warmth of a close, caring family.

PART
V

27

IN THE SUMMER of 1984, Torie's long-planned bombshell hit with sudden force. The fireworks started when she "leaked" to *Inquirer* columnist Clark DeLeon that she was planning to build a $248-million office building on a prime Center City site, two blocks from City Hall. The item would have been news in itself, even without the kicker: The proposed Di Angelo Tower would soar to a record sixty-two stories, shattering the sacred height taboo and topping Billy Penn's headpiece by 320 feet.

The furor was instantaneous. Screams of outrage came from as far as Delaware and New Jersey, setting off a conflict that divided the city into pros, cons, and a small number of indifferents who thought local officials should tend to more pressing matters. With the help of Ellory, her staff, and Mayor Borland (aiming for the State House in 1990), Torie waged a carefully choreographed campaign for public approval.

First, she gave a luncheon for press, politicians, civic and business leaders, and introduced Paolo Cava, the much-talked-about architect she had imported from Milan. His dramatic thirty-thousand-dollar scale model drew gasps, even from jaded reporters. Alternate bands of gray and black polished granite hugged a rectangular shaft emblazoned with the familiar twenty-foot-high "DiA" logo. Silver mirrored windows framed by aluminum grilles lent a quasi–Art Deco look to the exterior. The stunning structure was crowned with a three-story pyramid of gray-tinted glass.

A fine French restaurant would sit in the center of the rooftop solarium; around it, tables would revolve on a circular platform, affording diners changing views of the city. Di Angelo Tower would not only be the tallest building in town, it would also be starker, sleeker, more glittery and dazzling than anything currently gracing the Philadelphia skyline.

Before the luncheon ended, the hostess rose from the head table and gave a feisty, impassioned toast, part of which ran the next day in the *Daily News*:

"Ecclesiastes said there was a time for everything, and that time is now. It's time for an end to the folly of requiring all skyscrapers to be squashed, stumpy, and subservient to a statue. It's time for an end to the drabness of the stone, brick, and precast-concrete flattops that dominate our downtown. It's time for Philadelphia to burst out of the shadows of Washington and New York and take her rightful place as one of the most progressive, dynamic, talked-about cities of the nation.

"Like so many of you, I have a vision for Philadelphia. I see people flocking here to start careers. I see businesses and corporations setting up national headquarters. I see scholars and historians chronicling our brilliant architectural renaissance. With your help, we can make that vision come true. From now on, may our flat, drab skyline rest in peace. Here's to the *new* Philadelphia, and a skyline as rich and exciting as the visionaries who look up to it . . ."

Immediately following the luncheon, Torie was drawn into a maelstrom of appearances on radio and TV talk shows and at public debates, community meetings, and seemingly endless hearings before the City Council. (Tony Silvano excused himself from these sessions, saying it wouldn't be ethical to vote on matters concerning his cousin.)

Despite forceful, organized, and highly articulate opposition from locals who decried the "Manhattanization of Philadelphia" and saw no reason to "trade a cherished tradition for an office building and a developer's ego," Torie stuck with her crusade, even when the barbs became anti-Italian, anti-Catholic, and openly sexist. The personal attacks only rekindled her rage and resentment, particularly when three-year-old Michael came home from nursery school wanting to know what a "dagobich" was. Yet she managed to keep control. No one knew better than she that without the council's permission, the project was doomed.

As her name recognition continued to grow, so did her speaking abilities and personal magnetism, and her fiery conviction that what she was doing was *right* for the community. Slowly . . . gradually . . . the climate began to change. The more the citizens got used to the idea of shedding their image as a staid old Quaker towne, the more attractive Di Angelo Tower started to look. Torie took quick advantage of the shift to sweeten her offer to the council by increasing the amount of useful public space. She added a health club, open to the public and more street-level shops and areas available for art displays, and she doubled the seating capacity of the lobby.

After an exhaustive, bitter, seven-month battle, her efforts and determination paid off; City Council voted to approve Di Angelo Tower. The height change would be incorporated into the zoning code and Torie could proceed—if not with the council members' blessing, at least with their grudging permission.

In January of 1985 Torie was pleased (though not altogether surprised) to hear from Mayor Borland that she had been picked as the official developer for Penn's Landing, a seven-block stretch of riverfront running north and south along the Delaware. The city's goal, he announced, was to build the site into a tourist and commercial mecca to rival Boston's Rowes Wharf and Baltimore's Inner Harbor.

Torie's plan called for the construction of a hotel and office building, an entertainment center with a movie house, waterfront condominiums, a six-level shopping arcade with outdoor restaurants and terraces, a seventeen-hundred-car parking garage, and a central spire-topped tower (concealing an antenna) to serve as symbol for the project. Its height would be 548 feet, exactly that of City Hall. She wasn't about to jeopardize her recent victory by seeking another variance—at least, not right away.

Once again, she commissioned the brilliant but temperamental Cava. His preliminary sketches for the $1 billion complex, which included placements and concepts but not the actual architecture, were displayed at a news conference in the mayor's office. Reporters duly noted that the donor of the embellished decor and the developer chosen by the city were one and the same, but they were fair enough to add that the refurbishing had been done during the previous administration, and that (in response to cries of corruption and favoritism) the Penn's Landing proposals had been submitted anonymously.

Not that anyone believed such a fable, least of all Torie, who had carefully "let slip" to the mayor and key friends on the council that *her* plan had a needle-topped tower. In an earlier chat with Borland, she had confided her intention to take advantage of the fact that the site was separated from the rest of the city by two major highways, Delaware Avenue and Interstate 95. The Landing, she insisted, was another chance for Philadelphia to break free of its architectural rut and endorse a futuristic development so fresh and exciting that it "defied physics." She would proceed cautiously, however, and keep the scale model "on ice" until plans were farther along.

After the press conference, Torie asked Cava and several others on her staff to stay and answer questions, while she slipped out the rear exit and down the stairs to her limousine.

Moose was standing by the car, his face a study in frustration. "Sorry, Miz Torie," he said, opening the door. "You got company."

"Company?" She peered inside and gasped. Tony Silvano, resplendent in a polka-dot ascot, checked sportcoat, and black slacks, and his short, blunt-nosed aide, Max Lemo, were comfortably settled in the back seat.

"*Ciao, bellissima.*" Tony sat up and patted the leather. "Come in, come in. We've been waiting for you."

"So I see. I'm late for a meeting."

"That's how you greet your own flesh and blood you haven't talked to in four years? You know Max, don't you?"

Torie sighed and climbed into the car. It would be useless to ask them to see her in the office. Whatever was on their minds, they wanted to discuss it at *their* convenience, not hers. "Yes, I know Max. What do you want?"

"Don't be mad, Vittoria. I don't hold grudges, why should you? Bygones are bygones, no? We were foolish young kids."

"I haven't time for grudges, Tony. Please say whatever you have to say and let my driver come in out of—"

"Your driver will wait outside." Tony started to shut the door, when Moose's long arm restrained him. "It's mah-ty cold out here, suh. Mind if I get my scarf?"

"Make it fast," snapped Max.

Moose opened the front door, reached into the glove compartment, fiddled around a few seconds, then extracted a wool muffler. "Yessuh. Thank you, suh."

Tony turned to his cousin. "Congratulations on Penn's Landing. One more feather in your hat—a nice, fat billion-dollar one. You realize that even though it's not in South Philly, it *is* in my district."

"So?"

"You're going to create a mountain of work for my staff and my office."

"I don't know why. The mayor and the council already agreed to lease me the land."

"You know better than that. Verbal approval is merely the start of the long legal process. Right, Max?"

The aide nodded approval. "We gotta set da wheels in motion, Miz D'Angelo. Councilman Silvano gotta write a whole new zoning ord'nance. And after he writes dis ord'nance, he gotta make sure it passes. *Comprenda*?"

"What if I don't *comprenda*?"

"I'm sure you do, *piccina*. Without—let's call it—a personal commitment on your part, the holdups and delays could be endless. And we both know that when a developer has a project on the books, time is money."

"I see." She eyed him coldly. "How much do you want?"

"It's not for *me*, I assure you, only for expenses in connection with your magnificent venture. I think a million—a drop in the bucket to you—would allow me to hire the extra personnel needed to hasten the paperwork and *almost* cover our outlay for office expenses."

"A million dollars buys a lot of Scotch tape."

"You joke about a serious matter. Do we have an agreement?"

She looked thoughtful a moment, then asked, "How would I pay you?"

"That would be worked out. All I need to know today, so I can rush to my desk and start getting to work for you, is that we have an understanding."

"I can't tell you today. I'll have to think it over. I could lose my license if it ever got out that—"

"*Dio mio!* How could it get out? No one knows what we talked about here."

"I'll still have to sleep on it, Tony. I'll call you tomorrow."

"No," he said, firmly. "No calls. Sleep on it if you must. Max will contact you. Remember, there's no way you can develop Penn's Landing without the support of me and my district."

His message thus delivered, the councilman and his aide climbed out of the car and disappeared into City Hall.

Moose hurried back to close her door. "Y'all right, Miz Torie?"

"Yes. You must be freezing. Get in."

He slid into the front seat. "Somethin' sure do smell rotten in here."

"You've got a good nose. Those two thugs want to blackmail me."

"For what?"

"Not blackmail. I mean extortion. They want money in return for a political favor. I'm not about to give them a red cent and for *two* cents, I'd file charges. But I couldn't prove anything. It'd be my word against theirs."

"I was watchin' you every second."

"I know you were. I also saw you slip that gun out of the glove compartment with your scarf. You took a big chance. If they'd seen you—"

"I wasn't gonna let nothin' happen to you, Miz Torie. Jes' say the word, and me and my friends'll—"

"No, no, Moosekins, I don't want you tangling with the mob." She smiled warmly. "But I love your loyalty."

To no one's surprise, the February 1985 issue of *McGarren's* magazine listed the newly renamed Di Angelo Corporation (formerly Di Angelo Enterprises) as Philadelphia's top developer, with assets worth upwards of $700 million. (Torie was always quick to point out that most of the properties were financed up to 90 percent or more, so the worth of the developer was far smaller.) Since 1983, the company had made its headquarters in Di Angelo Parc, a striking monolith of glass and blue pearl granite on Chestnut Street, overlooking Penn Center and the financial district to the north and Rittenhouse Square to the south. The starkness of the façade, save for the ever-present "DiA" logo, was somewhat relieved by an inner courtyard with fountains, flowering shrubs, and stone benches where working and residential tenants took their breaks, gossiped over sandwiches, or simply enjoyed the fresh air.

In keeping with the building's exterior, Torie's office on the thirtieth floor was bereft of extraneous decoration. Hailed by *Architectural Digest* as "a glittering collage of milky textures, Miesian-clean, geometrically pure and spacious, with a paradoxical feeling of intimacy," the all-white room featured "floating" wood beams, curved windows, and the world's most photographed desk—white wrought-iron with insets of blue, green and violet glass. Beside it stood a high-tech communications center, complete with film projector and stock-quotation machine. First-time visitors often felt as if they were aboard a space ship.

"Can you imagine a little sperm swimming all that way knowing he was going to turn into Tony Silvano?" Peggy's nose wrinkled as she approached her employer's desk. "Bad news, T. D. The FBI says you have no case."

"How do I make one?"

"You have to wear a wire and tape a conversation."

"What if they search me? The hoods, I mean."

"I asked that. The agent said they can hide the bug in your purse or briefcase, but it's safer to put it under your breast. If anyone touches you there, you kick 'em in the crotch."

"Swell. You know what happens if you fight those guys? They slice up your face. For starters."

"Exactly. That's why you're insane to even think about tackling the mob. My suggestion is to forget it. Just tell Tony it's no deal."

"What? And lose a chance to put that shyster behind bars? I might not—oh, c'mon in," she called, to a rap on the door. "Al, Ralph, have a seat. Pig, you stay, too."

The staff architect and head accountant took chairs around her desk. "This won't take long. You all know my driver, Moose. He spoke to me a few days ago about his church, the Holy Hope Baptist something-or-other—Jane can give you the name. Anyway, the foundation's crumbling and the city's threatening to condemn it if it isn't repaired."

Ralph rolled his eyes.

"It's not what you think. Moose has never asked me for a cent. All he asked me to do was intercede with the city and get a delay so they can raise the money. But I *want* to do something. I'd like you to fix up that church, Al. Do whatever it takes, up to a million bucks. And Ralph, use the funds in my charity trust."

"Ellory'll have a stroke," said Peggy.

"Probably. But as of right now, Ellory's through telling me where to give money. I'm tired of his advice and I'm tired of giving a fortune to causes I don't give a damn about, just to get on some board or some list of names. From now on, I'm giving where *I* want to give. Oh, and, Peg, I want no publicity on this. Just tell the church it's a gift in honor of Ben Moose."

*   *   *

The following week, a female FBI agent came to Torie's office and taped a small bugging device to the skin under her breast. Torie had told Max Lemo she would deal *only* with Tony, and when the councilman picked her up for a drive in his car, she handed over her first payment of a hundred thousand dollars. The bug was later retrieved, the conversation transcribed, and the FBI began the long, slow investigative process needed to bring charges.

After rewriting her will to make sure Michael, Papa, Lisa, Peggy, and Moose would be taken care of for life, Torie wasted no time pondering the wisdom (or otherwise) of her action. Setting her staff to work on Penn's Landing, the Gersten Park trade center, and various other projects, she turned her attention back to Di Angelo Tower. Drawing up plans and getting approval had only been the beginning. Now that she had official sanction, she would have to put together a package of marketing studies, tax abatements, and creative inducements attractive enough to generate financing.

Her immediate challenge was to find a lead tenant, and after careful perusal of the reports, she knew exactly whom to target and what incentives she could offer—one by one—to ice the cake. Blue Star, a national health insurance company, was her biggest prospect, but the company was adamant about wanting "signage," its logo on the façade. There Torie balked. Only one logo would grace her buildings.

The ill-timed (from her point of view) release of a Coldwell Banker survey pointing up a nationwide glut of office space only spurred her determination not to let Blue Star get away. The sugar-coated package she offered was enticing: plush office furniture imported from Denmark, extra parking space, a gym and locker room with showers for employees; and the capper: six months of free rent. Even though Di Angelo Tower wouldn't be completed for two years, she was finally able to charm Blue Star into taking twenty-two floors. Soon after, two separate law firms signed up for a total of thirteen floors.

Armed with the tenant contracts, she and her corporate lawyer, tax lawyer, and chief accountant walked into the office of Putney Vickers, president of the Liberty Bell Savings & Loan Association. From previous deals, she knew him to be as tough, sharp, and focused as she was; neither wanted to bother with small talk.

"Monopoly time?" he asked, shaking her hand.

"I hope not," she said, smiling. "In Monopoly, only *one* person wins."

Thus began a series of give-and-take negotiations that kept them in closed chambers for twenty-three hours but eventually ended in a joint venture—a partnership agreement that gave Liberty Bell 50 percent of the building in return for putting up 98 percent of the financing.

The day the papers were to be signed, however, Vickers called to say the deal was off; his board had decided the project was too controversial. He was sorry, but she would have to find a new equity partner.

28

A CARTOON IN the Sunday, August 17, 1986, edition of the *Inquirer* caught Torie's eye: A tilt-nosed brunette with "DiA" monogrammed on her collar, sleeve, purse, and briefcase, was staring up at a gleaming half-built tower. Two hard-hatted construction workers were talking, and the caption read: "I *told* you she doesn't give a damn for tradition. She won't even pay off the mob."

The spoof followed the week's sensational announcement, seventeen months after the FBI began its investigation, that a federal grand jury had indicted Councilman Tony Silvano and his chief legislative aide, Max Lemo, on four counts, including a one-million-dollar extortion attempt.

"When are you coming in, Mommy?" called a voice. "You promised you'd play with me."

"Be careful, darling. I don't like you splashing about without your water wings." Torie set down the newspaper, swung her legs to the ground, and tucked her short hair into a bathing cap. She tightened the straps of her yellow Latex suit, well aware that it clung to her trim body, and for an instant she regretted that there was no one around to admire it.

"When are you coming *in*?"

"Right now, ready or not!" With a leap to the end of the diving board, Torie held her nose and jumped into the pool, landing with a squeal and a splash.

Michael clung to the side as she swam to him. "That's not how you're s'posed to dive."

"That wasn't a dive. Want to go piggyback?"

"Yeah!" He wrapped his arms around her and pressed his small body to her spine. "Giddyap, horsey!"

"What do you say?"

"*Please* giddyap, but don't let me fall off."

"Why not?" She started a slow breaststroke. "You're such a good swimmer you don't even need your water wings. Why are you afraid to fall off?"

"I'm not afraid, I just don't like it."

"I guess that makes sense." She laughed and carried him to the shallow end, singing nursery rhymes as she jiggled him on her back. Then she floated him on a raft across the pool and swung him around in circles until they both were weary and waterlogged.

"I think we've had it, Master Goldman," she said, supporting him as he paddled to the steps. "You're just in time, Ingrid."

A blond woman in a white uniform lifted Michael out of the water and blotted him with a towel. "Our swimmer needs a shower and some dry clothes before dinner, yes?"

"Are you going out tonight, Mommy?"

"No, darling, but you are. Don't you remember? Daddy and Fran are taking you to the country for a week."

"Kin Ingerd come?"

"Ingrid's going to take her own vacation. And when you come back Sunday, she'll be all rested up and *very* anxious to see you."

"Okay." He nodded approval and reached for his nanny's hand. "Hey, Ingerd, kin we play puppet show before you go?"

Alone in her spacious roof garden atop Di Angelo Parc, the building that housed her corporate offices ten floors below, Torie raised the lounge chair, rubbed sunscreen on her arms, and leaned back against the cushion. Ever since she had moved into her spectacular fortieth-story penthouse two years earlier, she had been planning to take a few weeks off to enjoy it. So far, however, time spent with Michael was the only pleasure she allowed herself.

Taking a deep breath, she tried to relax and get some perspective on her situation. True to the cliché, money *hadn't* brought happiness. The harder she worked, in fact, the more she realized how many other factors motivated her: the need to create something out of nothing; the desire to be a visible, positive force in the community; and, as always, the drive to wield power—the power to do unto others as they had done to her.

A columnist once asked if she agreed with Donald Trump's claim that making deals was an art form.

"No," she had answered. "Only a mammoth ego who'd lost touch with the world would call dealing with hard cash and real estate an art form. It's a game—a game of skill, luck, and a smattering of BS. But *honest* BS."

In her own mind, she was every bit as good a deal-maker as Trump, and maybe better. He had had advantages: being born a male and a WASP, attending Wharton, inheriting a successful business from his father. Yet all the traumas in her life had helped form character and build confidence. Today, she could join Trump or anyone else at the bargaining table and not feel intimidated.

After Liberty Bell Savings had pulled out of Di Angelo Tower, she had devoted her energies to finding a replacement and had finally signed up a major pension fund. Now, only a year from the day Mayor Borland had broken ground for the project, the dream so many said would never be realized was half-completed.

A sigh of frustration slipped out. No, money hadn't brought happiness. It hadn't bought her a close family or the home of her own she had always wanted. But thanks to Ellory, it *had* bought her a Vlaminck still life, a Degas dancer, a Brancusi bronze, and the services of the city's top decorator. Yet what good was it being surrounded by exquisite objects if she never slowed down long enough to look at them?

An iron railing, low enough not to hide the view of Billy Penn's hat and high enough to afford protection for Michael, circled the open deck where she sat. Japanese cherry trees, potted petunias, and Heavenly Blue morning glories provided a garden background for a large Henry Moore torso. Built-in heaters kept the temperature reasonably comfortable, and theoretically, she could sunbathe from May to October.

Luxuriating on the terrace, however, was not typed into her

schedule. Every hour of every day, including Sundays, when she still took Michael to visit Lisa and her father, was crammed with pressures and problems. At every public appearance she was beset by reporters, people with complaints, people who liked her, people who didn't, people who were simply curious about a rich, beautiful local celebrity. Whoever said being famous was easy?

Vowing to take a vacation with Michael as soon as she could set aside a few days, she reached for a Special Delivery envelope that contained the week's batch of clippings. Most were one- or two-line mentions, quotes, misquotes, and stories she had already seen. A *Newsweek* article, "Where Do You Go from the Top?," had brought comments from people who praised the piece, as well as from those who urged her to sue for slander. She reread the last two paragraphs without emotion:

> Charges that Di Angelo is unsophisticated may be right. She has narrow, limited tastes and little interest in historic preservation. Efforts by architects to incorporate traditional elements in her buildings go unheeded. Yet sophisticated or not, she has unerring instinct for the kind of sleek, majestic tower the public wants.
>
> What revs her motor is not the quest for societal improvement or artistic integrity, but a personal drive to stamp her own identity on colossal self-assertions of steel, glass, and granite. Di Angelo's creed can be summed up in seven words: "I can do anything—and I will."

Another clipping drew her attention; it was one she hadn't seen before, by Connie Morris of *Celebrity Times*:

> A new type of celebrity has emerged in the last two decades: the real estate developer. Contrary to the stereotyped oil-rich Texan in boots and cowboy hat, whose favorite art works are Cadillac showrooms and *Playboy* centerfolds, the 70s–80s breed has radically transformed the image.
>
> Manhattan-based Donald Trump brought out bold ideas and the money to match. Leona Helmsley, wife of developer Harry Helmsley, used glitz and guts to fire up her husband's empire. And now, Philadelphia's Torie Di Angelo combines Trump daring and showmanship with Helmsley chutzpah, and once again, life imitates art, producing a real-life soap opera star . . .

"Are you decent, beauty? Your beast is here."

Torie sat up with a start. "Oh, it's you. C'mon over."

"You *did* say I could nip by this afternoon." Ellory Davis dragged a chair under her umbrella and fanned his sweating brow. Time and a heavy cocaine habit had been unkind to the man; his face was haggard, his jowls sagged, his dilated pupils seemed unable to focus for more than a few seconds. When he spoke, his hands gestured nervously. "Reading all that good press I got you?"

"I don't know how good it is. I don't mean it's your fault. I'm just not thrilled to be called a soap opera star."

"I wish someone would call me that. All they ever say is that I remind them of Truman Capote—" He stopped to cross himself. "Rest in peace. I saw Michael on my way in. Most five-year-olds have all the charm of a dissected fly, but that little tyke is incredible. I'll bet he photographs like a million."

"Your job is to keep him *out* of the media, remember? He's enough of a kidnapping target as it is."

"Pity. I could get him a cereal commercial tomorrow." He eyed her suspiciously. "He doesn't look very much like a Goldman. Are you sure about his parentage?"

"What a question. Of course I am."

Ellory stroked his chin. "He looks more like Tony Silvano to me. A little hanky-panky in your past?"

She chuckled. "You really are a shit-disturber, Ellory. I pray nightly that they throw the book at that scumbag."

Her occasional profanity no longer bothered him. At least now she knew better. "Splendid PR on your part, calling in the FBI. It's done wonders for your image. I heard some man on a talk show say, 'The Mafia targeted Di Angelo for a shakedown and she turned 'em in. That broad's got balls.' If you'll recall, I remarked about that particular asset years ago."

Torie leaned back in her chair. "You didn't 'nip by' to discuss anatomy, Ellory. What's on that wicked mind of yours?"

"Several things. God, how I despise lovely summer days!" He wiped his forehead and pulled out a notebook. "First of all, Helen Gurley Brown wants to assign a writer to interview you for *Cosmo*. Before you say—"

"That's fine. I adore Helen."

"Wonderful! What about a second interview with Connie Morris?"

"*Cosmo*, yes, Connie, no. I can't stand that bitch. Whatever I say she'll twist and distort."

"If you refuse, she'll only be bitchier. And *Celebrity Times* has a wide circulation."

"I don't care."

He knew better than to push. "All right. Next question: Is there anything we can do about that house in West Mount Airy?" He said the word "house" as if it had been condemned by the health department. "Can't we get your family a more stylish address?"

"I've talked to Papa till I'm purple. I've offered them a beautiful apartment with a view, I've offered to send them on a cruise, I've offered a car and driver; they simply refuse everything. They don't approve of the way I earn my money so they're not about to help me spend it."

"Real estate was a good enough profession for your father."

"It's fine for a man. But God gave women wombs, you see, and if they're not hatching babies every five minutes, something's wrong. Besides, Papa blames me completely for the divorce. He's convinced Jeff and I would still be married if I didn't have a career." She tapped a cigarette on the table. "He's probably right."

Ellory offered a light. "Did you tell him you didn't want the divorce?"

She blew the smoke over her shoulder. "He has selective hearing. Hears what he wants to hear. And Lisa's the same. Do you know the one thing she broke down and let me get her for Christmas? A new freezer for the church. Some gift. Any more questions?"

"Yes. Would you offer a dying man a drink?"

She laughed. "The refrigerator in the cabana has fruit juices, diet sodas, champagne—help yourself."

"Are you crazy?" He groaned and covered his eyes. "You expect me to walk across this—this misplaced sun deck? Are you forgetting my acrophobia? I deserve a bonus just for coming up here. Got any diet champagne?"

"No, but there's vodka and bouillon."

"Hold the bouillon. And don't stint on the ice."

A moment later she handed him a tall glass. "How many questions to go?"

"Only two," he said, gulping noisily. "This one's a bit tricky, and it's not a question. I want you to start thinking about politics. You're a natural, you know. You've got everything it takes."

"God, I hope not. I hate politics."

"I'm not talking small time—except, perhaps, to get your foot in the door. I'm talking the big ticket"—he paused for emphasis—"the White House."

"Oh, good Lord!" Her hand went to her head as she returned to her chaise. "Don't talk insanity. You've got me sitting on the board of every cultural institution in this city. You've got me heading the fire-safety campaign, launching ships, sticking my toes in cement—"

"And I'm damn proud of it. You were nobody when I took you on twelve years ago. Today, you have ninety-nine percent name recognition in Philadelphia. You're CEO of the Di Angelo Corporation, you own twenty percent of the office space in Center City, and you're the envy of every developer in the Western world. I *made* you big, and I'm going to make you even bigger."

Ellory was starting to sound manic again, and she asked herself, as she did at least once a week, why she continued to pay him an exorbitant salary when she had little need of him and more media attention than she wanted. The answer was always the same: She was grateful, she was loyal, and most of all, she knew how much their association meant to him.

"Look, Ellory," she said, "I'm very appreciative of all you've done for me, but politics and politicians give me a royal pain. I have to deal with enough liars and phoneys in my business."

"That's what I'm saying. You're getting *marvelous* training." He stopped for a swallow. "I don't mean you should become active now. But we have to start grooming you. In twenty years, when you're fifty-four . . ."

"When I'm fifty-four, I plan to be sitting in a rocking chair reading to my grandchildren. No politics, Ellory. *N, O,* no. No City Hall, no State House, and the only time I want to see the White House is when the first lady invites me to lunch to meet Paul Newman, or the president calls me in to remodel his office."

"You'll change your mind." He drained his glass and set it on the table. "Last question. What's happening on Rittenhouse Square?"

She squashed her cigarette in the ashtray. "It's taken me three long years, but I'm finally getting my fourth building on the north side. The Historical Society Library on the corner isn't for sale at any price—yet. But I'm working on it."

"What will you do with that block when you get it?"

"I'm not sure."

"Why do you want it so badly?"

"I don't *know*, Ellory. You keep telling me I've got a hang-up."

"Well, you do. It's madness to be so obsessed with the past. You think you were the only kid who ever got snubbed?"

"I still get snubbed."

"Not true."

"Of course it's true. *My* generation accepts me. They invite me to their parties because I'm rich and pretty and good copy. But the Old Guard—"

"What do you care about the Old Guard? You want to get even with them for something that happened over twenty years ago? Maybe you'd like to tear everything down and build a whole row of Di Angelo Towers just to spit in their faces."

"Damn it, I *am* planning to raze two buildings for a hotel. I just haven't done anything about it yet."

"Torie," he said nervously, "don't even *think* about tearing down anything on Rittenhouse Square."

"Don't even *think* about trying to stop me. And quit frowning."

"I'm frowning, lovely, because up to now you've been deucedly lucky. The reporters who've dredged up the story of dear daddy's tilt with the law have seen it as a petty crime and haven't made a big deal of it—*or* your Silvano family connections and occasional mob mentality."

"My *what*?"

"If you don't like something, you want to blow it away. Bam! It's gone. Pure mafioso."

"That's the stupidest—"

"Even without the destruction, you're talking about subjecting the neighbors to months of dust and dirt and construction noises, making the area a magnet for tourists and gawkers—"

"Bringing new life, new jobs, new business—"

"Be *realistic*, for God's sake. Do you honestly think the people who live and work there are going to sit back and let you wreck their privacy?"

"You mean their semiprivate bastion of wealth and tradition and dumpy old buildings?"

"You're hopeless." He wiped his cheek. "If you don't realize they'll use every weapon possible to discredit you, you're tootier than a French horn."

"So what?" she said impatiently. "It's public knowledge that Papa went to prison. My enemies would've used that argument years ago if they thought it had any punch. Say"—she reached for his forehead—"are you all right?"

"I will be—when I'm back on terra firma." His breath was coming in gasps.

"I've dreamed of putting my imprint on that square since I was a child, Ellory. I told you once and I mean it: *Nothing's* going to stop me." She rose and started toward the penthouse. "You'd better get inside."

"I'm all right . . ." Staggering across the terrace, he followed her through the French doors, then sank down on the couch.

"We have a doctor in the building," she said, fanning his face. "I'll call him."

"No, no—not for a minor panic attack. I'll be all right in a shake—as long as I can't see the sky." He closed his eyes and, after a minute of deep breathing, managed a smile. "See? No more wheezing. Now tell me, if you insist on going ahead with this suicidal and totally maniacal notion, have you thought about an architect?"

"Well, it won't be Cava. He can't get along with his own shadow. Now he wants me to fire the interior designer so *he* can take over. '*Di Angelo Tower e un'oggetto di arte,*' he keeps screaming. We crass materialists shouldn't care about making a profit."

"Forget Cava. I've just had a brainstorm." Before she could comment, he went on: "Whatever you do on Rittenhouse Square, you're going to have tremendous opposition. And the only way I can think of to counter it is to hire the country's hottest and most celebrated architect—the man whose face graced the cover of last week's *Time.*"

Her heart took a leap. She collected herself long enough to answer, "Nielson Hughes would be ideal. His reputation's flawless, and as you say, he's the most dynamic architect in the country. But he won't work for me, so there's no sense discussing it. I've been thinking more along the lines of Portman or Lohan. Or possibly Rogers, who did the Pompidou Center in Paris."

"Why won't Hughes work for you?"

"We had a falling-out a few lifetimes ago. Nielson's not the type who forgives and forgets."

"How will you know if you don't try?" He rose and, somewhat unsteadily, headed for the entrance hall. "I've got to get out of here. But do think it over."

She followed him to the door. "You're looking awfully flushed, Ellory. Maybe I should ride down with you."

"*Ride* down? I'd step into an open grave before I'd get into an elevator from this height."

"You're going to walk down thirty-nine flights of stairs?"

"I most certainly am. God and my ankles willing, I should reach the lobby by midnight."

"If I don't hear from you, I'll send a search party." She pecked his cheek. "Thanks for coming."

"Think about what I said, ducks. If you *could* get Hughes, you'd neutralize your foes' main argument—that what we're doing will cheapen the area rather than improve it. There's not another architect in the world who can do what he can. Hughes may be New Scottsdale but he's Old Philadelphia. With his name on your hotel, it could be a national shrine . . . a model for other hotels . . . the envy of the *world*—"

"Don't get carried away. He'd never work for me."

"I've got a thousand dollars that says he will. I've seen you crack a lot tougher nuts than Hughes with some sweet talk and your special charms. But you have to ask in person or the bet's off."

"In person?" The thought of seeing Nielson again, after fifteen years, brought a tremor of excitement. In that short time, he had earned a reputation equal to, and in some ways surpassing, that of his father. Nielson Hughes was the man every contemporary student of the craft studied. At the age of thirty-seven, he was already a world-acclaimed architect whose name on a building stamped it as a classic, the work of a master.

Phrases from the *Time* interview ran through her head. Hughes "chooses his projects as carefully as other men choose their wives," observed the writer. "A compulsive perfectionist who spends long hours making intricate sketches, he constantly changes and reformulates concepts and details . . . studies and restudies every nuance of form and façade until the final design emerges . . . more times than not, a triumph of architectural purity . . ."

Nielson hadn't changed, she thought; he would still be impossible to work with. Yet both the Main Line bastard and the high school dropout from South Philly had come a distance. Both were reaching the peaks of their careers, both were attractive, outspoken, controversial. It would be absurd to imagine two such combustible entities as a team; and yet they had worked together once before and produced a winning product . . . just as they had produced powerful stirrings in each other . . .

"A thousand dollars for your thoughts."

"I can't take your bet. It's too much like stealing."

"In that case, I'll reverse it. You bet you *can* get Hughes and I'll bet you can't. Now will you take it?"

She laughed. "On one condition: When I lose, my money goes to the fire-safety campaign."

"And if you win?"

"*Your* money goes to the fire-safety campaign. We need it for new posters. But if I were you, I wouldn't be worried."

"On the contrary, I can't wait to write out my check." He kissed her hand and raised his head with a worried look. "It *is* deductible, isn't it?"

29
=

"MORNING, T. D." Peggy Shea breezed through the door of Torie's office, a writing pad and tape recorder tucked under her arm. Moon-shaped glasses and a wool tweed suit enhanced her executive bearing, as did the two strands of perfect pearls Torie had given her after fifteen years of professional togetherness. Everything about Peggy Shea appeared to be carefully planned, efficient, controlled. Even the once-flaming red tresses had settled into a subdued auburn-brown, swept back from her face and twisted into a bun—chic, not spinsterish. "How was the weekend?"

"Full of surprises. Michael started kindergarten last week and seems to like it, knock on wood. And Papa actually spoke to me yesterday." Torie's glance was approving. "Don't *we* look stylish. New suit?"

"No, old suit. Knock-off of a Chanel. It's the pearls. They make everything look real, even me." She crossed her legs and opened her notebook. "Here's the latest on His Lordship. The first letter went out to Mr. Hughes on 8/18/86. No reply. A follow-up letter went out three weeks ago, on 9/1/86. No reply. This morning I phoned his office and got some self-important prig who told me, quote: 'Mr. Hughes is not interested in working with the Di Angelo Corporation.' End of conversation."

Torie's face reddened. "That conceited ass! He couldn't even have his secretary answer our letters. Who needs him?"

"From what Ellory keeps saying, we do. What now?"

"What now is that I pay my thousand dollars to the aforementioned Mr. Davis, and we find ourselves another architect—someone who's brilliant, creative, gutsy, and has an international reputation."

Peggy shrugged. "Why fool ourselves? Nielson's is the only name that can slice through the opposition. I agree with Ellory. I don't see how we can sell the public on the hotel without him."

"I refuse to grovel."

"Who said anything about groveling? You haven't even put up a fight."

"Damn it, Pig, I'm not about to plead with the man. Who the hell does he think he is? The cover of *Time*—big deal."

"It is a big deal."

"Who cares? Screw him."

"You tried that. It didn't work."

"Oh, I don't know." Torie's smile lit up with mischief. "It got us the St. Francis Tower. Do you have any idea what that little nugget's worth today with the neighborhood so improved?"

"Maybe you should sell while he's hot."

"Not on your life. It's his first commission and it's a classic. When did you last talk to Ellory?"

"I never talk to Ellory, I listen. He's called three times this morning. He says Connie Morris is so pissed that you won't be interviewed, she's going around pumping everyone who knows you and gathering tidbits for a cover story. Strictly hatchet stuff."

"What am I supposed to do? Put out a contract on her?" She pressed the intercom. "Jane, get Ellory on two, please. No calls for ten minutes."

Seconds later, the publicist was on the line. "There's only one thing you can do about Connie. You'll have to counter her attack with a positive piece in a prestigious magazine like *McGarren's.*"

"No thanks, Ellory. Brayton McGarren's monthly masturbation is a bit too self-serving for my taste. Besides, it's aimed at the self-indulgent rich, not the working rich. Why can't we try *Fortune*?"

"Because *Fortune* tries to be fair and objective. If Mac likes you, he could take half the magazine to sing your praises."

"I'd rather be in *Fortune.*"

"They're not interested right now. I tried. Don't be so damn stubborn. Everyone knows Mac's a weird old bird with a cash register for a brain. But he's also publisher, emperor, dictator, supreme guru of McGarren Publications, and one hell of a journalist."

"And you want me to—?"

"Go to lunch with him. That's all I ask. He said he almost never dines out but he'll make an exception in your case."

"I guess that's a compliment. Say, didn't you try to get him to do a piece on me once before?"

"Yes, he turned it down. Felt you'd been overexposed. But this time I had a new approach . . . an appeal to his gallantry. I told him that a fellow Philadelphian was about to be skewered by a national tabloid spouting lies and inaccuracies. I said you deserved an honest, factual—"

"What did he say?"

"That he'd take you to lunch."

"All right," she groaned. "Check with Peggy and find a day. As to Nielson Hughes, he refuses to work with me, so I'll make out my check."

"When did you see him?"

"He won't even talk to me on the phone."

"Our bet was contingent on your making a personal appeal."

"Then our bet's off. I've got to run—"

"One last word, lovey. Don't underestimate Connie Morris's poison pen. She's going to give your opponents a heap of ammunition. If you care about building that hotel as much as you say you do, you'd better think twice about Hughes. You don't stand a rat's chance of getting approval without him."

"Okay, okay, I'll think about it." Banging down the phone, she turned to face Peggy's accusing eyes. "What's that look for?"

"Pretty emotional, aren't you? Why take it out on Ellory?"

"You know why I'm emotional. You're both bugging me to go charging after Nielson. What about my pride?"

"I understand your pride. I also think you want that hotel on Rittenhouse Square more than you've ever wanted anything."

"Damn right I do. Remember that wonderful story about Jack Kelly?"

"Which?"

"He was the world's champion oarsman, but the British wouldn't let him enter the Henley Sculls race because he'd 'worked with his hands' as a bricklayer and therefore wasn't a gentleman. So he decided to get even by entering all the other contests and defeating all the Henley Sculls' champions—which he did."

"It's coming back. Something about his son?"

"Right. Jack Jr. never worked as a laborer, so he *could* enter the Henley race about twenty years later. He won it, and flipped 'em the bird by wearing his father's old sculling cap. Then he wrapped that sweaty old hat in a box and sent it to King George VI, just to rub the royal nose in it. Don't you *love* it?"

"No, and I doubt His Majesty was amused. But if your heart's set on entrapping Nielson, I may have a plan."

Torie squinted suspiciously. "What're you about to dump on me, O'Shea?"

"I have a friend in Phoenix who got me some info. The Hugheses have an enormous spread in Scottsdale, but they've been in their La Jolla palace for the summer and won't be back for another week. Nielson's due in his office on Tuesday, September thirtieth."

"So?"

"So—you hop your jet to Phoenix. A car and driver meet you at Sky Harbor Airport and whisk you, not to Nielson's office, where you'd be persona non grata, but out to his house."

Torie looked up with interest. "To see Betsy? That's not a bad idea. If I could get to Nielson through Betsy—convince *her* that it's important for him to return to his hometown and create an architectural masterpiece that surpasses anything his birdbrain father has done—yes, that might appeal to Nielson's warped psyche."

"Then you'll do it?"

"I'm thinking . . ."

"Good. I'll reschedule your appointments and make plans for

Thursday, October second. That'll give Betsy two or three days to unpack and get settled before you show up on her doorstep."

"I'm just going to show up?"

"You can't let her know you're coming. She'd tell Nielson, and he'd forbid her to see you. So here's what I've worked out."

"What you've *already* worked out?"

"Correct. You call Betsy from the airport, tell her you're on your way to Taliesen West to interview prospective architects. Then—well, the rest is up to you. I'll go ahead and make the reservations."

"Better make 'em fast, because if I think about it, I won't go." She pressed a button. "Jane, find out if Doody Hellman's gotten word on those easement rights, remind Scott Newhall I need the space audit and predesign analysis by three o'clock, and check with Herb Caen in San Francisco about that Moller woman's reference . . ."

The sky was clear and crisp a week later, as Torie walked confidently into Le Bec Fin, a tiny, jewellike French restaurant on Walnut Street, a few blocks from Rittenhouse Square. She peered into the bar to the left of the entrance, saw no sign of her luncheon date, and approached the maître d'.

"Good afternoon, Miss Di Angelo." His greeting was polished and impersonal. Perhaps he saved his warmth for old money.

"Hello, Claude. Has Mr. McGarren arrived?"

"Not yet. Would you care to wait in the alcove or may I show you to the table?"

"The table, please." She smiled pleasantly, nodded to several acquaintances, and felt a wave of admiring glances wash over her as she followed him through the narrow dining room.

Strange, she thought, how little those stares meant anymore. Supposedly, she was the woman with everything: success, health, wealth, and beauty. Yet in the rare moments when she slowed down long enough to examine her life, she often felt that her visible assets were poor substitutes for the ones she lacked—a home that felt like a home and a loving family.

Divorce had been a shattering experience, leaving scars that continued to pain her. Part of her still missed the closeness and happiness she and Jeff had shared in the beginning . . . the wonderful peace of having a settled personal life . . . the comfort of having someone who cared for her, and for whom she cared in return. The few relationships she had had since the divorce had been so fleeting and unsatisfactory, she often preferred the company of her gay escorts to the hassles of dealing with an eligible male.

The maître d' moved her chair to the table. "Maurice is your waiter, Miss Di Angelo. He will take good care of you."

"I'm sure he will." Her watch said twenty-five to one, five minutes past the hour she was due. Perhaps she should have been fashionably late and avoided the minor discomfort of sitting alone. But that was not her way. She would never show how important she was by wasting other people's time.

"Hello. Am I late?" A tall man in a tweed sportcoat eased into the seat opposite her. His hair was windblown, his shirt open at the neck, his tie twisted like a pretzel. "Let's get you a cocktail. Let's get me one, too."

"I'm afraid you've made a mistake. I'm expecting—"

"Brayton McGarren. I bring you Mac's regrets. He was called to New York on business, and it was too late to cancel. I'm Keith McGarren. Nice to meet you, Torie."

She shook his outstretched hand. "You're his son—"

"I know I look more like his father. Or grandfather. I started graying in my twenties before they had Grecian Formula. Now I'm too old to change." He motioned to the waiter. "What'll you have?"

"A glass of white wine."

"Good idea. Bring us a nice Meursault and we'll order lunch right away." He lowered his voice. "I prefer California wines, but Mac won't think I did right by you unless I run up a bill."

She smiled. "That shouldn't be difficult here."

He nodded as the waiter brought menus. "I'm not much for chitchat. Would you mind if we got right to business?"

"Not at all." A slight abrasiveness to his tone, as if he resented having to "entertain" her, came across. On first meeting, Keith McGarren appeared to bear a strong resemblance to his famous father, who made an art of being cantankerous, and who was known for never using two words when one would do.

She leaned back in her chair, studying her host's face as he studied the menu. Despite the slightly disheveled appearance, he was a singularly handsome man: smooth brow, clear hazel eyes, straight nose, strong chin, and a full head of wavy gray hair. In a way, he seemed almost out of contact with his good looks— as if he knew they were there but didn't want to be bothered with them. "What'll you have?"

"Crab salad, please. Vinaigrette on the side."

"I'll have a steak, medium-well, with French fries." He tasted the wine and nodded to the waiter. "Here's to you and your accomplishments, Torie. I've watched you for many years."

"You have?" His remark—*almost* a compliment—startled her. Perhaps what she had sensed as resentment was simply the same old defensive attitude men affected when they met a successful woman.

"I've heard tales, too," he went on. "The latest is that you hate clutter so much you insist all your employees leave bare desks when they go home. Rumor has it you went back to work one night, marched through the entire office sweeping piles of papers off desks, and the next day found out you'd gotten off at the wrong floor and messed up the wrong office."

She chuckled. "Good story, but pure, uh, baloney. I'm no fan of clutter, it's true, but I try not to inflict my foibles on others. Let's talk about your magazine. It's fun to read . . . lots of sparkle and personality. I know Mac's the publisher. What do you do?"

"My official title is editor in chief, which is something like being vice president of the United States."

"You do none of the work and get none of the glory?"

He laughed appreciatively, showing a row of even white teeth. "No. I work hard and Mac is welcome to the glory. I do have the satisfaction of voicing my pains and pleasures in a monthly column. What I meant was that I don't have to put my life on display. I'm a recent bachelor and devoutly protective of my privacy. Mac would love me to become an international playboy, but I'm afraid I can't oblige him."

"You mean he'd like you to practice what he preaches?"

"Exactly—conspicuous spending, hobnobbing with the jet set, all that malarkey. He thinks it'd be marvelous PR for the magazine, and maybe it would. But it's not for me."

"Doesn't that make you a hypocrite?"

"Why should it? Do you think everyone on our staff has a penthouse and a yacht? Do you think you have to *live* a certain life-style in order to write about it? We make no secret of catering to the rich. Most of our subscribers are in the top tax brackets, so that's what we focus on: success . . . money . . . who's making it and how." He buttered a chunk of crusty bread. "Now, suppose you give me three good reasons why we should do a cover story on you."

His directness was confusing; she didn't know whether to be

amused or offended. "I haven't heard any mention of a cover story. Ellory's idea was that you might write a factual piece to counteract some of the distortions Connie Morris is going to print about me."

"Have you seen her article?"

"No, she's writing it now."

"How will we know what to refute if we don't know what she's writing?"

"I didn't say refute, I said counteract—meaning balance. Ellory thought you might want to do a candid, objective piece that exposed my weaknesses as well as whatever abilities I might have."

"Sounds pretty dreary."

"Perhaps it would be." She chose her words carefully. "Look, Mr. McGarren, I have no intention of trying to sell myself to you. When I agreed to this luncheon, it was with the idea that your father and I would discuss an article. I know nothing about a cover story and I'm not even sure I'd want one."

"Fine. Then let's just enjoy our lunch." He buttered bread again while she sat tensely, weighing alternatives. After a moment, he leaned forward. "Read any good books, lately?"

The lightness of his tone relaxed her. "Matter of fact, I've just finished one called *Money Madness*. Mac wouldn't approve. It's based on the premise that having money is terrific, but spending it is overrated."

He had asked about books jokingly, assuming she was too busy to read. The fact that she did intrigued him. "Isn't that a contradiction?"

"Not necessarily. *Having* money gives you security, confidence, power—and freedom from emotions like envy and worry. Spending it is incidental."

"Now aren't *you* being the hypocrite? Don't you enjoy the prestige of giving two or three million to charity every year? Don't you have a world-famous art collection? A fabulous penthouse? What did that stylish red suit you're wearing cost?"

"Enough to feed a family of four for three months. But the only possession I care about—and he's hardly a possession—is my five-year-old son, Michael. I don't buy expensive trappings for me, I buy them for image. The main reason I need money is to make me independent—to shield me from . . . well, from being hurt."

"If you believe money can do that, maybe it can." His expression made clear he had no such confidence; wealth had never insulated him from pain. The waiter set down a crisp steak and he reached for a fork. "Ever thought about politics? Running for office?"

"I'd sooner run for Miss Nude America. What was it Jimmy Carter's mother said? 'Sometimes when I look at my kids, I think I should've stayed a virgin.' I'm in favor of frontal lobotomies for most politicians and euthanasia for the rest."

"What about celebrities? Would you put them out of their misery too?"

"You'd have to define a celebrity. Do we agree on Daniel Boorstin's definition: someone well known for being well known?"

"Wouldn't that include you?"

"It might, depending on what you think I'm known for." She poked at her crab, suddenly more interested in talking than eating. "I like being called a visionary. I'd rather dream big and achieve one tenth of my goals than dream small and achieve everything. I want to have an impact on the world."

"Ego?"

She smiled. "Ego is the *visible* part of my drive. That's what the public sees. For instance, I won't deny I name everything I can get my hands on after myself. If I had my way, you'd be eating Steak Di Angelo in Di Angelo's Restaurant in Di Angeloville, PA. I have an insatiable drive to be famous."

"Why?"

"Well, originally—oh, it's too complicated. Let's just say that fame translates into dollars. According to *Newsweek*, my name on a property has come to be quite an asset."

"You mean it's all economics?"

"Of course not. But if I'm putting up a development, and someone tells me I'll do fifty percent more business by calling it Di Angelo Place rather than Seventeenth Street Place or Mabel McGlotchy Place, I'd have to be nuts *not* to do it." She deposited a crab shell on her plate. "To go any deeper gets too personal."

"What's wrong with personal? I thought you were going to be open and candid."

"For the article, maybe. For a stranger, no. Since you're not doing the story, I can be as obscure as I like."

He reached into the ice bucket. "These pedigreed French restaurants give me a pain. Forty bucks for wine and I have to pour it myself. But I hate to see an empty glass—"

A horrified waiter grabbed the bottle from his hand. "*Please,* Mr. McGarren!"

"Maurice to the rescue. Praise the Lord." His eyes returned to Torie. "Who said we weren't doing the article?"

"You inferred—"

"I implied. *You* inferred."

"Correction noted. I didn't finish school."

"What's that got to do with anything? Mark Twain said he never let schooling get in the way of his education."

"Well, anyhow, it's been an interesting lunch—"

"Interesting?" His brows shot up. "I detest that word. It says absolutely nothing except that something has grabbed the speaker's attention. Don't tell me this has been an interesting luncheon. Has it been a wildly stimulating luncheon? A gastronomic pearl of a luncheon? A maddening, frustrating wish-I'd-never-come luncheon?"

"Yes—to all." She couldn't help smiling. "Now it's your turn on the hot seat. How'd your family get into the magazine business?"

"That's easy." He laid down his knife and looked at her intently. "My ancestors came over from Ireland in the early eighteenth century. Timothy McGarren started a newssheet modestly titled *McGarren's Universe.* It flourished until the Revolution."

"And then?"

"Skip to 1802, when a gent named Chauncey Badimeer published a literary journal called *Byblos.* That folded in 1904. My grandfather, Dennis McGarren, was the editor. He rose from its ashes to launch a new effort called *McGarren's Monthly.* Are you asleep yet?"

"Not quite."

"Care for dessert?"

"Just coffee."

"Two coffees, Maurice, and a slice of your best chocolate cake with two forks." He pushed away his plate. "When that worthy journal became terminally ill, Dennis realized he'd have to give in to the pressures to take advertising. *McGarren's Monthly* finally began to make money, but Dennis couldn't live with the guilt of having 'sold out' to commercialism, and he died a year later. My father, who had no such compunctions, took over."

"He shortened it to *McGarren's* and prospered ever after."

"Hardly. Mac went through bankruptcy, lawsuits, and about

twenty changes of format before *McGarren's* began to catch on in the fifties. What you see today—what we like to think of as a more entertaining, personal version of *Fortune*—is the result of one man's unbelievable drive and stamina . . . his ability to shut out his family, his health problems, the world, every damn thing around him until that issue hits the presses."

The statement made her wonder if he secretly resented his father's intensity, and what kind of relationship the two men had. There was no open hostility, as there was between Nielson and his father, but neither was there the warmth and closeness of a Jeff and Mort Goldman. At least, not visibly.

She set her napkin on the table. "Thanks for sitting in today. I hope it wasn't too painful."

He signaled for the check and scribbled a name. "Do you have your car?"

"Yes. Need a ride?"

"No." He followed her to the exit and held open the door. "I enjoyed our lunch—most of it, anyway."

She laughed as Moose pulled up in the limousine. "Me, too. It was, well, interesting."

30
##

THE MINUTE TORIE stepped off the ramp in Phoenix's bustling airport, she hurried to a phone. If Peggy's "spy" had done her work well, Betsy Richardson Hughes would be waking up from her afternoon nap about now and getting ready to wheel herself around the garden.

The number rang once, twice, three times, before a man answered in a European accent: "Hughes residence."

Torie stayed cool. "May I speak to Mrs. Hughes, please?"

"Who is calling?"

"Miss Di Angelo from Philadelphia."

"One moment, madam."

Several minutes later, a cheerful voice came on the line. "Torie? My *God,* is that you?"

"Hi, Betsy. I wasn't sure you'd know my name."

The answer was a delighted giggle. "You're fishing and I shouldn't bite, but how could I not know you? Even though we've never met, you're a famous lady. Besides, I still take *Philadelphia* magazine."

"Then you haven't forsaken your hometown. I saw your dad a few weeks ago at the symphony board meeting. He looks fabulous."

"Isn't he amazing? Still living in that house, never remarried, still running around trying to save the world. And he's going on *sixty.* Now tell me, where are you?"

"I'm at Sky Harbor Airport—just here for a few hours. Going over to Taliesen West to interview architects. But I couldn't resist calling you. Maybe I can take a message back to your dad."

"Only if I can give it in person. You can't fly all this way and not say hello. Won't you come by for cocktails this evening? I'm sure Nielson wants to hear what's going on in Philly."

"That's sweet of you, and I'd love to tell your Dad I saw you, but I don't know what time I'll be through. Wait a sec—would you have a few minutes now?"

"Now? Well, sure, why not? Do you know where we live?"

"My driver does," she said, ending the conversation before Betsy could change her mind. "I'll be right over."

The chauffeur knew exactly where the Hughes estate was, on the east end of Scottsdale, in the so-called millionaire's ghetto. Everyone knew the location of the Hughes property, he explained, but the owner had been smart enough to surround it with a brick wall, hiding the fabulous mansion from view. If he hadn't, Scottsdale's most famous citizen would have had tourists cruising by twenty-four hours a day. The driver was delighted to be getting a closer look.

At the entrance, a voice from a black box checked their identities, and a heavy iron gate swung open, permitting the car to pass through. Torie's first view of the compound, spread over an area the size of a city block, gave her a surge of pleasure. A stunning flat-roofed house, molded with ease and grace, wound around two free-form swimming pools. Contemporary in design, with curves and countercurves as gracefully twined as the hands of a dancer, the adobe structure emanated a sense of peace and harmony against a backdrop of desert mountains.

Behind the house, rock pathways led through carefully landscaped gardens alive with tall saguaro cactuses, golden Arizona poppies, and pink and purple roses. A tennis court and a greenhouse were visible in the distance, and beside them what appeared to be a spa or gymnasium. No steps, curbs, or inclines cluttered the flow. The entire estate was as flat as the plain.

Torie was touched by what she saw, an obvious expression of Nielson's love. The style pleased her too, for it showed that he could turn his talents to streamlined structures when he wanted to. If only she could get him to realize that modernism had a place in Philadelphia as well as in Arizona.

The driver stopped at the front door. For a fleeting second, Torie's mind was back at Betsy's birthday party, twenty-three years earlier. Had she known then that one day she and Betsy would be meeting as friends and equals, she might have been better able to cope.

A butler in a white coat admitted her and led the way along a corridor lined with antique Indian cooking utensils. The living room they passed, furnished in earth tones of beige and brown with accents of orange, housed a collection of Native American baskets, dolls, and ceramic pottery. By some miracle of decor, a pair of bleached cow skulls over the fireplace managed to look smart . . . even elegant.

"There's the VIP lady." Betsy smiled from her wheelchair, parked by a window. Her sitting room appeared to be a working study, with book-lined walls and a desk with a computer. In one corner, bright threads dripped from a large loom. "Wouldn't you know it. You're even prettier than your pictures."

Torie hurried toward her, remembering she had said almost identical words the first time she met Betsy. "And you look like a teenager. You've found the fountain of youth."

Betsy's cheeks were rounder than she recalled, but her chestnut hair framed the same lovely features and flowed like silken ribbons down her back. And the same gracious smile lit up her face. They embraced warmly. "I feel as if I've known you forever. I'll never forget the note you wrote me after the accident. You put so much of yourself into it."

Torie debated telling her that they had met earlier, then decided against it. The reminder would only embarrass them both.

"I've always admired you, ever since I was a little nobody from South Philly and you were the mayor's daughter."

"You? A nobody?" Betsy's laughter filled the room. "I remember when you married Jeff Goldman—a darling boy all the girls liked. And they said *he* was lucky to get you!"

"I doubt he'd agree."

"Oh, I'm sorry. Touchy subject?"

"Not at all. We're friends now. Jeff's happily remarried, and I'm happily single—more or less."

"More or less single? Or happy?"

"Definitely single. Reasonably happy—and blessed with a five-year-old son."

"Then I'd say you're very lucky. Now sit down and tell me all the wonderful things you're doing."

"I'd love to." She settled into a brown leather armchair. "Will it bother you if I smoke?"

"It'll bother you. I hate to see people poison their lungs."

The reproach startled her. "I'm . . . sure I could stop if I made up my mind to."

"Well, make up your mind. This very minute. Then you'll at least have gotten something out of this trip. Because I doubt you'll find the kind of sophisticated architect you're looking for at Taliesen West—not among the students, anyway."

"In that case, I *will* quit. Here . . ." She tossed her pack of cigarettes into the wastebasket. "That's the end of this wretched habit—the absolute end—as God and Betsy Hughes are my witnesses."

"Bravo!"

"Thanks for caring enough to say something. Now, as to my quest for an architect—I can't be deceitful with you, Betsy. I *did* want to see you; I've respected and admired you all my life. But I didn't come here for Taliesen West. I came to try to hire Nielson."

Betsy shrugged pleasantly. "I'm not surprised. You're neither the first nor the last to try to get to him through me. But I might as well tell you right off. I have very little influence with my husband."

"I know how strong-willed he can be." Do I *ever*, she thought. "But I wouldn't be here if I didn't think I had an offer that would appeal to him. It's no secret why he left Philadelphia."

"Nothing's secret after that *Time* interview. They even wrote about where I buy my carriages—that's what Nielson calls my wheelchairs."

"He's right. A princess rides in a carriage. And you always were his princess, even when I knew him years ago."

"Well," she said, laughing, "maybe God doled out this sentence for a reason. I don't know that Nielson would have been so persistent if he hadn't felt sorry for me. And I can't imagine what kind of a life I would've had without him."

"I'm sure he feels the same about you." Torie hated herself for her hypocrisy. But her fantasies were so dim and deeply buried that by now they hardly mattered. "What I want to say is— I think the time has come for the native son and his wife to return to their hometown in glory and triumph. I don't mean permanently, just long enough to thumb your noses at the creeps who made Nielson feel unwanted."

"He's already proven himself."

"Yes, nationally. And internationally. But not to Philadelphia. Suppose he came back for a specific purpose. Suppose he were to design a superluxury hotel, so elegant, so majestic, so architecturally superior to any other building the city has ever seen—including all the works of a certain Robert Nielson— wouldn't that be a great satisfaction to him?"

"And where would this masterpiece be built?"

"On the north side of Rittenhouse Square, right opposite the Richardson town house."

Betsy stared curiously. "You mean . . . instead of the buildings there now?"

Torie's answer came fast. "We'd only have to raze two structures. One's a new office complex—a gross, overdecorated imitation of an Indian palace. It has no place on the Square. And the twin apartment towers next to it are so old and rundown, we'll have to strip them to their foundations no matter what we do."

"We? Do you own the buildings?"

"My company does. I swear to you we're not destroying anything of value. We're replacing an unsafe structure and a ghastly eyesore with what I know will be one of the finest monuments of the decade."

"What if Nielson refuses?"

"Then I'll get another architect." Torie leaned forward excitedly. "But I'm praying he won't. I'm praying that he'll want to build Philadelphia's most spectacular hotel. I'm praying he'll want to leave such an enduring mark on his city that his father won't be able to open a magazine or newspaper for the rest of his life without reading about his son's genius."

Betsy sat pensive a few seconds before asking, "How long would all this take?"

"About two years. You wouldn't have to be in Philadelphia the whole time, of course, but I'm sure your father would be thrilled to have you visit him. I don't suppose you've seen much of each other lately."

"No, and that *would* be an inducement . . . to me, anyway. Tell me, why'd you go to all this trouble to talk to me? Why didn't you ask Nielson directly?"

"I tried to, but he wouldn't take my calls. You see, when we worked together in 1971, on Nielson's first building, I made the mistake of mentioning his father in a news release. He got furious at me, stormed out of our press party, and hasn't spoken to me since. I thought he might have mellowed enough to forgive me but I guess he hasn't."

Betsy chuckled. "Forgiveness is not Nielson's strong point. Are you sure that's all it was?"

The question made Torie start. Could he possibly have told her about their affair? "We had plenty of clashes. I had to learn that you don't work 'with' Nielson, you work 'for' him, even if you're supposedly the boss. But I guess my goof at the end was the last straw. That's why I was hoping you'd talk to him."

"He'll be home soon. Why don't you talk to him yourself?"

At last, the invitation she had been both fearing and waiting for. She mustn't seem too eager. "When he sees me, I'm afraid he'll throw me out of the house."

"I doubt it. He only gets violent at football games." Betsy chuckled and wheeled herself to the door. "Come along. I'm dying to show off my garden."

The sound of the front door opening made Torie's heart pound. As much as she had tried to prepare herself for the confrontation, every nerve in her body was wire-taut.

"We're in the living room, dear," Betsy called out. "We have company."

Footsteps pattered along the thick carpet, and suddenly Nielson Hughes appeared—tall, stiff, imperious, and as outrageously handsome as ever. The sleeves of his white shirt were rolled up to the elbows, his collar was open, and one hand held a navy blazer slung over his shoulder.

His blue eyes flashed fire as they focused on the visitor, and he spoke without a second's hesitation. "What in God's name are *you* doing here?"

She laughed and walked toward him. "That's some greeting after fifteen years. I knew you'd be pleased to see me."

"What's going on, Betsy? Who let her in?"

"Don't blame your wife, Nielson. I called up and practically invited myself because it was the only way I could get through to you. What I have to say won't take more than ten minutes, and then I'll leave, I promise. My driver's waiting outside."

"I wondered whose car that was." Frowning, he strode across the room and poured himself a drink. "Didn't you get my message? I want nothing to do with you."

"Honey," scolded Betsy, "she's a guest in our home. At least hear her out."

"You keep out of this. Torie was a she-devil when I knew her as a student, and she's no better now. I don't need greedy little opportunists around me. I have my life ordered exactly as I want it."

"And you're just as rude and pompous an ass as you always were!" Torie grabbed her purse and headed for the door.

"Now, stop it, both of you!" Betsy's command halted all movement. "You're acting like spoiled brats. I don't know what kind of fights you had when you worked together, but you're too old to be snarling at each other like animals. Come back here, sit down, and try to act civilized."

Torie held her breath, waiting for Nielson to make a move. He stood silently a moment, digesting the rebuke, then, to her amazement, walked over to his wife and kissed her cheek. "You're right, pet. See what a pussycat I am, Torie? Marriage to this wonderful lady has taken all the tiger out of me. Come, have a chair."

Hesitantly, she walked back.

"Freshen your drink?" he asked, looking at her with interest for the first time. How incredibly she had changed, he thought— from that trampy little vixen with the hottest pants around to a stunning beauty with an air of confidence and success. There was still the same toughness, the same determination in the tilt of her chin, the same coiled energy ready to strike out and explode. But now it seemed channeled and controlled . . . or at least somewhat controlled.

"No, thanks. Sorry I blew up."

"You had good reason. Frank Lloyd Wright once said he had to choose between being honestly arrogant or a humble hypocrite. He opted for honesty and so did I. Now, what can the pompous ass do for you?"

She smiled and sat down, remembering how mercurial he could be—shouting with rage one minute, glowing with charm the next. That aspect of his personality hadn't changed.

Quickly outlining her proposal and all the reasons why she thought he should accept it, she ended by saying, "and you'd have absolute free rein to build this hotel whatever way you please. Naturally, I'd like it to be somewhat contemporary, but I remember your telling me that da Vinci didn't need anyone to help him paint the *Mona Lisa.* So you'll be completely on your own with the Rittenhouse North."

"Rittenhouse North? Is that what you want to call it?"

No, what she *wanted* to call it was the Di Angelo Regency, but she knew him too well even to suggest it. "Do you have a better idea?"

"I rather like the name, actually." He paused. "Have you got financing?"

"Not on paper. But I expect Berwick Bank will put up fifty-five million dollars for a construction loan, and Confederate Life Assurance will assume the balance—that would be another forty or fifty million, depending on your design. I'm also going to ask the city for a tax abatement—a waiver of all taxes on the property for fifty years."

"In exchange for . . . ?"

"Guaranteed rent payments with built-in annual increases, plus ten percent of the first half million net profits, after loan debts and expenses, twelve point five percent of the next one and a half million, and fifteen percent of net profits over two million."

"What makes you think the city will go for it?"

"They'd be crazy not to. They'll make just as much as I'd have to pay in taxes, and probably a lot more. You see, without a tax abatement, there's no hotel, and without a hotel, the city loses two thousand new jobs, the aforementioned share of profits, and the prestige of having a magnificent Nielson Hughes–designed masterpiece on its prime property."

"God, you're a bullshitter." He emptied his glass. "Planning to challenge the height limit again?"

"No, we'd never get past the zoning board . . . not on Rittenhouse Square."

"Have you applied for the site permit?"

"I can't do anything until I have your name on the project. Look, Nielson, I'm putting all my cards on the table. I need you for this project. Without your genius and your reputation, we stand a very slim chance of getting approval."

"I tend to agree. Do you have any idea what I get for my services?"

"I don't care. I'll pay your fee."

"Just like that? Without asking? How impressive. Are you very rich?"

"Not as rich as you are." She laughed, partly with relief. "But I've done all right."

"She's a hundred times richer than we are, Betsy." He cupped his mouth and pretended to whisper. "I saw an article that said she owns one fifth the office space in Center City. If I were to take the commission, I think I'd double my fee."

Torie tried to contain her excitement. He could quadruple his fee as far as she was concerned. She would gladly pay any amount for the prestige of having his design, and, especially, his name on the hotel, with all that would mean in terms of getting financing and approval. But she mustn't push too hard. He still seemed as volatile as nitroglycerin, and a wrong word, intonation, or gesture could explode her dream in seconds. "I'm grateful that you're considering the idea."

"Considering it, yes. But far from sold. What about room count? Price per room?"

She handed him an envelope. "All the information you need is in here, including my private number at the office when you've had a chance to look it over. I'm sorry, but I do have to catch a plane." She strolled over to Betsy. "I'll die for a cigarette on the flight home, but I swear I won't have one. Thanks for being so gracious. I hope I'll see you in Philadelphia."

"You might," she said. "Who knows?"

Nielson watched in surprise as the women embraced; then he walked Torie to the door. "I'll say this for you," he growled under his voice, "you've got more cheek than a barrel of bare-assed monkeys."

"I had the world's greatest teacher," she said with a grin. "Remember?"

31
==

THE EXTREMELY HANDSOME press kit Ellory Davis put together to herald Nielson Hughes's return to his native state, and to announce the Di Angelo Corporation's plans for the $125 million Rittenhouse North Hotel, made no mention of the architect's father. In true Philadelphia style, however, Nielson's brief biography noted that his "paternal antecedents" had been "among the first settlers on the Delaware . . . well established in their log-cabin colony by the time William Penn arrived on the *Welcome*."

Utter claptrap, Torie thought, sitting at her desk leafing through the folder, but whatever Nielson wanted, Nielson got. In the two months following her visit to him, her problems, particularly with Di Angelo Tower, had multiplied. Paolo Cava's report of structural errors had led her to fire the contractor in mid construction, file a lawsuit for damages, and hire a new contracting firm. But the harm had been done. City building inspectors found fire hazards in the elevator shafts and issued stop-work orders. Torie's lawyers were appealing; how could they repair the mistakes if they couldn't work? In the meantime, the cost of delays and legal services mounted.

Another setback was the wave of antipathy to Cava's "vertical bullets" plan for Penn's Landing. One reporter described the design as "a group of rocket ships lined up against a wall waiting to be shot." But it wasn't the architecture that worried Torie so much as the city's stagnant retail climate. The blue-chip corporate tenants she needed in order to get financing all seemed to be looking elsewhere.

Then there was the Rittenhouse North. Even with Nielson's name on the project, her tax-abatement proposal had met with vicious antagonism and outcries of favoritism, particularly from other hotel owners.

Public pressure was so strong that Borland had been forced to offer Torie very grim terms. Undaunted, and with the chutzpah of a TV preacher who denounces sin the day after being caught with a prostitute, she bounced back with a counteroffer. The astonishing result was that the council ended up giving her everything she originally wanted, except that the fifty-year tax abatement was reduced to thirty-five years—still a tidy deal.

Financially the Rittenhouse North was on its way, though technically and legally it had a long distance to go. Aesthetically—well, that was out of her hands. This time, she knew from the beginning that her tastes and her feelings would have no place in Nielson's work. No matter how strongly she yearned to influence his designs—no matter how desperately she wanted the hotel to be severe and spare, and to be faced in glass and granite rather than concrete—her silence was assured.

Nielson had seen to that. When he had called in late October of 1986, four weeks after her visit, he had insisted their contract stipulate that he could walk away from the project any time her actions (or anyone else's) became "objectionable." He had also upped his fee, as threatened, and made certain that in case of a dispute, he would be entitled to keep his initial retainer and all payments up to the day of his departure. The agreement was heavily weighted in his favor, but his terms were his terms, and not accepting them was unthinkable.

"Ready for the big show?"

Torie glanced up to see Peggy holding her full-length sable. "Do I have to wear that?"

"It's thirty-six degrees out, and you can't afford to catch cold." She helped Torie into the fur and turned up the collar. "Think Nielson might be on time for his own press conference?"

"There's an outside chance. That's why I accepted so fast when Matt offered to have it at the house. All Nielson has to do is walk downstairs."

Peggy slung a purse over her shoulder. "I can't believe I'm finally going to see the Richardson town house. Think you'll start promptly?"

"I hope so. Just before Christmas is a slow news period, so we should get good coverage." Torie rang for the elevator. "How do I look?"

"Much too attractive for a woman edging up to the advanced

age of thirty-six. If Nielson doesn't flip for you all over again, I'll be mighty surprised."

Torie frowned. "I've told you that's impossible. I have no interest in him other than—"

"I know, I know. And the Godfather made his money selling mozzarella."

"Damn it, Pig, he's devoted to Betsy, and for that matter, so am I. I wouldn't get involved with that—"

" 'Hunk' is the word." Peggy lowered her voice. "Do you think he and Betsy have any sort of sex life?"

"How would I know? And why would I care? Now quit trying to stir up trouble and check over that list of reporters so you can greet them by name."

"Methinks thou dost pro—"

"Shush, Piglet. I've got to rehearse my ad libs."

The wind was cold, the afternoon air frosty, and the blaze in the Richardson's fireplace glowed warmly. About twenty media people sat in rows of chairs, smoking, scanning their press kits, readying cameras and cassettes, nibbling canapés, and sipping champagne.

The instant Torie appeared, slim and startlingly beautiful in a pink Galanos sheath, shutters and tape recorders began clicking. Every eye followed as she crossed the carpet to the marble mantel, waited for silence, and then spoke in a clear voice. "On behalf of Matt Richardson and his family, and the Di Angelo Corporation—welcome to this historic event.

"It's truly a thrill," she continued, "to be able to introduce the world's most acclaimed master builder. His many credits and awards would take too long to mention, and are listed on a full page in your press packets. Suffice it to say, his talents are legendary, his genius unrivaled."

One enthusiastic young reporter broke into applause. Torie nodded appreciatively, then raised her hand for silence. "Our announcement of plans for Nielson Hughes's Rittenhouse North Hotel is admittedly premature. We estimate it will be two to three years from the date of last month's application for site permits until the final inspection for occupancy. But as you know, a man of Mr. Hughes's stature can't very well sneak back to his hometown unnoticed. So many tales and rumors have surrounded his return that we decided to tell you exactly what's happening. Without further ado, let me present to you the man of the decade: Philadelphia's own . . . Nielson Hughes!"

Torie turned toward the entranceway and, not seeing anyone, felt a shiver of apprehension. Ellory Davis's two-fingered circle in the air reassured her, however, and seconds later the architect made his entrance. His bearing was proud, his step quick and purposeful.

"I'm sure your applause was for my lovely predecessor," he said graciously, if not altogether convincingly. "Nevertheless, I thank you for your warm welcome. My wife, Betsy, and I have come home for two reasons. One is to see our family. Betsy and her father haven't had a chance to spend time together for many years, and while my esteemed father-in-law shows no sign of aging, I'm afraid my own gray hairs are sprouting rapidly."

He paused as the cameras focused on Matt, standing a short distance away. The former politician grinned and waved.

"The second reason I came back," Nielson continued, "is because this charming lady on my left made me an offer I couldn't refuse. The deluxe five-hundred-room Rittenhouse North Hotel will take up twenty-five thousand feet, or approximately one third of the Walnut Street side of Rittenhouse Square. My staff is working full-time at the drawing boards, and we hope to have a completed model of the thirty-story tower by February. When you've had a chance to look over the material in your kits, I'm sure you'll agree with me that this will be a crowning addition to the Philadelphia skyline of which we're all so proud."

"Have you seen your father?" came a voice from the back of the room.

Torie tensed at the question, but Nielson showed no emotion. "I hoped you might at least wait till I finished my statement."

A few reporters laughed; the rest were silent, anxious for his response.

"The answer is no, I haven't seen my father. We've had no communication for many years, and that's the way it is."

"What if he wants to see you?" asked a woman in the front row.

"The subject is closed."

A relieved sigh escaped Torie's lips. Thank God Nielson had learned how to handle the matter. She wondered if it was still as painful for him as it had been fifteen years ago.

"Miss Di Angelo," called a bearded man, "is it true that this hotel is only the start of your renovation project? How much of the Square do you plan to remodel?"

"My plans are to build this hotel," she answered. "Nothing else is planned at this time."

"What's the latest on Di Angelo Tower?"

"We've just gotten word that Di Angelo Tower will resume construction as of tomorrow. Barring acts of God and man, we'll meet our completion date of May next year."

"What occupancy?"

"Sixty-five percent when we open, eighty percent in a year, and one hundred percent in two years—or sooner."

"Penn's Landing?"

"That's on hold."

"Mr. Hughes!" "Miss Di Angelo!" A chorus of voices shouted questions. Shortly after four Ellory closed the conference, asking that further queries be directed to his office. Nielson disappeared up the stairs, presumably to see Betsy, who hadn't wanted to meet the press, while Torie found herself surrounded by reporters.

A voice calling her name made her glance over her shoulder. For a moment she couldn't place the handsome gray-haired man who beckoned her away from the group. "Keith McGarren," he said, as if reading her mind. "Could we have a word in private?"

"Oh, yes—about the article." Excusing herself, she followed him into the library, closed the door, and dropped into a chair. "Sorry I made it sound as if we had some big project going, but those reporters weren't about to leave. You saved me just in time."

"We do have a big project." He pulled up a bench and sat down beside her. "Mac's agreed to give that cover story a shot. He's willing to allot as much space as we need to do a first-rate layout. I'd like to get some feel for your background before I assign a writer."

"I'm not sure my life is worth all that space."

"It doesn't matter. Henry Kissinger says the great thing about being a celebrity is that when you bore people, they think it's their own fault."

"But you know the truth," she replied, laughing.

"You don't bore me. Whoever writes the story, you realize, will be interviewing your family, friends, enemies, and anyone he can find who knows you. What I want is a responsible profile of a woman who started with next to nothing and worked her way up to becoming one of the most successful developers in the world."

She smiled. "I'll have to think it over, Keith. Right now my head's too full of the Rittenhouse North to give you an answer. Could we talk after the holidays?"

"Yes, of course. Good idea." He rose and walked to the door. "I'll watch for you on the evening news."

The lively scene in the Richardson living room was replayed the following day with a different supporting cast and scenario. In place of journalists poised for confrontation, the top stratum of Philadelphia society stood chattering in small groups, enjoying tidbits of food and gossip, and appraising one another smugly.

At Matt's invitation, they had gathered to welcome back one of their own—his daughter, Betsy, appearing in public for the first time since the tragedy. With some encouragement they might stretch their welcome to include her husband, a man whose wealth and accomplishments might make him acceptable despite his very public profile and irregular birth.

Torie entered the room with Ellory Davis and greeted Matt and Betsy, who hugged her warmly, and then Nielson, who muttered a strained hello.

"What's he so uptight about?" asked Torie as they walked away.

Ellory chuckled. "My guess is that he doesn't feel very comfortable with Philadelphia's finest. While the rest of the world is bowing and scraping and falling over him, our bluebloods are checking him over to see if he's worthy of them. He probably feels like a slab of meat in a butcher shop."

"I know the sensation well."

"No doubt you do." Ellory guided her toward the bar. "I wonder if he appreciated the superb coverage we got last night."

"How would I know? I hardly watched it myself. Michael wanted me to read to him, and—"

"*Hello*, my dear." Ellory bent to kiss the hand of an imperious-looking woman with hawklike features and short white hair. "You remember Rebecca Rawley French, don't you, Torie?"

How could she possibly forget that scene at the music institute, where she had made the unforgivable gaffe of introducing the dowager to her date as Rebecca French. "Rebecca *Rawley* French," the witch had corrected, then turned her back and swept across the room.

"Good evening, Mrs. French. I'm Torie Di Angelo."

"You're the woman who broke the height limit? Who's doing all the building around town?"

Ellory laid an admonitory hand on her arm. "Now, Rebecca, you know very well who Torie is. She sits on several boards with you. Everyone in Philadelphia knows who Torie is."

"I'm not everyone, Ellory. And don't paw me!" She flicked his hand as if it were an insect. "I've heard a number of disturbing rumors about you. Are they true?"

"I don't know," said Torie, wishing she hadn't gotten trapped into conversation. "What have you heard?"

The woman stiffened. Her eyes narrowed and her jaw protruded like the beak of an eagle. "That you take no pride in our Philadelphia heritage—that you have no feeling for the fine old buildings and great architectural masterpieces that mean so much to the rest of us."

The criticism was not new. Torie had heard it many times before. "On the contrary. I care very much for this city and its aesthetics. I feel that my contributions have been a positive force in every way. If you disagree, that's your privilege."

"Of course I disagree! How could anyone with any pride of ancestry—any sense of background or history—have destroyed the Washington Theater? When I was a girl—"

The expression on Torie's face made Ellory nervous. "Now don't go on and on about the old days, Rebecca. What's done is done, and most people think that whole area is greatly improved. May I get you some champagne?"

"No, you may not. And stop trying to change the subject. I have something to say to this young lady and I intend to say it." She glared at Torie. "I'm told you now own that whole block of Walnut Street except for the Historical Society Library. The rumor is that you not only want to ruin the street with this monster of a hotel, you also want to tear everything down to build some kind of modern plaza with steel buildings and fake waterfalls and plastic trees and God knows what else."

"I assure you I have no intention—"

"As long as I've alive, Miss Di Angelo, you will *never* turn that square into a cheap tourist attraction. I'll go to my grave opposing you if I have to. Why can't you leave our architectural treasures alone? There's plenty of work to be done in South Philly. If you insist on tearing down monuments and putting up carnivals, why don't you go back where you came from and start there?"

In a flash the rebuke brought back memories of Betsy's birthday party: the humiliation of being unwanted . . . an outsider . . . unworthy . . . The blind, cutting snobbery she had suffered so many years ago had come back to attack her again in the very same house. But how could it? Now she had money and success and a name to protect her . . .

Ellory watched helplessly as Torie turned and hurried across the room; he had never seen her so shaken. By the time she got to the library, tears streamed down her cheeks. Shutting the door behind her, she buried her head in her hands and began to cry. Her whole body shuddered with sobs . . . until a noise startled her. A figure by the window was staring at her.

"N-Nielson!" she stammered. "W-what—?"

"Sorry. Didn't mean to scare you."

"What are you doing in here?"

"Same as you, I daresay—escaping that gaggle of illiterate coupon-clippers. What happened?"

"Nothing." She reached for the doorknob. "I'd better go—"

"Did someone say something?"

"Yes." She spun around to face him. "I guess I'll never see the day when I'm judged by my deeds, not by the neighborhood where I grew up. Mrs. French told me to go back to South Philly where I came from!"

"Oh, hell, Torie. You can't let that snooty old fishwife upset you."

"It's not just her . . ." Tears began to trickle again as she fumbled in her purse for a handkerchief. "It's this house . . . the garden . . . the memories . . ."

"What are you talking about? Did something else happen here?"

Before she could stop herself, she blurted out the story of Betsy's fourteenth birthday party, how the girls taunted her, how she had watched another boy tease him, how Betsy had come to his rescue, and how sorry she had felt for him. "I . . . never told you about it. I thought it would embarrass you. I don't even know why I'm telling you now."

"Because you're hurt, and you hate being seen crying. You want me to know you're crying for good reason, and you are."

He walked toward her and for a brief moment looked as if he might reach out for her. But if that was his impulse, he suppressed it. "I know what you're feeling. It's called rejection. I've lived with it, and with incidents like the one you remember, all my life. You can't take it to heart. Take it to your brain instead. Let their stifling stupidity wash over you like a stream of cold water and forget it."

"Forget it? When someone spits on you? You don't believe that for a second, Nielson. You believe in fighting back, and so do I. You came in here to get away from those snobs because you couldn't take it anymore, and you were afraid you'd lash out at someone. I know you did."

"In a way," he said, after a pause. "Another minute of their inane gibberish and quite possibly I would have exploded. I have more talent in my little finger than that whole mob of phoneys put together. They don't deserve to wipe up my spittle. Yet they treat me as if they're doing me a favor coming to meet me. No one's said a word about my work, my reputation, my achievements. It's all, 'Oh, so you're Betsy's husband,' or 'Welcome back to a *real* city, Mr. Hughes.' Your Mrs. French looked me over through her lorgnette and said, 'Too bad you can't get along with your father. Robert's such a *dear*.' One old coot did me the colossal honor of inviting me to his club for lunch 'if I had nothing better to do.' If I had nothing better to do—*me*! Can you believe it?"

"I can believe it." She wiped her eyes and looked up guiltily. "I'm sorry, Nielson. I'm really sorry that I dragged you back here to reopen all the old wounds."

"It's not your fault. Betsy's been after me to come home for a visit ever since we got married. I had to face it sooner or later. You were merely the catalyst. Now I can go away knowing that nothing has changed in the nine years since I left—and nothing ever will. God Himself could descend from the heavens and they'd want to know where He went to prep school."

"You're right." She managed a smile. "I wish I hadn't blown it with you, though. I wanted you to see me as a tough executive, not a whimpering . . . jellyfish."

"How *I* see you shouldn't concern you in the slightest. What should concern you," he said, touching the tip of her nose, "is how you're going to get that mascara off your cheeks. Are you sure you're all right?"

"I'm fine."

"In that case, I'll go back and suffer a little more of this abysmal evening for the sake of my dear wife and father-in-law. And afterward I shall make perfectly clear to them that I am here to work, not to be on display, and that I will be unavailable for any future gatherings of the A-clan or A-team or whatever one calls them, including half a dozen insipid parties planned in our honor. Now patch up your pretty face and go out swinging."

She nodded as she watched his tall, broad-shouldered frame disappear through the door. He had a kind streak in him, no matter how he tried to hide it. She would never forget the day she told him about Frankie, and how he had taken her to lunch and done his best to cheer her up. Or maybe it was just that he hated to see a woman cry. Whatever the reasons, she knew one fact for certain: That damn chemistry was still there. No other man had ever affected her the way Nielson Hughes did—and no other man ever would.

32

"PAPA DOESN'T LOOK well, Lis."

Torie nibbled a bite of fruitcake as she pushed aside an empty ashtray, proud that she hadn't used one for almost three months. Breaking a twenty-one-year habit had been difficult, at times near-impossible, but she was determined to keep her promise to Betsy. "What do his doctors say?"

"That he's amazing." Lisa stood up and began to clear the table. "They don't know how he's managed to last this long. He's got almost everything wrong with him that a person could have, including cardiac disease. But he's not strong enough for surgery."

Torie stared hard at her sister. "I wish you wouldn't be so stubborn. Why can't you take him on a nice cruise? I'll send the doctor and his wife along too. You'd be doing it for Papa, not for me."

"Save your breath. He wouldn't go. Where's Michael? Hadn't you better check on him?"

"He's okay. I'll help you clean up."

"No, I'd rather you were with Papa. He sees so little of you these days."

Message received. Lisa never missed a chance for a sermon or a jab. Torie carried her dishes to the sink. "Christmas dinner was delicious—as always. When you get to that nunnery and they discover your cooking skills, they'll probably lock you in the kitchen and throw away the key."

"I'll serve the Lord wherever I'm needed."

"Yes, I'm sure you will." Torie walked out to the hall. Each year that Lisa stayed tied down to their father and unable to join the convent, she grew more resentful, more martyred, more infuriatingly self-righteous.

Michael was in the living room, curled up at the foot of his grandfather's chair.

"Is he behaving himself, Grandpa?"

"Mom, shhh! We can't hear the tel'vision."

"Sorry, darling." She lowered her tone. "You okay, Papa?"

Frank opened his eyes and nodded. He seemed to sleep so much of the time now. Torie checked her watch. Frank's cousins had left half an hour ago, Michael was already tired of playing with his new toys, and Jeff would be coming by any minute, to take him away for the week.

She wished he would hurry. Not that she wanted to get rid of Michael; on the contrary, she never seemed to have enough time with him. But what a relief it would be to go home. Each year, the West Mount Airy house depressed her more. Lisa lived in a dream world, turned off to everything but God and the church, and Papa had grown stooped and frail and spent most of his waking hours playing solitaire, reminiscing about the old days in the old neighborhood, and "waiting for the Lord to take me." Yet for all his physical disabilities, his mind was remarkably clear.

Michael jumped up at the sound of the bell. "Daddy!" he yelled, and ran out of the room.

"Don't open the door." Torie hurried after him, peered through the peephole, then turned the knob. "Hi," she said. "Happy Chanukah."

"Merry Christmas." Jeff smiled and picked up his son. "You're getting heavy, buster, you know that? I think your mom's feeding you too well."

"Look what I got!" Wiggling out of his father's arms, Michael ran into the living room and pointed to a pile of toys and games. "Lookit all my presents!"

"Wow. You'll need a truck to haul that load."

"I got a truck. See?"

Jeff walked over to Frank. "Merry Christmas, Papa. How're you doing?"

"Fine, just fine." Frank's face came alive. "You look wonderful, Jeff. The family all right? Fran? The children?"

"We're all doing great. I'd like to talk to you and Torie if you can spare a minute. Let's go in the dining room so Michael can watch his program."

"Kin I come with you?"

"We have grown-up matters to discuss." Jeff ruffled the boy's hair. "You can come in when your show's over. What're you watching?"

"Nuts!"

"Must be something new. I never heard of it."

With a pout, Michael sprawled out on the carpet and propped himself on his elbows.

Moments later, behind a closed door, Jeff sat facing his former wife and father-in-law. He clasped his hands in his lap and spoke quietly. "Do you remember last summer when I took Michael to that ranch in New Mexico? Do you remember how much he enjoyed it?"

"I remember what a long plane ride it was," said Torie, instantly wary, "and sweating it out waiting to hear you got there safely."

"It's a marvelous ranch," Jeff went on. "Two hundred acres of apple orchards, alfalfa fields, grazing land for horses and cattle, mountains everywhere—and it's only eighteen miles from Santa Fe."

Torie listened with growing apprehension.

"We all decided," he continued, "that last summer was the best summer we'd ever had. Fran was happy, Michael and the babies were happy, and I was in heaven. There's an artist's colony close by—kind of a central marketplace for all the art of the Southwest. I did some of the best work I've ever done. Sold a few paintings, too. That warm, rustic atmosphere suits me to a tee. I'm not a city person. I never was."

"The point, Jeff?"

"The point is—I bought that ranch yesterday. Fran and I and the kids are going to move out there as soon as we can get packed. And with your permission, I'd like to take Michael with us."

"You what?" Her voice rose in shock. "You want to take Michael—to live in New Mexico?"

"Shhh—yes." Jeff leaned forward, his eyes intense. "For his sake, Tor, not for mine. It's not healthy for a six-year-old to grow up in a palatial penthouse with a mother as busy as you are. I'm not saying you're a bad mother. You're a wonderful mother and Michael adores you. All I'm saying is that—"

"I hear you," she said, forcing herself to stay calm. "You're saying that you want to take my son away from me."

"Please don't put it that way. Can't you see that your son— our son—needs fresh air, and trees to climb, and streams to fish in, and kids around him? He needs a normal life and a chance to have a childhood. He doesn't need a nanny hovering over him, telling him he can't play with his finger paints because he'll stain his lace shirt or spill on Mommy's antique carpets. He needs more than an hour in the park every other day. Don't you see, Tor? I'm only thinking of Michael."

"Have you thought about his grandfather? How do you think Papa would feel if—"

"I can speak for myself." Frank's voice broke in, shaky but clear. "I'd still see my grandson. He could come home for Christmas and holidays, couldn't he, Jeff?"

"Of course he could. It's only a few hours on a plane and Michael loves to fly." Jeff turned to his unexpected ally. "You have more influence with your daughter than I do, Papa. Maybe you can convince her that I'm speaking the truth. I only want what's best for Michael."

"That's what we all want." Frank shook his head sadly. "I worry too. A boy should be outside, playing with other kids after school, not cooped up in some apartment with a Swedish maid."

"You too, Papa?" Torie jumped up angrily. "You'd be willing to let your grandson live thousands of miles from his own mother? You think *that's* good for a child?"

"Michael needs a mother full-time," said Frank. "He doesn't need someone who's so busy making money and building buildings that she thinks all she has to do is give him toys and he'll be happy. He doesn't need a mother who's so selfish and so involved in being fancy rich that she can't see how lonely her child is . . . how much he wants to be like other boys . . ."

"Oh, *criminy*." Torie dropped back into her chair and turned to her ex-husband. "What about schools? Piano lessons? Doctors? Dentists?"

Jeff smiled. "Santa Fe's a very civilized city. There's a fine grammar school and a world-famous medical center only a short drive away. I'd love you to come out and see the place—you too, Papa, if you feel up to it. We have a nice guest cottage. I think it would put your mind at ease. Wait, I forgot." He reached into his pocket. "I brought you a picture."

She took the snapshot reluctantly. The sprawling pueblo-type ranch house, with its lush trees and gardens and backdrop of towering mountains, did indeed look inviting. "It's beautiful," she said, returning the photo. "I'm sure you'll be happy there."

"Michael will be too—won't he?"

"I don't know, Jeff. Don't bug me for an answer. I'll need a few weeks to think this over."

"We haven't got a few weeks. The movers are coming Friday, and we're leaving Monday. We'll be there just in time to get settled so Michael can make an easy transition. He can start school the day after Christmas vacation."

Before she could protest the door burst open and the boy charged in. "Show's over," he announced, scrambling onto his father's lap. "Hey, what's that?"

He grabbed the picture, looked at it, then grinned. "That's our ranch in Mex'co! Kin we go back this summer, Daddy? Please?"

Torie sighed. Now she would have three people pressuring her. "You really liked it there, darling? What did you do all day?"

"Oh, we played and stuff. Daddy and I found secret caves where no one's ever been ever before. Kin we go back there, *please*?"

"It's up to your mother."

"Mommy, say yes. Please say yes, *please*?"

She looked from her father to her ex-husband and back again to her father. His eyes were stern, unrelenting, almost commanding her what to do. They seemed to be underscoring his words . . .

telling her that she had been thoughtless and selfish too long. And her son's small face was anxious . . . pleading . . .

With a grieving heart, she raised her head.

"Michael," she said hesitantly, "Daddy and Fran just bought that house—that big ranch in New Mexico. They want to take you there to live with them and go to school there. I'd come out to see you as often as I could and you could fly back to see Grandpa and Aunt Lisa and me. Do you think you'd like that?"

"Yeah," he said eagerly. "Kin I bring my 'lectric train and my puppets?"

"You can bring whatever you like." Jeff's voice cracked with emotion as he rose to his feet. "Now go ask Aunt Lisa for a bag, and start piling in your toys. Go on—get moving."

"Oh, boy!" he cried, and dashed out.

"Thank you, Papa." Jeff grasped the old man's hand, then turned to Torie and kissed her cheek. "I'll come by tomorrow to pick up some of his things and perhaps you can send the rest. You won't be sorry. You'll see him often, I promise."

"Won't I see him again before you go?" she asked, stunned.

"It's best this way, Tor. If we go straight from our house, he won't have the heavy trip of leaving home and his mother."

She stood in numb silence, kissed Michael good-bye, and watched Jeff walk out of her life . . . just as he had done five and a half years before. A wave of despair and helplessness swept over her as she realized that this time he wasn't going alone; he was taking her precious son along with him.

Overwhelmed by sadness, she dropped to her knees and laid her head on her father's lap. "Oh, Papa, what have I done? I should never have agreed to let Michael go. I shouldn't have let Jeff talk me into it. Michael's happy with me—we haven't any problems. He's going to be so lonesome . . . and so am I. What am I going to do without him?"

For the first time in years, Frank's eyes were warm as he looked down at her. And he spoke words she had long despaired of hearing. "You made a good decision, Vittoria . . . an unselfish one. You did the right thing for your son . . . for yourself . . . for all of us."

He stroked her hair and melted into a smile. "I'm proud of you."

The following week, the final days of 1986, Torie worked punishingly long hours, trying not to think about Michael, or how much she missed him. Ingrid came back from vacation on New Year's Day, and rather than watch her pack up the boy's clothes and toys, Torie wrapped herself in a fur and walked over to the Square.

Shivering in the late-afternoon cold, she glanced up at the two buildings soon to be sacrificed to the steel-beam framework of the Rittenhouse North. Unlike the glittering showplace she had envisioned, the new hotel would be subdued and dignified . . . what Nielson modestly called "a magnificent synthesis of the noblest elements of classical and contemporary traditions."

His sketches gave every assurance that it *would* be elegant enough to please even the stodgiest of Philadelphians, including Rebecca French and her ilk, who were determined to keep the city in mothballs. Torie hoped that once the hotel started going up, probably in June, it would garner so much attention and such positive press that her other permit requests would attract little notice.

In a short span of time, Nielson's name had worked miracles. Neighborhood and preservationist groups still held meetings and rallies protesting the despoiling of the Square, but their opposition was balanced by the architect's international reputation, worldwide interest in the project, and public recognition of what it could do for the city's stature.

At the moment, all that stood between her and her dream of putting up her own building on Rittenhouse Square was approvals—legal, social, economic, and political. And yet she felt confident. Her carefully cultivated friends on the various commissions could easily swing the votes. She was sure of it.

Bundling against the chill, she turned up her collar and was starting to head home when a flash of movement made her look toward the Richardson house. To her surprise, a figure in the window stood beckoning her.

She recognized Nielson, waved back, and walked at an angle toward the town house. Maybe Betsy would invite her for dinner. She wasn't ready to return to the empty apartment yet, and an evening of distraction would be welcome.

Nielson opened the front door and shut it quickly behind her. "Are you mad? Only Eskimos and polar bears go out in weather like this. Come stand by the fire."

"Th-thanks. It is a bit nippy." She hurried over to the mantel, shaking with cold, and rubbing her hands together. The heat of the room and the warmth of the flames soon revived her.

"Brandy?" he asked, trying not to stare too hard. Torie would always be an enigma to him. This little nothing of a girl who had no education, no money, and no background, who had been no more than a convenient and very hot lay at the time, had managed to parlay a face, a body, a sharp mind, and the guts of a lion tamer into her present status—one of the country's richest and most powerful women. He would never have believed it.

"No brandy, thanks. I'll just thaw out another minute and be on my way."

"Come into the kitchen. The help's all off and Matt's in New York. I'll make us some tea."

"That does sound tempting." She dropped her coat on the sofa and followed him down the hall, trying not to notice his familiar proud stride or how well he filled out his white turtleneck cashmere and navy slacks. "Will Betsy join us?"

He motioned her to a chair. "She went home right after Christmas. Once she'd seen her friends and visited with her father, she saw no reason to suffer the cold and the inconveniences. She's quite helpless and dependent here, and she hates that. In Scottsdale, she's a different person."

"Yes, in that beautiful house—"

"By the way, she said to say good-bye to you, and to thank you for your kindness. She'll call you after New Year's."

"I'll look forward to it." Torie clasped her hands on the table, and tried not to think about where she was . . . or why. For the first time since Nielson had come back, they were alone together, and for some reason he was trying very hard to be pleasant. "I was touched when I saw the home you designed and built for her. You've been a wonderful husband."

"I've tried my best. She's an amazing woman." He filled two cups and set one in front of her. "Sugar? Cream? Milk?"

"No," she said, smiling. "Just the tea."

"Forgot that minor item, did I? Good thing I'm not a surgeon." Reaching into a cabinet, he took down a box of tea bags and set them on the table. "It just occurred to me that I haven't eaten all day. Are you hungry?"

"A little. I could fix us a sandwich."

"I feel like a good meal—no offense. I've been working on those plans till I'm bleary-eyed, and I deserve a break. The decent restaurants will all be closed today, but I know one that might be open. Wait here. I'll get my overcoat and be right down."

How like him not even to ask if she wanted to go . . . or if she *could* go. "What about our tea?"

"Pour it down the sink," he called from the stairway.

"It doesn't seem like fifteen years since we were here." Nielson hung their coats on a brass rack and slid into the booth beside her. He didn't know why he felt a sense of excitement being with Torie, and it didn't matter. He had long ago made peace with his emotions; anything he did was all right as long as it didn't hurt Betsy. "Or is it sixteen?"

"One or the other." Settling back in her seat, Torie glanced around the room. He had amazed her by taking her back to the South Philly trattoria where they had dined together to celebrate the completion of the St. Francis Tower. Her memories of that night were disturbingly clear; she had been desperately in love with him and full of schemes to get him involved in her next project. But only a week later, he had stomped out of the press party in a rage. "The plastic grapevines on the wall haven't changed. Neither have those horrendous murals. How'd you happen to remember this place?"

"I remember it quite well. I remember looking at you across the candlelight and thinking that I'd never seen skin so soft and translucent. That hasn't changed. If anything, you've grown lovelier."

His compliment was surprisingly personal, but his tone was casual and he neither dwelled on his words nor gazed into her eyes as he said them, which gave her some reassurance that he wasn't about to get romantic. In her vulnerable mood, with the holidays over, and missing Michael as much as she did, any real warmth on his part might be more than she could handle. "What else do you remember about that night?"

"Great food."

"I remember that too." She laughed and unfolded her napkin. "I also remember having a terrible crush on you and knowing it wasn't returned. Did you know that?"

Of course he knew it. "In my younger days, I suppose I felt all women had terrible crushes on me and that was a fact of life. My work came first, as you know. I never took you or any other woman seriously."

"Except Betsy."

"Well, yes. She was always in the back of my mind. I'd planned to marry her ever since grammar school, and the accident wasn't going to change my feelings. If anything, I felt she needed me more." He motioned to the waiter. "Bring us a '65 Cabernet Sauvignon."

"We no have, *signore*. I take your order?"

Nielson studied the menu. "We'll share one portion of cappellini *al dente* to start, then two veal piccatas, à la carte, two mixed green salads with vinegar and olive oil—be sure it's *pure* olive oil—some hot garlic bread, buttered, no margarine, and, umm, a large bottle of your best Chianti. All right, Torie?"

"I can't eat that much."

"I'll help you." He nodded to the waiter. "Bring the wine and the garlic bread right away, please."

"*Si, signore*," he said, scribbling on his pad. "*Subito*."

By the time the espressos arrived, Torie was feeling replete, relaxed, and slightly giddy from the wine. Nielson had done 90 percent of the talking, entertaining her with tales of his work, his honors and awards, and how his life had changed after the *Time* cover story.

"It was phenomenal," he went on, with a gesture of helplessness. "Overnight I became a kind of cult figure . . . a national hero . . . almost a deity to some people. The day the article appeared, one of my office staff—a rather good-looking woman, actually—stopped me in the hall to tell me she had talents I had never taken advantage of. Can you imagine? Here's this female I've been working with for six years, and suddenly she throws herself at me."

Torie coddled her wineglass and pretended only a passing interest. "Did you catch?"

"Good Lord, no, I ran the other direction. Nothing turns me off more than a public drinking fountain." He dropped a sugar lump into his cup. "I make no pretense of having been faithful to Betsy, but whatever I've done has been with the utmost discretion and respect for my wife. I would never do anything to shame or embarrass her. Deep in my heart I think she knows I've strayed now and then. But she also knows that I love her very much and always come home to her. I don't see anything callous about that, do you?"

He could change personalities faster than she could blink. One minute she admired him, and the next she found him impossibly smug. "You mean—considering your gargantuan ego?"

"Hmmm. How quaint of you to put it that way. I suppose

you're right, actually. And because Betsy—well, our sex life is rather limited. The strange thing is that I *have* been faithful for the last two years."

"Why?"

"All these new diseases make sexual relations with strangers decidedly unappetizing. AIDS is a heavy price to pay for an orgasm. And then there's my increased visibility as a public figure. Not only would I be subject to blackmail, I'd be risking a scandal that could damage my family and my reputation. I rather like the rarefied air on my pedestal."

She nodded. "I know what you mean. I couldn't stand to have some guy spreading lies about me, or selling 'intimate details' to the tabloids. It seems easier to stay uninvolved—although it does get lonely."

"Lonely at the top." He motioned for the check. "One of life's better clichés—and truer ones, regrettably. The greater a person's success, the more he or she becomes a target. What *do* you do for companionship?"

"If you mean sex, I try not to think about it. I'm wildly busy, just as you are." She debated telling him how much she missed Michael, then decided not to. Sharing her sadness would not lessen it. "I might even get married again, one day. I remember how nice it was, in the beginning, having someone to come home to at night . . . having someone you could count on . . . having all your emotional needs solved."

"Nonsense. If your emotional needs had been solved, you wouldn't be divorced." He laid a hundred-dollar bill on the check and handed it to the waiter. "Keep the change."

"Thanks for dinner," she said, happy to move to a new subject. "You're an excellent orderer."

"I do have a certain flair, don't I." He turned to her with a perplexed frown. "Look here, I'm not ready to go home yet, and it's too cold to run around to nightclubs. Any suggestions?"

"I know a bar over by The Bourse that has a fireplace."

"I don't feel up to mingling with the hoi polloi. Do you have any cognac in your apartment? Is there a separate entrance so we don't have to pass the doorman?"

"Yes to both questions." She laughed to relieve the tension. Why did he want to go to her apartment? Why was it so important to bypass the doorman? Was he thinking the unthinkable? Didn't he know what temptations . . .

"Where is this private entrance?" he asked, helping her into his car.

"You follow the driveway to the garage. My remote control opens the door, you drive in and park, we take the basement elevator up to my door, and no one sees us or spreads tacky rumors—that is, unless someone happens to be in the elevator."

"I'll run the big risk if you will."

He was teasing and yet he wasn't. If they were seen going up to her apartment together at that hour of the night, that *would* be hard to explain. A warning voice told her to say no—to plead tiredness or an early-morning appointment or anything that would get her out of taking him back with her. But what could happen? He hadn't made any advances, he had explained why he had been faithful for the last two years, and they both loved Betsy too much to do anything that could hurt her. Thus reassured, she turned to him with a smile. "Why not," she said. "I've always been a gambler."

The stereo played Bach, a single ceiling spot highlighted the delicate Degas painting by the piano, and Nielson stood with his back to his hostess, perusing her liqueurs. "Ah, Champagne Cognac, V.S.O.P.—may I pour you some?"

The same impossible snob, she thought. Wealth and success hadn't made him any more democratic. In truth, very little about him had changed. He was no less conceited, though he could couch his arrogance in humor when he wanted to, and no less belligerent toward the world, even though it had finally recognized his genius. Nor had success changed his feelings toward his father. She could still feel anger and resentment well up in him whenever Robert Nielson's name was mentioned. "About three drops, please. Snifters are in the cabinet to your left."

He carried the goblets to the coffee table. "Why are you sitting in the chair? Afraid to join me on the couch?"

"Why would I be afraid?"

"That's what I'm asking. It's not as if we're those two rutting adolescents thrashing about on the floor of my drafting room."

So he did remember. "I'm sure I wasn't the first—or the last."

"Did I say you were? Now be a good hostess and come sit by me."

"I'm fine where I am."

"You can't possibly be." He took her hands and pulled her

to her feet. "For the sake of making a point, I'm going to kiss you and show you how little you affect me."

"Nielson, please! You mustn't—"

He silenced her with his lips, holding her tightly as she struggled and pushed against his shoulders and tried desperately not to respond. The more she fought, the more aroused he became, pressing his stiffness against her, driving his tongue between her lips and opening her mouth . . . until suddenly, helplessly, she felt all the resistance run out of her body.

Her arms crept around his neck, and soon she was meeting his mouth with equal fervor, letting her tongue glide in and out to touch his, then sliding her hands over the expanse of his back, down to his tight buttocks . . .

He tried to draw her to the couch but she pulled away.

"No, no—not here." Breathlessly, she led him through the hallway to her bedroom. A lamp glowed softly on the night table, and the turned-down sheets gleamed invitingly. Her conscience surfaced for a brief instant, telling her it was not too late to stop. She could still say no to him, still maintain it was unfair to Betsy . . . but her heart and her body were throbbing insistently, and her brain wasn't listening to reason.

Fumbling in the semidarkness, he unbuttoned her dress and let it slide to the floor, then slipped off her bra and cupped her taut, full breasts in his hands. "You're as beautiful as you ever were," he said intensely. "Only more so. You've filled out. You've become a ripe, luscious woman and you turn me on even more, if that's possible. Remember what I once told you about passion?"

"Yes—but we weren't hurting anyone then." Except me, she almost added.

"We're not hurting anyone now." He set her down on the pillow and lay alongside her, staring hungrily at her breasts. "Betsy understands," he said, caressing her nipples and feeling them erect to his touch. "She knows she can't answer all my needs. She won't ever find out about tonight, and she would understand if she did."

He stilled her protest with a long, slow kiss that generated a burning electricity as he moved her hand down his body and placed it where he wanted it.

Almost unable to believe what was happening, Torie told herself that this was *Nielson* she was lying next to . . . it was *his* sex she was stroking and fondling . . . the man of her fantasies . . .

the only man she had ever really loved. And he was right. She *had* matured sexually and every other way, and she was anxious to prove it. That panting little puppy who would roll over and spread for him was long gone.

With deliberate restraint, she opened his zipper and ran her tongue and lips over him, teasing him, bedeviling him, knowing she was driving him as mad as he was driving her. "Jesus," he moaned, "where did you learn . . ."

His groans increased as her exquisite pleasure-torture continued, his needs becoming more and more pressing, until finally, unable to hold back any longer, he pulled himself from her hands and slid over on top of her.

Groping in her silky underpants, he touched her where he knew she loved to be touched, and felt a violent tremor as she arched high in response. All he wanted was to sink into her tight, warm, wetness, and he helped her squirm out of her panties . . . straining . . . moaning . . . and finally slamming himself in and out of her with the force of his urgency.

She cried aloud, repeating his name, receiving him avidly . . . all controls gone as their motions accelerated. Her gasps and calls grew shorter and faster, and soon he felt her surrender to the supreme convulsion as a rocket of fire and energy surged through him.

And when they came back, he looked down into her face. "You see, Torie?" he whispered. "Kissing you doesn't affect me in the slightest."

PART
VI

33

THE PHONE BROKE into Torie's sleep. One hand flailed out and reached for the receiver. " 'Lo?" she mumbled.

"Oops, did I wake you? I was told you bounced out of bed every morning at six."

"Who is this?"

"McGarren. Keith McGarren. Shall I call later?"

She grabbed her clock and set it down again. Three minutes to seven. Nielson had left only two hours ago. "Oh, no, thanks. I usually do get up at six. Last night . . . I . . . had trouble falling asleep. What can I do for you?"

"Could we meet today after work?"

"I'm sorry, Keith. I haven't had a minute to think over your offer. Could you give me another few days to make a decision?"

"What are you talking about? Ellory Davis gave me your answer two weeks ago."

Damn Ellory. So that was how Keith had gotten her private phone number. "What did he say?"

"That you and he had talked it over and you were thrilled with the idea of a cover story. He sent over four scrapbooks of press clippings—including one I wrote myself in '65 when I worked for the *Evening Bulletin.*"

"Sixty-five," she repeated. Then the realization struck. "Oh, my God! I *knew* your name was familiar. You wrote the piece about my father—the editorial saying his sentence was too harsh. I carried that clipping around with me for weeks. You were the only reporter with the guts to stick up for him. You'll never know what that meant to our family."

"Your father was a victim—a scapegoat. He shouldn't have gone to prison for doing what was common practice in those days. We'll mention that briefly in the article and set the record straight."

"That would mean a lot to Papa. Ellory would like it, too. He's worried my enemies will use it against me."

"You do have a few challengers. I brought up your name at a dinner party and got quite a reaction. I had no idea people felt so strongly. They either love you or want to run you out of town."

"Mostly the latter."

"I wouldn't say that. Even your enemies give you credit. One man told me—let's see, I wrote it down: 'She's sharp, tough, and tenacious, and she has a knack for knowing what to buy and when. There's never been a hint of corruption in her empire. But she has no feeling for the thousands of tenants she's evicted, the contractors she's driven crazy with her demands, or the visual pollution she's created with her glitzy shopping malls and her obsession with overtall skyscrapers. Her arrogant dismissal of the past is destroying the city. Someone ought to stop her before she turns Philadelphia into a poor man's Manhattan.' Care to comment?"

She chuckled into the receiver. "That's what I wanted to think over—whether or not I want to be skewered. I can't believe Ellory made the choice for me. He never said a word about talking to you."

"You're not going to make a liar out of him, are you?"

"He already is a liar." She threw off the comforter and sat up in bed, acutely conscious of her nude, tingling body. Whatever regrets she had about the previous night, she was grateful to Nielson for a resurgence of vitality . . . for the awakening of long-dormant responses. "Since you've taken the trouble to record such a flattering statement about me, I guess I've no choice but to defend myself."

"A drink after work?"

"Sounds great." She reached for her robe, then let it slide to the carpet and walked over to her window. The sun was beginning to rise in a clear blue sky, and the city—her city—looked deceptively peaceful. The day would bring pressures, tensions, explosions, hostility . . . but she flourished on battle and felt eager to take on all contenders. "Why don't you stop by around six, Keith. Do you know where I live?"

"Yes, I know where you live. I know where you were born, and I know where you grew up. I even know your middle name,

Vittoria Francesca. And now I know that I'll see you at six this evening."

"Okay, but don't expect—" A click on the line told her the conversation was over. Keith McGarren was not a telephone person.

Dressing for work, Torie found herself thinking more about Keith and what she would wear for their meeting than about the Swedish stud, as Peggy called him, whom she had loved—or fancied herself in love with—for half her life.

The two men were as different as caviar and chocolate, she realized, choosing a lavender cashmere dress she knew was flattering. Nielson was neurotic and patronizing and clearly hadn't planned to resume their affair any more than she had. Despite his stubborn refusal to be compared with his father, it was obvious that he had come back to Philadelphia for only one reason: to prove himself the greater architect.

Yet much as Nielson hated and resented his father and claimed to have locked him out of his psyche, she felt certain he would have little hesitation if Robert Nielson ever opened his arms and said, "It's time we got together, son."

Keith had a paternal situation too, but he seemed to be far less complicated. He gave the impression that he had no time for brooding or evasiveness and preferred to approach people openly and directly. If anything, he erred on the side of bluntness—a bluntness she found strangely appealing, and not without kindness and sensitivity.

But then, Keith was a communicator by profession, and Nielson, although articulate when he wanted to be, had closed off certain areas of consciousness and simply refused to deal with them. After making love to her a second time, early that morning, he had dressed and gone home without saying a word about their relationship, without showing any sign of affection, without giving her any indication of when they would see each other again. It was, in a way, as if they had picked up their affair of fifteen years ago and gone on as if nothing had happened.

Nevertheless, she thought, as she fastened a long strand of pearls, his behavior was appropriate. The less said about the previous night the better. She could forgive herself a one-time incident with a man she had loved, but she must never let it happen again. Having sex with him had done something nothing else could have done: It closed the chapter and put to rest her infatuation . . . forever. The sex was still good . . . great . . . *fantas-*

tic, if she had to admit it. But it was animal sex, purely carnal. Lust without love.

In such circumstances, an ongoing affair would be both foolish and unconscionable. No matter how much he'd protested that Betsy understood, an unfaithful husband was something no woman "understood"—even a woman in Betsy's heartbreaking condition.

The second day of 1987 started off with an appearance at Tony Silvano's trial, in a courtroom packed with reporters. Once the FBI had begun digging, they had unearthed enough corruption to bring four separate felony charges against the councilman. Torie's testimony was brief and convincing, and she looked the defendant straight in the eye as she left the courtroom. His accusatory expression evoked no regrets or sympathy. A prison term would be too good for the slimebag.

The rest of the day was filled with appointments, visits, calls, and constant calculations on a yellow legal pad. Di Angelo Tower was back under construction, still aiming for a May completion. (As expected, several other businesses, including a bank, a trade center, and two major corporations, had also gotten zoning permits to exceed the height limit.)

Penn's Landing remained a giant headache. Prospective tenants all seemed to be waiting to see if Di Angelo Tower really would set off a building boom and energize the city's retail climate. Without tenants, no one would discuss financing—not even John Loder, the banker who had denied her first big loan request, and who now called regularly *wanting* her business.

Representatives of a group of Rittenhouse Square residents came by late that afternoon, at first polite and reasonable, then angrily threatening lawsuits if she didn't take her hotel elsewhere. She had no intention of taking her hotel elsewhere and she so informed them, pleasantly but firmly.

As usual, she didn't leave her office until early evening. When she finally walked into her apartment, Keith McGarren stood waiting in the living room.

"Hello," he said brightly. "You're right on time."

She set down her briefcase. "You seem surprised."

"I shouldn't be. You were prompt for our lunch date." He glanced around the room. "I had a brief chat with Ingrid. She's delighted you're keeping her on. You must miss Michael a great deal."

"Boy, you don't waste a minute." Torie settled into a chair and appraised her visitor. Like it or not, this man was there not as a friend or a suitor but to pry out buried facts and secrets—to probe into her private life for the sole purpose of revealing them to the public. A momentary wave of resentment swept over her. She wasn't selling perfume or running for office. Why should she have to put up with a stranger nosing into her affairs? He'd already informed her he wouldn't be writing the article himself, so she wouldn't even be dealing with Keith McGarren.

And that, she mused, would be a shame. The more she saw of the good-looking editor, the more she was intrigued by him—by his straightforward approach, his professionalism, his confident, easygoing masculinity. He stood about six foot one, she guessed, was mid-fortyish, lanky, fond of tweed sportcoats with patched elbows, and not given to small talk or idle flirtation. Unlike so many men in positions of power, he didn't use his considerable assets to play ego games.

Ingrid appeared, took their drink orders, and vanished. "Did you have a busy day?" he asked. "Or am I asking the pope if he prayed."

She smiled. "His Holiness and I both do what we do best—instill faith and shoot for the heavens. It was a good day. My New York investment counselor sold off forty thousand shares of Bickman Oil and racked up a six-figure profit."

The numbers made little impression. "You don't handle your own investments?"

"Not in the market. Bernard Baruch said one should never speculate unless it's full-time. So I stick to what I know—real estate—and hire experts to do everything else. Sometimes you've got to give up power to get power."

"Isn't that hard to do?"

"It was at first. My ego had to accept that I couldn't become an authority on everything."

"Yet you have time to read Baruch."

"Reading's my only real escape. Besides, he was right. My portfolio's averaged an eighteen-point-two-percent profit in the last five years, and I haven't lifted a finger. Oh, God, that'll sound so smug in print. I *do* have reservations about this story—"

"Then why are you doing it?"

"Hmm. I'd like to say Ellory volunteered me, but that isn't entirely true. I pay him a fortune to keep my name before the public, so I can't complain when he does his job. The name recognition's been good for business, and good for me, personally. I get kind of a publicity high when I read something positive about myself."

"Why?"

"Insecurity, I suppose. Goes back to childhood. In South Philly, you were a big shot if you got your name in the papers—except for going to jail."

"That's true everywhere."

"Is it? I just know I've spent too many years striving for acceptance and approval in this narrow-minded town not to be pleased when I get them."

"What if the publicity's negative?"

"You get used to it. Ellory taught me that people love underdogs. You have to be battered a bit, otherwise—oh, excuse me, that might be Michael." She reached for the telephone. "Hello?"

"Torie?" Nielson's voice caught her off guard. "I know a small out-of-the-way place that has the most superb *goujonettes* of Dover sole you've ever tasted. I'll pick you up in front of your building in fifteen minutes."

The man was unbelievable. "Sorry, I can't make it tonight."

"Of course you can make it. It's me—Nielson."

"I know who it is. But I have company. Perhaps another time—"

"Get rid of the damn company."

"I can't do that."

"What about later?"

"I'm tied up all evening."

The silence on the phone told her he was stunned. If he expected her to be that same lovestruck girl who would drop everything, at whatever hour of the day or night he called, and rush to be with him, it was time he realized those days were over. "Give me more notice in the future, will you?"

"Notice!" His voice rose in anger. "You want an engraved invitation?"

"That's not necessary, and I don't care to argue." Replacing the receiver, she turned to Keith in embarrassment. "Forgive me for answering, but I thought it might be Michael. It wasn't."

"So I gather. Lover's quarrel?"

"No."

"Was that the man in your life?"

She regarded him at first with irritation, then amusement.

"None of your business who that was. Frankly, the only man in my life right now is my son."

"That's hard to believe."

Ingrid reappeared with their drinks, and Torie raised her goblet. "Calling me a liar?"

"No, paying you a compliment." He clinked glasses. "Here's to our story. You're right, of course—your personal life is none of my business. But even journalists have ethics. If you tell me something's off the record, that's where it'll stay."

"I've heard *that* line before. And I've gotten up the next morning to read my off-the-record comments in headlines."

"Every profession has its turkeys. You wouldn't want to be judged by the tactics of a third-rate developer. Why judge me and my magazine by some unethical reporter?"

"You've got a point." She chuckled and passed him a bowl of nuts. "I still don't trust you."

He took an almond, than handed back the dish. "Suppose I were to do something I've never done before—let you read and approve your quotes before we print them."

Her eyes widened slightly. "Are you serious?"

"Word of honor."

"Why would you do that?"

"Because you've been burned, and I don't want you to be burned again—especially by us."

"There must be a quid pro quo."

"There is. I want this to be a sensitive, human story that will grab every reader, male and female, young and old, rich and semirich—"

"*Semi*rich?"

"I can't say poor. Our readers *aren't* poor. We don't appeal to the average American or the *Money* magazine family trying to balance its budget on a schoolteacher's salary. Our subscribers are mostly executives, chairmen of the board, upwardly mobile yuppie-types. That's why I want this feature to go deeper and be more revealing than anything ever written about you. And the only way I'll get that is if you can let your guard down and talk freely and honestly, without fear of being misquoted. *That's* the quid pro quo."

"In that case," she said, reassured, "It's a deal. I assume you came here to see how difficult I'm going to be."

"No, I came because I like to give my writers a handle—an

idea as to what direction I want the story to take." He slipped on his brown-rimmed spectacles. "Ready for a few questions?"

"Start the inquisition." The glasses, she noted, were most becoming. They made him look like a middle-aging Clark Kent. She would like to ask a few questions too. How old was he? Did he have children? Did he live alone? Was he unattached at the moment?

For the next half hour, she answered his queries as honestly as she could, elaborating on some subjects, steering away from others, and, despite her wariness, opening up to him more than she realized. He surprised her by volunteering information about his own background, and when she felt it wouldn't sound improper, she asked how "recent" a bachelor he was.

He nodded, as if the question was expected. "I'm a twenty-year veteran of marital disharmony, with an ex-wife and two grown-up kids. My daughter's at Hartley's Fashion Institute, and my son's an economics major at Harvard. He's thinking about coming to work for me after graduation."

"*Thinking* about it?"

"Well, Carter knows *I* had other jobs before joining the magazine. He feels he might get a better offer."

"Sounds like a smart young man. Maybe I should hire him."

"Be my guest," he said, with a grin. "Teach him all you know, and then I'll steal him away from you."

"On second thought—never mind." She smiled, nibbled a nut, and tried to sound impersonal. "What broke up your marriage?"

"To quote a charming young woman, 'None of your business.'" He rose. "Listen, I have to go."

"Was it her lover, your mistress, or both?"

He laughed. "You're worse than I am. All right: My ex and I married young, and when we grew up, we had about as much in common as Mr. T. and the tooth fairy. She liked to sleep till noon and party all night, and I like to get up early, work like a madman for ten hours, and relax at night. It went much deeper than that, of course. We disagreed about practically everything, and made each other miserable for a long time. When Carter went off to college two years ago, we split up. She's remarried now, and living in Paris. The kids say she's happy, and I hope she is."

"What about you?"

"Am I happy?" He shrugged. "If happiness is the absence of pain, I suppose I qualify. More accurately, I'm in limbo. Married to my job at the moment. It keeps me from thinking about what's lacking in my life."

She followed him across the room.

"I'm heading for the Poconos tomorrow for some easy downhill skiing," he went on, talking as he walked. "I'll be back Tuesday and have a writer for you by Friday. Think you can wait?"

"I'll force myself." She smiled and opened the door. "Have fun on the slopes."

By Saturday morning, Nielson had cooled down enough to call back; insisting he had vital matters to discuss, he convinced Torie to see him that evening. Over dinner in a small, candlelit restaurant on South Street he told her his latest ideas for the Rittenhouse North, and the time schedule he had mapped out for construction.

She listened to him, enjoying his growing enthusiasm for the project, and at the same time promising herself that she would not invite him back to the apartment, would not go to bed with him that night. He didn't wait to be invited, however, and on the way home he grabbed the remote control and drove into the garage.

"You can't deny yourself to me," he said, ignoring her protests as they rode up in the elevator. "You've awakened passions that have been dead in me for two years. I'd almost forgotten what it was like to feel the soft, smooth body of a woman under me . . ."

"That's the point, Nielson. I'm just a woman to you. I could be anyone. I didn't care for the role when I was twenty, and now that I'm almost thirty-six I care even less."

"Don't talk nonsense. You want me as much as I want you." He bent down to her lips and once again his touch—the feel of his body heat—electrified her.

There was no refusing him that night. The next morning, she swore to herself on her mother's honor that she had slept with him for the last time. While the sex was still wild and intoxicating, she reminded herself that she no longer loved or cared for him. All the fantasies she had kept alive over the years, even during her marriage, had been just that—fantasies. In the flesh, Nielson was a brilliant, spoiled, phenomenally self-centered man who needed a Betsy, or someone like the old Torie, to adore him unconditionally, put up with his moods and tantrums, and ask no questions. The tender, affectionate lover she had built up in her mind was a phantom. He didn't exist in the person of Nielson Hughes, and he never had.

Despite the orders Torie had given not to be disturbed while she penciled out an estimate Monday morning, the light on her desk flashed insistently. She finally pressed the intercom. "Are my ten o'clock people here, Jane?"

"No, it's a gentleman to see you, a Mr. McGarren. I told him you couldn't possibly—"

"That's all right." Instinctively, she reached for a comb and mirror. "Show him in, please."

Keith's appearance in the doorway, several minutes later, brought her to her feet with a gasp. Both his hands were in casts supported by shoulder slings. A white bandage covered his brow and wound around his head like a skullcap.

"It's all your fault," he growled. "You told me to have fun on the slopes."

"I didn't tell you to *kill* yourself." She pulled up a chair for him. "Are you all right?"

"I'm not dead, if that's what you mean." He dropped onto the seat. "Lousy damn sport. Tripped over my own skis and tried to break my fall with my hands. Fell flat on my head."

"Oh, dear. Did you hurt the snow?"

"Very funny. And so original." He exhaled loudly. "Two sprained wrists, a conk on the noggin, and a bruised ego are my main battle scars. But I have to wear these goddamn splints, and I can't type, can't write, can't even hold the phone. Mac said I was driving everyone crazy and threw me out of the office. I said fine, I'd take sick leave and see him in three weeks."

"What about your work? Your column?"

"My column's written, and Mac's taking over my editing chores. Talk about a disaster. He slashes copy like Jack the Ripper, scribbles a three-word critique, and signs it, 'Mac the Knife.' Last time I came back from a leave, half my staff was ready to quit. I'll probably lose my best people before the month's up. And all I can do is flop around like a goddamn mummy and bang my flippers."

The sight of the big, macho editor sitting there with his fingers poking out of the casts, reduced to helplessness by a very *un*-macho accident, was too humorous to resist. "I'm sorry you were hurt," she said, trying to keep a straight face, "but you're breaking me up."

"Your choice of words stinks."

"How about: 'You've got me in stitches?' " His disapproving scowl dissolved her last bit of reserve, and she burst into laughter.

"I'm glad one of us is amused," he said, glaring.

"I'm s-sorry, really I am. Even if it doesn't sound like it." She wiped her eyes with a tissue. "You came here for some sympathy, and all I do is go off in hysterics."

"I *didn't* come for sympathy. I came to tell you that I found you a writer."

"Oh?"

"You're looking at him—old plaster paws himself. I need a project for my convalescence. I can't take notes, but I can babble into my recorder. Any objections?"

"I don't know. How do you plan to proceed?"

"I plan to observe you in the office a few days, ride around with you, get a feel for how you operate, how you meet people, what you do in an average twelve hours—"

"If you mean you want to shadow me and eavesdrop on all my conversations, the answer is no. Why don't you take your flippers and go to the zoo? Go see a play—or a movie. There must be something you can do besides snoop on me."

"I will *not* be snooping. I'll sit quietly in a corner, and you won't even know I'm here. If you have something private to discuss, I'll leave."

"For good?"

"No. What are you afraid of? I promised you could see your quotes before we run the story. How can you get hurt?"

The lights on the intercom were flashing, her ten o'clock appointment was due in three minutes, and Peggy was standing in the doorway with a batch of letters.

"Oh, all right, we'll give it a *try* for one morning. If it doesn't work, out you go. No two weeks' notice, no severance pay, nothing. Come on in, Piglet. Meet Keith McGarren, and then forget he's here."

"Nice to meet you, Mr. McGarren. I've heard a lot about you." Peggy appraised his casts with a raised eyebrow. "I see you've run into problems. Does that mean we won't be getting our February issue?"

34

KEITH'S PRESENCE IN Torie's office caused little, if any, disruption. Peggy provided him with a chair, a table, on which he kept his recorder, tapes, magazines, and a pitcher of ice water that he gradually became adept enough to pour himself.

True to his promise, he was not intrusive, and although Torie introduced him to all visitors, only a few asked that he leave while they talked business. Most recognized his name and were pleased to meet him, or enjoyed the prospect of being mentioned in a national magazine.

To her amazement, Torie quickly adjusted to having Keith around and even began to look forward to their chats between appointments. He was keenly alert to people—to their needs and motives—and his instant appraisals were generally accurate. His grasp of economics was equally impressive. While he was not obsessed with money, as he had once explained, he clearly understood matters of finance.

Checking her calendar on a Monday morning late in January, Torie realized—with conflicting emotions—that it was Keith's last day in her office. She would be glad to be able to talk freely again and not have to worry about every word she spoke and how it might look in print. At the same time, she would miss seeing him sitting across the room, watching her with his detached, half-cynical expression—or occasionally, when he thought she wasn't looking, letting a glimmer of pleasure or a hint of admiration cross his face.

She would even miss having him accompany her to various construction sites, bank appointments, corporation interviews, political caucuses, and board meetings—although his observations had not always been flattering. Once, when she asked him

320

how other people saw her, he told her that very few cared about her as a person. The so-called friends who sucked up to her wherever she went, he felt, were about "as sincere as the vegetarian actress who does 'real beef' commercials."

The main disadvantage to his presence, however, had been the embarrassment she felt at having to ask him to leave the office when she wanted a private chat with Peggy or her architects, or to make calls to Michael and, once, to Nielson.

Typically, and most unprofessionally, Nielson had flown back to Arizona without thinking to notify her. When she phoned his office in Scottsdale, she was told he was "not available," but a secretary called back to say that he had his drafting staff working overtime, and that he would be returning to Philadelphia on Sunday, February first, with a set of new, improved plans.

The prospect of his return made her uneasy. She had less than a week to figure out how to tell him their brief affair was over— if indeed it had ever really begun. How many sex acts constituted an affair? she wondered. Perhaps, after going home to his wife and taking time to reflect, he would realize the foolish risks they had taken.

"Knock, knock. Anybody here?"

Torie looked up to see Keith standing in the doorway. His arms, still in casts but temporarily out of their slings, dangled at his sides. All that remained of the head bandage was a yellow-gray bruise on his brow. "Good morning."

"It's a very good morning for you," he said, approaching her desk. "As soon I get the rest of this apparatus off, you'll be rid of me forever—almost."

"Only almost?" she asked, feigning disappointment.

"Okay, here's the situation. I've got a pretty fair idea of how you tackle projects, how you use your brains and charms to great advantage, and how you rule your empire. What I don't know is what makes Her Majesty run . . . what keeps you going . . . what motivates you. Why the fixation—if that's what it is— about Rittenhouse Square?"

"I told you, I don't want to discuss that."

"Why not? What comes after the Rittenhouse North? Why have you spent half the national debt trying to buy up that block? Why the hush-hush meetings with your architects? I keep hearing that you want to tear everything down and put up some glitzy new development. Why *can't* you talk about it?"

The direct question sent Torie's brain spinning. She knew rumors were circling like vultures over a carcass. Still, she faced him defiantly. "I'll make my announcement when I'm ready."

"That's not good enough. I want to hear the story from *you*, and I want to hear it now. I want to know what the hell you've been plotting all these weeks and why you haven't seen fit to trust me. I'm keeping my part of the bargain and I expect you to keep yours. That means honesty."

"I haven't lied to you. I just haven't told you everything."

He glared at her in angry silence.

"Oh, Christ, Keith," she finally said, slamming down her legal pad. "Sometimes you can be so damn patronizing. Okay, they're right. All the rumors flying around are right. The dumb dago bitch from South Philly who has no regard for history or tradition or Mrs. French's bleeping ancestors is about to send this mausoleum of a town into orbit. Got that?"

"Go on," he ordered.

"I *am* going to tear down those crumbling relics. I own that whole block of Walnut Street except for the library on the corner, and it can rot away to eternity, for all I care. I *am* going to put up a development around the Rittenhouse North—a dazzling office high rise, and a glittery new shopping complex with a bridge to the park. And you know what I'm calling it? Di Angelo Center. Di Angelo Center on Rittenhouse Square."

"Fascinating," he said, without emotion.

Her head tilted defiantly. "You think I can't?"

"I think the residents would sooner approve a brothel."

"Then you're in for a surprise. Money buys a lot of friends. It's like manure. You spread it around and it works. Even preservationists need money."

"Perhaps." His voice was once again friendly as he asked, "Do you remember telling me you never let personal preferences affect your business judgment?"

"Yes." She was as anxious as he was not to argue. "But this is different, Keith. I don't care about making money in this deal. I don't care if it costs me millions. I can't explain any further. It's just something I have to do."

"I'll quote you on that—subject to your approval, of course. In the meantime, can we meet after work and chat briefly about your personal life?"

"What personal life? I called Michael yesterday, and he said he missed me, so I'll fly to New Mexico this weekend. That's my thrilling personal life." She glanced at her watch. "Now, when's *your* big moment?"

"About an hour. At approximately eleven o'clock, God and Dr. Brophy willing, I will regain control of my manual extremities. And in case I haven't told you I appreciate your putting up with me these past weeks. It's been most therapeutic having something to do with my time."

"I hate to admit it, but it hasn't been *too* terrible having you around."

"Thanks, I think." He slipped his left arm into the sling. "What about this evening?"

Before she could answer, the door opened, and Peggy marched in, carrying a cupcake with three burning candles. She set it down on Torie's desk and beamed at Keith. "Happy wristday."

"*Pour moi?*" He lifted the pastry with a delighted grin. "I'm speechless!"

"That'll be the day," said Torie, looking pleased.

Peggy tapped his arm. "We wanted to give you a 'cast' party—get it? Now blow out your candles, one for each week, and make a wish."

"Thanks, Piglet. You're a special lady." He doused the flames in a breath, then glanced at Torie. "What about tonight? Are you going to help me celebrate?"

"Celebrate, my foot. All you want to do is ply me with liquor so I'll pour out all my secrets for your article."

"I thought you didn't have any secrets."

"Excuse me, dear ones," said Peggy, "but someone around here has to get to work. Good luck, Keith. Don't be a stranger now, just because you have hands."

"Take care, Peggy." He kissed her cheek. "You have an open invitation to tour our premises anytime you like. I'll guide you personally."

The moment she left, he took a card from his pocket and set it on Torie's blotter. "This is a formal request for your company. That's my address in Chestnut Hill. It's a big old rambling house I never got around to selling."

She picked up the card. "I know those old stone mansions west of Germantown Avenue. We tried to build apartments there a few years ago and got chased away so fast it made me dizzy."

He chuckled. "Chestnut Hillers would kill to preserve their

provincialism. They like to say that the high-profile rich live on the Main Line, but true aristocrats prefer the Hill. Their snobbism is the purest you'll find anywhere in the world."

"Doesn' it bother you?"

"Not really. The need to feel superior exists at every level—Chestnut Hill, South Philly, Camden, for all I know. I've never lived anywhere but the Hill. I was born there, went to Chestnut Hill Academy, and grew up a spoiled only child with the run of the family home, better known as Brayton Place. My ex grew up on the Hill, too. When we got married, there was no thought of living anywhere else."

"So you bought a house and you've lived there ever since."

"Yes, I kept it after the divorce. She was off to conquer Paris before the ink dried on our decree. As to snobbism, I'd like nothing better than for everyone to live the way I do, but I know it's impossible, so I try not to be two-faced. I support all causes anonymously and go out of my way to avoid charity balls—especially the kind that feature caviar centerpieces sculpted in the shape of starving Ethiopians."

"If you're not two-faced, what are you?"

"A capitalist. A realist. And realistically, I'm going to be late for my doctor's appointment. What about dinner tonight? My mother's off in Europe, so Mac's coming over at seven-thirty. Will you join us? I could pick you up at seven."

"Thanks, I have Moose."

"Then you'll come?"

"Well, I . . . yes, sure. I'd love to." Even if she weren't curious enough about his house, a chance for a quiet dinner with Brayton McGarren was an opportunity she could not refuse. "I'll look forward to shaking your hand—gently."

"Very gently." He gave a cheerful thumbs-up sign and hurried to the door.

Benjamin Franklin Moose drove to the top of a steep slope overlooking Fairmount Park, passed through an open gate leading into a driveway, and finally stopped in front of a reddish-brown stone mansion. Two tall spruce trees stood sentinel duty on either side of an arched entranceway.

"Here we are, Miz Torie. Don' forget to give Mr. Keith my regards. I sure miss havin' him drive 'round with us. He's one fine gentleman."

"I'll tell him."

"Don' forget now."

"I won't."

"A real special gentleman, Miz Torie."

She sighed and crossed her arms. "All right, Moose, spill it."

"Oh, nothin', ma'am."

"Moosekins . . ."

"Well . . ." He turned around in the front seat and faced her. "It ain't no good for people to live alone, Miz Torie. I've met lot of nice folks in my life and I ain't never met no one like Mr. Keith. A pretty lady like you—"

"I get the message." She leaned forward. "How's the church coming?"

"Mercy, they's men all over that place like ants on a cupcake. Folks is so excited, they talkin' of namin' a special room for me. What you done, Miz Torie . . ." His voice broke with emotion.

"If I'm so nice to you, how come I get such crummy service?"

"Oh, Lordy." He grabbed his cap, jumped out, and came around to help her. "Now, you have a good time, and stay jus' as long as you want. I don' mind sleepin' in the car all night."

"Thanks, Cupid," she said, chuckling. "I promise you won't have to."

The front door opened almost as soon as Torie touched the bell, and a cheerful Keith ushered her into the hall. He grinned and held up his fists. "Care to go a few rounds before dinner?"

"Darn, I forgot my gloves." She bent down for a closer look. "No scars? No discoloration?"

"Nature's one hell of a healer. C'mon in. Mac and I have a wee headstart on celebrating."

She gave her coat to a young French maid, picture-perfect in a black uniform set off by a starched white apron, then followed Keith into the living room. The sight of it brought a gasp of pleasure.

Instead of the expected Oriental rugs and floral chintzes, the decor was in solid colors, mainly burgundy and shades of brown, accented by leafy plants in teak containers. Inviting-looking chairs and sofas were grouped before a marble fireplace filled with crackling logs, their glow reflected in the rich patina of the wainscoting. To complete the homey atmosphere, the aroma of roast lamb and fresh-baked bread wafted in from the hallway.

Before Torie could comment, a man rose to his feet. "Hello, young lady. You *are* pretty."

She shook hands apprehensively. "Nice to meet you, Mr. McGarren. You're not bad-looking yourself."

A flicker of amusement crossed his face then vanished. At sixty-six, the publisher resembled a short slim Einstein. His shiny pate was bald, save for a fringe of wild white hair that matched his bushy brows and mustache. Balancing on the edge of the couch, he looked like a wildcat ready to pounce. Keith had once told her he had never seen his father sit back and relax. No matter where he was, he always seemed to be on his way somewhere else.

"The name's Mac. My son tells me you put up with him for three long weeks. I can't imagine why."

"Neither can I. But it wasn't too bad. At least he was bound hand and foot—almost."

"I suppose the cad played on your sympathy."

"Well, I did feel sorry for him, seeing him so helpless and frustrated. Now that he's mended, he's all yours again."

"I resent being tossed back and forth like a bean bag." Keith handed Torie a glass of wine. "Shall we drink to my newly unveiled hands?"

"By all means, and here's to you, too, Mac."

The older man raised his goblet. "Life's a short trip, kids. Live every second as if it's your last."

Determined to break through to the publisher, Torie started him talking about the magazine. To Keith's surprise and delight, his father began to open up to her, chatting and gesturing with animation, pausing only long enough to sip his Stolichnaya or sample an hors d'oeuvre. The same restless energy carried through dinner, prepared by a skilled chef and elegantly served by the maid and a young Frenchman, presumably her husband. As soon as the meal was over, Mac kissed Torie on both cheeks, embraced his son, and disappeared in his limousine.

"What a fascinating character," said Torie as she and Keith returned to the living room. "You seem to have a great relationship."

"We're about as compatible as fire and kerosene." He pulled up a chair for her, then sat down on the couch. "If we didn't love each other, we'd have clawed each other to pieces long ago."

"Really? It doesn't show. I get a strong feeling of paternal pride from him. In fact, this has been a great evening all around.

Dinner was fabulous and I'm in love with your house. It has a quality I can't describe . . . you feel warm and at home the minute you step inside. Even the host is charming but I can't tell him so."

"Why not?"

"You never compliment anyone who's writing about you. It sounds insincere—as if you're trying to buy kind words."

"Go ahead, sound insincere. I promise I'll respect you in the morning."

She laughed. "No way. There's this constant nagging voice warning me to be careful around you—to watch everything I say and do. Even now, I get the feeling you're observing me, wondering what I'm thinking—"

"What *are* you thinking?"

She debated how to answer. Honesty was out of the question. How could she possibly tell him that she found him bright, stimulating, masculine, and very much an individualist . . . that she wished their relationship were not based on the damn article . . . that the attraction she felt for him was getting stronger by the minute. "I guess I'm wondering—"

"Miss Di Angelo," a French-accented voice broke in. "There is a call for you. The madame says it is urgent."

"Oh, dear. Excuse me, Keith." She rose and followed the maid to a phone in the hall. "Hello?"

"It's me, T. D."

"Piglet! What's wrong?"

"Lisa just called. She didn't know how to reach you. There's some bad news . . . about your father—"

"Oh, no. What is it?"

"Look, I'd better come over."

"What is it? Is he—?"

"I can't tell you on the phone. I better—oh, hell. Lisa said he suffered a stroke in his sleep about half an hour ago. No pain. He never woke up. I'm afraid . . . he's gone."

"Oh, my God! Is Lisa—?"

"She's okay. The doctor's there. They want you to come to the house."

"Yes—yes, I'll go right away." She swallowed hard. "Thanks, Peg."

She turned to see Keith come hurrying toward her, his brow furrowed. "What's wrong?"

"Papa," she blurted, as the tears rolled down her cheek. "He had a stroke and d-died in his sleep."

"I'm so very sorry." He moved toward her without thinking, and suddenly she was in his arms, trembling and shivering, and sobbing against his chest.

"It's all right," he whispered, holding her tightly. "It's all right. You were a good daughter. He lived to be proud of you. He must have loved you very much."

"I—I have to go. Moose will—"

"Moose will nothing," he said firmly. "*I'm* driving you to your father's house."

35
==

THERE WAS LITTLE Torie could do in West Mount Airy that night. The doctor confirmed that Frank had suffered no pain, and Lisa, though grieving, had immediately called the church. Father Miles scheduled the wake for Wednesday, and the funeral and mass for the dead would be Thursday.

Keith waited in the car for Torie, then drove her home, promising to call the next day, which he did. That evening she went back to the house to help Lisa handle the parade of friends and relatives.

Many were faces from the past: the Stumpos, their longtime tenants on Snyder Avenue, Jock from the South Philly office, Frank's boyhood chums, his doctors—even his lawyer. The sight of Tony Silvano appearing at the door gave Torie a shock. He had aged dramatically since the start of his trial, now in its final days. The chalk-white hair and sunken eyes made him look older than his fifty-six years.

"I didn't expect to see you," she said, trying to hide her reaction.

"It's family."

"So it is. I'll tell Lisa you're here."

"Wait!" He grabbed her arm and spoke in a hate-filled voice. "You ruined me, Vittoria. You jabbed a knife through my heart and God will make you pay for it. You're a murderer. Worse than Hitler. You killed your own cousin in cold blood."

She shoved away his hand. "What about what *you* did, Tony? Do you ever think about ruining Papa's life? Do you ever think about the fact that Frankie would be alive today if it weren't for your laziness and bad advice? Do you ever think about pulling one of the dirtiest tricks I've ever heard of to cheat me out of a nineteen-million-dollar contract? Do you ever think about blackmail and extortion and strong-arm tactics? Or telling me you were getting a divorce when nothing was further from the truth?"

"Grace and I haven't lived together for a year. And I never meant to hurt Frank or Frankie. I loved them."

"I loved them too," she said, biting her lip. "But Papa's gone now, and I trust you'll turn his will over to my lawyers. Lisa's been waiting years to join the convent, and she's very anxious to get on with her life. Mervin Lewis will call you in the morning."

"*Che dice!*" He stared at her in fury. "What are you saying?"

"I'm saying that I don't want you or your office processing Papa's will."

"*Puttana*," he sputtered, "I can't *stay* in this house. You are lower than a whore!" Barely controlling his rage, he turned and stomped out the front door.

The evening strengthened Torie's resolve to be cremated and spare her loved ones—if she was lucky enough to have any—a similar ordeal. She detested funerals and the fanfare that went with them; the grotesquerie of an open casket particularly appalled her. Papa deserved better than to be made up like a mannequin and laid out to be gawked at. But he had insisted on being buried in the style of the old neighborhood, and by tradition, a closed casket would have been a scandal.

Shortly before nine, Keith's unexpected arrival gave her a lift. She set down the tray she was passing and hurried to greet him. "I hope you're not here as a reporter. I couldn't bear to have you—"

"I'm here as a friend." He glanced past her into the dining room. "That's quite a spread. I see I should've brought food."

"Thank God you didn't. Everyone's been bringing antipasti and cheeses and salads and pastry . . . Italians seem to think if you eat enough, the pain'll go away, or get better, anyway."

"How are you holding up?"

"I'm not. Come with me." She took his arm, guided him into the kitchen and closed the door. "I'm talked out, cried out, pooped out—just plain beat. I'd give anything to sneak away, but I can't leave Lisa with all these guests. Why don't they go home?"

"They're trying to show support. Most people don't want to be alone at times like this. They want their family and friends around."

"For five hours? Besides, they're not my friends, they're Papa's and Lisa's friends, except for you, and poor Piglet out there trying to practice the Italian my brother taught her. The only phrases she can remember are 'Pour the wine' and 'Let's go to bed.' "

"I'll spare you the obvious. Where's Ellory? I thought sure he'd be here."

"So did I. He hasn't even called. It's strange, too. I know he's in town."

"What about Piglet—does she need rescuing?"

"She did the last time I looked. I'd better go give Lisa a hand. You were very thoughtful to come, Keith, but there's no reason to stay—"

"Yes, there is," he said. "I sent Moose home."

"What reward can I give you? My body? My soul? A ten-pound box of money?" Peggy scampered up the stairs, followed closely by Keith. "God must've heard my prayers and sent you to deliver me."

"Torie heard your prayers. And we'd better slow down or no one will believe you're taking me up to treat my psychosclerosis."

"Your what?"

"Hardening of the brain. Very common ailment."

Peggy chuckled and led the way down the hallway. "I left my things in T. D.'s old room. One quick cigarette, then I depart. Keep me company?"

"My pleasure." He entered the white-walled chamber and glanced around with interest. A tall chest of drawers faced a wooden bed with a faded yellow chenille spread. Beside it, a lamp and a wind-up clock sat on a table. Droopy curtains framed the windows. "So this is where Torie grew up. How old was she when the family moved here?"

"About sixteen. I was heartbroken when she left South Philly. I didn't think I'd ever see her again."

"Were you very close?"

"Like sisters." Peggy took a chair and lit her Salem. "We used to spend hours and hours playing games."

"What kind of games?"

"Off the record?"

He nodded.

"We used to pretend we lived in the Richardson house on Rittenhouse Square. T. D. was usually Betsy, I was one of the servants or one of her beaux, and we'd dream up these wonderful romances. One day, Papa had to go see the mayor on business—for real—and he took T. D. along. She got to meet Simone and Betsy in the flesh."

"Was she thrilled?"

"At first . . . before it got traumatic."

"What happened?"

"Well, she'd always loved the Square, especially that house and what she thought the people in it were like. Then Simone invited her into Betsy's birthday party. Betsy was nice—darling, in fact—but when she wasn't around, the other girls ganged up on Torie. They made fun of her dress and the way she talked and where she lived. She was so upset she didn't tell me about it till years later."

"I can understand that."

"Yes, you can imagine how it hurt someone with her pride and sensitivity. Then, when Papa got—" She stopped herself and put a hand under her cigarette, pretending to look for an ashtray. "Oh, dear—"

"It's okay, Piglet. I'm well aware of Frank's conviction." He handed her a ceramic dish. "It was a bum rap. He was no threat to society."

"He certainly wasn't. Anyway, that was another tough period. Some of her school chums thought prison was a badge of honor, but most of them were brutal. I think that's when she made up her mind she was going to show them . . . show *everybody* that she was as good as they were, or better. And damned if she isn't doing it."

Keith scratched his ear. "But why this compulsion to remodel

Rittenhouse Square? If she loves it so much, why can't she leave it be?"

"She made a vow to herself a long time ago that the score—Torie versus Philadelphia—won't be even until she leaves her mark on the Square. She doesn't mean to be destructive. She thinks of Di Angelo Center as a renovation project'."

"You're her closest friend. Can't you knock some sense into her head?"

Peggy rose and grabbed her coat. "If I could it'd be the first time in my life. Thanks for the rescue."

By eleven that night, only Father Miles, Sister Margarita, and two other nuns remained in the living room. Lisa found Torie having coffee in the kitchen with Keith.

"Please take my sister home, Mr. McGarren. She looks exhausted."

"No way, Lis. I'm not leaving till you go to bed. Let's start bringing in the food."

"Please go. The sisters will help me."

Torie set down her cup and stood up. "I haven't had a minute to talk to you tonight, but you've been fantastic, making all the arrangements and being so nice to everyone. I know how hard it must be—"

Tears of gratitude filled Lisa's eyes. "Was I really okay?"

"You were better than okay. You were sweet and gracious and hospitable . . . exactly as Papa would have wanted." Impulsively, Torie grasped her hand. "You're going to have a good life from now on, Lis. You've spent so many years taking care of Papa. Now it's your turn. And we're going to see more of each other, I promise. I may even get to church one of these days."

"You mean that?" Lisa drew back to look at her.

"Well—now and then. Don't expect me to be a regular."

Lisa burst into laughter, Torie joined her, and then quite suddenly, they embraced.

"I love you," Torie whispered, holding her tight.

"I love you too."

"Wherever Papa is—I know this is making him happy."

"I feel so relieved about my sister," Torie said to Keith, as they drove away. "We've had such a standoff all these years—my fault as much as hers. But tonight we could actually relate to each other and say we loved each other—and mean it. My heart goes out to her. She deserves some happiness."

"I'm sure she'll get it. The nuns like her. And you were very generous offering to remodel the convent as a gift."

"I'm cynical enough to think they'll like her even better if her sister spends a few hundred grand sprucing up their quarters."

"You'll probably take one look and want to tear it down and start from scratch."

She regarded him quizzically. "Oh?"

"Now, don't get touchy. You *do* have a penchant for building new buildings rather than restoring old ones. You don't deny that, do you?"

"I'm too tired to talk about it." Her tone closed the subject, but her voice was warm again as she said, "You're not planning to attend the funeral tomorrow, are you?"

"Do you want me to?"

"Heavens, no. It'll be a long, grueling day—driving out to the gravesite after the service, coming back to the house for hours . . . God knows when I'll get home. And you've got three weeks of work awaiting you."

"And a Friday deadline." They drove in silence for several miles before he asked, "Still flying to Santa Fe this weekend?"

"Yes, I'm anxious to see Michael. I don't look forward to telling him his grandpa's gone to heaven, but he's got two other grandfathers, so I guess he'll handle it. What are you up to? Not taking a twirl on the slopes, I hope."

"Nope. I've decided skiing is for the young and demented. I'll be in my office. My secretary's transcribed all the tapes, and I'm hoping to finish your story this weekend, except for a few odds and ends. By the way, the pictures we took came out beautifully."

"Any chance of touching up the wrinkles?"

"Nothing to touch up. I should have a printout of the story by Friday. Can we meet after work for a last interview?"

"Sure. Check with me in the morning."

He stopped the car in front of her building as the doorman came running over.

"Don't get out, Keith. Thanks for everything."

"Be strong tomorrow," he said. "I'll be thinking of you."

The funeral on Thursday went smoothly, and the two-day visit with Michael served its purpose, reuniting mother and child, and reassuring Torie that her son was happy and reasonably well adjusted. As always, seeing him left her feeling depressed, and freshly aware of the void in her life. His lack of reaction to the news that his grandfather had gone to heaven disturbed her and renewed old feelings of guilt for having deprived her father of his grandson. But that was what Papa had wanted, and much as he had missed Michael, he had never complained.

Shortly after she got home Sunday night, Nielson called, wanting to come over. She pleaded fatigue.

He insisted he had pressing matters to discuss, however, and *had* to see her. He also said he couldn't walk through the lobby in his jogging suit and finally persuaded her to admit him through the basement.

"I called as soon as I got in," he said, setting down a manila envelope on the bar and helping himself to a brandy. "Your maid told me you'd gone to Santa Fe to see your son, and that you hadn't been to your office since Tuesday. Tough break about your father. My condolences."

"Thanks, it hasn't been my best week. I'm sure I show it, too." She had changed into jeans and a sweatshirt for his visit and had taken off her makeup; the last thing she wanted was to look enticing. "How's Betsy?"

"She's fine." He sat down opposite her. "What's the latest?"

"It looks good," she answered. "Mervin says that as long as you agree to the steel frame reinforcement, they're ready to grant the variance. One of the planning commissioners wants us to lop off four stories because they cast a shadow on the park for half an hour a day, but I'm sure he'll be outvoted. We should get full approval by the end of this month. Everyone's very impressed with your designs."

"Everyone but you."

"Not true." She crossed her legs beneath her, Hindu-style. "Contrary to what you may read in the press, my projects don't all have to be snazzy and streamlined and a hundred stories high. I'm thrilled about the Rittenhouse North. It won't be the biggest or flashiest hotel in the world, but it *will* be one of the most elegant and beautiful . . . another sparkling addition to Nielson Hughes's long list of triumphs."

"It will be that, yes," he murmured distractedly. His gaze drifted down to her breasts, then back up to her lips. "You know, I rather like you this way. You're much more approachable without all that garbage on your face."

"Nielson . . ." She sat up and set her feet on the floor. "I am *not* approachable tonight or any other night. My father died less than a week ago, which should tell you something about my mood. And what happened should never have happened. You're married, we both love Betsy, and neither of us wants to hurt her. Am I reaching you?"

"Quite," he said, getting up and walking toward her. "Let's talk about it in the other room."

"No!" She rose and faced him with folded arms. "I am *not* going to bed with you. You said you had urgent matters to discuss. Was that a ruse?"

"No, it was not. My needs are extremely urgent, and you do the most splendid job of satisfying them."

"Come any closer and I'll scream."

"What, and bring the security guards?" He started to grab hold of her when a raspy throat-clearing made him halt.

Torie looked toward the doorway and blanched. "Ellory!" she exclaimed. "What are you doing here?"

"Oh, dear God. My timing's been off all week." The publicist removed his glasses and fingered them nervously. His cheeks were flushed with embarrassment. "The doorman told me you were alone and Ingrid let me in. I'd better go—"

"No need to, Mr. Davis. I was just saying good night." Grasping Torie's arms as if it were the most natural gesture in the world, Nielson kissed her cheek. "The new designs are in the envelope. You'll want to get them to the commission right away."

"Yes—thanks. I'll see you to the door."

"Don't bother, I know where it is." With a parting nod, he vanished through the archway, leaving her staring after him.

"Shall I go?" asked Ellory, settling into a chair.

"Soon, please. I'm glad to see you, but I'm beat." She sank down on the couch, relieved to have Nielson gone, yet aware of the new problem facing her. She gazed at her old friend curiously, saddened to feel that she hardly knew him anymore. Over the years she had watched him grow increasingly enslaved to his habit, but somehow she had always felt he had himself in control. She no longer had that confidence. In the last few months he had seemed constantly agitated, excitable, impossible to talk to. Once, when she offered to send him to a drug clinic at her expense, he had turned half-apoplectic and screamed at her to stay out of his personal affairs. "What's on your mind, Ellory?"

"What's on my mind? What do you *think's* on my mind after that tender scene I just witnessed? Do you realize what a major scandal could do to both your careers? What if that leaks out?"

"What if *what* leaks out?"

"Don't be coy. I heard his remark about how well you satisfy his needs. I doubt he was referring to your cooking."

"Very funny." She shrugged. "We had a brief affair years ago, when we were kids. Big deal."

His brow furrowed in anger. "What do you take me for, Torie? I know what I heard and I know what I saw. I also know you must've sneaked him in through the basement so the doorman wouldn't see him. Was that so you could discuss neoclassicism?"

"Ellory, you're pushing me too far. Say what you came to say and go home."

"I came to give you some thoughts for the *McGarren's* piece," he said, shaking a finger at her, "but you'd better hear me out. You're playing with explosives fooling around with that man. We're not talking tabloids, we're talking international headlines: DI ANGELO–HUGHES LOVE TRIANGLE! PARAPLEGIC WIFE RE-FUSES—"

"Shut *up,* Ellory! I don't need you to create problems. In case you've forgotten, I just lost my father and I'm in no mood to be preached at. By the way, where were you all last week? Couldn't you have called me?"

"What for? You want sympathy? Look in the dictionary. You'll find it between 'shit' and 'syphilis.' " His fingers drummed the table. "The reason I didn't call you is because I'm no hypocrite. It's too bad your father died, but from my point of view, it's the best thing that could've happened. He won't be around to remind people of his prison record anymore, and that baboon-faced sister of yours will be off to a convent. With those two losers out of the way, my work will be a lot easier."

Torie's face went pale. She rose unsteadily and spoke in barely controlled tones. "I don't appreciate those remarks. You'd better get out of here right away."

"I'm going," he said, rising. "But I warn you, *you'd* better stop pussying around with Hughes. I have my own reputation to worry about. I'll be damned if I'll work for a slut and a home-wrecker!"

"A—what?" she gasped. "What did you say?"

"Nothing wrong with your ears. You heard me."

"You needn't worry about your reputation any longer," she shot back, trembling with anger. "You're fired!"

"Fired?" He turned to confront her. "You *can't* fire me."

"I just did. As of this minute."

"So be it." He took several steps toward the door, then stopped and whirled around, his face contorted with bitterness. "You were a trampy little nothing when I found you. You dressed like a whore and swore like a sailor. I was the one who taught you what to wear, refined you, polished you, molded you out of mud and common clay. I had great plans for you—for both of us—all the way to the White House. Now it's too late for that. Everything I've done for you—the hours I've slaved to get you where you are, the years of busting my ass and using all my friends and contacts—none of that's worth a damn to you now that you're ensconced on your throne. Well, remember this, Madam Rich Bitch: I put you up there, and I can knock you off just as fast."

"Go to hell! Get the hell out of my life!" She slammed the door and strode back to her bedroom, white with rage.

Let him do what he would. Anything would be better than another minute of his vicious tongue.

Torie had just crawled into bed that night when her phone rang.

"It's Nielson," said the voice in her ear. "I didn't wake you, did I?"

"No. Sorry about Ellory. He had no right to walk in like that—even if he did save me. We had a horrible fight after you left."

"About what?"

"He said you and I were having an affair, and that it might get out and hurt *his* reputation. He made some unforgivable remarks and I fired him. I should have done it long ago."

"Is he likely to tell anyone about us?"

"There's nothing to tell. That's all over."

"Don't be absurd. I want to see you—now."

"Nielson, how do I get through that thick skull of yours? How can I make you understand?"

"By letting me come over. I'm only two blocks away. I'll be there in five minutes."

"No. I won't let you in."

"Why? You have strong feelings for me. I know you do."

She was silent for a moment. Then she answered slowly, "I *did* have strong feelings for you. I thought I was in love with you ever since our first night together. Even when I was married, I used to dream about you. I followed your career in its fantastic climb. Ironically, it was Ellory who convinced me to try to bring you back. He knew our plans for the Rittenhouse North would cause opposition, and he felt that if we could hire the world's greatest architect, we'd have it made."

"I applaud his wisdom. Then you met Betsy—and all of a sudden you stopped caring for me?"

"I'll never stop caring for you, Nielson. I always want us to be friends. But yes, seeing Betsy did change my feelings."

"Then you don't know Betsy. You don't realize that she would understand and not blame us—either of us. At the same time, I don't want to hurt her any more than you do. Look here, I loathe this long-distance communicating. Won't you let me in your bloody basement?"

"No."

"Very well. You're tired and you want to go to sleep. But we *will* be together soon, because we belong together and you know it. There's no one worthy of you but me and vice versa. There's no one either of us can trust. And this very moment, I want to make love to you so badly, I could break through a solid brick wall—"

"I'm hanging up the phone," she said quickly. "We'll talk in the morning."

36
==

MONDAY MORNING WAS chaos. Paolo Cava's ego had been sprouting in direct proportion to the growth of Di Angelo Tower, and when a section of the new building was not to his liking, he ordered it torn down. Bitter arguments from the project manager and the head structural engineer had failed to change his mind, and Torie had had to step in and offer a compromise.

Penn's Landing was at an impasse. Because of Cava's increasing tantrums and lack of budgetary concern, because she hated to keep losing money, and because the tenants she sought refused to make a commitment, she made the reluctant decision to pull out of the development and so advised the mayor, her staff, and all concerned.

In the meantime, her phone never stopped, nor did the stream of invitations—invitations to speak, to chair dinners, to head drives, to serve on boards, to attend parties at the homes of people who had once refused to attend hers. There were lawyers and lawsuits (two that she initiated and four against her), internal meetings, a visit from the city planning commissioner, a bid to endorse an airline, and the usual ongoing negotiations for deals in the works.

Not until Peggy handed her a velvet box containing a small gold brooch in the shape of a pig did Torie realize it was the day before her thirty-sixth birthday. Beaming, she pinned it to her collar, hugged the giver, and then it was back to business.

The accountant stopped by to confirm that he had arranged for Ellory's severance pay and other details of his "resignation," and Jane informed her that the Design Arts Company had completed their model of Di Angelo Center and was ready to deliver it.

"Have it sent to my apartment," said Torie. "I don't want it seen around here until we make our official announcement."

Later that day, she sat in her conference room discussing the Center with her two chief architects, her developments manager, two lawyers, and a representative from the Goldman Corporation. Her former father-in-law had broken off relations after the fire at Di Angelo Plaza, but now, almost six years later and needing the business, Mort Goldman had been sufficiently pragmatic to shake hands and resume their dealings.

The meeting was almost over when Torie got a frantic call to return to her office. Excusing herself, she hurried down the corridor, wondering what the commotion was about—until she heard Nielson's angry voice.

"There's the female Judas!" he shouted as she came through the door. "Did you think I wouldn't find out about your bloody Di Angelo Center?"

"Jane, I'll talk to Mr. Hughes alone."

"Be my guest." The secretary departed quickly.

Torie faced him with pretended calm. "Would you please stop screaming? Of course I knew you'd find out. I was going to tell you myself this week. What's all the fuss?"

"You know damn well! Do you think I want my hotel to be part of some sleazy amusement park? Do you think I want my name associated with tearing down city landmarks to put up those oversized plumbing fixtures you call buildings? At our press conference, some reporter asked how much of the Square you were planning to remodel, and I thought he was a lunatic. Turns out *I'm* the damn-fool lunatic!"

"You're nothing of the sort. I don't know who's been feeding you lies—"

"I'll tell you who. Your former flack, Ellory Davis, claims he walked out on you last night because he couldn't take your duplicity. He gave full details of your unconscionable plot to that Rawley French woman, who called me—and it's a good thing she did. I'm taking my name, my designs, and my reputation, and getting as far away from here as I can." He headed for the door. "I'll still build my hotel, but it won't be on Rittenhouse Square!"

Torie felt the blood drain from her face. "Wait—please! You've got to hear me out!"

He turned and glowered at her. "Where is it written?"

"It's true, Nielson, I didn't tell you about the Center. I wanted to hold off till I could show you the plans. But I swear, they're not the least bit sleazy. It's going to be a spectacular luxury development—contemporary, yes, but in the best materials, the best designs, and the best of taste. And right smack in the middle will be the gem of the complex: the classic, elegant Rittenhouse North."

"As lost as silk on a sow's rump."

"It won't be lost at all. Remember when the Pompidou Center was built in '76? The Parisians complained that a modernist building was out of place amid all that traditional French architecture. Yet today people travel miles to see it, the French adore it, and the whole area's improved. Your hotel will be the same, only in reverse. A classic structure in a striking postmodern setting—a wonderful contrast to its surroundings, and an enduring monument to the timelessness and greatness of your style."

The flattery rolled past him. "The terms of our contract permit me to walk away from this project anytime your actions become 'objectionable,' and that time is now. Your actions are not only objectionable, they're unspeakable. That you can willingly instigate such desecration—that you can even *think* of razing those landmarks—"

"Yes, I can think of it." Her patience was fast disappearing. "And Mrs. Rebecca Rawley French knows what she can do with her beloved rotting buildings. Preservationists—damn necrophiliacs! They understand *nothing* of the present or the future."

"And you? What do you understand of the past?"

"That's it's over. Dead. Gone. But that doesn't mean the Rittenhouse North won't . . . Nielson, where are you going? You can't walk out on me!"

"Who's going to stop me?" He glared at her from the doorway. "Go ahead and build your razzle-dazzle Coney Island. Build your superstreamlined hotel just the way you want it. The hell with what the people want. The hell with the surroundings. The hell with any linkage to the past. Let's hear it for glass cartons, cold, hard steel, and massive slabs of granite. Let's blaze DI ANGELO SHRINE across the front in neon and have a brass band strike up 'Hail to the Chief' every time you walk through the lobby. That's what you want, isn't it? That's what you've wanted all along. You needed my name for city approval, but you never gave a damn about my designs—not fifteen years ago when we tried to work together, and not now. And if you say otherwise, you're a goddamn liar!"

Too stunned to cry or protest, she watched him stride angrily down the hall.

The next two days Torie spent in frantic consultations, spelling out what she wanted to her staff. Her advisers vetoed the idea of hiring another big name to replace Nielson, and she agreed. Her own chief architect was familiar with the project, and by Wednesday evening, in fact, sketches for the new hotel—one that would retain the best construction features of Nielson's blueprints—were under way.

According to terms of the contract, Nielson would keep his five-million-dollar retainer as compensation for his aborted efforts and would be free to take his plans elsewhere. But the redesigned Rittenhouse North would secretly have the benefit of many of his ideas, and she would make *sure* his name stayed linked with it. He could hardly sue for a credit spread by word of mouth.

Progress would be delayed while the revised blueprints were being drawn, but this time, the hotel would embody the fresh exciting spirit of the whole Di Angelo Center and blend in with the other buildings. The complete package would be submitted for city approval as soon as it was ready.

Her lawyers predicted fierce opposition, even though Torie still had a strong ally in Mayor Borland—who still had his eye on the governorship. At least nine of the commissioners owed her favors, and five aspired to higher offices. In general, the prospect of getting approval looked stormy . . . but possible.

Torie barely had time to shower, change into a blouse and slacks, and have a bite of salad before Keith arrived at a few minutes past eight that evening.

"Sorry I'm late," he said, handing her a chocolate petit four. "I stole this for you. Mac was honored at a museum reception. You got an invitation, didn't you?"

"Yes, and I wanted to go, but the office was hurricane city today—even worse than usual. How was it?"

"Same old faces. Same platitudes. Same outstretched hands. Mac outraged everyone and wrote a fat check. He'll get good press and we'll sell a magazine or two. That's about it."

"I'll drop him a note." She bit into the pastry, and finished it in seconds. "Ooh, that's sinful. I can feel my hips growing already."

"Your hips are perfect." He moved toward her and took her hands. "So is the rest of you. It's been a long week without you."

Their eyes met. She knew what he was feeling because she was feeling it too. Even with all the pressures, she had missed him tremendously—his warmth, his companionship, his support, the mutual attraction that was getting harder and harder to ignore.

"I have to talk to you," she said, drawing gently away and walking into the living room. They sat down, and she asked, "Did you know Nielson resigned from the project?"

"I've heard rumors. I'll be at your press conference tomorrow. What will you say?"

"That he hadn't foreseen how long the project would take, that he had too many other commitments, and that he decided—with regret—it was better to resign now than be forced to abandon the hotel in mid-construction."

"You think the media will buy it?"

"Why shouldn't they?"

"The story I heard is that you didn't like his designs. You wanted something more modern. True or false?"

"False!" She shook her head for emphasis. "Only a total idiot would hire a brilliant, world-celebrated architect, pay him an outrageous fee, and then try to tell him what to do. Nielson had free rein to indulge his genius. His blueprints were *not* subject to my approval, and anyone who says they were is absolutely wrong."

"Then what happened?"

"Off the record?"

"You know our agreement."

"Well, Nielson found out about Di Angelo Center and blew a fuse."

"I knew it!" Keith stood up and began to pace. "I knew that damn project was going to backfire. And you haven't even announced it yet. I wish you'd try to look rationally at what you're doing."

"What do you mean?"

"You know exactly what I mean."

"Now *you're* going to tell me I'm a monster too? That we should keep this city a graveyard—a city forever stuck in the past? I'm sick to death of antiquity-worship, and I'm tired of being told I can't breathe vitality into this town. For God's sake, what's *wrong* with the new?"

"Nothing's wrong with the new. But there's some question about destroying the old."

"Nostalgia for its own sake isn't worth a damn. I don't expect everyone to share my taste in buildings any more than you expect everyone to agree with what you write. Architecture, by its nature, is a few imposing their designs on the many. Even Rittenhouse Square drew opposition when it was first conceived. If we tried to please everyone, we'd still be crawling around in caves."

"Perhaps." He tried not to show his apprehension. "How do you propose to get zoning permits?"

"Zoning laws are a farce today. Cities everywhere know they have to accommodate developers if they want to grow. Zoning regulations are merely negotiating points. For instance, I'll agree to put in a public courtyard and a few other amenities, and in return the city will increase the FAR—the floor area ratio, or amount of office space I'll get in relationship to the square footage of the lot."

"Why does everything have to be a deal with you?"

"Why not? Dealing's what I do best. I'll also explain to the commissioners the advantages of giving a huge boost to the construction industry, and of luring firms away from New York with cheaper rents. I'll point out that Di Angelo Center will create thousands of new jobs and new sources of tax revenue, and that the city's image will be tremendously enhanced by having one of the most daring, exciting plazas in the world."

"You have at least four boards to pass. Do you have friends on all of them?"

"Off the record—sure. I'll call in my markers. I'm not doing anything illegal. That's just the way the game plays."

"Strange game, isn't it?" He sat down again and faced her. "Your father goes to prison for attempted bribery; you give money to commissioners in exchange for favors and become a national celebrity."

"Keep my father out of this! He was under tremendous stress and coerced by an evil man. Mine's a different matter entirely. Are you saying I'm a criminal?"

"Of course not." He shrugged. "You're just doing what the average businessman does every time he makes a campaign contribution and knows he's buying a politician's ear. Or what the U.S. government does when it aids foreign countries where it hopes to build bases."

"Then why are you giving me a bad time?"

"I'm merely raising questions. In the case of Rittenhouse Square, old is good, and new is good too, and one needn't be at the expense of the other." He hesitated, choosing his words carefully. "Look, I know something about your particular passion. Peggy told me about the birthday party and the games you used to play. But that's no reason to let emotion rule your judgment. Why does Di Angelo Center have to be built *there*?"

"Because that's where I want it to be. Maybe you'd better go home," she said wearily. "I don't feel like arguing."

"I still need some facts from you, and I'm not leaving without them." He set his recorder on the table. "Now tell me, when you were a child . . ."

The resentment slowly began to drain from Torie's voice as she thought back to the early years, chatted about Frankie, how she used to memorize his technical manuals and pester him with questions, how her father had insisted that real estate was no profession for a woman, how she had gradually taken over the business . . . even Tony's role in her father's downfall.

The more she talked, the more she felt Keith's eyes penetrating her defenses. Their brief skirmish had shown that they could disagree, but they could also live with their differences and not let them dilute their feelings for each other—feelings that neither could deny much longer. The attraction was growing intense, she was becoming distracted . . . forgetting her words and getting confused in the middle of sentences. If only his eyes would stop sending signals and straying up and down her body . . .

The hall chimes rang ten o'clock, and Ingrid came in to say good night. "I almost forgot, madam. That large package you were expecting arrived this morning. I put it on the dressing table in the guest room."

Torie jumped up eagerly. "That's the model I've been waiting for all week. Come on, Keith."

He followed her down the hall, unable to ignore the faint outline of her panties under her slacks. He was sure they were pink bikinis, edged in lace, but if she was wearing green boxer shorts, that would be all right too.

She closed the door and turned on the light, her fingers trembling as she ripped away the brown paper. When the last piece of wrapping came off, she stood back and gasped. Stretched out before her was a full-scale replica of Walnut Street on the Square, exactly as she had envisioned it: a forty-story office tower faced in red granite and black-tinted glass, and a spectacular domed shopping complex with a bridge to the park. The Rittenhouse North Hotel, modeled after Nielson's design before he had walked away from the job, was aristocratic and elegant—yet, as he had predicted, overshadowed by its glistening neighbors.

"Oh, God, Keith, isn't it fantastic? Have you ever seen anything more breathtaking?" Her shaking hands caressed the plaster spire, sliding up and down the shaft as she imagined its cold hardness, its raw soaring power. "I've waited so long for this moment . . ."

He stood behind her, watching her revel in her vision, sensing her elation . . . and before he knew it, his hands were on her arms, gliding along the silky folds of her sleeves. The heat and electricity in her body were almost tangible as she quivered to his touch. Moving closer, he brushed his lips against the back of her neck, then reached his hands around her waist, slowly inching up to her breasts.

Her head dropped back as he began to undo her blouse, and then her bra, and she closed her eyes while her garments slipped from her shoulders and fell to the floor. He watched in mesmerized silence as she turned to face him, unzipped her slacks, stepped out of them and stood there in her panties—tiny, pink, and lacy. Her breasts were startling in such a small woman, and she looked even more delectable than he had imagined.

He folded her in his arms and their mouths came together with that tingling erotic expectancy of a first kiss.

"Torie," he whispered, his hands roaming up and down her back. "I've ached for you so long. You must know how I feel about you."

"And I, too . . . I want to surrender to you. My heart . . . my being . . . everything . . ."

Her movements conveyed urgency, and he carried her to the bed and switched off the light. Then he quickly shed his own clothes and lay beside her in the darkness. Feeling the heat of her nakedness, he began to explore the creamy flesh of her inner thighs.

"You're an amazement," he said. "So complicated and yet so simple. Underneath all the rough-and-toughness there's a soft, vulnerable girl-woman who wants to be loved for herself—and to love back. I felt that the day we met."

"Keith . . . I only know that I want to be yours."

Her words inflamed him, and he kissed her smooth belly and moved downward, instinctively knowing where to please her, enjoying her low groans, and staying there for a long time.

When he could stand it no longer, he rose up and entered her and felt her joyful, uninhibited response. His movements were gentle at first, and he kissed her eyes, her cheeks, her lips, her chin, and spoke her name as he made tender love to her. Their bodies arched and swayed and found a rhythm, and sometimes he stopped for control and stroked her face, saying that he didn't want it to end . . . and then he would start again, with unhurried motions, prolonging their pleasure until it was almost time.

"Fly away with me, darling," he finally whispered, and he grabbed her hips and let himself go, driving and plunging with abandon, until her low, purring moans became a cry that sent them both spinning over the edge . . .

Moments later, lying entwined in the dark, he brushed back her hair. "You're my woman, Torie," he said. "From now on— you belong to me."

37
=

AT TEN A.M. on Thursday, twenty-four media people crowded into Torie's office and heard her read a prepared statement about Nielson Hughes's resignation. An equally beautiful Rittenhouse North Hotel was in the works, she announced, and in a few weeks, as soon as the designs were completed, she would release them, along with her plans for a revitalization of the Square.

Rumors about the new plaza were widespread, and the reporters threw questions at her, all of which she politely declined to answer. Ginny Goodwin, a young woman on her staff who had taken over press relations after Ellory's departure, was about to close the meeting when a clamor at the door drew everyone's attention.

Torie watched in stunned silence as Rebecca Rawley French, swathed in black crepe held together by a huge diamond eagle brooch, and accompanied by a pudgy-faced man, elbowed her way through the crowd and marched up to her. Grabbing the microphone from Ginny's hand, she spoke in loud, clear tones: "Ladies and gentlemen of the press—my name is Rebecca Rawley French." (Pause.) "My son, Silas Rawley French, and I came here today to *save* Philadelphia."

Ginny seemed ready to panic, but Torie nodded to let the woman continue.

"I was born and reared here," the dowager proclaimed, "as were my son, my grandchildren, and great-grandchildren—as were my parents, grandparents, and great-grandparents before me. I represent six generations of Frenches and seven generations of Rawleys, and my august relatives and I do *not* intend to let this woman lay waste to our beloved city without a fight."

She inhaled deeply, lifted her chin, and resumed her monologue. "Miss Di Angelo's former publicist has informed me that Nielson Hughes did *not* resign because of work commitments. He resigned because he learned of her plans for Rittenhouse Square—plans that include the desecration of not two but four revered structures on Walnut Street—the entire block, in fact, save for the Historical Society Library, which, thank the Lord, was not available for sale.

"In place of these classic monuments," she went on, "Miss Di Angelo intends to erect brassy, tasteless modern structures in total contrast to everything Rittenhouse Square and the people of Philadelphia stand for. She also plans to bestow upon this atrocity her very own name—the same name as that of her late father, an ex-convict who served time in prison. Do you deny my statements, Miss Di Angelo?"

Her eyes blazing, Torie snatched back the microphone. She started to speak, then caught sight of Keith's face in the crowd and instantly mastered her anger. "Allow me to remind you— this is *our* press conference, and I have no desire to stoop to name-calling. Mrs. French has a right to question, not to slander. When I'm ready, I'll answer her allegations honestly and completely, and I'll expect equal time from the media. Until then, friends, I wish you good day."

Ginny jerked the plug from the microphone and hustled Torie out a side door, then went back to dispel the mob. Reporters crowded around Mrs. French and her son, shoving mikes at them, taking notes, snapping pictures. Keith McGarren slipped through the exit and headed for Peggy's office, where he found Torie surrounded by chattering members of her staff.

"Thank God you're here!" She hurried over to him. "Do you *believe* that dragon lady? Crashing my press conference? Boy, if I could—"

"Shhh. Calm down. Is there someplace we can talk? Alone?"

"Yes." Taking his hand, she led him back up the corridor, turned a combination lock, and entered a well-furnished room, complete with lounge chair, sofa, and dressing table. "This is my secret hideaway. When people do a number on me, I come here to blow off steam."

"Wish I'd known about this before." He shut the door and reached around her waist. "I'd have wanted to test your casting couch."

"It's not a casting couch, it's a daybed." Her arms circled his neck. "You're trying to make me forget that I'm practically homicidal. Was what I said all right?"

"You were controlled and dignified and handled yourself like the perfect lady you are."

"Really? Perfect? Are you prejudiced?"

"Damn right I am." He bent to touch her lips. "I'm also wildly, madly out of my brain about you. Have I told you that standing close to you gives me a greater thrill than microwave popcorn?"

She laughed, and in the comfort of his arms, she began to relax. "Will I see you tonight? I'll have the cook fix steak and French fries. About seven?"

"I'll be there." He released her gently. "I have to go back to my office, but first, some good news. Tony Silvano was convicted on all four counts. Looks like he'll serve hard time."

"Hallelujah! The justice system *finally* works. I hope they lock him up for life." She reached for a tissue and gently blotted his mouth. "The bad news is that I won't see you for eight hours. And you'd better not walk out of here wearing lipstick. People might talk."

"One of these days," he said, kissing her fingers, "we'll give 'em something to talk about."

DI ANGELO PLANS TO RAZE RITTENHOUSE SQUARE blared the Friday morning headlines, and beneath it the subhead announced: "Hughes Dumps Hotel, Returns to Arizona."

Torie sat in bed clutching the paper and reading nervously:

Torie Di Angelo, wunderkind of the real estate world, wants to put her stamp on Rittenhouse Square. Or, according to her increasingly vocal opponents, stamp it out. As if owning an estimated billion-dollar empire isn't enough for the brash thirty-six-year-old, a reliable source reports that she will soon seek civic permission to level the whole north side . . .

Throwing down the page in disgust, Torie headed for the shower. Wouldn't she *love* to start slinging back the manure. A brief statement to the press about Ellory's coke habit would muzzle his big mouth and reduce his precious flow of party invitations mighty fast.

As for Rebecca French, she would simply point out the woman's "august" background. Her years of private schooling;

her membership in exclusive country clubs and genealogy societies; her involvement in whites-only causes, politics, and philan-
thropies; the three homes she maintained in restricted
neighborhoods—all were evidence of a selfish, privileged life
based on racist and religious bigotry.

But further dirt-tossing would only upset Keith. Were it not
for her desire to maintain the ladylike image he had of her, she
would have fought back like a wildcat at the press conference . . .
and that would have been a mistake. Keith was himself a scion
of an old and prominent family, and even with his scorn for pho-
niness and hypocrisy, he shared some of Rebecca French's senti-
ments.

Torie prayed that their differences would not become an issue.
Her feelings for him were deep, tender, and passionate, and
growing more so every minute they spent together.

For the next forty-eight hours, the press continued to report
whatever facts or rumors they could gather about Nielson's sudden departure and Torie's plans for Rittenhouse Square. Letters
to the editors poured in, praising and blasting her; Clark DeLeon
at the *Inquirer* did another column on her; TV commentators
babbled pro and con. Almost everyone in Philadelphia, it
seemed, had an opinion, and most were unfavorable. Amidst all
the chaos, a second bomb dropped—courtesy of Connie Morris.

Torie was home studying the revised designs Saturday morning when Keith, sounding upset, called from the lobby and said
he was coming right up.

"What's wrong?" she asked, opening the door.

"Everything!" He marched past her into the living room and
slapped a copy of *Celebrity Times* on the coffee table. "What I
want to know is how much of this horseshit is true?"

"I don't know, sweetheart. I haven't read it. I told you to expect the worse of Connie Morris. When did the magazine come
out?"

"It hit the stands about an hour ago. Mac called and told me
I'd better get a copy. Were you having an affair with Nielson
Hughes?"

"What?" The blood drained from her head as his question registered. "Is . . . that what she says?"

"Were you?" he demanded.

"Honey, you can't—"

"Answer me!"

"I will. But let me—"

"No, I won't let you think up any lies. I want the truth. Were you sleeping with Nielson Hughes or weren't you? Yes or no?"

She sank into a chair. "Yes," she said, almost in a whisper, "when we were very young. I was nineteen years old and I thought I was in love with him. We broke up, but I continued to care for him for a long time after that. Our relationship was unresolved in my mind until I offered him this commission and had a chance to get to know him again. Then I realized how foolish I'd been. I'd loved a teenage fantasy. He wasn't that man at all."

"Connie Morris says he went back to Scottsdale because you wanted him to divorce his wife and marry you."

"That's a damn lie! Keith, you *have* to believe me. Even if I'd been wildly in love with him, and I swear to you I wasn't, I would never do anything to hurt Betsy. Nielson left town because Rebecca French told him about Di Angelo Center. He was furious that I hadn't mentioned it, and he didn't want his hotel surrounded by modern buildings. That's the *only* reason he left."

Keith sighed and bit his lower lip, wanting desperately to believe her.

He sounded calmer as he asked, "Then you haven't been sleeping with him since . . . you and I . . . ?"

"How could I?" she replied. Her voice was soft and pleading. "Don't you know how much you mean to me? Do you really think I could be the way I am with you . . . the way we were last night . . . and not love you with all my being?"

"No." He started to move toward her, but the ring of the phone stopped him. "You'd better answer, darling. If it's the press, say the article is full of lies and you're preparing a statement."

"Must I answer?"

"Yes. Sound mad as hell. Your denial should go right out over the wires before the public has time to read that bilge and think there might be any truth to it."

With a sigh, she lifted the receiver. "Hello? Yes, this is she. From where? Scottsdale? Sorry, I can't—I'm not—oh, hello, Nielson."

The voice in her ear was enraged. "Did you see that piece of fecal matter called *Celebrity Times*?"

"Yes, I saw it. I mean—I haven't read it but I know what it says. I'll talk to my lawyers and issue a statement of denial."

"Denial? How can you deny we were having an affair? What if she has proof?"

"That's impossible." She glanced fearfully at Keith, hoping he couldn't hear the other end of the conversation. "I can't talk to you now. I have to—"

"Quite right. We can't talk on the phone. We'll talk in person. I've got my plane waiting. I'll be there sometime this afternoon."

"But why? That's stupid!" Her tone rose in panic. "I don't want to see you and we have nothing to talk about. You can't leave Betsy now. She must be terribly hurt by all this, and your place is with her. Make a statement to the press that it's pure horse hockey—some garbage Connie must've gotten from Ellory—and you're calling your lawyers. You'll only make things worse if you come here."

"Nonsense. I have something important to say to you." A sudden click ended it.

Swearing under her breath, she replaced the receiver and turned to Keith in confusion. "I—I'm sorry. I have no idea why he's coming here, unless—unless he wants us to make some sort of joint denial."

"Or confession? That phone call, the first night I came to see you—the guy who wouldn't take no—was that Hughes too?"

"Yes, but it wasn't what you think. He only wanted—"

"I can guess what he wanted!" Clenching his fists, Keith strode out of the room and slammed the front door.

Torie pulled herself together and immediately called Scottsdale, leaving word that she would be out of town and unavailable to see Mr. Hughes that day, or at any time in the future. Then, telling Ingrid to take messages and not say where she was, she packed an overnight case and drove to the office.

Setting all the files and plans for Di Angelo Center on her desk, she tried to forget her misery in work, spending the rest of the day reading, revising, making notes, additions, changes . . . her brain functioning, but her heart detached from her once-favorite project. Finally, too tired and too depressed even to undress, she took a Valium, curled up on the couch in her office, and fell asleep.

Late Sunday morning, after four more hours of reviewing the plans for the Center, and still unable to revive her old enthusiasm, she dressed and drove home, confident that she had stayed away long enough to avoid Nielson—that is, if he had been stubborn enough to fly in, despite her message.

All she could think about was Keith . . . how she could break through to him . . . how she could make him see that Connie

Morris and Ellory Davis and Rebecca French and all the other vicious people in her life were of little consequence compared with what she felt for him. Yet he was the one who had accused *her*—condemned her without a trial, and walked out in a jealous rage. No, damn him! She had her pride. It was up to him to call and apologize.

She twisted the key in the lock, opened her front door, and stepped back with a shock. Nielson Hughes stood in the archway of her living room, still the same haughty, imperious figure, as startlingly handsome as he had always been, his blue eyes glaring. "Where the hell have you been?"

"None of your business. I told you not to come here. Why did Ingrid let you in?"

"Because I said it was urgent and it is. Now quit acting like a prima donna and come with me into the living room. I've been waiting forty minutes and I have something to say to you."

Frowning, angry and frustrated that her elaborate plans to avoid him had been for naught, she followed him. Had she thought about it, she would have realized that he never arrived anywhere on time, even by plane. "What do you want from me?"

"Did you read the article?"

"Yes, I read it. It's a crock from beginning to end."

"So it is. Did it occur to you what kind of effect that will have on my career?"

How typical of him, thinking only of himself. "How can it affect your career? People will gossip for five minutes and then forget about it. This is tabloid stuff. Locker-room talk. It doesn't make your work any less brilliant. It doesn't make you any less the great architect you are."

"On the contrary. My work is brilliant because it has integrity and purity. It's the quintessence of *me*—a reflection of everything I value and believe in. People admire me because they know my personal life is equally strong and pure, or has been up until now, with no hint of scandal—no separation between what I build and what I am."

She eyed him irritably. "What rot, Nielson. How can you say that to me, of all people? What are you getting at?"

"Our secret is no longer a secret. The public knows that two famous, glamorous people in the prime of their youth and talents are drawn to each other like steel magnets. We can't hide our attraction, so we might as well use it to mutual advantage. Don't you agree?"

"What's your point?"

"I'm suggesting a merger."

"You mean . . . a business team?"

"I mean a life team. I told Betsy the article was pure fiction and I was coming here to set the record straight. Her last words to me were 'You don't have to explain anything. I accept your needs . . . whatever they are.' She knows she can never be a real wife to me—a wife in every sense of the word." He paused for impact and lowered his voice. "But you can, Torie. There's no limit to what you and I could do if we put our minds and resources together. I want you to marry me."

She stared at him in amazement.

"Betsy would give me a divorce without a question," he went on, almost oblivious to her reaction. "She's told me so a hundred times—that she loves me enough to want to see me happy. She's the sweetest and gentlest soul on earth, and it pains me very deeply to leave her, but I've known for a long time that she holds me back—that I can't reach my full potential tied down to a woman who can't travel, who can't wear fabulous clothes and give marvelous parties and be photographed with me all over the world. She can't even stand by my side greeting heads of state—"

"You're insane!"

"I always knew that someday I might meet the woman who was the perfect mate for me—and I have."

"I won't listen to another word."

"You *will* listen, Torie. You and I could be married right away and I would tell the world, in essence, 'My beloved wife is a paraplegic. I've been devoted to her for many years, but now that she's strong enough to face life on her own, she doesn't need me anymore. And I can't lead a double life. I demand the same integrity in my personal life as in my work. Therefore, Torie and I are going to legalize our union and make it permanent.' "

She swallowed hard. "You seem to have it all figured out."

"Quite so. This way, instead of looking like an adulterer, I come out a hero—a man who has made tremendous sacrifices for his wife all these years but finally succumbed to an irresistible attraction and now steps forth to save the honor of the woman he loves."

"Loves?"

"Well, so to speak. We don't have to love with our minds as long as we love with our bodies. I doubt we could ever 'love' each other any more than we could build a hotel together. Our problem with the Rittenhouse North was that we were thinking small—way too small."

His eyes gleamed as he continued, excited by his own words. "Listen to me, Torie. With the money, the resources, the glamor and influence we would wield as a pair, there's no limit to how far we could go. What I admire so much about you, besides your physical beauty, is your energy . . . the fabulous, inexhaustible supply of energy that drives you and everyone around you to the most incredible achievements. With your business abilities and my artistic talents, you and I could literally move mountains . . . convert wastelands to huge medical complexes or space exploration centers or universities . . . create whole towns . . . villages . . . entire cities! Don't you see? We could become one of the most powerful, exciting couples in the world!"

She listened to him, dumbfounded.

"Well?" he insisted. "Don't you agree?"

"No—I don't." Her own response surprised her. "That's not what I want out of life."

"What do you mean you don't want it? You can't sit there and tell me you don't want power. You've striven for it ever since you were a young woman. It drove you to seek me out the first time we met in that church. I knew then what you wanted, and I know now. I don't buy your denial for one second."

"I don't care what you buy, Nielson. For the first time in my life, I'm beginning to know what I want and how to order my priorities. What I don't want is to hurt Betsy. I also don't want a marriage without love."

"Didn't you say you'd always care for me?"

"Yes, and I will. I thought I loved you for a long, long time. It was a schoolgirl infatuation I never outgrew. I would've given up anything for you at one period in my life, just as I would've fought to the death to build Di Angelo Center—two days ago."

"What are you saying?"

She hesitated, weighing a decision she might regret. But when she finally spoke, her voice was strong and confident. "I know you respect passion—and I've always had a passion for Rittenhouse Square. When I was little, it represented everything that was rich and beautiful and solidly established. Everything I was deprived of and wanted in this world. As time went on, it became even more of a symbol to me. Eventually, I came to believe that I could somehow erase the painful memories of the past by erasing its buildings. I thought I could prove myself by 'possessing' the Square—by putting my name and my imprint on it. I wanted to get even with all the people who made me feel less than I am."

She paused for a quick second, then nodded to emphasize her words. "I'm just now beginning to see how wrong I've been—how vain and petty and narrow-minded."

"You mean you're—"

"Yes," she said softly. "I'll leave Rittenhouse Square as it is. I won't touch a brick, except to repair and restore. There's no reason to build Di Angelo Center. There never was. What this city *really* needs is an exciting new performing-arts center on a site that's not already developed. I'm going to put all my energies toward finding that site, and filling that need."

"I'll be damned." He shook his head and sank into the couch. "Are you *sure* that's what you want?"

"I couldn't be more sure. The other thing I want is for you to go back to Betsy and tell her how much you love her. She's a saint, you know. A woman of flesh and blood and human feelings, but a saint. You'll never find another woman who loves you the way she does."

"You're quite right about that." He rose with a sigh, and started toward the door. "I suppose I'd better take my battered ego and go home. It's not every day I fly across the continent to propose and get turned down."

"You weren't serious. We both know that. And don't worry about *Celebrity Times.* I'll put my lawyers on it and get a retraction."

"Yes . . ." he murmured absently. "Good idea."

"Give my love to Betsy. Tell her I haven't had a cigarette in four months."

"I'll mention it." He glanced over his shoulder as he opened the door to the elevator. "Well, good-bye, then. Keep in touch about your performing-arts center, will you? I might want to take a stab at it."

She grinned at him from the doorway. "I thought you'd never ask."

Back in her bedroom, Torie set down her suitcase and leafed through the stack of mail and messages on her desk, disappointed to find no word from Keith. The hell with him, she thought, and then . . . the hell with pride. Nothing else mattered except seeing him, talking to him, trying to make him understand that she loved him, that all she cared about—

"Beg your pardon, madam."

"Oh, Ingrid. Is that for me?"

"Yes, Mr. Keith dropped it by earlier. I told him you'd be home soon, and he asked that I be sure to give it to you as soon as you came in."

Torie took the envelope. "Did he say anything else?"

"No, that was all."

Snatching an opener, she sliced across the top, pulled out a note, and read his scrawled message. "The story's finished, but it needs an ending. Please choose either: (A) heroine decides love and career incompatible; or (B) heroine marries jealous fool who adores her. To discuss further possibilities of (B), meet me at noon—say, Rittenhouse Square?"

She checked her watch—twelve exactly—and dashed out the door, arriving at the park in minutes, flushed and breathless. He spotted her and came running across the lawn.

"You had me half-crazy," he said, wrapping her in his arms. "I was afraid you weren't coming."

"I just—got your note," she gasped. "Oh, darling, I can't tell you—"

"Don't say a word. It doesn't matter." He pressed her head to his chest. "Don't try to explain anything. Whatever happened before we met isn't worth a damn. All I care about is what happens now. And for the rest of time."

"That's all . . . I care about, too." She clung to him tightly, still catching her breath. "What about Mac? Do you think he'll approve of me?"

"Approve! He's been pushing this since the night you came to dinner. After that bitchy article, he called and offered to fly you and me and our families to his ancestral estate in Ireland for our wedding."

"Oh, no," she said, laughing with relief. "God help us."

"My thoughts exactly. But I told him we wouldn't turn down the use of his jet for our honeymoon—that is, if you can stop Di Angelo Centering long enough to marry me."

"That's what I wanted to tell you." She drew back and looked around her. Two fat pigeons strutted along the cobblestone walk, a leaf floated down to the fountain, and the delicate bronze lady on her pedestal still pointed her finger to the sky. "The Square is beautiful the way it is—the way it was meant to be. I've decided to forget Di Angelo Center. I'm going to build an arts center instead—on a site where there's nobody to displace and nothing of value to tear down."

"Are you serious?" He tilted her chin to see her face. "I believe you are. When did all this happen?"

"After you left yesterday, I couldn't stop thinking about us . . . about the Center . . . about everything. You're right about the Square. So is Rebecca French, battle-ax that she is. Just because I don't appreciate certain buildings, it's no reason to deprive other people of them."

He listened in astonished silence.

"The catalyst," she went on, "was seeing this whole mess drag on and on for months, and causing more and more problems and friction between us. I made that mistake once—putting my career before my marriage. I'm not about to do it again."

"Those are the words I've been waiting for." He smoothed her hair, blowing in the breeze, off her face. "I've been thinking, too. What we have is much too precious to jeopardize. I predicted a bloody battle over the Square, but I knew you were determined to fight, even with the odds against you. And I was prepared to detach myself from the project, difficult as that might be. Now, I don't have to worry. The war's been canceled, no one will get hurt, and you're putting your talents and your efforts where they'll be appreciated. I wouldn't be surprised if Madame French herself comes out in support of a performing-arts center. By the way, do you have an architect in mind?"

She looked up in alarm. "Would you object terribly if—?"

"Not at all," he said, laughing. "Hughes is the man for the job. I bear no grudges. He's the loser. I got the girl. And exclusive rights from now on?"

"I'll sign in blood—that is, if I can write. Do you think you could find some sustenance for your future wife? I haven't had a bite since yesterday."

"Now that you mention it, I haven't had much appetite myself." He grinned and took her arm. "Come on, we'll walk over to the Barclay."

"Ah, yes," she said, "the Barclay."

Torie stopped by the pillars at the entrance to the Square. "Just look at that dreary old façade, darling. What I wouldn't give . . ."